Sca

Raki and Piyanah are born as outcasts into an American Indian tribe, many thousands of years ago somewhere in the West—but they are outcasts only because Piyanah's mother, who raises them both, is strong enough to defy tribal customs—and the chief. Once Piyanah's mother dies, however, the two children must integrate themselves into the rest of the tribe—and prepare themselves for their destiny—to form a new tribe which will be able to break the bonds of superstition and tradition that have infected the old tribe. To become the joint chiefs of the new tribe, however, Raki must live the life of a young squaw, and Piyanah must pass all the tests of a young brave.

''During the last twenty years, seven books of mine have been published as historical novels which to me are biographies of previous lives I have known.''

Joan Grant.

BOOKS BY JOAN GRANT

Far Memory Books:
Winged Pharaoh
Eyes of Horus
Lord of the Horizon
So Moses Was Born
Life as Carola
Return to Elysium
Scarlet Feather

———

Far Memory

———

The Scarlet Fish and Other Stories
Redskin Morning

———

The Laird and the Lady
Vague Vacation
A Lot To Remember
Many Lifetimes *(with Denys Kelsey)*

SCARLET FEATHER

by Joan Grant

ARIEL PRESS
Columbus, Ohio

First published in Great Britain
by Morrison & Gibb Ltd. 1945
First Ariel Press edition 1990
Second Printing

This book is made possible
by a gift from M. DeSales Gilson
to the Publications Fund of Light

ISBN 0-89804-148-1

FOR

VERA SUTHERLAND

WHO WILL FIND IT SO EASY TO ANSWER
THE QUESTION OF THE GREAT HUNTERS

author's note

The Redskins of this book belonged to a much earlier epoch than is covered by the recorded history of the North American Indians. My present knowledge of the United States is very limited, three months in New York when I was seven, so I have as yet had no opportunity of trying to identify the country crossed by the Tribe of the Heron on their migration.

SCARLET FEATHER

PART ONE

Raki and Piyanah

Raki and I, Piyanah, were together from the beginning. His mother died when he was born and I was three days old, so we were suckled together. There were two of everything: two babies in the cradle, two breasts when we were hungry, two voices to comfort us if we cried. Later we recognized the voices as Mother, who was the most important, and Ninee, who helped her to look after us. All things were happy because they were in pairs; even the rocks and the trees had each a shadow to stop it being lonely.

Raki and I shared all our discoveries; the hard, hot feeling in your mouth before teeth happen; the shape of stones; the interesting taste of grass and earth; the texture of skin, and rush-basket, and moss; and the beautifully loud noise we could make by shouting.

We used to lie naked in the sun and watch the dance of the leaves, or play in the shallow water which jumped up to laugh with us when we banged it with our hands. We learned that there are different kinds of warmth: Mother, and sunlight, and the deep, sleepy warmth of the beaver pelts in which we were wrapped together at night. Fire was warm too, but sometimes it got cross, like Ninee, and hurt so badly that you had to cry.

Cold took longer to learn; there was the friendly chill of wet grass in the early morning; the sharpness of spring water and the beautiful coolness of licking shadowed stones on a hot day. Suddenly one morning the great white cold happened: it was soft and lovely, but when it grew tired of playing with us it hurt nearly as much as fire. It stayed on and on until we couldn't remember there had ever been anything but white-

3

ness outside the tepee.

Raki knew what hot ashes felt like when my hand was burned, and I learned about ants when they stung his foot. I thought I should always follow Raki because I was his shadow; and the first time he went away from me I was so frightened that I screamed until Mother came to comfort me. She explained that I must learn to crawl too, so I did. After that I was careful to learn everything as fast as he did, so that we shouldn't be parted again.

We learned to swim on the same day, and if he fell and cut his knee I nearly always cut mine before sunset. Once he ate some berries that gave him a very bad pain; I hadn't eaten any, but I pretended I had, so that he shouldn't have the pain all by himself. Ninee made us drink something very dark and bitter; after that we both had a pain, so I didn't have to pretend any more.

Mother played with us and told us stories: she knew everything, and could even make fire and moccasins. Ninee didn't know very much, and scolded us when she thought Mother wasn't listening; but she was nice when she was in a good temper.

When we were five, Mother told us that we were all going to a new place. We were sorry at first, for there were so many special rocks and caves and trees that would be lonely if we went away. Then Raki said it would be a wonderful adventure, so we were both pleased.

I don't think Mother wanted to go on a journey, for the night before we left I was too excited to sleep and I thought I heard her crying. I still thought so, even when Raki said I must have made a mistake because grown-ups didn't cry. I had tried to find out where we were going and why; but Mother only said that we were going to a new ''place of the corn-growing'' because the tribe needed fresh hunting-grounds.

We did not know what the tribe was, but Raki thought it was something to do with the people we occasionally saw in

4

the distance. I wondered how we should be able to carry our two tepees and the wooden chests which took care of our clothes; but I needn't have worried about them, for one day Mother took us into the distant woods, as she had often done before, and after we had walked a very long way I asked when we should be going home, and she said:

"We are not going to turn back, Piyanah. Tomorrow, and tomorrow and tomorrow will all be in a new place...a new place that has no memories."

Then she walked ahead, and we did not ask any more questions, because we knew she was unhappy and didn't want to talk. Then Raki pointed to knife cuts on the trees and we knew someone had blazed a trail for us to follow. Further on there were many footprints in the dust, so we knew that many people were making the journey too. They must have been kind, if not friendly people, for at the end of each day we found a shelter made for us to sleep in, with food and a cooking-pot beside it. Mother said they were the tribe, but when we asked what a tribe was, she said we didn't need to know yet.

When Raki or I got tired of walking Mother carried us on her back. We came to a river and waited for several days while canoes were built. Then Ninee came back from collecting firewood and said all the canoes had gone, but they had left one for us...we found it tied to a stake which was driven into the bank.

Mother paddled in front and Ninee at the back; Raki and I sat in the middle and were allowed to trail our hands in the water so long as we didn't splash Ninee. Sometimes we saw other canoes ahead of us, and then Mother drew into the bank until they were out of sight. We thought it curious that she never wanted to thank the tribe; for they went on being kind, and every evening we saw a bunch of feathers, hanging from a branch or tied to a stick in the bank, which showed us where they had prepared our sleeping-place. Sometimes a fire had been lit and the food was ready for cooking...on those days

5

Ninee was good-tempered and the food tasted better. Raki and I always ran on ahead to see what had been left for us: usually it was meat or wildfowl, but sometimes it was only a little corn-meal, and then we had to look for a stone on which Ninee rolled the dough into flat cakes which she baked in the hot ashes. It was early spring and the nights were cold, but that didn't matter as Mother had brought the beaver robe for us to sleep in.

When Ninee was cross she used to mutter to herself, and we found out that she thought we ought to live with the tribe, and that somehow it was Mother's fault that we didn't...but when we questioned Ninee about it she wouldn't answer. The tribe were incomprehensible, like the weather...something which affected you but had to be accepted without argument. Ninee would only say they were looking for a new ''place of the corn-growing'', and that if they didn't find it we should all go hungry next winter. I asked how they would know when they got there, and she said, ''The Chief will tell the Elders.''

When I asked her what a Chief was, she said, ''Your father''; then gasped as though she had swallowed a fly, and, grabbing hold of my arm, said, ''If you tell your mother I said that I shall slap you so hard that you'll scream the moon out of the sky!'' So I knew that my father being the Chief must be very important. Raki and I decided not to say anything about it to Mother, because when Ninee was cross she made things so disagreeable.

We knew that everything had a father and a mother, but animals always had parents like themselves. We agreed it was a pity that I only had a ''Chief'' and Raki only a ''Scarlet Feather'' for a father...we used to think that a Scarlet Feather was a kind of bird, but Mother said it was a specially brave kind of man. When Raki asked what his father's name was, Mother said she didn't know, for her sister, who was Raki's mother, had never told her.

It was exciting when we came to a rapid. Ninee was

frightened of them and used to pull a blanket over her head so that she couldn't see the rocks...she pretended she did it because it kept her dry. Mother knelt in the prow of the canoe, and just when we seemed to be driving down on a rock she would twist the paddle so that we slid past it down a green slope between the white waters into the calm beyond.

When for three days there had been no rapids, the river found open country with hills only in the distance. On the south bank there were gentle hills which grew steeper as we went further, and on the other there was grass-land, for a distance it would take two days to cross, and then a ridge of high mountains. It had been rather dull that day, then suddenly, as we came round a curve, we saw many canoes tied to the bank. On a half-moon of close turf, protected by a steep cliff on all sides except where it flowed down to the water, men were setting up the posts for tepees...some of the tepees already had their hide coverings in place and were like the one we had lived in before.

I looked for the bunch of feathers which would have showed us where to land, but Mother stared straight ahead and paddled on down-river. I wished she wouldn't go so fast, for I wanted to see what the tribe looked like...it was disappointing that they seemed quite ordinary people, no different to the ones we had sometimes seen in the distance. Then Raki pointed to a ledge in the hillside above the encampment: on it there was a tepee much larger than the rest and it was covered with brilliant patterns in red and blue and yellow. A man stood before it...or was it one of the Great Hunters? His head was crowned with feathers, many, many feathers which swept right down to his feet.

I heard Ninee say under her breath, ''The Chief has come to watch us pass.'' So that was the Chief, my father! I felt proud, and then ashamed that even for a moment I had been glad of a father who let Mother pass by without a greeting.

We rounded a spur of rocks which guarded the eastern

side of the encampment and hid it from our view. Mother let the paddle trail through the water and leaned forward as though she were suddenly tired. Ripples slapped against the side of the canoe as we drifted in towards the bank. I saw a bunch of feathers tied to a stake and knew that we had come to the landing. I couldn't see any tepee for us, but there were signs that someone, or perhaps two or three people, had recently come down the bank. So we followed their tracks...it was a steep climb, and Ninee began to grumble that it would be hard to carry water up from the river. She grumbled too soon, for when we came to an open glade encircled by great trees we saw a tepee and beyond it could hear a stream singing.

"It is *our* tepee," Raki shouted. "I thought we should never see our own tepee again."

We ran forward and unlaced the flap. Everything was there, just as we had left it moons ago: the winter blankets Mother had woven, and the wooden animals she had carved for us to play with when we were small...even the bow which Raki had started and not had time to finish.

"The tribe can't be unkind," I whispered to Raki, "or they wouldn't have bothered to bring things which were important only to us. Or do you think it was the Chief who told them?"

There was a smaller tepee for Ninee, though not the same one she had had before; we were glad she wouldn't have to share ours, for on the journey she had been cross if we talked when she wanted to sleep.

That night I woke soon after moonrise to find that Mother's bedplace was empty, so I told Raki that we could go out to explore before she came back. The trees stood watching the smoke rising from the cooking-fire which was still smouldering...perhaps it was the first smoke they had ever seen. The shadows were black and sharp, and the silence clear as water. We went through the wood and crossed a stretch of open ground in the direction of the encampment. Beyond the sharp line of the cliff edge there was a pool of darkness which hid the tepees, and on the far side a great rock pointed to the sky: something moved on it...a bear? An eagle? Raki saw it too, so we lay flat to watch unseen.

"It is the Chief," whispered Raki.

The moon escaped the clouds that were chasing her, and the light was so brilliant that we could almost see the colours of the feathered headdress. If the night had not been so hushed we should never have heard Mother say, "Na-ka-chek...Na-ka-chek...."

She was standing in the shadow of a soaring pine above the river...the cliff was like a bow, and she and my father held the string through which it lived, the bow in whose protection the tribe were sleeping. Again I had heard her say, "Na-ka-chek"; and realized it was my father's name, and that she was crying.

I wanted to run to her, but Raki held me back. "Lie still, Piyanah. She wouldn't like us to be here....I don't know why, but I know she wouldn't."

I watched her turn away and vanish into the shelter of the trees. Now the far rock was empty also, and their singing bow was only a curve in the cliffs above a river.

The Tribe

Our tepees were much closer to the encampment than they had been in the old "place of corn growing", and we often saw people who belonged to the tribe. Mother told us that when we could not avoid going near them—for instance, if we met them on a narrow path where there was no place to hide—we were to walk straight past and pretend not to see them. She made us promise that even if one of them spoke

9

to us we would never answer.

Ninee sometimes went down to the encampment, but only when she thought Mother was with us and wouldn't know about it. Food was left for us every evening, on a flat rock at the top of the cliff; so it was difficult to understand why we had to keep away from the tribe, when they were friendly enough to provide us with everything we needed... even fine deer-skin for tunics and coloured beads to decorate our moccasins. The Chief was my father; yet my Mother never told us anything about him and we never saw him except in the distance.

Sometimes Mother took us into the mountains during the hot weather. At night we slept under the stars and she would tell us stories about them: how each star was a torch set in the sky by someone who had entered the Land beyond the Sunset, and how the larger ones were two torches that belonged to two people who loved each other very much; so we knew there would only be one new star when Raki and I were dead.

There were several different places where we could go when our bodies grew too old to be exciting to live in any longer. I thought the nicest was the Land beyond the Sunset, which is sometimes called the Land without Shadows, where there is no winter and the flowers never wither nor the trees lose their leaves. The rivers are always summer warm, and you can swim in them with the freedom of fish; through those woods you can run swift as a deer; in that sky you share the horizon of eagles.

Before you can enter the Happy Hunting-Grounds, where live the Great Hunters whose younger brothers are the Lords of the Trees and the Lords of the Animals, you have to answer the challenge of Great Grizzly, Great Trout, Great Deer, and even Great Gopher. If you have betrayed any of their people, they make you return to Earth to seek forgiveness. Great Pine and Great Silver Birch question you too: if you have deliberately hurt a tree, or used it for the centrepost

10

of your tepee without being properly grateful, they also send you back to learn kindliness. Each Lord of the Trees has many spirits who look after his forests; they are very powerful, but kind unless you annoy them.

Ninee believed in demons, and was always threatening to send them to punish us when we were disobedient. She was so good at describing them that sometimes it was difficult to be sure they would not happen. There were fat ones who hopped like toads, and thin ones with sharp teeth, who hid in thickets and were always ready to pounce when you went past. The most horrible were like enormous bats, with bloated, furry bodies, who dropped from trees and smothered you if you went out of the tepee at night without asking permission. When Mother discovered that Ninee had been telling us about demons she was so cross that Ninee wept and then sulked for days.

Raki and I agreed that being with Mother was even better than being by ourselves. She never tried to stop us climbing trees, as Ninee did, but showed us how to swing from one branch to another and how to be careful not to rely only on one hold at a time. She taught us how to recognize all the different birds, and to imitate their calls so well that they often answered us. When we were seven she gave us our own canoe, which we kept down-river where there was a long stretch of water without a rapid. She taught us how to carve and to use bow and arrows; and always realized that Raki and I must do everything together to enjoy it.

She was with us when we found the grizzly cub. His mother must have been killed by a hunter, for otherwise she would never have deserted him. He was curled up beside a rock, whimpering because he was cold and frightened. Mother carried him home; at first he wouldn't eat, but she made a little bag of doe-skin and taught him to suck goat's milk through it. He was different from other grizzlies, for he had a white blaze running from his right shoulder down the fore-leg. We called him Pekoo, and when he got used to us

11

he followed us everywhere, and whimpered on the bank when we went out in our canoe.

There were only three "specially forbidden things": going too near the encampment, speaking to any of the tribe, or nearing the sound of a particular waterfall which fell into a pool in the forest. Mother said this pool was a very magical place and that we were not old enough to go there yet. As she so seldom told us not to do anything, we accepted these as being things she knew about and we didn't; and we were nine before they began to seem important.

We had found a new way up the cliff above the river, and had crawled along a narrow ledge until it widened enough for us to be able to lie on it. Far below we could see the encampment; the air was so still that the smoke of the watch-fire was straight as a pine, and the man sitting beside it looked small as a gopher.

"I have got an idea," said Raki.

I interrupted him, "So have I!" Let's both say it at the same time, so that we can be sure we both thought of it first."

He picked up a stone, as he always did when he wanted to be sure we really had thought of the same thing, and threw it as far as he could—which was a long way, for he was very good at throwing and the hill being so steep helped a lot. When it stopped rolling we both said, "Let's have an adventure with finding out about people in it!"

"I'm glad you had it too, Piyanah. I wasn't sure I ought to tell you about it until I had found out if it was very dangerous."

"If you had done it without me it *would* have been dangerous...being without each other always is."

"Not always," said Raki. "Remember how I found the grizzly's cave the day you cut your foot and couldn't come with me?"

"That doesn't count," I said firmly, "because the grizzly wasn't in it. If it had been, you might have been too silly

12

to run away before it got cross."

"We needn't bother about that, because it isn't the grizzly day, it's *now*, and as 'now' is when we've decided to find out about people we had better make a plan. The best thing to do when you start having a new adventure is to decide which the most dangerous part is likely to be, so that you will know what to do if it happens, and not have to decide when you may be in a great hurry."

"That's not very difficult," I said, "for if it's a nice, small Danger, you go on with what you're doing and pretend not to notice it, and if it's an extra large Danger, with teeth or a horrid noise, you practise running, in the opposite direction, and forget it ever happened."

Raki sighed. "You can't always go on doing that, Piyanah. Mother has told you, and so have I, that pretending dangers aren't really there is quite often very silly and hardly ever at all brave."

I thought he was probably right, so I said, "Well, when it stops me doing the things you do, I'll stop it, but I like being comfortable, and if I start thinking about all the things there are to be brave about, I mightn't be brave at all. Then you might start having adventures without me...and that's the most uncomfortable thing I can think about."

"Do stop talking, Piyanah. I'm trying to think."

"So am I; and I'm wondering at the same time."

"Well, *don't*."

"But you can't help wondering if you're doing it...and anyway it's an *important* wonder. Why does Mother let us go out all day by ourselves...and at night too if we want to, except when there is a full moon: why does she let us climb trees, even unfriendly ones: why does she tell us never to be afraid of animals, even mountain lions: why does she let us have our own canoe and even go down the small rapid alone: why does she let us do nearly everything we want to, except go near the encampment or speak to any of the tribe? *Why?* *That's* my wonder...and you needn't be surprised that it's important, because I told you it was going to be!''

''Perhaps the Chief's children are always kept away from the others.''

''No, they're not. I heard Ninee talking to Mother, when she thought I was asleep; she thinks it's wicked of Father to let Mother and us live away from the tribe. Ninee only stays here because she promised she would; she says she misses being with the other squaws.''

''Then perhaps they hate us, and Mother is afraid they would kill us if they got the chance.''

''I don't believe that. No, Raki, of course they don't hate us. We've often been quite close to hunters, and they could easily have killed us if they had wanted to, and do you remember when we met the file of Braves, and honestly hadn't got time to hide; they didn't *hate* us, Raki.''

''Then why did they turn away as though they couldn't bear to look at us?''

''Because they were *frightened*. I know it sounds silly, but I *know* they were frightened of us.''

''How do you know?''

''Because two of them didn't turn away, and their eyes were dark and wide open, like Pekoo's were until he got used to us.''

''Perhaps you're right,'' said Raki slowly. ''I've thought so too, sometimes, but it seemed too silly to be likely.''

''Let's make sure we're right, and then instead of asking Mother why we mustn't go near people—and that's the only question she will never answer—we can say, 'Why are people frightened of us?' and she'll probably tell us before she realizes it's a new way of finding out the same thing.''

''But she'll probably say, 'Of course they are not frightened of you,'...and that will make us feel silly, as I did after I boasted of killing the deer with the arrow you made for me, and she wouldn't believe me...and I thought she would have to when she saw the body. And then she found it had been dead for days and was full of maggots.''

"Don't think about that," I said hastily. I hated thinking about it myself, for it had been my fault that Raki thought he had killed the deer. It had gone bounding off, and I suppose I imagined I saw the arrow sticking in its shoulder. We searched for it all day, and when we saw the dead deer...we knew it was dead because a buzzard was sitting on its head, I convinced him that it was the same one, and hurried him back to tell Mother about it before he had time to look properly. It was such an uncomfortable memory that I buried it, in a hole I had been scratching in the sandy ledge, and put a white stone on it to remind me not to dig it up again.

"There's one way we could make quite sure about their being frightened, talking very loudly so that they couldn't help noticing us, and if you're right and they're frightened, they will hide, or pretend to be too busy to see who we are."

"And if I'm *not* right?" I asked, feeling anxious because it had only just occurred to me that this adventure would include doing the most dangerous of all things, quite slowly and on purpose.

"If you're not right, I expect we shall be full of arrows."

"Full enough of arrows to be dead?"

"Quite dead, I expect; but that won't matter because Mother says the Great Hunters will welcome us to their country, and it's more exciting there than it ever is down here."

"Well, if we're *both* full of arrows, it won't matter at all," I said...and hoped that Raki thought I meant it.

Neither of us spoke until we were climbing the path which led up from the encampment. I wondered if Raki had been as frightened as I had, or if he had even found it equally difficult not to run. Would an arrow have felt like being stung by a hornet...only even hotter and sharper? I hoped that I should never find out!

"I am glad that's over," said Raki. "Were you frightened too?"

15

That ''too'' made me love him even more than usual. ''Horribly frightened,'' I said, glad to be able to admit it without shame. ''Nothing really happened, but it was horrible.''

''Which did you think was the worst part?''

''Do you mean the worst of the things that happened, or the worst of the things I was expecting?''

''The things that happened.''

''When the old man by the fire looked straight at us and pretended we weren't there...he pretended so hard that I began to believe it. I thought that arrows might be quite different to hornets and so we had been killed without us noticing. I daren't look back in case I saw our bodies lying on the ground. I pinched myself so hard that it still hurts...to make sure I wasn't only a spirit.''

''It wouldn't matter much if we had been, so long as we didn't notice being killed.''

''Oh yes, it would,'' I said. ''Mother says that it's very important to know when you're dead...for if you don't, instead of asking the Great Hunters to let you go to their country, you wander about, feeling lonely...and getting so cross with people for not seeing you that you get more and more disagreeable. That's why some dead people hide in the shadows and make frightening noises to chase you away from the places where they live.''

''Then I hope it never happens to us.''

''It won't, because we'll never forget to ask the Great Hunters to look after us.''

''Does anybody?''

''Of course they do, or there wouldn't be so many spirits. Mother says you don't get anything until you ask for it. I expect the spirits were people who thought they got carried up to the Happy Country without doing anything about it for themselves: as though they were worms, and the Great Hunters behaved like hungry birds who swooped down and carried them off. Was it frightening to you, Raki...our

16

adventure, I mean?''

''Yes, very. My worst bit sounds much sillier than yours.''

''Which was it?''

''Did you notice the two small children playing in the dust near the large tepee?'' I nodded, and he went on, ''Well, they saw us, but they weren't surprised or frightened, until a woman came out of the tepee; and when she saw us she ran to the children and snatched them up and fled into the tepee as though we were a pair of angry grizzlies.''

''So *small* children aren't frightened of us,'' I said slowly, ''but women are, and the old man pretended we weren't there. Why, Raki?''

''We shall have to ask Mother.''

''She will be angry: we have done the worst of all the 'specially forbidden things'.''

''But her being angry won't last nearly so long as our not knowing.''

''We had better think about it first.''

But we didn't have to think, for I looked up to see Mother standing waiting for us, on the rock from which you can look down into the encampment. She didn't seem angry, but as though she were suddenly very tired.

''So you have been there,'' she said. ''I knew I couldn't keep you away from them much longer.''

It no longer seemed a brave adventure. It was as though we had deliberately done something mean and unkind. My eyes felt as though they had got sand in them, and I knew that if I wasn't very careful I might cry. Raki took my hand and held it, hard. ''It was *my* idea,'' he said. ''I shouldn't have let her come with me.''

''No, it was my idea, really it was.''

''It doesn't matter now,'' she said. ''It isn't your fault that the tribe is stronger than a woman...even if a woman loves her children very much, she can't protect them from the tribe.''

17

"They didn't hurt us, Mother. It wasn't at all important...we thought it was going to be a tremendous adventure, but we walked through the encampment and nothing happened."

"Are you sure?"

"Quite sure, Mother," said Raki. "Nothing is changed by our having been there."

"You don't want to know why you are different?"

"Yes, of course we do," I said, "but knowing can't do us any harm."

"I was older than you are when I knew," she said softly, as though she were speaking to herself. "Would I have been happier if I had never seen beyond the water?" She sighed, a deep sigh as though she put down something very heavy which she had, been carrying a long way. "Of your own choice you have done the first of the 'specially forbidden things'; now you shall do the third. I will take you to the Place of the Falling Water, and tell you what I saw there... and why, because of that seeing, you and I are 'different'."

the Other Side of the Water

The water of the high fall seemed only a greater intensity of the light flooding down from the full moon. It fell into a circular pool whose sides were of smooth rock. Then I realized why it was different from other falls: the pool must have been bottomless, for the smooth circle of rock was unbroken by any outlet...however deep one dived there would only be water and more water.

"Now you know why I never let you come here," said Mother. "This is one of the hidden places, an entrance to the country on the 'other side of the water.' Even the tribal Elders dare not come here at the full moon. They are afraid to see themselves as they were before they were born; they are afraid to see the Before People looking up at them. But I have brought you here to tell you my story, because it was at a pool very like this where I learned the courage to break the laws of the tribe....

"When I was young, the story-teller brought us legends which were much older than those told by his successor. He told us about the beginnings of things, and because I was eager to listen, he did not hide from me what he knew of the Before People."

"Who are they?"

"Those who came before we can remember."

"Before the Totem?"

"Before any totem. He told me that if I had the courage to look into still water, at the foot of a high fall when the moon is full, I might be able to see his legend come alive. I saw more than a legend, Raki and Piyanah; I saw a way of life forgotten by the tribes, a way of life which must make men and women find only a familiar joy in the Land without Shadows."

"What do the Before People look like?" said Raki.

"They differ from us, yet they have not the faces of strangers. I saw pictures of their country beyond the water... and the pictures were more real than everyday things, not cold like lines on the wall of a cave. They must have stayed a long while in the same place, for they had built their tepees of stone, and there were wide stretches of cultivation, instead of only enough to grow corn for the winter. They wore tunics of colours we cannot make, the blue of a jay's wing, and a dark, rich crimson, and orange of the moon in autumn. Many of their trees were different; some had fruit on them, scarlet and yellow and green, so large that one would fill your hand. There were men and women; I saw them walking hand in hand, and sharing their days. I knew they talked with each other as equals, and when one wept, so did the other; and it was together that they laughed, and worked, and loved."

19

"Then what made them so different from us...except the colours of their tunics, and their stone tepees?" said Raki.

Moonlight was shining full on her face, and for the first time since she had known we had been to the encampment I saw she smiled. "That you can ask such a question shows that I am not altogether a failure. You are Redskins, male and female, and you find nothing surprising that men and women should love each other, and wish to live together through all the seasons?"

"How could we be surprised?" I said, wondering why she didn't go on with the exciting part of the story.

"When I realized that men and women could live like that, I made a promise to the Great Hunters...because I knew their way of life was the same as the Before People's, and that they wanted me to follow it again. I promised that if I had a child I would try to keep it free of the laws of separation, and that I would never leave its father, to go back to the Squaws' Tepees."

"What are the Squaws' Tepees," I asked, "and why did my father want you to go there?"

"The Redskins have forgotten the Before People; even the Elders have forgotten, so deeply that they cannot learn wisdom from the wild-duck, who know that the great secrets can be learned only in pairs."

"Then Raki and I shall learn a lot of secrets," I said contentedly, "because we are always in a pair."

"How do the rest of the tribe have children if they don't love each other?" said Raki.

"In the early summer each Young Brave chooses a squaw, and takes her away into the woods so that she can have a child. He does this because it is his duty to the tribe, not because he loves her. I told you that the Redskins are less wise than the least of the animals!"

"What happens to a squaw after she knows she is going to swell up and have a baby?" I asked anxiously.

"She goes to the Squaws' Tepees, and not until it is more

20

than a year old may its father, or any other man, notice her again. If they meet on a narrow path, she must stand aside for him to pass, and he will pretend even to have forgotten her name.''

''Don't squaws hate the fathers of their children?'' said Raki.

''I don't know...perhaps if they have never known love they are not disturbed by hatred either.''

''It is a pity that my father is the Chief,'' I said, ''otherwise I could kill him for making you so unhappy. Do you hate him very much?''

''No,'' she said, ''I love him...and he loves me, though only a little and not enough to make him break the law of the tribe. You were born because we were happy together, while he had forgotten everything except that we were young, and alone together in the summer weather. And I was happy, because I believed that he would never wish to send me away after I had told him of the Before People...but you see, Raki and Piyanah, he never believed that they were real.''

''Why didn't you make him look into a pool too?''

''I did. I could see the Before People so very clearly...two of them, a man and a woman, held out their hands to us. But your father said there was only moonlight on dark water.''

''He loved you and he wouldn't *believe* you?'' said Raki, incredulous.

''Perhaps he couldn't believe me...because he wanted to go on believing that the only duty of a Chief is to carry on the pattern set on the loom by his father and his father's father. He said that if he took a squaw to live with him all through the year, the Braves would never trust him to lead them to battle. He said that even the squaws would despise him. But at least he did not make me go back to the squaws, for I said that if he did not allow me to live away from the tribe I would drown myself, and take his child with me to the 'other side of the water.' My sister chose to come with me; but she died when Raki was born, so I suckled you both. It is because

Raki has taken milk from me that Piyanah's father can declare him to be the next Chief.''

''Has he no other son?'' said Raki.

''No. Perhaps I made him distrustful of all squaws, or sometimes, when I am happy, I think it is because he still loves me. We are under his protection, and that is why food is left for us on the rock where I was waiting for you...that is why Ninee stays with us, and why no one dares to molest either of you.''

''But why are they afraid of us?''

''Because you are my children, and they know that I have seen the Before People. And because you have already broken one of their laws, and not been punished for it.''

''Which law?''

''Raki is a boy who still lives with his mother after his seventh year, and he is straight, and swift, and full of health. The men are afraid of the squaws seeing him, for it might make the squaws rebel against the law which says that if a boy stays with his mother after his seventh year he will be crippled before the next moon, and mad before the second, and dead before the wane of the third. It was clever of the men to think of that 'punishment,' for without it they could not make the women obey them. I have often heard a squaw weeping, night after night when she thought the others were asleep, because her son had been taken away; and I have seen a woman stand by the path while a boy walked past without any sign of recognition that she was his mother.''

''Then the women ought not to hate us!''

''Women must either believe that this tribal law is false, or else that you are under the protection of some powerful spirit, and to the foolish all spirits seem evil; or they must know that they have been betrayed for generations...and it is easier for them to cling to their false loyalties.''

''Do all tribes think the same?'' I asked.

''Each tribe has its own totem, and the hope by which I live is that among them there is at least one tribe that remembers the Before People. Every seven years the tribes meet for the Feathered Council. When your children are old enough to find their mates, go to the Gathering of the Tribes, and I think the Great Hunters will allow them there to find the ones who will be to them as you are to each other.''

The fear that this story had brought disappeared like mist before the sun. Mother knew that Raki and I would never allow ourselves to be parted...he would never be a Brave, nor I shut away from him in the Squaws' Tepees.

''If Piyanah's father chose me for the next Chief, would the tribe acknowledge me?'' said Raki.

''No, that is why he will not choose you.''

''I am glad,'' said Raki. ''We should have to try to lead them away from their unhappiness, and Piyanah wouldn't like to live among people who hate us, and neither should I.''

''Shall I be able to see the Before People?'' I said.

''I hope so, Piyanah. Not a day has passed since you were born that I have not asked the Great Hunters that I might share with you my perilous sight.''

''Perilous?''

''There is always danger in being 'different'.''

''Can I try to see them...now?''

''When the pool holds the circle of the moon.''

Side by side Raki and I lay on the smooth, cold rock, staring down to the troubled water. It was dark, for a cloud had hidden the moon: when it shone clear I knew that the moment had come.

I watched a stick carried round and round by the current. I tried to send my spirit diving down, down, so that it could tear aside the dark water which was hiding from me the country beyond the water. ''Great Hunters, please let me see them,'' I whispered, over and over again.

But the water was only water, driving on and on under the force of the fall.

''You see...nothing?'' It was my mother's voice.

23

"Nothing..." The desolation of the word made it difficult not to cry.

"Nothing," echoed Raki; and I knew he shared my bitter disappointment.

"Perhaps when you are older you will see them," and I knew Mother was desperately trying to believe this might be true.

Raki put his hand on her arm. "It doesn't really matter, Mother; it doesn't really matter if we can't see them, because you have shown us how to believe in them. Piyanah and I would never be able to forget them, even if we wanted to, for every time we thank the Great Hunters for letting us be together we shall be remembering the Before People and thanking them too for showing us how to be happy."

"Yes," she said slowly, "I had forgotten that. You have each other. I had only...them."

Later, when we asked Mother why the Before People had been forgotten, she said:

"I have told you, many times, the legend of how the Father of the Great Hunters made the Earth in the morning of the years. First he made the rocks, then the plants and the trees, and then he made the animals. When Earth was ready for man, each pair of animals brought forth a strange cub, the first men and the first women; and the tribes who are decended from them still honour their first ancestor in their totem animal.

"But the Father of the Great Hunters had an enemy who is old as the sky. At the dark of the moon he came down to Earth; he made treacherous rocks which betray the climber; poisonous fungus and the death-berry; the rattle-snake and the viper. The hornet and the tek fly are his children also, and he made the bat and the carrion crow. These also brought forth men and women, and of all these the descendants of the carrion crow, the Black Feathers, are the most fearsome.

"Many times did the Black Feathers fight against the chil-

24

dren of the Great Hunters, but always were they vanquished, for the happy people were led by an oriole whose wings were bright as the sunrise, and it sang to them of the morning of the Earth.

"Then the Lord of the Carrion Crow fought with the Oriole, and stole her feathers, and hid his evil in her bright plumage. And the people believed the Sorrow Bird, the first of their enemies, because he came disguised as their protector.

"The Sorrow Bird told them that pleasure is only the conquering of pain, and joy the overcoming of sorrow; that freedom comes only through endurance, and courage is born only of fear. So because they listened to the Sorrow Bird they left the quiet valley which had been prepared for them, where the trees were heavy with fruit and the meadows parted by singing waters; for they thought it was wicked for them to live in a place which demanded neither pain, nor endurance, nor tears. Some of the women suspected that the Sorrow Bird was evil, but because they loved their men they followed them into exile. Yet even in the cold lands of the North they still vanquished the Black Feathers, for the love between them was stronger than arrows.

"Then the Lord of the Carrion Crow brought another great evil to Earth. He told the Sorrow Bird to lead the people to a wide plain where they must build two fires, a hundred paces apart; round the first fire gathered all the men, and round the second all the women...and the people who had once been happy obeyed.

"Then did the Lord of the Carrion Crow gather up the power of all black clouds, and with it he drove a great cleft into the Earth between the fires, a cleft which stretched from horizon to horizon without end, and was deep as the black night.

"Yet still the Black Feathers could not defeat the people, for across the cleft they spoke of the love between them, and the love built a bridge over it. Then did the Lord of the Car-

25

rion Crow go down into the canyon he had made, down into the depths below the Earth. And when men and women spoke to each other he caught the words and twisted them between his fingers, so that the word of love was heard as hatred, and unity became the sound of separation.

"He is still there, the Lord of the Carrion Crow, and only people who love each other, as do you and Raki, need not fear him. The bridge over that canyon is firm under your feet, and though he roars in fury, to you the sound is less than the shrill squeak of a bat; even if he takes your bridge in his hands and tries to snap it like a dry bone, it is less disturbed than is a rock by the shadow of a dragon-fly."

Then my mother said, "Remember always, Raki and Piyanah, that the two great enemies of mankind are the Sorrow Bird and the Canyon of the Separation; but both are powerless when a man and a woman keep the strength of the love between them, for love is stronger even than the Lord of the Carrion Crow."

It was nearly two years before we again saw the Pool of the Before People, for Mother had asked us not to go there until she thought we were ready to see to the "other side of the water." She came with us, as she had promised. My father carried her in his arms; for she was dead.

He had wanted to bury her under the great pine tree which grew solitary above the encampment. But he listened to Raki and me, this tall, remote stranger, and said that as it had been her wish, he would give her body to the pool.

Sharp and clear in the vivid moonlight he stood on the high rock that shone with the spray of the fall. My mother's body looked as though it was carved wood, stiff and unyielding; yet it remembered her, and could still smile at the things they used to do together, she and her body.

Raki's hand was warm and reassuring, yet I knew he trembled as I did. "*We* can't see them, but they are waiting for her," he whispered. "All the beautiful people of the Before Country…and it isn't cold and dark down there. The fruit trees are shining under a kindly sun, and the people have put on their most brilliant tunics to welcome her. She was lonely here, with only us to talk to; and they have been waiting for her since before we were born.''

I saw the Chief's lips moving, but could not hear what he said because of the sound of the fall. He raised up her body on his outstretched hands, as though he were offering it to the night sky.

Then he knelt, and let her rest on the water, still supported by his arms. Gently the current drew her away from him. Three times she passed us, quiet and serene, as though she were asleep on the breast of the pool.

Perhaps the Before People were waiting to take her feet in their hands, to set them on the steps which led down into their country, for at the centre of the pool she raised her body upright…and then we couldn't see her any longer.

''Did you see them?'' I whispered to Raki.

''No,'' he said, ''I didn't see them. But there was a light round her before she disappeared; it may have been their sun shining up to her…or perhaps it was only the moon reflected on the water. I shall never be quite sure.''

the Choosing

Only a circle of earth scorched black by the cooking-fire was left to show where we had lived with our mother; even the holes which had held the centre-posts of the tepees had been filled in and the ground trampled hard and smooth. I saw a gleam of scarlet among the scattered ashes and picked up a small bead…one of those which Mother had used to decorate our moccasins. ''This is all we have left, Raki…all that is left of the place where we used to belong.''

"Na-ka-chek has given us our own tepee," said Raki, "and he lets us do whatever we like."

"As though we were bear cubs he was trying to tame! He is afraid we shall run away if he is not very careful."

"Are you being quite fair, Piyanah? He gives us everything we ask for."

"Didn't we give Pekoo honeycomb every day when we first found him?"

"We always did...when we could find any."

"Yes, but we did it because Pekoo liked it, not because we hoped it would keep him with us. When the Chief is sure of us, he will try to make us obey the laws."

"Well, we can wait until that happens," said Raki cheerfully. "I am sorry for him in a way...living all alone as he does. Even the Braves are so much in awe of him that they never speak in his presence except to answer a question."

"I'm *glad* he's lonely," I said passionately, "terribly glad. He is so proud of being the Leader of Braves, and we are the only people who know he is a coward."

"He's not a coward," said Raki indignantly.

"Yes, he is! A brave man can be frightened of his enemies, but only a coward is frightened of his friends. It was because he was frightened of his own tribe that he wouldn't let Mother be happy with him. If he had had even a little of her courage, the others might have followed him...instead of being so disgustingly miserable that they don't even realize that they *are* miserable."

"You can't be miserable without knowing it," said Raki, in the voice he kept for the times when he thought I was being deliberately unreasonable.

"Oh yes, you can! And it's the worst kind of misery there is...when it's so deep that you have to make yourself believe that there's nothing better to compare it with. They won't admit that anyone can be happy...that's why they still hate us, even though they daren't show it now that Na-ka-chek has declared that you will be the next Chief. We keep on reminding them of the things they have missed...we are the hind that escaped from the hunter, the fish that was too agile for the starving fisherman, the canoe that shot the rapids in which theirs always foundered. That's why they hate us... and why they always will!''

''They won't believe us *yet*,'' said Raki, ''But that's only because they don't take any notice of anyone who hasn't won a feather for his forehead-thong. When I am the Chief they will have to recognize the truth of my laws...and they will recognize you too, for you will always sit with me in council. When they see we go on being happy together, they will have to believe us.''

''It will be a long time before they let you win a feather, Raki, and what shall I do while you are training to be a Brave?''

''I expect they will go on letting us share a tepee...if they don't, I shall refuse to attempt the ordeals, and that would make your father so ashamed that he would soon change his mind. I am afraid it will be horrid for you having to watch me undergo the ordeals, but you will have to think of how useful the feather will be to us in making people listen.''

''You and I have only known days with both of us in them, Raki. A day would seem longer than a moon if we were apart.''

''But we shan't be apart.''

''You will have to be trained by the Brown Feathers, like all the other boys who want to be Braves. They will make everything as difficult for you as they can, to try to prove that a boy who is brought up with a girl is always weak and a fool.''

''They'll soon get tired of trying that!''

''You are stronger and quicker, and much more wise than any of them...but there are tens of them and only one of you.''

''Well, they can laugh at me...and I can fight. They will find it more difficult to laugh with a split lip and some of their teeth missing! If your father had meant to part us, he would have said so by now.''

But I didn't trust Na-ka-chek to understand about Raki and me; he was too cold, too spare, to know the hearts even of his own children. So Raki's confidence in the future brought me little comfort.

Although Ninee had refused to eat for three days after Mother died, we knew she was glad to be back with the tribe. Nona, her mother, was the eldest squaw; a woman so old that only her eyes seemed really alive, yet her word was never disobeyed in the Squaw's Tepees. Her voice was thin as the echo of a cracked cooking-pot, but when she told stories even the shadows crept closer to listen.

She never spoke when Raki was there, but sometimes, when he was with the other boys learning to build a canoe, I used to let Ninee take me to her. I pretended that I only went there to hear stories which would make Raki laugh, but sometimes it was difficult to remember that they were not really frightening.

Nona seemed to believe that everything was hostile to women: the tree spirits were jealous if a woman brought forth a child, and scornful if she was barren. The animls hated her because she sewed their skins which the hunters had stolen from them, and cooked the flesh that, but for women, the hunters would have been too lazy to kill. The spirits who lived in quiet pools were especially dangerous, for they would catch a girl's reflection and carry it away, so that she lost her memory and died. For a woman to kindle a flame was so deeply to anger the spirit of fire that she would die before the next noonday, and only after humble supplication might she take a brand from the watch-fire to the place of the cooking-pots.

So many trivial things might lead to disaster: if a girl wore more than a hundred or less than ninety beads in her forehead-band, she might go blind; if one of her bracelets broke, it was certain that her first two children would be born dead. But of all the things the squaws accepted without question, the most surprising to Raki and me was the Choosing.

This took place every year, at the full moon before mid-summer, and was the only tribal feast in which the women played an important part. All squaws between sixteen and thirty-two were concerned in it; the first to be Chosen were girls who had not yet been taken into the woods, and then, in order of age, the women whose last child was more than a year old.

For days the Squaws' Tepees buzzed with preparations like hollow tree-trunks full of bees. I was asked to admire moccasins embroidered with coloured beads and even to advise whether a doe-skin tunic could be improved by another porcupine quill stitched to its hem by the stem of a feather. The tepees smelt of rancid grease, for during the growing moon the women plastered their hair with the fat of those animals whose virtues they wished to possess...deers' fat for swiftness, beavers' for industry, owls' to make them wise at night.

I tried to find out why they wanted to be Chosen, whether they hoped to find someone like Raki among the strangers, but they stared or giggled, and instead of answering ran away. Nona's power over them seemed to have suddenly increased, and whenever she spoke, they listened attentively... even when she only grumbled at them; and they vied to make her notice them by trying to please her. Raki and I decided that they must think she could help them to get something they wanted if they could persuade her to be genial; but neither of us had any idea what it was, until Ninee told me that at the Choosing each squaw must have one of the Old Women to speak for her at the wrestling.

Raki told me what to expect at the wrestling, for he had watched the young Braves practicing for it. A man who wanted a squaw had to fight for her if another man chose her too; and all were allowed to take part in the Choosing after they had become full members of the tribe by gaining their

31

Brown Feather. In my grandfather's time no one could become a Brown Feather until he had taken the scalp of an enemy warrior, but now there were other ordeals instead; for we had known peace for more than fifty years, and the scalps that hung in the Tepee of the Elders were so dry and withered that it was difficult to believe they had ever grown on human heads.

So that between us we could see as much of the Choosing as possible, I decided to watch it with the girls while Raki stayed with the boys. The Old Women, wrapped in the blankets with coloured patterns that they kept for ceremonial occasions, sat in a semi-circle on one side of the watch-fire; and opposite them were the Elders, seated on each side of the Chief who wore the Feathered Headdress. The Elders wore feathers too, but reaching only to their shoulders instead of hanging down to the ground as did Na-ka-chek's.

Behind the Old Women stood the ''not yet chosen'' and the women who had already borne children. I was with the younger girls, and the women who were not going to take part, either because their babies were too young or they too old. The ground sloped up towards the cliff, so I was able to see everything that happened. Raki must have been on the opposite side of the encampment, among the boys, but the crowd was so thick that I could not pick him out. A white stone had been put near the watch-fire and round it a space marked by a rope tufted with coloured feathers...another rope closed off a square between the two main groups of spectators. The woman sitting beside me held her son on her knee; I was rather puzzled at her sorrowful expression until I realized he must be nearly seven...the age when he would be taken away from her and given to the Brown Feathers to begin his training. If Mother had stayed with the tribe, Raki would have been taken away from her, and instead of our being together always he would belong on the other side of the encampment....I suddenly felt cold and wished I had not had such a horrible thought.

32

A group of men and boys had collected behind the Elders and there was a hush as the crowd waited for the ceremony to begin. One of the Elders called out the names of two boys, and at the same time Nona spoke the name of one of the girls who were standing behind her. The girl walked forward and stood on the white stone, and the two boys came to take their place on each side of it. Then one of the Old Women went up to the girl and in a loud voice began to proclaim her advantages, pausing between each statement to allow it to be given full attention. Her name, her age...the boys stared without displaying any interest, and the Old Woman's voice became more urgent.

"Her hair...see, the braids are thicker than my wrist and they have never starved for good grease...her teeth are as strong and white as a musk-rat's...and she is lively as a chipmunk."

The boys began to walk around the girl, noticing each point that the old woman described with such enthusiasm.... "Look at her moccasins, that fine beadwork which proves she is intelligent and has nimble hands! Her shoulders are strong enough to carry a deer; her feet are broad and can walk far uphill without tiring."

The girl stared in front of her, her face expressionless; not a muscle quivered, even when one of the boys prodded her ribs as though she were a carcass being tested for the cooking-pot.

The Elder who had called them forward asked whether either wished to choose her. Both boys held up their right hand, the sign of assent. At this, a ripple of excitement ran through the crowd, for it meant they must wrestle for her. I had often watched Raki wrestle, so it wasn't very interesting, though I saw one of them win by a new hold that sent the other spinning over his head.

Then the victor shouted a challenge which could be answered by any boy of his own age; but no one took it up, and without looking at the girl he walked off towards the roped square, the girl following him.

Neither of the second pair of boys chose the next girl, although the voice of her sponsor grew shrill. "Look at her thighs, strong as a cougar's. Only one tooth missing, and that was broken by a stone." She was offered twice more, but each pair of boys showed increasing disinterest in what had already been rejected. Even though she struggled to remain impassive, I saw tears on her face as she ran through the crowd to seek sanctuary from this open humiliation. I longed to run after her, for though I thought her lucky to have escaped, I knew she was suffering a desperate shame. Only by being chosen next year or the one after could she hope to end the jeers of her companions, for if she was three times rejected she would have to spend the rest of her life doing the most disagreeable of the work for the other squaws.

A great deal seemed to depend on the words of the Old Women, though to me they all sounded equally vehement, for two girls whom I considered much uglier than the rest were chosen by Brown Feathers, for such uninteresting qualities as endurance and a special skill in the preparation of food.

When a woman had already borne strong children they were displayed with her. "See, twice she has brought forth strong sons, and these wide hips would be a fine cradle for a future Scarlet Feather."

And of another Nona said, "Look, her son is more than a year old and yet her breasts are still proud with milk. Her children will never be starvelings to disgrace their mother!"

A third woman had three children; they huddled against her, and wept when she followed the man who had chosen her and left them to be taken away to the tepees. Because they had cried in the hearing of men they would not be allowed to share in the feast, so I decided to try to take them something to eat, for tonight there would be plenty for all.

The Scarlet Feathers did not wrestle for their women—I suppose they thought it undignified to display so much interest in squaws; and the men who had just won their brown feathers only wrestled because they enjoyed displaying their strength before the tribe.

After the Choosing, the men, each with his squaw beside him, sat in a large circle while the Old Women and the Elders served them with food as a mark of honour. Only after they had taken all that they wanted were the rest of us allowed to share the feast. Deer had been roasting since early in the day over the cooking-fires and there was as much as we could eat; and there were cakes made of corn-meal and honey, pigeons stuffed with sage, and rare delicacies such as fungus fried in fish-oil.

Suddenly the noise of the crowd stilled, as the drum began the opening phases of the Betrothal Dance. At first the pulse was so quiet and slow it seemed to tremble on the edge of hearing; gradually it grew louder and more insistent. The girls linked hands in single file, and pacing in rhythm to the drum, wove into a circle...faster and faster they padded round while the crowd swayed from side to side in harmony with them.

The men made a wider circle round the women: leaping high in the air, spinning on their heels, yet always drawing into a closer circle. The women were no longer separated by their linked hands...they drew nearer together until each had her hands on the shoulders of the woman in front: their bodies were pressed close; a wall of women drawing into a narrower spiral, until they were a pillar of women on whom the men were closing in. Shouting, leaping men, their bodies glistening with sweat...men who had thrown off their impassivity and roared like stags in autumn.

Then, as the drumming reached a new peak of frenzy, the men broke into the whirling cone of women, who screamed and struggled and pretended to try to escape. Or was it pretense? Were those real screams of terror? I was frightened, and wished that I had stayed with Raki. I looked at the women among whom I was standing: there was pity on some of the older faces, but the younger seemed only envious or excited. So I hoped that the screams were only part of the ritual...like the brandishing of tomahawks in a war dance.

As each man caught his woman, she ceased to struggle; he slung her over his shoulders like a deer, and carried her across the encampment to fling her down before the Totem. Beside it stood an Elder and one of the Old Women...whom I recognized as Nona. The man held out his hands, and into the palms they put something that they took from two pottery jars...later Raki told me it was blood and corn. The girl still lay face downward on the ground, but when the man spoke her name she crept to his feet and raised herself until she could lick the palms of his hands. This seemed to make them become ordinary again, for the man walked away and the girl followed five paces behind him until they took their place with those who had already done homage to the Totem.

At moonrise, the tribe gathered in two long rows, the women on one side, the men on the other. Through this avenue of people walked the Chosen: the men leading, the squaws walking docilely behind them. We watched them take the path to the woods. Some would return before the next full moon, others not until the moon after; but they would never speak of what had happened to them, nor might they mention, after they had returned to the Squaws' Tepees, the name of the man who had taken them away.

It was difficult to remember that these people were of the same blood as Raki and me, for nearly everything we said to them seemed beyond their understanding, as though an oriole tried to explain to a beaver the freedom of wings. One day I asked a girl whether she was happy, and she stared at me as though she didn't know what the word meant.

Raki said the boys were just as strange. They did everything with terrible determination. When they speared a fish they must always try to get more than the next boy, even when they didn't need fish to eat; they must always try to paddle their canoe faster than the others, to find more difficult ways up a cliff. They thought it splendid to go without moccasins on stony ground, and felt proud instead of foolish when they came back with their feet clotted with blood.

"Can't you make them understand it's silly to suffer *unnecessary* pain?" I said to Raki.

"No, I can't. I tried, but they stared at me as though I was mad, and then began to jeer, shouting, 'Raki is afraid of being hurt! Raki is a coward!' I tried to explain that I didn't mind pain if it was any use to anyone...but they only laughed."

"None of them really laugh, Raki. The girls make a kind of shrill giggle, and the boys laugh *at* people...but they never sound as though they were properly happy."

"Perhaps they never are. Their favorite ambition is to have a face which doesn't change with their thoughts. One of the Braves earned his scarlet feather by smearing himself with honey and letting fire-ants crawl over him while he didn't twitch a muscle...they stung him so badly that he nearly died. The boy who told me about it looked horrified when I said it didn't sound very *useful.*"

"The girls want to be impassive too. They tickle each other and put pads of nettles between their thighs, and some of them drive thorns under their nails."

"*Why* do you suppose they do it?"

"I suppose it's because they still listen to the Sorrow Bird....Mother said it was the greatest of all enemies except the Canyon of the Separation, and that until everyone knew it was the great enemy they would never remember the Before People."

"And they love the Sorrow Bird," said Raki sadly. "I think it's the only thing they love at all."

37

Shadow of the Totem

After the Choosing, I kept away from the Squaws' Tepees, for I disliked being reminded that I was female; and I made Raki repeat his promise that he would never let me go to live with them.

"Of course you'll never be a squaw!" he said indignantly. "We two are a *pair*, like two chipmunks, or two grizzlies, or two of anything that isn't stupid enough to belong to a tribe."

"The terrible thing is, Raki, that the squaws don't realize that the laws are unfair...they look on them as something which can't be altered, like the winter being so long and cold. You happen to have been born a boy, and so, if you wanted to, you could be first a Young Brave, and then a Brown Feather, and then a Scarlet Feather, and then an Elder, or even a Chief. But all that a girl can expect is to be Chosen...which is probably very disagreeable, and then to have babies...and if those are boys, they are taken away from her just when she's grown really fond of them and they are old enough to be interesting. Then, years and years later, she could become one of the Old Women, and enjoy bullying the younger ones and telling them horrible and unlikely stories. Males have got everything and females nothing; even the worst-off man has a better time than any woman."

"Not the Naked Foreheads," said Raki.

"Well, they hardly count," I said unfeelingly. "If they choose to go in for their silly ordeals and then fail so that everyone despises them, they can't expect pity."

"They can't help being born into the tribe," objected Raki. "At least no one expects anything of a woman, but if a boy happens to be naturally afraid of things, it must be terrible to know that he has either to do them or lose all privileges. I talked to a Naked Forehead yesterday; he was so surprised that I spoke to him as an equal that I thought he was

38

going to cry. He couldn't climb rocks without getting giddy and falling, and they wouldn't let him do some other trial instead...at least they offered to let him take his canoe down the Great Rapid, but he thought that was even worse than climbing. So eventually the Elders declared he would never win a feather and so must become a Naked Forehead as he would never be worthy to wear the tribal mark.''

''Apart from being ashamed, the Naked Foreheads don't have such a bad time, do they?''

''They have to take orders from the Old Women...though they oughtn't to mind that, of course,'' he added hastily, ''and they have to do all the scavenging, and carry game the hunters have killed, and clean and skin the deer.''

''Why shouldn't they do it? If they didn't, the women would have to.''

''You don't understand, Piyanah; for a man, it's shaming to have to do things like that.''

''It's just as disagreeable for women to have to do them, and if women aren't ashamed, it only shows they've got a little more sense than I thought.''

''Naked Foreheads can't take a squaw at the Choosing.''

''Do they ever father children?''

''No, and if they get even a little interested in a woman they are branded on the forehead...and I think other things happen to them as well, and they are then exiled from the tribe.''

''Perhaps I had better try to remember that Naked Foreheads are not really men, and then it will be easy to be nice to them.''

''Do you hate *all* men, Piyanah?''

''I like a few of them, but they are people like us who got into a tribe by mistake. The ones who enjoy the laws of separation are enemies....I wish I could turn them into slugs and then squash them with a heavy stone!''

39

Braves made their own arrows, but all the other skilled crafts were done by the Half-brothers, men who had been injured and could no longer fight or hunt, but earned their right to the protection of the tribe in other ways.

Tannek, the canoe builder, could only hobble leaning on a stick, for the muscles of his right leg had been torn by a mountain lion; below the knee it was withered and the toes curled under like claws. No one was so wise as Tannek in the selecting of birch-bark, or in knowing the grain of wood to make the ribs, or in choosing the sinews, which go to the making of a canoe.

Raki and I often went to watch him working on the one he was building for us: he carved a pattern of feathers on the prow and made the paddles, one for each of us, from red birch. In a canoe he forgot he was a cripple, and took us down rapids that until then had been forbidden to us. He named the rocks, telling us how to recognize their characters; which ones were kindly and fell sheer into deep water, and which pretended to be harmless and then thrust out a jagged ledge just under the surface to rip open the canoe of the unwary. He taught us to know water by its colour and where to watch for eddies; how to paddle so quietly that we left only a ripple that might have marked the passage of a moor-hen; how to make a canoe leap forward even against the current, and where to cross to the other side of the river, using the flow instead of fighting against it.

The Half-brothers each had a small tepee of their own in a clearing up-river from the main encampment. Tannek's tepee smelt of new wood and deer-sinews, except when he was boiling fish-glue and then there was no room for any other smell.

Minshi, who was much older than Tannek and rather surly, was also lame. He would never speak of how he lost his foot, but one of the boys told Raki that he had been burned in a prairie fire and a demon had prevented the wound from healing until the foot rotted off. He made all the pottery, except some of the roughest food-bowls used by women, and beside his tepee he had a small pit full of red clay which was brought by canoe four days' journey down-river. From this he made water-jars, the bowls used by the Chief and the Elders, and everything considered worthy of decoration. Most of the decoration was wavy lines and dots and sometimes a row of little crosses. Tannek had warned me that they meant snakes and stars and even birds and animals, so I was able to admire them properly, which pleased Minshi so much that he gave me some of the clay to make a food-bowl for Raki. Shaping it was much more difficult than it looked, but Minshi said the unevenness didn't matter and he put it into the oven, a hole in the ground lined with stones, with a fire above it, to bake until the colours were set. Pigments were made from special rare clay, yellow and a dark, rich red. This was baked, ground to powder, and then mixed with white of egg. It was not always easy for Minshi to get enough eggs, so Raki and I used to find them for him...usually along the river bank; they had to be fresh or else they spoiled the final colours.

Narrok, the tribal drummer, was also a Half-brother, for he was blind...though neither of us realized this until we had seen him several times, because he walked fast and without hesitation. Tannek told me he lost his sight through the ordeal which he hoped would have made him a Scarlet Feather, the highest honour to which any Redskin can attain, and before that he had been a famous tracker. Gradually, pace by pace, he learned the ground in every direction from his tepee, so that he no longer had to rely on a guide.

Raki and I had been up-river in our canoe and were returning in the early evening when we heard the muffled beat of a drum. We took our paddles from the water and drifted in silence to listen where the sound came from. It seemed to come from a thicket of young alders on the south bank, so we tied the canoe to a tree growing by the water and crept through the undergrowth until we reached a glade.

41

Narrok was sitting on the trunk of a fallen tree with the drum between his knees. He was tapping it with his long, flexible hands, the rhythm steady as the heart of a man asleep, and my heart steadied to the same beat. His eyes were open; they seemed to see us, and beyond to a far horizon. The sound belonged to the trees, and to the water and the rocks, and to us, as though we were all part of a living body whose heart was the Great Hunters. The rhythm changed: it spoke of courage, and splendid battles, and the war cries of Braves in victory. Then it grew slower and heavier: it was after the battle, and Death Canoes were going down-river to their last sunset...the Chief was standing by the ''pool of falling water'' holding my mother in his arms before he gave her to the Before People. I felt a tear slide down my cheek, and yet the sadness of the drum was beautiful as the crying of curlews through the mist of a winter evening.

I do not think he can have heard us, yet when his hands let the drum fall asleep, he said:

''There are two people listening...young and happy. Is it Raki and Piyanah?''

We came forward and sat on the grass beside him.

''I am glad you understand the language of the drums,'' he said. ''There are very few who understand. What did they say to you?''

I tried to tell him about the trees and the rocks being part of a living being who is the Earth, and of the joy of battle and the sorrow which followed after.

He smiled. ''So I have not betrayed my drum. When my eyes said they would no longer serve me, I asked the Great Hunters that I might learn to use my inward sight. For a long time I thought they had not heard me, for the night in which I lived remained unbroken. The tribal drummer was old and could no longer keep rhythm from dawn until sunset...and I was young, and blind...and useless. It was the Chief who asked me to learn the language of the drums in service to the

42

tribe; and for the first time the long night was a kindly darkness.

"I am no longer blind, Piyanah. There are eyes in my hands, and they know the texture of bark and of leaves, the colour of a stone, the humour of a plant, whether it is sad or singing. Out of the darkness I have made a little Earth: I know each path and where the trees are spaced; even if I walk a long way I know what the next pace will bring, turf or gravel or smooth rock to my feet. And in the drum I can see battles which have been forgotten, and mountains we have never crossed, and sunsets which belong to the generations."

"Can you see the Before People?" asked Raki eagerly.

"Are they the Singing People...who laugh, and are young even when their bodies grow old?"

"They must be the same," I said. "They had white houses, and trees with yellow fruit, so heavy that I could only hold one of them between my hands."

"I cannot remember their houses...only their songs. I hear them always behind the voices of my drum, between their sound and silence."

After this, Narrok was our friend, but he told us not to tell anyone that we talked to him. "For," he said, "it is only with you I wish to share my silence."

His loyalty to the Chief would not let him speak against the tribe, but he let us understand that he, too, felt a stranger among them.

"I loved my mother," he said, "but she never told me the name of my father, only that he was a Scarlet Feather. She made me promise to be worthy of him...she died soon after I went to live with the boys, so I could not ask her to release me from my promise. I was a Brown Feather when I was seventeen, though I found it difficult to remember the importance of endurance, to believe that a cliff was a challenge to the climber and not a curve against the sky to be enjoyed.

"Perhaps that is why my eyes deserted me, because I refused so many things they brought me and kept them about

43

such ordinary tasks. They told me to delight in a flock of white birches on the mountain-side; and I said to them, 'Birches? How far are they from the river? Is their bark ready for canoes?' They showed me trout, fluid as water among the reeds; and I said to them, 'Where is the exact place to cast a fish-spear?' They showed me a doe, standing with one forefoot lifted in dappled shade; and I said to them, 'She is in her third year; meat for the cooking-pot.' They showed me the river in flood; and I said to them, 'The pack-ice will make it too dangerous for canoes; our journey must be delayed three days.' My eyes offered me joy, but I valued them only because they were useful in little things that do not matter to the spirit.''

''When did your eyes go away?'' I said.

''At the Gathering of the Thirty Tribes, which takes place every seven years. The Braves vie with each other, and the Chiefs boast which of them has the most wearers of the Scarlet. To earn the title of Scarlet Feather you must be a full member of the tribe and then pass an ordeal to prove that you have overcome fear. The ordeal is chosen by the Chiefs in council, and they make very sure that it tests you to the utmost. At the Place of the Gathering there is a rock above the river, called the Eagle Rock. It leaps from the water the height of twenty men standing on each other's shoulders, and the pool below it is so narrow that only a perfect dive can end in safety.

''Many had died there in the past. I thought beyond the water I might find the land of the singing; but if this was denied to me I should have fulfilled my promise and wear the Scarlet in my forehead-thong. I knew as I fell towards the pool that I was too far from the rock. I felt my hands break the surface; then a dull blow and a whirling darkness...a darkness that has gone on and on....There was no welcome for me beyond the water, so I wait here until the drums of the Great Hunters tell me I am free to go.''

feathers of the future

The actions of the Chief cannot be questioned, but we knew that the tribe were anxious and disturbed because one morning my father's tepee had been found empty and for seven days he had not been seen.

Without being told, we knew he had come back, for the encampment suddenly lost the feeling of unspoken tension. We had just finished the dawn meal when he sent for us. If he had been an ordinary person instead of a Chief, I should have thought he was embarrassed, but that was impossible, for he was too remote and austere to know what real people felt like.

"It is not customary for a Chief to claim he has made a false decision, nor for a father to admit error to his children; but it is now necessary for me to do both these things, in loyalty to your mother." His face was impassive, but I knew that to say this was causing him great effort.

"Your mother told you of the Before People." He said this not as a question but to tell us that he knew it, so neither Raki nor I spoke.

"She told me of the Before People, but because of my pride I did not believe her: how could the son of the Chief learn wisdom from a squaw? But now her spirit has come to me, at the pool where I said farewell to her body; though of what I saw there I cannot speak even to you. To her I made an oath, the oath of a Chief which can never be broken; that what remains of my life on this side of the water shall be used to make reparation, so that one day she will take me to join her in the Land beyond the Sunset."

I felt a warm spring of affection for him bubble up inside me. He *had* loved my mother, and he still loved her. It was only because he had forgotten how to let love shine out of him that he seemed so cold and alone.

"The words of your mother, to which I had not the wis-

45

dom to listen, have become to me the law greater than all other laws. She said that the way of the Before People was the way of the Great Hunters. I had not the courage to believe her, but now she has shared with me her courage, which was always greater than mine even though I am a Scarlet Feather and she a woman.

"She told me that the meaning of the legends was not understood even by the Elders, and that of all these the legend of the First Red Man has been the most distorted. For generations, men have believed that they are the children of the Great Hunters, who, when they have passed the last ordeals, will return to the Land without Shadows. We have been taught that women have no such immortality; that woman was given to man only to bring forth the fruit of his seed and to do for him such tasks as are too lowly for him. We believed that Earth was made for man; the fish for him to spear, the deer for him to hunt, the corn for him to plant. We believed that the seasons of the year are sent to teach him their qualities; so that he may grow strong in the conquering of winter and gain endurance from the long heat. All this I believed: because I had not learned that in your mother's voice was wisdom; and in mine, only the utterances of a blind man who says there are no stars because he cannot see them."

"When are you going to tell the tribe that they must follow the Before People?" I asked eagerly.

"They would not believe me. Why should they, when I did not believe your mother?"

"But if you told them, they would have to believe you, because you are the Chief."

"Had I taken your mother to live at my side they would no longer have acknowledged my authority. It is the new Chief, Raki and Piyanah, to whom they will listen."

"*Both* of us to be the Chief?" I asked.

"Both of you; and you need not wait until my death, for you will lead your own tribe when you have become 'proud with feathers'."

46

From the cedar-wood chest he took the great headdress which he wore in council and on all ceremonial occasions. ''This has been worn by my father, and my father's father, for nine generations. With you it must find new life. Each feather should be a symbol of something the Chief has brought to the tribe: scarlet for an act of special courage, yellow for the wisdom of a new law, white for a vision of the unseen things.''

''There are three black feathers. What do they mean?'' said Raki. ''I thought that black feathers always belong to the Enemy.''

''They are supposed to record a victory, in the far past, over the children of the Carrion Crow. But your mother told me they should mean that the Chief had gone down into the Underworld to rescue one of his people from the Lord of the Dark Moon.''

''Is the Underworld the same as the Cavern of the Blind Fish?'' I said, remembering the legend of the boy who had gone there to get the second pair of eyes which restored sight to his twin brother.

''I cannot tell you; for I have never been there.''

''Do the Blind Fish exist, or are they only a legend?''

''I cannot tell you; for I have never seen them.''

''What ordeals shall we have to pass before we become 'proud with feathers'?'' asked Raki.

''It is to tell you the nature of these ordeals that I have brought you here,'' said Na-ka-chek. ''Your mother, whose voice is truth, told me that even if my Braves increased ten-fold, no arrow of theirs could kill the Sorrow Bird while men and women are still divided against each other. She said that the strongest warrior was a cripple if he had not a woman for his dear companion, and that a squaw who had borne many children was barren unless she loved their father. In you and Raki I have seen the truth of her words; now you must learn to teach her truth to your people.''

''If they won't listen to you, why should they listen to

us?'' said Raki.

''Because you will become the bridge by which they can cross the Canyon of Separation. Each of you must learn to be neither man nor woman. Raki will be the 'not-man,' Piyanah the 'not-woman'. Each of you must gain a brown feather; but during the seven years that will prepare you for the ordeals, Raki will live as a squaw; until he has learned to think as a woman, and can speak to them in a voice which they understand because it is their own. Piyanah will live as a boy; she will learn to think as they do, feel as they do, challenge their hard endurance with her own. Only when they have had to accept her as one of themselves will they believe that woman is the equal of man. In Piyanah, their fellow Brave, they will see all women as worthy companions. In Raki, all squaws will see the men they need no longer fear, the men who will no longer despise them. Then will Raki and Piyanah be the Chief of a new tribe, in which the men and women will honour each other in equality, and bear children in whom the Before People will live again on this side of the water.

''At the next full moon Raki will go to the Squaws' Tepees and Piyanah will join the boys. It will be as though the Canyon separated you also: Piyanah who has begun her warrior training will not speak to Raki the squaw. But in seven years *two* Feathered Headdresses shall be made, for Raki and Piyanah, the Chief of a tribe whose happy voices will be heard by your mother in the Land without Shadows.''

Then, without waiting for us to answer, he told us to leave him, but as I went out of the tepee I heard him say softly, ''When your mother hears their voices perhaps she will allow Na-ka-chek, who was blind, to come to ask for her forgiveness, because she knows he has fulfilled her dreams.''

When we left the Great Tepee, Raki led the way among the winter birch trees to the rock where Mother had waited for us, when we first learned why we were not the same as other people. The silence was deep as a snow-drift; far away, muffled by the cold, I heard the hunting bark of a coyote. Raki stood looking across the falling shadows of the lower slopes to the distant mountains. Then he said:

"Everything we can see, even the patterns our snow-shoes made yesterday, is unchanged; only you and I are different. We are going to follow the Before People, and because of us the squaws and the Braves will laugh together, and their children will not be frightened by legends, for we shall have killed the Sorrow Bird."

One phrase of my father's stood out like fresh blood on snow, "For seven years you and Raki must live apart." Surely Raki had heard it too?

"Raki, you are talking as if it were really going to happen. Didn't you hear him say it would be seven years before we passed the ordeals and could be together?"

"Until we are ready to lead our own tribe."

"I don't want to be a Chief! I want to stay as we are, you and I together, always."

"Because we love each other we can never really be lonely, but we can't let the rest of the tribe go on living as unhappy strangers just because we haven't the courage to be parted for a little while."

"Seven years *isn't* a little while! Raki, don't go away from me. I'm frightened, Raki, and you never let me be frightened by things other people tell us."

He jumped down from the rock and put his arms around me. "You're crying, Piyanah, and you never cry. Think of how we are going to teach other people to be happy."

"How can we teach them to be happy when we shall have forgotten what it feels like! Mother told us that it was because the tribe had forgotten how to laugh that they couldn't remember the Before People. Don't you remember her story about the girl and the hunter, whom the animals protected because they had the light on their foreheads which comes from loving someone more than yourself? We've got that light, Raki, and if we are parted it will go out and we shall be alone in the dark.''

''It will be very difficult for a girl to become a Brown Feather,'' he said slowly. ''If you are less swift, they will say you are a stone in their moccasins; and if you are better at the things they do, they will be jealous, and cruel.''

''I'm not frightened of *them*. It's being parted from you I'm afraid of.''

''It's only for seven years. Perhaps it will be less if we learn very fast.''

''You talk of seven years as though they were seven days! Being without you will be worse than being without food or water; it will be like not being able to breathe.''

''Seven years is a very long time....I had forgotten how long it was going to be before we shall be ready to lead our own tribe.'' Then, as though thinking aloud, ''Three died in the ordeals last year. It will be worse for Piyanah than for me...her body is not so strong as mine.''

''Then you agree, Raki, that we can't let them part us?''

He sighed. ''Can we betray the Before People?''

It was dark when we got back to the encampment. The others had finished the sunset meal, but food had been left in our tepee. I tried to talk of the things we should do when we had our own tribe to look after. But louder than the words, my thoughts kept saying, ''Soon we shan't be together any more, any more, any more,'' on and on, like the feet of a weary runner.

Every day Raki made me practise all he had taught me of a boy's training. Time after time he went over the wrestling holds, showing me the exact spot where pressure on an arm snaps the bone like a dry twig, and how to turn an opponent's strength against himself. I used his bow, which was heavier than mine, for the one I should soon be given would be longer by a handspan than any we had yet bent.

So as to try to get used to the new life we should soon have to lead, when we thought there was no chance of us being seen, we changed clothes and he pretended to be my squaw. He wore the bracelets and necklaces which had been Mother's and the embroidered tunic I had worn at the Feast of Midsummer. I was showing him how to plait his hair, because soon he would have to do even the ones at the back himself, when I suddenly realized that the notes of the mocking-bird I had been hearing were made by a human throat.

Tekeeni, a boy two years older than us, swung down from a tree on the far side of the glade. He was laughing. ''Poor Raki! Piyanah has turned him into a squaw! When he has learned still more of the ways of women there will be a great wrestling at the Choosing, for all the Braves will want Raki—the prettiest squaw of them all!''

Then he came towards us, mimicking the postures of the Betrothal Dance.

''Poor Tekenni will feel humble when he has been beaten by a woman,'' said Raki calmly.

Tekeeni had obviously not intended to provoke a fight, for when he saw Raki was unembarrassed he said airily that he couldn't stay to talk to us as he had to visit a snare he had set.

But Raki taunted him, ''Tekenni is a child! He would run even from the Old Women in case they should smack him! Tekeeni dares not take three paces towards Raki, for if he did, he knows it would be a challenge!''

Tekeeni hesitated, and then took three steps towards us. Raki and I usually fought people together, but this time I knew he wouldn't like me to help.

The fight was soon over, though Tekeeni didn't give the sign which accepts defeat until blood was pouring from his nose and a loose eye-tooth hung from his upper jaw. He lay panting on the ground and then scrambled to his feet.

''If all squaws fought like you do, Raki,'' he said with a grin, ''it would be the women who carried the war bows and the men who stayed behind to wash the cooking-pots.'' He pulled the loose tooth and held it out to Raki. ''Here's something to add to your bear's claws when you get them.''

51

His smile was crooked because of his split lip, but I knew by his eyes that we had found a friend.

One of the necklaces had broken in the fight, and after Te-keeni had gone we searched for the beads which had been trodden into the snow. Raki stood holding one of them in his hand. "I shall not be able to fight everyone who mocks me," he said ruefully, "or I shall never learn to 'Think as a woman, live as a woman, feel as a woman.' " He sighed. "I shall have to become impassive as the Elders!"

I didn't want him to become impassive! I wanted him to go on laughing easily as a spring, not to turn his face into a mask which hid pain, and sorrow, and joy...if a Brave ever felt joy, even from me. Had I at last found a way to turn him from the path he had accepted? Mockery might have shown him how difficult the lonely years would be; would he let me suffer mockery?

After this I no longer tried to conceal my dread of the future. I told him that I might fail in the ordeals, and that I was frightened of dying; I did not tell him that I was more frightened of my heart turning into stone than my body into dust. But I could not make him promise to run away from the tribe; and we still had to count the days we had together. Eight, seven, six...time burning away faster than a pine-torch.

When there were only three days left to us, the fear of separation was stronger than the fear of arguing with the Chief.

Na-ka-chek heard me without interruption, then he said: "I have already told you that you must become the man and the not-man; the woman and the not-woman. You must obey my laws until you are a Chief and ready to make your own."

I thought that if I could break through his impassivity I might be able to make him believe me, so I tried to make him angry. "You are asking Raki to betray me as you betrayed my mother!"

"You are asking me to send you to the Squaws' Tepees while Raki passes the ordeals alone. If he knew that you had not the courage to win the right to the Feathered Headdress, he would choose another squaw to bear his sons."

"Raki would never choose another squaw! My mother said you had forgotten how to be happy and that was why the arrows of your Braves would never kill the Sorrow Bird. Please let us go to the Brown Feathers together, and then we will prove to them that because of love we are stronger than they are."

"Why should they believe that love gives strength when you are already showing that it makes you a coward?"

"A man is not a coward if he says he will not be able to fight if you cut off his arms! That's what Raki and I are like without each other...cripples! How can a cripple fight?"

"You must be strong alone before you can be double strong together."

"Why should we be separated so as to learn how to become one again? If only you would let us train together, we will each win *four* Scarlet Feathers; no one has ever done that!"

"You mean that you hope Raki will win eight feathers, and give half his honour to you. You must learn to wield authority in your own right before men will accept your words: if you returned from the ordeals in Raki's company, the men would say, 'She is like the squaw who carried home the deer for the hunter...and claimed the kill for her own.' "

"If you make me leave Raki, men will say things that make bitter hearing for you! They will say, 'Piyanah, the daughter of Na-ka-chek, is a coward! Na-ka-chek was foolish to have called her his son.' "

There seemed no ember of kindliness in the cold ash of his eyes. "I have spoken; and the word of Na-ka-chek is not questioned by one of his tribe."

I managed not to cry until I thought Raki was asleep. The tears only increased my grief, but I could not stop them. Suddenly I knew he was awake. As he gathered me closer into the shelter of our fur robe, he said:

"You needn't sorrow any more, Piyanah. We *are* going to lead a new tribe, but now, not after seven years. It will be a small tribe, of two people who love each other."

the little valley

The moon was up when we crept out of the tepee, and weaving shadows from the watch-fire patterned the black and white of the open space we had to cross before reaching the shelter of the trees. Thin snow crunched under foot; across the valley a wild dog began to bark, and another took up the challenge.

It was very cold, but Raki's hand was warm and secure. I wondered if the big grizzly, whose spoor we had seen two days earlier, had gone back to the high ground or was lurking near us in the darkness. I heard a thud, and thought it must have been caused by some large animal, but Raki said it was only snow falling off an overloaded branch. Except where the trees grew close together, the track was easy to follow in the brilliant moonlight, yet it seemed longer than I expected before we reached the place where we had hidden our bundles the previous day.

We had bread, enough for three days, strips of pemmican, a bow with four extra bowstrings, fish-hooks, line, a rope of plaited raw-hide, two knives, and a small tomahawk. These were divided equally between us, but Raki carried two water-skins, one empty and the other full of seed maize, and a small cooking-pot. We each wore a second tunic and a blanket, and carried a spare pair of moccasins in our belt. I was glad that Raki had let me bring only the things he considered essential, for the thongs of my pack soon began to chafe my shoulders.

It was moonset when we reached the edge of the forest; we had to wait until the thin grey light brought the ground out of the shadows and it was safe to go on. We heard the roar of the water before we came in sight of the river, so I knew I could no longer cling to the hope that we should be able to cross on the ice lower down the valley.

Raki knew what I was thinking, for he said confidently, ''It's not really a very difficult climb. You have done harder ones for no particular reason except that they were an adventure. This is an adventure above all the others, so you are sure to be steadier even than usual. Now we are our own tribe, the Great Hunters will give us counsel...they always do to Chiefs.''

''I'm not frightened,'' I said firmly, ''not even right down inside of me.''

''Of course you're not, but it's easier to climb when your hands are warm; give them to me and I'll thaw them.'' He pulled open the neck of his tunic and held my hands against his chest until the fingers were supple.

Then he said briskly, ''Now; before we have time to think about it any more. Would you like me to lower you down this first bit until you can stand on a ledge?''

I was afraid of having to watch him do the climb, for if he fell, I might not be able to get down to him. He knew it, otherwise he would have gone first as he always did.

''I'll go now, while my hands are warm,'' I said.

''Take off your pack. I'll lower them both down afterwards.''

I lay face down and slid my feet over the edge of the cliff. The spray of the rapids far below reached me, fine as mist. Raki was lying flat holding my wrists.

''Go slowly. You'll feel the first ledge in a moment; the rock is honest; I tested it yesterday.''

I couldn't find the ledge and felt my fingers slipping from their hold. I nearly shouted to Raki to let go my wrists, for I thought I should pull him over with me. Then my foot found something to take my weight. ''It's all right, Raki, I can stand now.''

''Edge along three paces to the right; then stretch out your hand until you feel a thorn bush; its roots are quite firm.''

He let go my wrists. I felt as though the dark water below was trying to pull me backwards by the hair. Flattened against the rock I groped sideways, afraid that the narrow ledge was going to crumble before I could find a foothold. I reached the thorn bush and swung by it to the other ledge.

His voice steadied me. ''There's a fissure in the rock a little farther on; follow that down till you come to a broad shelf. Wait there till I join you.''

I heard the packs bumping against the rock-face as he lowered them down, then the thud of the coiled rope as he dropped it after them. The spray was swirling up from the fall like steam from a cooking-pot. My hair was grey with damp and I blew on the fingers of the hand I was not using to hold on with, to make them warm enough to be obedient. As Raki climbed down I tried not to think of what would happen if he slipped....

Then he was beside me, saying, ''It isn't a difficult climb, really, is it, Piyanah? It's only that it *looks* difficult from the top. No one will think that we came this way, and even if they can follow our tracks so far, they will think we must have turned back to try to cross the river at the ford higher up. Or if they follow this bank till they reach the marsh, they will know they have lost us when they find no tracks there. If the ice hadn't broken, we might have crossed almost anywhere, so they would have searched the whole of the far bank, but now when they find no sign of us beyond the ford, they may not try anywhere else....I expect they will believe we have been drowned. It's worth three days' start, the ice breaking.''

I tried to thank the Ice Spirit for bringing the thaw before we had crossed, but thought it would be easier to be properly grateful when we had reached the far bank.

''I'll go first this time,'' said Raki. ''Slide over the ledge when I tell you. I'll put your foot in a safe hold; it's rather difficult to find unless you know where it is.''

The rest of the climb down was easier than I had expected, but I knew Raki was nearly as relieved as I was when we reached the foot of the cliff. We tied on our packs, and Raki wound the rope round his waist. I was used to balancing on slippery rocks above a torrent, for we often did it when spearing fish. The ice was moving faster now; and the slabs grinding together sounded like skeletons being gnawed by Great Cougar. The noise was too loud for us to hear our voices, but we could see each other laughing, and there was no longer fear behind the laughter.

From boulder to boulder we jumped or scrambled, sometimes creeping forward on hands and knees, sometimes poised for a leap over racing water. The sun had cleared the mist before we reached the far bank. We spread our dripping clothes over a bush, and ran about naked in the sun till the air only felt sharp and clean, like cold water when you are thirsty, instead of being an enemy with arrows of ice. We ate some bread; there was no time to make a fire even if we had caught fish to cook in it.

Spring had come before the Day of Spring, and all round us we could hear Earth stirring into life. From the forest we heard snow crashing from the branches, as trees held up their arms to the sun. Even when we struck north, away from the river, the sound of running water was with us, for each melting drift added its note to the spring chorus. There was heat in the sun now, and it was good to walk naked, and forget that the night would be cold.

We decided not to make a fire until we were certain that its smoke would not betray us...perhaps it would be safe after dark, if we could find somewhere to hide the light. We came to a small stream which was running freely, and walked through the shallow water for a long way, further to hide our trail.

The country between us and the hills was flat and stony; there were no trees, for only stunted bushes could nourish themselves in the sandy ground. We had expected to be able to make a shelter out of branches, but here there was not even a rock high enough to keep off the night wind. Winter crept back with the lengthening shadows. We put on our tunics, and thought of the fur robe which had been too bulky to carry...by moonrise it would be bitterly cold. We were hungry enough to have eaten raw fish, but we couldn't see any in the stream. I helped Raki to set a snare over a gopher hold, though it didn't look very promising as there were no fresh droppings near it.

A sullen wind began to blow from the north; it raised the sand in little eddies and disturbed the dry twigs of the huddled bushes. Long ago the stream must have been much larger, for now it threaded its way through a bed wide enough for a river. Beside it we were hidden from anyone who was not standing directly above us, and Raki wanted to risk making a fire; but I was more afraid of being taken back to the encampment than of the cold.

I wondered if we should ever live in a community again, ever be part of a life which went on in the same pattern day after day. If only Father had not been so cruel, it would have been pleasant to see the Old Women stirring cauldrons, and the Elders smoking, remote and sombre, by the watch-fire. Even a bear needs the security of her den and the beaver her fastness under the bank...but Raki and I did not need a tepee, or people, or familiar things...we only needed each other. To be apart would be a coldness which no fire could warm, and a hunger which even deer-stew could not satisfy.

"Piyanah," he said, "we must dig a hole to sleep in. The bank is loose enough to pull down with our hands. Pile the earth on the windward side."

It was nearly nightfall before we finished. The sky was green as ice, and the wind dark as a crow's wing. We huddled together like cubs whose mother has gone hunting, and I could hear the long, steady beat of his heart.

"When we return into the sky, Piyanah, men will see one new star instead of two. The brightest stars are two people who have loved each other; they will take us into their tribe...and it is a greater tribe than follows the proudest Lord of Feathers, and its brotherhood is closer than blood-tie."

"Nothing else matters except being together, does it, Raki?"

"Nothing else matters," said Raki.

It took us two days to reach the mountains beyond the plain, and another to find the pass by which we crossed them. On the northern side, the foothills folded into narrow valleys, each separated by a sharp ridge, and it was in one of these that we found our "place of the corn-growing."

A stream leapt down five falls, and then sang through a meadow, a gentle slope of about two hundred paces, enclosed by wooded slopes which drew together beyond it so that the water flowed down into the open country through a narrow cleft. Instead of a tepee we made a shelter against the face of a steep rock; three small trees growing close together made the uprights, and between them we put closely interwoven branches until it was secure against wind and rain. Beside it there was a great pine with twin trunks, and this became our Totem; every day we put flowers at its foot to remind the tree spirit to look after us.

Windrushes grew in the bed of the stream; from their stalks we made a covering for the floor, and a heap of the dry leaves was warm to sleep in. After Raki had made a trap below the largest pool, we had plenty of fish, and in the woods we found several kinds of plants which we knew were good to eat. There was a colony of gophers lower down the hillside, and though I hated to kill them, we had to set snares there, becuse their flesh was useful for stew and we needed the skins to make a curtain to close the entrance to our shelter. He carved me a needle out of a chipmunk's bone, but it was difficult to sew the skins together without deer-sinew, for the gut of small animals is brittle unless it has been treated with oil or bear's grease.

It took us nearly a moon to prepare a plot of ground, for though the soil was dark and rich, it was difficult to get it ready for the sowing without any proper tools; but soon we could watch the green shoots of our own corn getting taller and stronger every day.

Though we made several expeditions into the Uninhabited Country we couldn't find any salt, and often wished that we had remembered to bring some with us. Sage and garlic helped to make our stews more interesting, but it was always exciting when we found something that was a change from fish or gophers. Occasionally Raki got wildfowl from a lake about three hours' running distance from our little valley, and severals times he caught a porcupine, which we wrapped in clay and baked in hot ashes, until the clay was so hard it could only be broken with a heavy stone and the quills came off with it. The best find of all was a hollow tree full of honey-comb; I got badly stung taking this, but there was enough to fill four jars, which we had baked from red clay at the same time as we made our food-bowls.

I was lying on the bank of the stream, enjoying the feel of the grass, warm and alive against my skin, while Raki plaited a rope from strips of raw-hide which had been part of the deer he had killed a moon earlier...the flesh we had made into pemmican and the sinews I was keeping to sew winter tunics and moccasins. As I watched him I wished that I could draw his face so that people in the future would know the colour of his thoughts. The pictures we had seen in a cave were only a few scrawls of red chalk, and yet the bison were so alive that I could almost feel the ground shudder under their thundering hooves. I should draw Raki's nose and forehead in a single line: the shadow under the cheek bone would be difficult, and the listening stillness of the eyebrow....

He leant down: the straight black hair swung forward and hid his face; and I got up to push the logs nearer to the centre of the fire, whose heat was soaking down through the sand to a teal wrapped in leaves and clay. Then I remembered the water-jar was empty. There had been very little rain, and now that the flow over the rocks was only sufficient to keep them glistening with moisture, we drew our water in the shade of a rock that guarded the pool below the meadow.

As I bent over the water my reflection stretched out her hands to me and I smiled at her. The polished surface rippled, though there was no breeze. I thought, ''If Nona saw this, she would say my spirit was in danger.''

The water was smooth again: suddenly I realized that what I was now seeing was more than my own reflection. The girl was like me, yet older...and she wore the Feathered Headdress. The lips moved, and though I could not hear her voice, I knew what she was saying:

''You must follow the way of the Feathers; you cannot hide from them, Piyanah, for you are only the girl I used to be. You were born to the Feathers; though you cannot see them, they are part of you, as the pinions of the eagle are in the unhatched egg.''

The pool quivered, as water in a cooking-pot trembles with the heat. I saw my own face looking up at me, with fear in the eyes.

Clearer than the call of the blue jay in the tree above me I seemed to hear my father's voice:

''You cannot escape the future, for with the past it is the other half of the present. They are the two wings by which the bird of the spirit flies to the Land without Shadows.''

I answered him as though he were standing beside me, ''Raki and I are not bound by the past; we are children of the present, and the future is our own! We are secure because we are together. We are bound by no tribal laws; we are free to live. Why should your ambition bring down our swift joy like a roped bison?''

In the listening silence it seemed that all the things I had ever feared came out of the shadows of the trees to watch me. The sunlight had grown cold, and the stream was weary as slow tears.

I heard Raki calling me, shouting that he had found a wild duck in a snare, so that tomorrow we should feast like the Chief of seven tribes. As I ran towards him, the thoughts which had come to haunt me slid away behind the barriers I had built against them. There was no longer a cloud over my sun; Raki's hand was on my shoulder and he was laughing down at me.

I wanted to tell him about the ghost in the pool, but the memory of how my father had nearly taken him away from me made me afraid. Hidden in my mind was the fear that something even stronger than the love between us would call him back, for I knew that if he had heard the voice as I had heard it, we should be setting out to cross the pass, every step bringing us nearer to the desert of seven years which we must travel alone.

A few days later I was standing on a rock waiting to spear a fish when again I saw the water tremble. For the flash of a dragon-fly I saw the woman...then flung my spear at her so that she was hidden by the spreading ripples. I told myself she was not Piyanah of the future, she was only a dream of my father's, looking up through the water in search of a mortal who would give her breath. Yet I found myself speaking to her as though she were a real person:

''Poor Piyanah of the Feathers, you will never be born; because I, Piyanah, who is eleven years old, am stronger than you. You and your feathers belong to the land of dreams, and you will never be able to make me fulfill your destiny. You can't understand me because you are only a legend...I belong to the firm earth, where trees are rooted and I can hear Raki laughing.''

After that day I filled the water-jar only where there was a flow, for I dared not look into still water. It was the first time I had ever concealed something from Raki. I knew in my heart that he wanted to bring the Before People alive; he was like a carver who sees a totem pole hidden in a tree, calling to him to release it with his knife. He had seen the old truth hidden in the past, and he wanted us to bear it into the present, even though we walked as mourners under the burden.

Dark Smoke

Through the mellow autumn days we made ready for the winter. Enough firewood to last until spring thaw was stacked beside the shelter, and beyond it we had dug a pit, in which our hoard of nuts, and pine-kernels, and roots, were stored in dry sand protected from the weather by branches.

As the corn ripened I hung the cobs from the roof, and though the pemmican we had made was rather harder than usual, it was quite good to eat if soaked for two days and cooked very slowly.

Already there was a chill in the air before dusk, so I pulled on a tunic when we went up to the top of the ridge to watch the sunset. Suddenly Raki stopped, tense as an animal scenting the wind. To the east, in the Uninhabited Country, a column of dark smoke was thrusting up towards the evening sky.

I thought it was a prairie fire, and said unconcernedly, "It's a long way off. Even if it spreads, we shall be safe, for it's beyond the river."

"It will not spread...unless the man who tends it is careless."

Even then I saw no menace in the smoke. "I expect it's

63

only a hunter...and there's nothing to bring him here.''

''Does a hunter need to cook for three hundred?'' While he was speaking I saw new threads of smoke rising up near the first fire. ''They must be a strong tribe, Piyanah...and they have come out of the East!''

I tried to reassure him. ''Perhaps it's only one of the tribes who used to trade with our people in the summer. They must have crossed the plain from the West without our seeing them.''

''We have watched from here every dawn and sunset since we made this our place of the corn-growing, and we have never seen smoke. You know that a tribe does not travel without lighting a fire every night, and the swiftest runner could not reach there from the western horizon in less than two days. That fire has been lit by people who are so strong that they need not conceal their numbers—and they have come out of the *East*.''

''But no one lives in the East.''

''The Chief told us that the Carrion Crow also had children.''

''The Black Feathers! Raki, they are only a legend made to frighten children.''

''Would the Braves be honoured by the tribe if there were no enemies?''

''You think the Black Feathers are *real*?''

''Do spirits need to build cooking-fires?''

''They'll never find us here, Raki. Even if they go to the Lake of the Wildfowl and see our snares they will only think a hunter had been there and forgotten to take them up.''

''They may not find us, but if they travel southwards they must mean to cross the pass. By tomorrow night we shall know if we have to go back to warn Na-ka-chek.''

''We can't go back! Not now, Raki, not when we're so happy. We must hide from them. We can't seek Father's protection after we ran away from him.''

Suddenly I realized that Raki was angry. ''We could leave

64

the tribe when it was secure; but would you let our people be massacred because you were too proud to return?''

''But, Raki, even if we have to tell them that the Black Feathers are coming, they can't keep us there. It would be against the laws of the tribe...we could be driven out, but not kept there against our will.''

''The Chief, your father, will not run away from his enemies. Our Braves protect what is rightfully their own, and I shall fight with them.''

''Then you must promise to let me fight beside you. You won't tell me to hide with the squaws...promise me that, Raki, and I'll do anything else you want.''

For the first time since we had seen the smoke, he smiled. ''Of course we shall fight together. We do everything together, and your bowstring could sound no war song in a squaw's tepee.''

''Will the Black Feathers be very terrible? The story-teller said they are twice the height of ordinary men; their teeth are filed into points because they eat flesh warm from the kill, and the fingers of their women are taloned and can rip open a man's belly like a eagle feeding on a gopher.''

''I expect they have grown in the telling. We needn't be frightened, at least not very frightened, for I expect we shall *both* be killed. Does it matter *very* much if we live here or in the Land of the Great Hunters, so long as we are together?''

''They might kill you, Raki, and forget to kill me. The story-teller said they killed all the men and children and carried off the women who were not too old.''

''You shall wear a breech-clout and I'll paint your face with the tribal marks before battle. You are nearly as tall as I am, and we wear our hair the same way, and your breasts are too small to betray you. If I am killed first, you will just have to go on fighting until you join me.''

I felt comforted. Now that I accepted the fact that Raki and I were both going to be killed, I found that death wasn't frightening, if we both met it together. It was too dark to watch the smoke any longer, so hand in hand we went down to our little valley.

Before going to sleep we had decided that as we could do nothing until the direction of the fires next evening told us whether the Black Feathers intended to cross the pass, we should try to keep what might be our last day in the valley unshadowed by fear of the future.

"We must be careful not to think that this might be our last day," said Raki when he woke. "We must keep it as a memory to feed on if we are ever joy-hungry...as though it were bread to take on a journey."

"If we *do* have to go, Raki, we had better take bread with us; it's easier than anything else. We can pretend we're only baking it because we want to take it on an adventure which will be too exciting to bother with looking for food."

"Yes, we had better make bread...it will be the first we have eaten here."

Together we stripped the cobs into the round hollow of a rock which served as a grinding-bowl. Then, while I kneaded water into the meal, Raki scraped an opossum pelt with a sharp flint to remove the fat, and began to scour it with gravel before pegging it out to dry. I wondered why he bothered to do this, until I realized that it was part of his plan for keeping today away from tomorrow.

Everything must go on as though nothing unusual had happened. I must make myself believe that day by day we should see the stack of firewood getting lower, and count the corn-cobs to judge how many must be saved for the spring sowing. I wondered if he would remember to cut withies for snow-shoes; yesterday he had said that it was time we made them.

I tried very hard to copy Raki, but I kept on finding myself thinking, "This is the last time we shall be able to watch the shadow of the twin pine cross the meadow. Perhaps a patch of wild corn will grow here, year after year, when a storm has blown down our shelter and scattered the grain over the blurred furrows. When the snows melt, the fish-traps will be washed away, and our fur robe that I made from so many little skins will rot, and every autumn be buried deeper under the dead leaves.''

''Are you burning the fish you will catch tomorrow on today's fire?'' said Raki.

''I am sorry. I started thinking about the rest of the corn, wondering what was going to happen to it. We were so sure that we should winter on bread of our own planting.''

''I think we always eat of our own planting, Piyanah: though the food may be life, or death, or victory, according to our seed.''

''Will it be cold on the other side of the water?''

''I think it will be like Earth, only more beautiful. You have only to look at the reflection in still water to see the spirit of a bird, or a rock, or a tree. We shall be able to fly like birds and swim like fishes. Do you remember how you always wanted to see into the cave at the bottom of the pool where Mother would never let us swim? We can go to that cave now...when 'now' is after we have been killed. Do you remember what it felt like before we ran away? There were so many things which might happen that it was like trying to steer a canoe down a rapid when the river is so high that the rocks are hidden; yet we came into calm water. Try to go back to that moment when we stood looking down the cliff and heard the ice-packs growling below us. Do you remember how the climb was much easier than we thought it was going to be? We laughed while we were crossing the river...do you remember how we could see each other laughing, though we could not hear our voices? As soon as we crossed the river we heard spring coming back...everywhere the sound of the earth being born again. Then we found this valley. Don't you realize, Piyanah, that what is going to happen to us is only the journey here over again? You are frightened now, just as we were frightened when we crept out of the tepee and started off alone through the forest.

And when we see the Black Feathers coming towards us we shall only be standing looking down the cliff, and the battle will be the climb. I think we shall be afraid of seeing men die while it's actually happening, but our own death will be crossing the river...and we laughed when we crossed the river, Piyanah.

"Whoever stands first on the far bank will wait there for the other. Even if the country on the other side of the water is strange at first, we shall feel our spirits getting used to their new freedom, like streams when the ice melts. Then we shall find ourselves in another meadow, the Place of the Garnering of the Corn; and we shall see each other in the light of our single star. We shall be so close that it will be like being one person, and we shall never have to grow old, or be afraid any more."

"Can the place we go to after we are dead be just like this, Raki? I don't want it any better, I want it exactly the same."

He smiled. "Wouldn't you prefer the pool a little deeper so that we could dive into it, or the shelter set so that it faces the morning sun?"

"No, Raki, not at first. I want everything to be just as it is now. You can change it afterwards if you like, when I'm used to being dead."

I threw down two corn-cobs. "I even want those to be there, just as we left them. I'll pick them up after I am dead. You won't forget about the cobs, will you, Raki?"

"We will ask the Totem to arrange it for us."

Hand in hand we stood before the twin tree. "O great spirit who knows us on both sides of the water! If we meet death without shutting our eyes against him, and cross the water without fear, may the Great Hunters let us return to this place, and may we find it exactly as we see it now. May we stand here together and say, 'Tomorrow and yesterday are one day: Raki and Piyanah are one star'."

It was sunset when we reached the head of the pass. We stood in a pool of warm light, looking back at the plain which was already nearly engulfed by shadows flowing down from the mountains. A day's journey behind us we saw the smoke that to us was more terrible than the cloud which is the forerunner of a tornado.

"There is no chance of their turning back now, is there, Raki?"

"None. The river crossing will delay them, for they must go half a day up-stream before they find a place to ford. They are travelling faster than I expected, so we must make full use of the moon, resting only between sunset and moonrise, and in the darkness before dawn."

When running had become a weariness which grew into pain, the journey took on the unreality of a grey dream, in which the only sound was the soft padding of our feet as I followed Raki, further and further away from happiness.

On the third day we hoped to see one of our own people who could take on the warning more swiftly, but there was no sign of man in the blazing autumn of the woods. Last night we had seen smoke between us and the foothills below the pass, and knew the Black Feathers would give no further sign of their swift approach.

The river was low and water curled lazily between the rocks, but we were both so tired that it was difficult to swim across. I hoped that the enemy would arrive before I stopped being tired, for then it would be easy to die unafraid. Already I felt separate from the girl who still ran on and on although her moccasins seemed to be made of stone: my spirit would be free with Raki, and her body would be glad to lie in the quiet earth, knowing that it would not have to carry me any further.

At sunset we dared not rest, for we knew that if we fell asleep we should never wake at moonrise. It was too dark to find the track through the forest, so we had to take the longer way beside the river. The water held an echo of daylight, shining through the dusk like the track of a snail.

We saw the watch-fire through a cleft in the rocks which guarded the east side of the encampment. The flaps of the Squaws' Tepees were closed, but two of the Elders were still sitting by the fire. They looked up as we passed, but made no sign of recognition.

My father was standing beside the Totem; he remained impassive as the carved wood while he watched us running towards him. I was panting so hard that I couldn't speak. "Are you tired of each other's company that you have returned to me?" he said.

I heard Raki say, "The Black Feathers! The Black Feathers are coming out of the East...they will be here before noon tomorrow!"

"Do you hope to win the office of tribal story-teller?"

"Father, you *must* believe him! We have seen them. We must all fight....Raki and I are both going to fight with you and it doesn't matter if we are killed."

"You both look as though you had run a long way. Did you meet a grizzly, or frighten yourselves with your own imagination?"

I felt as though I were trying to wake from a nightmare in which I was screaming a warning into a silence too heavy to break. I had been ready for the turmoil of preparation, had seen it while we ran on and on to bring our warning: the Chief giving orders to the Braves, telling them where to hold their ground, where to fall back so as to lure the enemy into ambush. The young squaws taking the children to hide with them in the woods, while the Old Women heated cauldrons of water and pitch for the staunching of wounds. I had seen men trying to pluck arrows from their throats, or staggering forward with eyes that had begun to glaze like a dying deer's....I had heard the bowstrings sounding the song of death. But because I could not make my father share my vision, our people were going to be massacred.

I saw Raki run towards the Great Tepee, and realized that

70

he was going to blow the horn used only by a Chief to summon the tribe in time of danger. For any but a Wearer of Feathers to touch the horn meant death, in expiation of sacrilege. But the tribe would have been warned, even though the deep note rolling across the valley would tell the Black Feathers that we were prepared.

I saw my father follow him, silent as a shadow. His hands were on Raki's shoulders, holding him back, and I heard him say, ''Had you forgotten that it is death to touch the Horn of the Gathering Together?''

''No, I had not forgotten.''

''You are not afraid to die?''

''How could I be...when there is no other way to warn the tribe?''

My father called me, and I went and stood close to Raki so that I could feel his shoulder against mine. Almost it seemed as though my father was smiling.

''You are both ready to die for your people now that you think a black cloud has come out of the East to shut away our sun. Why did you not stay in your little valley where the danger would have passed you by? You need not answer: your presence here has done that for you. You thought you owed no allegiance to your tribe and were free to live your own lives without accepting responsibility. It seems that the ties of the Totem are stronger than you knew.''

''We should never have come back except to warn you,'' I said.

''But you came back. I did not expect you until tomorrow. To travel so swiftly from the high pass shows that already you have learned something of the endurance of Braves.''

''How did you know we were coming?'' I said, bewildered.

''How did you know how long it took us to get here?'' said Raki.

''How do I know that it was at sunset five days ago that you first saw the smoke in the East? You took it for a great tribe because there were many cooking-fires springing up near the first and largest of them. How do I know that the next night the fires were nearer to us, and that when you crossed the pass they were only a day's journey behind you?''

I said, ''You saw it in the pool, just as I saw the woman you want me to become, the Wearer of Feathers. You made me see that vision, you thought it would make me come back, but I wouldn't look into still water again. You can't take me away from Raki!''

Raki was saying slowly, ''Who lit those fires? You had them lit, didn't you?''

''Yes,'' said my father. ''It was my smoke which called you home.''

''You knew that we should remember the legend of the Black Feathers. You snared us by lies...another Nona who frightens children into obedience! Piyanah and I won't stay with you. You can't keep us prisoners. There is no law which can keep anyone in the tribe who prefers the freedom of exile!''

''Have I kept you prisoners? Have I imposed my wishes on you? You thought you had escaped me, and that we searched for your bodies below the rapids. But you were wrong, my children. Senchek, the finest of my trackers, followed you. He told me of your climb down the cliff, and how that night you slept in a hole by the stream. I knew when your corn ripened, and where you set your snares by the Lake of the Wildfowl. He has often brought me news of you; and there was pride in my heart at what he told me.''

''And yet you betrayed us!''

''I knew you would be too proud to return, for to you it would seem defeat instead of victory.''

There was despair deep as my own in Raki's voice. ''We have been defeated—by fear, that was born of black smoke and fathered by a legend.''

''The Black Feathers are not a legend. Three moons ago one of our hunters returned from the Unknown Country and

72

brought this back with him.'' He held out his hand, and across the long, narrow palm was a crow's feather, knotted to a forehead-thong.

I looked at it with scorn. ''Is that a brand from the fire whose smoke is lies?''

''No, my daughter. This is another sign that the days when men dared to forget the legends are passing. Now we must be strong in wisdom which is behind our symbols: the scarlet feather must be more than a symbol of physical strength, and the feathers of the headdress must be winged in truth. The Great Hunters have given you into my care: the voice of the past has spoken, saying, 'The two who are one must of their own choice become two, then shall their united strength be mighty.' Already the bond between you is wiser than the commands of your father, older than the laws of your Chief, stronger than the security of your tribe. Now must you gain the twofold wisdom; the right hand and the left hand; sunset and sunrise; man and woman. You were ready to die for your people: now you must live for them. No longer will it be remembered that Piyanah's body tires more easily than a man's, that for her the bow is heavier to bend. Her companions may not find their tolerance increased when they discover that she is only a woman by name, for it will make them less confident that man is superior to his squaw. They will find this thought disturbing, but through it they will learn that tradition must be weighed against the Feather of Wisdom before it can be accepted.

''Raki will live among the squaws, until he has learned to think as a woman, to feel as a woman. He must learn how to fringe a tunic, to make cooking-pots, to look after a sick child...all the humble things which fill their days. The girls who have not yet been Chosen will try to find ways of re-minding him that he is a man, and at times he may find it diffi-cult to forget that he is an arrow and not a quiver. He, too, will undergo the ordeals of a warrior, and the others may scorn him because he is dressed as a squaw.

"Neither of you may explain that you are learning to bring back the wisdom of the Before People: you may say only that you obey the commands of the Chief. It may be thought that I have done this to humble you for running away, but that will further strengthen you, for no one who is strong of heart need fear mockery. When the not-man and the not-woman have passed the ordeals, then shall they lead forth their own tribe under a totem of your own choosing, and the contentment of the unborn generations shall be your heritage."

There were no words strong enough to fight against Na-ka-chek. He had said, "You were ready to die for your people, now you must live for them"; and Raki had heard him. Raki would never be happy if we went away: for even when we laughed together he would still hear an echo of the people we had betrayed to the Sorrow Bird.

I had thought that with Raki I was stronger than visions of the future, stronger than the call of the tribe. But we were children who had tried to escape into a world of our own, children watched by grown-ups, who could afford to be tolerant because time was their friend, not ours.

I was no longer the Piyanah who was brave and confident because she was secure with Raki in our little valley. I was a child who obediently drank the bowl of broth that Na-ka-chek put into my hands: a child who struggled against an aching weariness, until her father realized she was going to fall into tears and carried her back to the tepee that for this last night before the Separation she would share with Raki.

Someone must have come into our tepee without waking us, for new clothes were lying ready and our own had been taken away. For me there was a breech-clout and a strip of brown cloth, which I couldn't think how to wear until I remembered that I was to bind my breasts.

My fingers were clumsy as I helped Raki to plait his hair smoothly under the forehead-band of white beads, to put on the tunic of a squaw and the two wide bracelets he must wear above the right elbow. There was a look in his eyes which reminded me of Braves making the yearly dedication of arrows before the Totem, and I whispered to the Great Hunters, "Please don't let me cry. Raki is living in the far future where the present cannot hurt him...please don't let me drag him back."

I thought he was going out of the tepee without speaking to me, but he paused before he unlaced the flap. "We must always remember that the not-man and the not-woman are still Raki and Piyanah. If one of us dies, he will wait for the other in our valley. Even the corn-cobs will be there, just as we left them. I daren't say any more...they mustn't know we are afraid. You aren't crying, are you, Piyanah?"

"No, Raki, I'm not crying."

Then I watched him go away, across the clearing, to join the squaws.

Everything looked just as usual: the box where we had kept our clothes, the beaver robe in which we slept, both wrapped in it together; even the little canoes that Raki had carved for me still followed each other round the circular shelf of the centre-post. Everything looked just the same, yet nothing would ever be the same any more. Raki would never come back to put on those moccasins. I should never see him smiling as he woke; smiling because we were together on a new day.

I put on Raki's belt, the one he always wore because I had made it for him. I took his knife and filled his quiver with arrows. Then, carrying his bow, I took the path which led away from childhood.

PART TWO

fIRSt BeaR's Claw

The boys, and the Braves who were training them for the ordeals, lived to the west of the main encampment. Dorrok, the Brown Feather to whom I had been assigned, was standing before one of the tepees. He beckoned me to approach him, but made me wait before he spoke.

"Here you are not the Chief's daughter; you are Piyanah who obeys me. You will share this tepee with three others: Kekki, Barakeechi, and Tekeeni."

Before I could answer he turned away and went down the path towards the river. The tepee was smaller than the one Raki and I had shared, and had no centre-post. My new possessions had been put beside the dry reeds on which I was to sleep: two blankets, one with a neck-slit to wear in cold weather, a pair of moccasins, and a tunic of coarse leather, roughly patched together from the hides of small animals. I picked it up; it was hard and some of the skins had not been properly cured, so it had a disagreeable smell. There was also a food-bowl of yellow clay, made by an unskilled thumb.

I was glad that Tekeeni was going to be with me, and wondered if the others were angry at having to share their tepee with a girl. I went out and looked down the slope towards the Squaws' Tepees. I could see three women plodding up from the river with water-jars, but there was no sign of Raki. When I heard the others returning I pretended to be setting the feathers in one of my arrows. I looked up as the boys came in and waited for a greeting; but even Tekeeni was careful to avoid looking at me.

Through the open flap I could see two Naked Foreheads carrying a cauldron by a branch threaded through its handle. I realized that I was very hungry; except for the broth Na-ka-chek had given us the night before, we had eaten nothing but bread for four days. I watched the others pick up their food-bowls and go out of the tepee. I followed them, and saw that the boys were crowding round a Naked Forehead who was ladling stew into bowls they held out to him. By the smell I knew the hunters had made a kill, for it was fresh deer meat. I wondered if Raki was having some too, or whether there was not sufficient to spare for squaws.

No one spoke to me; they either stared or pretended I was not there. Then one of them began to wind an imaginary bandage round his chest. His mimicry spread to the others, who began an obscene parody of the Betrothal Dance. I wanted to run away, but knew that would only give them a victory. I ate my stew very slowly, knowing that when it was finished I would have to think of something else to do.

A little spring bubbled out of the rock, and each boy rinsed his food-bowl there when he had finished eating. Through a gap in the trees I could see down into the encampment: three women were scouring cooking-pots...no, two women, for the third was Raki. I wished that I were really a man, and that it was the time of the Choosing, for then he could be my squaw, and we would go into the woods and never come back.

One of the Naked Foreheads picked up the empty cauldron to take it to the place of the cooking-fire. I wondered if he was resigned to being despised, or if sometimes he longed for the privileges he had forfeited. It must be lonely to live so near the squaws and yet be allowed no woman.

The tepee was empty when I went there. I wrapped my-self in a blanket and when the others came in pretended to be asleep. I had not yet learned that after the sunset drum the boys were not allowed to talk, so I thought they kept silence because they did not want me to overhear.

I woke before the others and crept out without waking them. In the thick half-light I ran down to the pool where

77

Raki and I used to bathe every morning. I hoped that he might be there, but though I waited as long as I dared, he never came. The day before I had pulled the bandage too tight, and my breasts were sore. The water was very cold, and in the grey stillness the brooding trees looked like sorrowful ghosts.

As I went back, I saw a group of boys, led by Dorrok, moving off towards the high pasture. Tekeeni was there, but I was uncertain whether I ought to join them, until he dropped behind the others and beckoned to me. He stayed beside me long enough to whisper, ''I saved your bread. I couldn't bring it with me, but I've hidden it under your blanket. We don't have another meal until sunset, so you will be hungry.''

I smiled to thank him, and before running ahead he said hurriedly, ''Don't let the others know I'm trying to help you. They will soon accept you for one of themselves. Don't forget the Chief is your father, and I'll see they don't forget it either!''

I felt much braver now that I was not quite alone. Tekeeni had been Raki's friend, and it was almost like having a shadow of Raki with me. I wished I had been nicer to the squaws, for then there might have been women to help him because of their friendship to me. I wondered why my father had decreed that Raki must spend a moon with the squaws before, still dressed as a woman, beginning his training for the ordeals. Even then I should have very little chance to speak to him, for the boys were divided into two groups, and I was sure he would be kept away from me; and he would eat with the squaws and sleep in their tepees.

I repeated the conversation I had so often held with myself since I left Raki, ''You must live as a boy, think as a boy, act as a boy...only then can you and Raki be together again. Raki has to be a squaw, so I will make all these boys realize that a squaw is better than they are. I will smile every time they mock me, but I will remember each boy who starts it until I can turn his mockery against himself. I will make myself beat him at whatever he is most proud of doing. I won't let them hurt me. I will study the habits of the ones who are enemies, as though they were grizzlies that I was watching to learn the weakness in them through which I can capture their claws.''

In my imagination, Raki and I, both dressed as women, were receiving homage from all the tribal Braves. I had forgotten to be watchful, and Gorgi, the boy who had led the mimicry, tripped me so that I fell and cut my knee. I ran on as though I had only stumbled. It didn't hurt much, but I could feel blood trickling down my leg. I knew that I was being watched to see if I looked down to find out if it was a deep cut, so I didn't. They were going to be disappointed...for they had forgotten that Raki had taught me to share everything with him!

After we had been running for some time we came back to the river, which had made a wide loop round a hill. Here Dorrok told us that we could rest before the diving practice began. The boys sprawled on the ground, panting after their long run. I wanted to lie flat, to relax all the aching muscles which were still sore after their journey from our little valley; but I sat cross-legged, looking across the river to the mountains which were already covered with the first snow.

Though many of the squaws were strong swimmers they were not taught to dive. I felt a comfortable satisfaction, as a hungry man feels when his food-bowl is warm between his hands....''They think I shall be frightened of diving. I hope Dorrok leaves me to the last. I wish the pools in our valley had been deeper, for it is more than a year since I could practise every day. I shall pretend that Raki is here watching me, and then I shall go in very straight, without a splash. Great Hunters, please let me do better than the best dive I have ever done!''

The boys were taking off their breech-clouts and tying back their hair with their forehead-thongs. I wondered

79

whether I ought to take off my breast bandage, and decided to do so because it would be so uncomfortable to wear if it was wet. I saw Gorgi taking off an imaginary necklace and armlets, and pretending to unwind a bandage from his chest: several of the others were grinning with him; they thought it clever to copy whatever he did. I decided that Gorgi should be the first bear's claw on my spirit neck-thong!

The river swirled past the foot of the cliff, but in a backwater there was a deep pool. Above it the rock formation split into a series of ledges, natural steps from which a diver could choose more than twenty different heights. The youngest boys went off a ledge lapped by the water. Dorrok watched them, usually in silence, but sometimes shouting instructions. After they had finished, four boys collected on the next ledge. Then I realized that each ledge was taken in turn, and that the boys knew which height they were expected to choose. Dorrok had expected me to join the youngest boys, but when I pretended not to see him looking at me, he must have thought that I had never dived before and decided to let me watch the others as it was my first day.

The eldest boys, Gorgi among them, were fourteen. They all moved towards the fourth ledge, but at the last moment he stood back and let the others go up to it without him. They looked surprised until he pointed to another height, on a level with their shoulders. My heart began to thud....I was determined to go off a ledge as high as any of the others, but even the fourth ledge was more than I had ever done. The ledge Gorgi had chosen was narrow and difficult...and the one above it stood above the water three times the height of a man. It looked fairly easy from where I was standing, but I knew what it would look like from up there.

If I made myself go up there, I should *have* to dive. If I went in flat and knocked the air out of myself, I should be pulled out of the water like a drowning toad. They would never stop laughing at me, and have much more to laugh at than my being a girl. I would be a vanquished boaster...and even Raki laughed at boasters!

Until then I had pretended to take no notice of the divers. I felt Gorgi staring at me, so I turned and looked at him. He was smiling, and there was a swagger in his walk as he went forward to climb to the ledge. Before he dived he looked down to make sure I was watching him. Suddenly I knew one of his weaknesses; he despised me because I was a squaw, and yet he longed for the squaw's admiration. He was thinking of the Choosing: he wanted all the squaws to admire him, to envy the girl he took into the woods. It would be pleasant to be wanted by the Chief's daughter...and he would never be able to forget that her name was Piyanah...for I would make him remember it, to his discomfort!

He dived well, and I saw Dorrok sign approval...."I have *got* to go off the ledge which is higher than the others."

Slowly I climbed the rock. Dorrok looked surprised that I intended to dive, and pointed to the lowest shelf. I took no notice and went on climbing, ledge by ledge. I thought Dorrok was going to call me back when I reached the fifth ledge, Gorgi's ledge: then I scrambled up to the one above it.

It was a good place from which to dive, for the rock overhung the pool. The water looked very far away, and hard as stone. "Please, Raki, don't let me go flat. Please, Great Hunters, and totem, and spirits, and *everybody*, don't let me go flat...or, if I do, please let me hit a rock and be killed...."

I dived. It seemed a long time before I felt the water part smoothly under my hands. It was dark and safe under the water. I came to the surface and swam to the bank.

Dorrok was smiling at me. "Piyanah dives better than his brothers," he said loudly, so that all the others could hear.

I saw Gorgi swimming away from me across the pool. Now the neck-thong was no longer empty: on it was my first bear's claw.

the Squaws' tepees

After I had shamed Gorgi, the others ceased to mock me openly, but they made no attempt to be friendly. The only time I was close enough to Raki for us to have spoken was when I was in a file of boys returning from practice with the fish-spear and he was with a group of squaws who were ahead of us on the path. They stood aside for us to pass; none of the boys glanced at the women, and Raki pretended to be watching a cloud as though he had forgotten he must give precedence to boys.

The following day completed the first moon of our separation, but I knew that even when he began his warrior's training he would still have to sleep in the Squaws' Tepee. Dorrok said that we were all to set off before dawn, one by one, as we were not to follow each other, and that before nightfall we must bring back one of the plants which only grew high on the moraine above the snowline.

Raki and I had discovered the best way up there two years before, and to my joy I found him waiting for me. We climbed fast until we found a sheltered ledge where we could talk without fear of interruption. I asked whether he had seen me the previous day. He smiled.

"When I can wade through a stream and not know that water is wet; when I feel no warmth coming from a fire, and the winds make no sound among the branches, then I shall be near Piyanah and yet be unaware of her!"

Then he asked me to tell him everything that had happened, and to hear how I had gained my first bear's claw made him laugh as though he were really happy.

"Has it made Gorgi an enemy or a friend?"

"I am not sure, but I think he is still an enemy. Half of him hates me for hurting his pride, and the other half would like to have a squaw whom men fear...or perhaps only a squaw who is the Chief's daughter."

82

"You can trust Tekeeni; his heart is all of one colour."

"He gave you a tooth of friendship. We must have two necklaces, Raki. Claws for vanquished enemies, and teeth for friends we have won."

"Then I have two teeth for my second necklace, but the other thong is still empty."

"Tell me about them...and tell me everything else too."

"When I first had to walk across the clearing dressed as a squaw I thought everyone would stare at me. I had forgotten that women are almost invisible to men, because they have for so long been ignored! But I think nearly all the women must have gathered in their largest tepee to wait for me. They were making tunics or moccasins, or kneeling at the looms; but their eyes were bright with curiosity, all watching me, all very conscious that my body was different to their own...and wondering how much they dared do against one who might in the future choose a squaw among them!

"Ninee was sitting, wrapped in a blanket, by the centre-post. She took no notice of me until she had a chance to speak without being overheard. Then she said that my presence among the squaws was only another game we had invented to plague her, or else that her warnings had come true and our spirits had woken up in the wrong bodies. Do you remember how she used to say that we should become each other's reflections, so that when I wanted to use my right hand it would be your left hand which moved? I gave her the squaw's greeting with the wrong hand, and she was so startled that she called me 'Piyanah'. I saw her stare at my arm, and knew she was trying to see if you had brought your scar with you into my body!

"Perhaps some of the squaws believe Ninee and think I am you, or else they find it more comfortable to believe I am a girl. Anyway, after the first few days they lost interest in me, and went on with their work or suckled their children as though there were no stranger among them...which is much better than when they whispered about me all the time."

"Who shares your tepee?"

"I am with the young girls who are still 'unchosen'; the Old Women and the mothers with small children sleep in the smaller tepees."

"What do they talk about...are they *terribly* dull, Raki?"

"Most of them seem to think of nothing but the next Choosing. They weave patterns for blankets or sew beads on their moccasins, or count over the little horde of treasures which each keeps in a box by her sleeping-place."

"What kind of treasures?"

"Necklaces and bracelets, and some have pots of bear's grease, or oil to make their hair glossy."

"Did you hate the first day *very* much?"

"Yes," he said frankly, "I never thought it was possible to feel so helpless! Such small things were difficult...like wondering how I was going to plait my hair without you to help me. I pretended that they were a hostile tribe among whom I had gone as a spy...and it was easier when I wore my clothes as a disguise. It is going to be very difficult to learn to *think* as a woman, Piyanah, for most of them don't seem to think at all! I keep on trying to remember two things your father said, 'A man who is sure of his own judgment need not fear mockery,' and 'Man and woman are part of the same whole'. If they were only at all like you it would be easy, for I should be proud of being like you; but they seem so stupid!"

"They *are* stupid, or they would never have allowed men to make life so dreary for everybody!"

While Raki was talking we had both forgotten that we were supposed to be climbing to the top of the ridge and must not be seen together. Above us someone must have trodden on a loose boulder, for a shower of stones came down the hillside: we were sheltered by an overhang, so the stones passed harmlessly overhead and we heard them go rattling down the slope.

We climbed up a dry water-course and every few moments

84

stopped to listen in case anyone else had found the same route. The air was so still that voices carried a long way, and though the sky was cloudless, the sun seemed to give only an illusion of warmth, like the reflection of torches in water.

"Raki, you haven't told me about the friendship teeth yet."

"One is Yeena, the granddaughter of Ninee's sister. I noticed she was much slower at weaving than the others, and I found that the loom she used had been mended with fish-glue, but so roughly that the threads kept on catching. So I made her another one, and she was like a child with a new toy. I said I would teach her to use a knife if she would teach me to weave...she was very clumsy at first and cut her fingers, but now she is quite good at it."

We had climbed fast and decided it was safe to rest for a little while. "And the second tooth?" I asked.

"Her name is Rokeena. She fell and hurt her leg when she was six, and now she is fifteen and still crippled. She hardly ever spoke, just lay staring up at the roof or else fingered a necklace...berries they must have been, but now so old and wrinkled that they have lost their colour. I knew they must have some special value for her by the way she touched them, and when she thought anyone was watching she hid them away. Making friends with her was like taming a chipmunk, she was so timid. I think the others grudged helping her... she can't even crawl to the scavenger pit or fetch her food, for when they saw that I always took her food-bowl to the cooking-pot they left her to me. I knew she really trusted me when she no longer hid the necklace, and at last she told me why it meant so much to her."

And while Raki told me Rokeena's story I felt as though I was hearing her speak:

" 'I, Rokeena, have not always been held in contempt by the Great Hunters. When I was little, your mother used to let me play with you, and she told me not to believe my grand-mother's stories about demons who are always waiting to punish disobedient children. You were never wrapped in the bandages which the other babies wore to protect them from jealous spirits who live in barren trees, but lay naked and laughing in the sun. She said you were different from other children, and that I would be 'different' too. One day I wanted to make a necklace, so I went to the high pasture to search for berries. I found some, red and smooth and beautiful, and then I saw others which were even more brilliant...but they were on a creeper which was growing up a dead tree. My grandmother had told me that it was dangerous to climb a dead tree; it was like disturbing a grave, for in it the tree spirit was buried. But I was proud of not believing her stories, so I climbed the tree. I got three of the berries...they found them still clutched in my hand, after I fell. You see, I had forgotten that a Chief's woman is honoured by the spirits and so need not fear them, but Rokeena was only an ordinary little girl who had made them angry.

" 'They must have been *very* angry, Raki, for they have left me lying here for so many summers, and autumns, and winters. Even the Great Hunters have no pity for me, for though I have twice dragged my body out into the snow, they have told Nona to fetch me back before I was quite dead. Now there is only this necklace to link me with the girl who was not afraid of trees. Sometimes when I hold it the berries are not withered any more, and I am no longer lame....I am the girl who was free of the high pasture, my legs can run fast, and my feet know the kindliness of moss, and the coolness of shadowed stones on a hot day.'

"Then she looked up at me and said, "You took more than milk from the woman who suckled you, Raki; you took into yourself her power of taking fear away...for while I was talking I had almost forgotten that I am being punished, and that a squaw must always feel humble to the spirits as well as to men.' "

"Oh, Raki," I said, "I wish we had our own tribe, now,

so that she wouldn't have to lie there for seven years before we can take her away with us. Can we do anything to make her leg better?''

''We must try, because I know the Old Women have got salves, but they pretend it is useless to do anything when the spirits are angry.''

''What does her leg look like?''

''She wouldn't let me see it until yesterday...she was too ashamed until I made her believe that it was *not* a punishment. It was wrapped in some kind of bandage they use for their newborn babies, the ones that have been soaked in water from the underground lake which they think will blind the evil spirits. I had to cut the bandage off with my knife, for it was too stiff with dirt to unwind...she had had it on for a long time. When I saw her leg I knew that squaws can be braver than warriors. There were sores on it, Piyanah: old sores where the scabs were ready to fall off, and open sores crusted with yellow. The leg is so thin that the foot looks like a bird's claw, but it is not deformed.''

''Dorrok has a jar of salve in his tepee! Tekeeni had some of it put on his arm only three days ago. I can get some tonight while they are all having the sunset meal! If we hurry, Raki, I can get it before the others return.''

The loose shale of the moraine was already covered with thin snow, but soon we each found a root of the plant we needed. We saw some boys in the distance, but they were too far away to recognize us. Instead of descending by the water-course we decided to take a quicker way down, and as we dared not risk being seen together, Raki went on ahead, having said that he would wait for me in the wood above the boys' encampment.

When I joined him, he told me that as the place seemed deserted he thought it would be safest for me to go openly to Dorrok's tepee, so that if he were there I could say I had come to give him the plant which showed I had done the allotted climb.

The tepee was empty: at first I could not see the jar, for it had been sunk in the ground to protect it. The mouth was covered by a bladder, and while I was trying to undo the thong which held it in place, my heart beat so loudly that I was afraid of not hearing Dorrok if he came back...for I knew how severe were the punishments for theft. The jar was half full of pungent green salve, thicker than bear's grease. I looked round for something to scoop it up in; there was nothing I dared take, so I fetched my food-bowl, though its absence would be difficult to explain at the next meal. I crossed the clearing without being seen...the few paces between the tepees seemed longer than a day's run!

I took a handful of salve and then tied on the bladder...wishing that I had taken more care to notice exactly how the thong had been knotted. When I rejoined Raki I asked him whether I could come with him to see Rokeena.

''No, there are sure to be other women there at this time. I'll manage somehow to see you tomorrow or the next day to tell you what happened.'' Then he noticed the bowl and said quickly, ''Why did you bring it in this...is it your own?''

''Yes, I couldn't find anything else.''

''But you'll need it tonight....''

''I'll make some excuse. I can say I broke it and forgot that I ought to have kept the pieces.''

''You can't do that, or they will make you miss a day's food to help you to remember. I know that's true, for it happened to me. There are some broken pots behind the cooking-place: I'll put the salve in one of them and bring back your bowl. Don't wait for me, in case it makes them suspicious. When you find the bowl you will know I've hidden the salve...it will be a way of saying good night to each other''.

Outside Dorrok's tepee there were some boys waiting to give him their plants. If I had not been busy with the salve, Raki and I would have been the first to get back...but Rokeena was much more important than annoying the boys!

88

When I went into the tepee it was difficult not to look at the jar to make sure that I had put the cover on straight.

The food-bowl was lying at the foot of a pine tree: and as I picked it up I whispered good night to Raki.

It was three days before he had a chance to tell me more about Rokeena. ''To find out if the salve would hurt her,'' he said, ''I rubbed some into a cut on my thigh; it was fiery as a hornet! I decided that if I could make Rokeena think of it as a test of courage, instead of as yet another 'punishment', it would be easier for her to stand the pain. So before fetching the salve—I had hidden it under my blanket—I told her about the Ordeal by Fire.

''Her leg must have felt as if it were being roasted in hot ashes; but instead of crying out she suddenly went rigid, with her eyes wide open though I knew she didn't see me. Then she began to speak; the words were quite distinct, but they sounded as though she were far away. 'I am no longer Rokeena. I am not a squaw. I am not a cripple. I am a man who will soon wear the scarlet feather in his forehead-thong. I have scorned the anger of winter and mocked the torrid heat. I have fought for my tribe; yet when the arrow of an enemy entered my body it could not harm me, for I was beloved of the spirits and they caused my clean flesh to heal without a scar. I am not afraid of pain, for even if it comes when I am very tired I savour it as though it were good smoke. The tribe has gathered to see me win the Scarlet which will make me a brother of the fire.'

''Suddenly the power seemed to go out of her; she began to tremble and give little whimpering moans. She shut her eyes, and before she opened them again I had covered up her leg and hidden the salve. She thought she had been asleep, for she said, 'I had a dream, Raki: a dream in which I wasn't afraid. The spirits were not angry...I was clean. I can't remember any more, but I *know* that the spirits no longer hate me....' Then she said, 'My leg hurts, but it's not a dirty, grey pain. It's like a flame, or a shining arrow-head.' I watched beside her, and when she went to sleep she was smiling—I had never seen her smile, except when she made her lips curve to hide her sorrow.''

The sores on Rokeena's leg were slow in healing, but by the early spring, clean skin had grown over the raw flesh. I had told Raki that when one of the boys who shared my tepee had torn the muscles of his arm, Dorrok had made him rub it with fish-oil. Squaws made the fish-oil, so Raki was able to get plenty for her: it seemed to help her foot to become more supple, and soon she was able to move the knee-joint.

Until Raki looked after her she must have been half starved; but now it was always the best pieces which went into her food-bowl. As she grew stronger we decided that as soon as the sun had real warmth he would carry her every day into the open air; but when Nona found out what he intended to do she forbade him to take her out of the tepee.

''I have never seen Nona so angry,'' said Raki. ''She shouted at me, 'It will offend the spirits if they see that one who has angered them is given shelter in our tepee! We have hidden her from them: is that not enough? Must you bring down thunder on our heads, or make the trees fall when we walk under them? Why should we all suffer because of the lame one?'

''I told her that she was a foolish old woman, which annoyed her exceedingly—especially as the other women had gathered to listen to our quarrel. They enjoyed seeing Nona defied, until she said that the spirits would revenge themselves on all the squaws, who would either return barren from the woods, or else have babies too weak to suck. There seemed no end to the evils which she promised: snakes hiding in the woodpile, fish stinking before they reached the cooking-pot, corn blighted so that we all starved! Most of the squaws began by being scornful, but she scattered fear among them until they began echoing, 'Rokeena must stay hidden or the spirits will be angry with us. Why should we suffer for Rokeena?'

90

"Then I got angry and shouted, 'Rokeena will not stay in the tepee unless it is by the command of the Chief! I will ask him to decide between us,' and I strode off towards the Great Tepee, leaving them staring after me in horror. They have got so used to me that most of them have forgotten that I am not a squaw, a squaw who would never dare to expect a hearing from the Chief!"

"What did Na-ka-chek say to you?"

"I forgot to give him the squaw's sign in greeting, but he didn't seem to mind. He said it was better that I should fight against superstition than against enemy Braves, for it was more dangerous to the tribe. I even told him how you stole the salve from Dorrok, and I think he was pleased, though of course he didn't show it."

"Then he must realize that we still see each other."

"I think he knew it already...just as he knew we were in the Little Valley."

"And can Rokeena leave the tepee?"

"Yes, and I could see he was angry with Nona. He said, 'If the sun makes Rokeena strong, that in itself will be a great thing, but a greater will be if the other squaws see that the words of the Old Women cannot be trusted when they speak of the Unseen. When you and Piyanah rule together, women, if they have proved themselves worthy of a feather, shall belong to the Council; but while they are shackled by legends whose true meaning has been forgotten it is well that they should be confounded out of their own mouths.'

"I thought it might be a good opportunity to tell him what a bad influence the Old Women have on the younger ones, but I suppose he thought he had agreed with me enough already, for he said coldly, 'The Old Women know many things which the young should be glad to receive. They know how to ease a woman when she brings forth a child; how food should be prepared so that the skill of the hunters is used to the best advantage;

they can make oils and weave, embroider and dress hides. You will find that there is much for Raki to learn from them.' ''

The Quarry

I was always glad when Dorrak said we were to practise tracking, for it meant being alone all day, which was much better than being with anyone except Raki. The boys worked in pairs, a quarry and a hunter. The quarry was given a start and had to return to the encampment at sunset: if he had been caught before then the hunter was the winner. I preferred being the quarry, for Raki and I had always been good at hiding, and often, by leaving a false trail and then climbing a tree, I could have time to forget I was supposed to be a boy and think of the future when Raki and I would no longer be apart.

But when for the first time I was told to act as Gorgi's quarry I knew I should need every trick to keep ahead of him, for since the dive he had always tried desperately to win when we were matched against each other. It was a difficult day, for there had been heavy rain during the night and Dorrok said we were to keep in a south-westerly direction, which meant following tracks now sticky with mud where it was almost impossible not to leave footprints.

Gorgi was fast, so there was no time to make a detour through the woods, and thrusting under low branches when every leaf was weighted with water-drops always left a trail easy to follow. I put my moccasins in my belt, for it is easier to run barefoot on slippery ground. It was cold when I started, but when it began to rain I was glad not to be wearing a tunic, which would soon have been sodden and heavy. The rain grew thicker, and I hoped that it would obliterate any tracks I had left. Streams which at this season were usually only a trickle among the stones were in full spate, and I had to struggle across two of them with water up to my waist.

In case Gorgi hadn't yet lost me, I waded up the third stream and climbed a fall where the water arched out from an overhanging rock. Between me and the grey sky there was a curtain of water that hid the mouth of a small cave which Raki and I had found three years earlier. It was a wonderful place to hide in, though very wet, and until I began to shiver with cold I considered staying there for the rest of the day.

When I was higher up the hillside the rain stopped abruptly, though the air was alive with the sound of water dripping from trees. The sun came out: I wanted to sing with the good warmth—and should have done so if I had forgotten Gorgi. I climbed a tree from which I could gain a clear view of the lower slopes. There was no sign of him, and I whistled to amuse myself...bird-calls, so that he wouldn't realize it was me even if he heard them.

I found a wide branch on which I could lie almost full length; the sun was so hot that the wet bark began to steam. I pulled off my forehead-thong and spread out my hair to dry. When it had frozen last winter the ice had chafed my shoulders till they bled, and I had almost envied Raki his woman's plaits.

The branch was so comfortable that I nearly went to sleep and only saved myself from falling by gripping with my knees: the ground suddenly looked a long way down, although it was only the height of fifteen men. I was glad that heights did not make me giddy, for several of the boys found it difficult to stand on the edge of a cliff, holding their ankles and looking down the sheer drop. Then I remembered that Piyanah used to hate climbing down cliffs...she had expected sympathy from Raki, and always got it. But the new Piyanah never felt sympathy when she saw weakness—she was delighted as a hungry man who realizes that those who share the cooking-pot are too weary to eat.

I was separated from Raki until I was ready to share the headdress with him...and I was getting less worthy of it every day. This was a very unpleasant thought, and I couldn't hide from it. I was learning endurance, learning to live as a boy and to beat them at the things they were taught. Even in the wrestling I had thrown Kekki, and twisted his arm so badly that he couldn't use a bow for half a moon...it had given me a warm satisfaction, of which now I was suddenly ashamed. I looked on the boys as my enemies, and yet from them must come our new tribe. I was preparing myself to be a Chief, like my father and my grandfather...honoured for endurance and impassivity. But Raki and I had agreed that a Chief should be chosen because his people loved him.

I had done everything I could to get myself envied...and disliked. Every jeer and slight I had carefully hoarded; to be returned with the arrow sharpened, and, I hoped, from a stronger bow. Already Raki had made Rokeena happier, freed her from pain and many of her fears; and there were five others with whom he could talk of the laws we would make in the future. But I had made no friends, though I had gained a small measure of grudging respect.

Tekeeni had tried to be kind, but I thought that to accept his help would be to acknowledge weakness...and now he seldom spoke to me. I had known Kekki was ashamed because he grew dizzy on high branches, but instead of being sympathetic—and if I had tried, how easy it would have been, for I well knew the horrible queasy feeling in the pit of the belly—I had dared him, in front of the others, to climb higher than I; and rejoiced when I saw the sweat bead on his forehead and knew that his hands were so slippery that he had to cling on while the rough bark scraped the skin off his wrists and fingers.

I had lost in understanding...and what had I gained? I could run further without getting tired. The soles of my feet were hard enough to cross sharp gravel or rough ice without doing more than ooze blood. I could swim in the river when the pack-ice had only just cleared and keep my teeth from chattering. I could make the tribal marks on the calf of my leg with a glowing stick, and then rub salt into the blisters, without flinching: salt stolen from the place of the cooking-pots to show that I could dare the penalties of a thief.

What had the year brought me? Thick skin on my feet; stronger jaw muscles; the scars of several burns...and the recognition that I had worked hard, to change man's contempt to a bitter hatred. Instead of helping Raki to build a bridge over the Canyon, I had cut away my edge of the cliff and made it wider. My jeers at myself were louder than any that Piyanah had heard. Clever Piyanah! Brave, wise, impassive Piyanah! So Proud with Feathers!

I listened: and wept.

I had made everything much more difficult for myself, but perhaps I could go back to the beginning and start again. If I told Kekki that I often felt dizzy, it might help. I wished I had not thought about Kekki before I got down to the ground... swinging by my hands and then dropping to a lower branch was suddenly unpleasant; so unpleasant that I had to cling to the trunk until the tree felt steady.

I decided to try to find Gorgi and then give him a chance of picking up my trail. Poor Gorgi, he might have been quite nice if only I had not been so determinedly horrid! I saw him, coming up the slope. He didn't seem to be taking any trouble to conceal his movements, so I supposed he had lost all hope of finding me. I fell flat behind a boulder, more from habit than any real wish to hide. I thought a bird-call would be too obvious a way of helping him, so I dislodged a stone and made it roll down the hill. I knew he heard it, for he dodged behind a tree. It was no longer important to escape from Gorgi, only an interesting game. Perhaps if I stopped minding about everything, training with the boys might be quite enjoyable: but of course I should never stop minding about being separated from Raki.

I crawled across an open space, and noticed that the gravel

felt unusually sharp, before I reached a spinney of alders and white birch. The small trees grew so close that it was impossible to pass between them without breaking off twigs which I knew would betray me. I broke several, and did not even bother to avoid stepping on dead sticks. I reached a plot of turf surrounded by brambles and realized the reason I wanted to stay there: not because it was a clever hiding-place or I was getting tired...I wanted to talk to Gorgi. That Gorgi was the kind of person whom Raki and I would want to talk to had never occurred to me before.

Perhaps a friendly tree spirit had spoken to him too, for when he saw me, instead of leaping to claim me for his quarry, he pretended to be surprised.

"Oh, you're here! If you don't want to go back until later, I can tell Dorrok I didn't come up with you until just before sunset." He paused and then added abruptly, "Do you want me to go away?"

Yesterday I should have said that it could not have the smallest effect on me whether he went or stayed. "Please don't go, Gorgi...unless you want to, I mean."

Gorgi broke off a branch and began to slice the bark away: the silence was so solid that he might just as well have carved it instead of a stick to conceal our embarrassment. I felt as though I were hesitating before a dive, and then plunged into a spate of words:

"Gorgi, I've been thinking—and it wasn't at all a pleasant think. I've deliberately tried to be as horrid as I could. Until I left Raki I had never been mocked, and it made me angry and bitter and small. I wanted to prove that girls could be the equal of men if only they had the chance...and I have done everything to make you all hate me."

"I don't hate you," said Gorgi.

I was so moved that I was glad I had done my crying for the year earlier in the day, otherwise I might have started in front of him. "I am very grateful, Gorgi; really I am. I have done so many things to make you hate me...and to Kekki and

Barakeechi and Tekeeni too. I thought you were all jeering at me, so I never stopped looking for things to jeer at in you....I even asked the tree spirits to help me. I was glad when Kekki was dizzy; glad when Barakeechi broke his leg; glad when your canoe overturned and you were nearly drowned...horribly, disgustingly glad! So it's very kind of you to say you don't hate me, for of course you must.''

''But we don't, Piyanah. We wanted to at first, because we were insulted at having to work with a girl. But when we saw that you were brave, and clever at our kind of things, we tried to be friendly...and you wouldn't let us.''

''I know I wouldn't...that's what I'm trying to explain.''

''Now that you've understood you will find it's much easier,'' said Gorgi warmly. ''When Tekeeni offered to lend you his moccasins, the day you cut your foot on the ice, he ought to have explained that he didn't make the offer because you were a girl but because you were one of us.''

''I'm not really one of you....I mind things and you don't.''

''We have to pretend not to mind in front of Dorrok and some of the older boys, but among ourselves we can admit that we dislike being hurt. But you would never admit it, Piyanah, so whenever you were there we had to pretend to *enjoy* being uncomfortable!''

''But you all try so desperately hard in everything.''

''Of course we do...when you're waiting to mock the loser! And you're always so serious, Piyanah. If we play a joke on anyone, you look scornful and walk away.''

''You'd be scornful of jokes too, Gorgi,'' I said hotly, ''if it was always your blanket that was full of nettles, or your food-bowl that had been rubbed with gall so that you couldn't eat your meal, or your tunic that had been smeared with honey to attract fire-ants, or your bowstring that had been cut nearly in half so that it snapped with the first arrow, or your canoe that leaked!''

''If only you had laughed, or even got angry or played the

same tricks back on us...or even wept, we would have stopped. But when you sneered and pretended we were idiot children, of course we tried to think of something still more annoying.''

''You never asked me to share in the interesting things: I even had to find an excuse not to go to the last tribal feast, because I was ashamed of sitting alone: I didn't want Raki to know that no one would talk to me.''

He patted me awkwardly on the shoulder. ''I am sorry, Piyanah. It must have been terribly lonely for you...but can't it be different now?''

I gulped, and hoped that Gorgi thought I had swallowed a fly instead of a sob. ''I should so like it to be different! It's supposed to be a secret, but Raki and I are trying to learn how to teach men and women not to hate each other...and I've been such a fool that because of me men will hate the women they take into the woods...and then the women will hate them, and the Canyon of the Separation will get still wider.''

''I shan't hate *my* squaw because of you, Piyanah. I shall remember that she is better than me at diving, better at tracking...and that she got seven arrows in the target yesterday while I got only five. And I shall remember that a cut on her foot hurts her just as much as it would have hurt me, though she is too proud to admit to pain. When I have a squaw I shall never let her go back to the women if she wants to stay with me. She shall be my equal in all things, and I shall only be proud when she speaks my name and I shall honour her with the Scarlet Feathers.''

''Oh, Gorgi, dear Gorgi! then I haven't entirely failed?''

''You haven't failed, Piyanah. Perhaps one day in the woods you will understand how much you have won.''

He put his arm round me as Raki might have done. ''This is not the wood in which I can tell you...it is nearly sunset, and I must take my quarry back to Dorrok.''

Then we walked down the hillside: even the shadows were friendly and the evening star did not speak of loneliness.

three hunters

After I had killed my first deer, a stag in its fifth season, several of the boys apparently accepted me as one of themselves; but Gorgi and Tekeeni, with whom I now shared a tepee, were the only two who were pleased when Dorrok said I had done well, so I was glad when the three of us were chosen to hunt our first grizzly together.

To kill a grizzly was considered the first important stage towards becoming a Brown Feather, and to wear its claw on a neck-thong meant that you could give orders to any boy who had not yet gained the same honour: I looked forward to giving orders, for I had not forgotten how difficult some of them had made my first months with them. Grizzlies are easier to kill in the early spring, when they are stupid after their long sleep, but as their fat is poor then, the ones needed by the tribe are hunted in autumn.

We were told which spur of the mountains to search for the bear, but all decisions as how best to attack it were left to us. If we had not succeeded within fifteen days we must return to admit failure, and if we made a kill we must come back as quickly as possible so that Naked Foreheads could be sent to bring down the carcass.

For days the three of us talked of little else. Arrow after arrow was discarded, either because the haft was not perfectly balanced, or else we thought the set of the feathers might be improved. Each of us took a deer-skin bag of pemmican and corn-meal, for on the high ground it might be difficult to find food; we also took a sling for bringing down small birds, a heavy club with a stone head, and a wooden bar bound with raw-hide which Gorgi believed might be thrust into the bear's jaws if it tried to crush one of us. I hoped that we should never have to use it!

It was not until the night before we were due to start that I remembered Pekoo. Raki and I used to give him honey when we could find any, putting some in the bottom of his food-bowl which he held in his front paws, standing upright in his excitement to lick out the last trace of sweetness. When he was small he whimpered if we didn't take him with us, but as he grew older he sometimes disappeared for days, then suddenly came back and followed us everywhere, pretending he had never let us out of his sight. He was away when Mother died, and he never came back. We hoped he had found a mate who didn't like humans, so that he would keep away from hunters: we knew that they hadn't found him yet, for none of the bear-skins they had brought in were marked by the white blaze on the left shoulder which made Pekoo different from all other grizzlies.

I tried to forget about Pekoo. Grizzlies were large, and dangerous, and the pride of hunters: they had never been small, lonely cubs who snuggled up beside Raki and Piyanah for warmth. Hunters killed grizzlies and were honoured by the tribe who needed their skin and their grease, and ate of the flesh which brought strength and cunning. Piyanah was a hunter, not a child with a pet bear.

We left at dawn: the air was clammy with mist and Tekeeni's footprints showed dark in the grey damp of the turf. We led in turn, for it was easier to follow in made tracks than to be the forerunner who must choose each footstep. Following, you can run without thinking, for training has made your stride the same length as your companions'; only a skilled tracker can tell if two or twenty have taken the same path, and sometimes even he is deceived.

Later in the morning Gorgi saw some pigeons and got three of them with the sling. We were hungry, and as we did not want to waste time making a fire, we ate them raw, sprinkled with salt. We were moving south-west across the slope of the foothills, for it was in this direction that we had seen the tracks of several grizzlies during the previous moon. It was not easy country to cross, for there were many steep water-courses, and woods where thick undergrowth forced us to follow winding game tracks which often led us in the wrong direction.

The first night we caught some trout and roasted them in hot embers, and next day Tekeeni killed a small deer, a doe in her first season, so we had more fresh meat than we could carry. There were still nuts to be found in the thickets, though it was late in the year for them, so we had plenty to eat. When we got above the tree line, we could see patches of snow higher on the moraine. The rocks were covered with the lichen which some species of deer prefer to any other feed, and we saw several stags in the distance who had not yet been driven down to the lower ground by the snow.

On the evening of the fourth day we found the spoor of a large grizzly, probably a solitary male, as there was no track of a second one though usually they pair before winter. We drew lots from the spoor, as is the custom, to decide who should have the first chance to make a kill. I hoped that I looked sufficiently elated when it fell to me. It is useless to send an arrow against a bear until you are within twenty paces, or through the thick fur it is unlikely to do more than wound and make the bear turn on you. The hunter should advance slowly towards the grizzly, when, if he is lucky, it will stand upright, so displaying its softer under-parts through which a heavy arrow can bring a clean, swift death. Tracking a wounded grizzly is a thing no hunter enjoys; he knows he cannot leave it to die without incurring dishonour not only with his tribe but also in the land of the Great Hunters, where animals who have suffered needless pain give judgment against him before the Lords of the Animals.

We spent the next day casting a wide semicircle until we found where the tracks converged; always the tracks of the same bear, so we knew he had chosen his winter cave and probably already spent most of his time there. Soon after dawn next morning we saw the mouth of a cave, opening on a ledge of the ridge above us. Snow had fallen during the night and there was only one set of tracks, going towards the cave, so we knew he must be in it.

I tried to pretend the feeling in my belly was hunger—we hadn't eaten since early the previous day except to chew strips of pemmican. But I knew the feeling was fear—a different kind of fear from that I had felt in being parted from Raki, a little like diving from a new height, but slower and heavier, and very disagreeable.

We were down-wind of the cave, but we crawled forward, using every small irregularity in the ground for cover. If the bear was awake and saw us, he would either escape up the mountain or else charge us before we were ready. At thirty paces from the cave I stood upright and notched an arrow. Gorgi with his club, and Tekeeni, with an arrow in his hand but not set to the string, stood ten paces behind me. Until I had wounded the bear, admitted failure, or asked for their help, they were not allowed to take part in the kill.

The sunlight poured down on the snow, and except for an eagle wheeling in wide circles above me everything was still. At twenty paces I halted; no hunter will go into a cave which he believes to be occupied, unless a demon has afflicted him with madness, for he would be blinded by the sudden darkness while his quarry saw him clearly outlined against the daylight. I began to feel sick, and the fear in my belly got harder and more sullen.

I knew it would be wiser to wait until the bear came out of the cave, for if he was not aware of me he would probably be sleepy and half blind in the sudden brightness. But suspense spoke louder than wisdom; I picked up a stone and flung it up to the ledge and heard it clatter against the mouth of the cave. Then before the echoes died away, I flung another, and another.

A large dark head against the darkness...and then the largest grizzly I had ever seen came out into the sunlight, his head swaying from side to side as he scented the wind for an enemy. I shouted and he stood upright. But before I released the straining arrow I saw that the left shoulder was white...white, as no other grizzly had been, except Pekoo.

I was no longer Piyanah the hunter; I was part of Raki and Piyanah and Pekoo, who had been happy together. To kill him would be to kill part of us, to let the present stain the happy past we shared.

Gorgi ran forward. "What's the matter? Why did you lose that chance? Quick, Piyanah...there's still time!"

"I can't kill him," I said flatly.

"Piyanah...you're not *afraid*?" There was horror in Gorgi's voice.

"I *can't* kill him."

"Then I will," said Gorgi, and started to draw his bow.

"Put it down! You have got to obey me. He is *my* grizzly."

"You've had your chance and thrown it away...now I'm going to have mine," said Gorgi.

"He's my grizzly, *mine*, do you understand? He belonged to Raki and me before we joined the tribe."

I saw that neither of them believed me....I must make them believe me or they would kill Pekoo and betray us.

"If I go up to him and he lets me stroke him, will you believe he knows me?" I said desperately.

"You're mad, Piyanah," said Tekeeni. "There must be demons up here and you've been listening to them. No one ever had a pet grizzly; they are much too fierce."

"I will show you...I will prove to you. You have *got* to obey me until I ask for help. You've got to, or else you have broken the law of the hunters."

"You're mad," said Tekeeni miserably. "We'll never tell the others you were frightened. They'll think that Gorgi had the first chance and then me. It's very brave of a girl to come on a grizzly hunt: and it's not cowardly for a girl to be afraid. We'll never tell anyone, Piyanah, if only you'll admit that it's our turn now."

103

"I'm *not* a coward, and I'll prove it! Stay here: I *order* you to stay here!"

And before they could argue I began to walk slowly up the slope towards Pekoo. Had he forgotten me? It was four years...more, it was five years, since he had seen me. If only the wind would change, he might remember my smell. I began to whistle, the tune Raki and I had used to call him. Had he remembered?

He dropped down on all fours and swayed his head from side to side.... "I don't think he's seen me yet. It is difficult to whistle when your mouth is dry. I must go slowly or he'll think I mean to attack him.

"Pekoo," I said, "Pekoo!" Was he going to charge? He began slowly walking towards me. "Shall I stand still and wait for him, or go forward?"

He stopped: I could see the blaze more clearly now, so I was quite sure he was Pekoo. "I must forget that I am a hunter and that he is a grizzly...and remember that we were both small and friendly, and that neither is afraid...."

Suddenly I found I wasn't afraid...the greyness had gone; I must talk to him as I used to. "Do you want some honeycomb, Pekoo? We must go and find Raki. Milk, Pekoo?"

Very slowly I went forward, holding out my hands. He stared at me, sniffing, undecided whether to trust me or to attack.

"Honey, Pekoo! Don't you remember the honey?"

I whistled, and this time he pricked up his ears. Now I was so near that I could smell the warmth of him.

"Where is Raki, Pekoo? Beautiful, small Pekoo." I put my hand on his forehead and rubbed him behind the ears. He flinched and drew back: then he sat up on his haunches and put up his chin for me to scratch him on the throat.

For a little while he remembered me, or perhaps it was only my smell or the sound of my voice that he remembered. Then he shook himself like a dog after a swim, and ambled away, pausing only once to look back at me.

Gorgi and Tekeeni were standing where I had left them. We were all too embarrassed to speak. I was still caught up with the young Piyanah who was so fiercely lonely without Raki and resented any other companion. If they jeered at me for loving a bear I should hate them, and then the awful loneliness of the first moons would come back. If only the bear hadn't been Pekoo I should be feeling proud and brave...or else by now I should be safely dead, and not have to keep on trying to remember whether I was a girl or a man.

Gorgi stared at the ground and shuffled his feet. I supposed he was feeling a fool because he had ever accepted me as an equal. Then, to my astonishment, I heard him say:

"I never knew a girl could be as brave as a Scarlet Feather."

And Tekeeni said, "I am sorry I thought you were frightened, Piyanah. Need you tell the others that Gorgi and I were fools?"

Then Gorgi said, "Because of you and Raki we will honour all squaws, and ask you to take us into your tribe."

Suddenly the three of us were happier than we had ever been before; we hugged each other, and shouted with laughter, and pelted each other with snow...and forgot that the lives of hunters are hard and difficult.

LORE OF THE FEATHERS

I was never sure what Gorgi told Kekki and Barakeechi, and the others who had begun to be friendly, but they changed towards me so completely that if I had not recognized their faces I should never have believed they were the same people. Every day I liked them still better, and it was so restful not always to be on my guard that I felt twice as strong as I had ever done before.

There was an extraordinary relief in being able to admit that the smell of warm intestines when I had to gralloch a deer made me feel sick; and, instead of laughing, Barakeechi did it for me, unless one of the other boys, who might tell Dorrok, was there. Even a cut foot hurts very little with a friend to share a grumble, and sympathy brought quicker healing than green salve.

We agreed that in front of the others we must hide our friendship, for we who belonged to the future tribe had secrets which could not be shared by people content with the Separation. Some of the older boys must have suspected, for instead of ignoring me they tried to be tormenting. It was a moment warm and beautiful as a sunset, when I saw Kekki being held down by four of our future Braves while they painted him with fish-glue and rolled him in burrs: then they pegged him down, like a drying hide, by thongs tied to his wrists and ankles, until the glue set hard. I stopped Tekeeni putting belly-berry into another enemy's food-bowl, for I knew he wasn't sure how much of it was safe. They had tried the same joke two years earlier, and the victim had squatted until he nearly died of exhaustion.

After that the enemies kept away from me; which was lucky, as Raki did not seem to think the jokes were funny; I felt rather ashamed of having enjoyed them, though he agreed that sometimes it was necessary for a Chief to be firm.

As Na-ka-chek seldom spoke to us, Raki and I decided that so long as we went on training for the feathers we could prepare for our tribe without asking his permission about details, and that it would be a good idea for Gorgi and the others to have a chance to know some of our squaws.

Rokeena could walk quite a long way if she went slowly, so I was able to meet her without Nona or the women finding out. She was very shy at first with Gorgi and Tekeeni, but soon got used to them, though she still tried to hide her scarred leg. It was Tekeeni who cured this fear; instead of pretending not to notice it he showed her a bad scar on his arm, where he had fallen on a fish-spear when jumping from a slippery rock, and said it was a better scar than hers because it was longer. After that Rokeena talked about her leg with him as though they were two girls comparing the patterns of their moccasins.

Through Raki and Rokeena, I came to know the life of the Squaws' Tepees almost as well as if I were living there myself. Only women over seventy years could claim to know how to propitiate demons, and this claim was the real source of their power. Demons did not seem very intelligent, for the bad ones were sent scuttling away by a small packet of herbs worn under the right arm for three days; and even those considered specially dangerous, which crept up the nostrils and jumped about inside the head causing great pain to their unwilling host, were often killed by five drops of porcupine oil in the left ear, if at the same time certain magical words were whispered into the other. The flesh of water-rats was prized for coughs, and beavers' bones, dried and crushed to a fine powder, must be given to a child whenever it loses a tooth, otherwise the second teeth will not grow properly.

One of the first laws we made for our tribe was that there should be no Old Women, for if we could not survive without their medicines we would only be wasting time in starting out. Dorrok had promised to teach me how to treat a broken bone and the way to sew up a jagged wound with gut and a bone needle. I already knew how to pin a flap of flesh in place with a long thorn, but it did not always heal very cleanly.

I was surprised when Rokeena asked how our tribe would have children if we did not take at least one of the Old Women with us. "What use would they be?" I said. "Raki told me that no woman over thirty-two ever has a baby."

"It is when the baby is born that the Old Women are needed," said Rokeena. "The mother and the baby both die unless the proper rituals are carried out."

"I don't believe it," I said firmly, for the prospect of taking a person like Nona with us was impossible to accept. "There can't always have been Old Women...certainly not among the Before People, and animals manage perfectly well by themselves."

"No one under seventy must go near a mother or her baby until it is seven days old. If it is a male child, the belly slits open downwards from the navel, and only if the wound is properly bandaged can it heal without a scar."

"I could learn to bandage," I said, "and so could Raki."

"But we couldn't get the right bandages. They have to be steeped in water to which a lot of secret things have been added....I know they use salt, but there are many other things as well. They must be kept in the dark except at the full moon when they are exposed to her rays for three nights...so that the moonlight soaks into them and blinds the demons. The baby has to be bandaged too, as soon as it is born, otherwise a demon can use the body for its own."

"Rokeena, you must try to stop believing in demons! Tree spirits, cloud and fire spirits, are quite different....they are messengers between us and the Great Hunters, and always friendly...unless one is rude to them, and of course one never is. But demons are invented by Old Women...and I shouldn't be surprised if the Elders help them."

"Don't say that," she said, and there was real fear in her voice. "Don't say that, for one of them might be listening."

"An Old Woman, or a demon?"

"A demon: they are *everywhere.*"

I began to feel cross with her. "Raki cured your leg, and that should be quite enough to convince you that he is much stronger than demons."

"I *know* Raki is stronger...and so are you," she added hastily. "I only meant that it's no use pretending demons don't exist."

"They don't: unless you believe in them. They are like

108

death-berries: they don't jump off a branch and dive down your throat...if you ignore them, they are quite harmless. Unless you learn that, Rokeena, we shan't be able to take you into our tribe.''

''Please don't say that, Piyanah! If you won't say that, I'll tell you a very important secret...which proves that demons are real. The Old Women would kill me if they knew, so I shouldn't dare to tell you if I wasn't worthy to join your tribe.''

I knew she really meant 'Raki's tribe', but I only said, ''What secret?''

''All babies don't come out of a slit in your belly! Before I fell and hurt my leg I was in the woods when I heard someone groaning. It was a young squaw: she had torn off her tunic, and was lying doubled on her side, and there was a baby on the ground beside her...it was a female baby and it was crying. I forgot that if anyone goes near the Birth Tepee they bring death with them, and I ran towards her. She saw me and screamed at me to go away...but my shadow had already touched her. I ran, but I had seen her belly, and there was not even a mark on it.''

''Why didn't you tell Raki? He has been trying to find out about babies because he knows it will be important to us, but no one will tell him anything.''

''I didn't tell him because I knew he was happier not believing in demons. I *know* they are real; because the squaw never came back to the tepees.''

''What happened to her? What happened to the baby?''

''I think, though I am not sure, that one of the other women took the baby...there was a new one and no other squaw had been away to the Birth Tepee.''

''The mother died?''

''Yes, the demons killed her. *I* killed her, because I saw them both before the baby was seven days old. That's why I knew the demons were angry when they threw me out of the tree, and why I couldn't believe that Raki was going to cure me. I didn't know then that Raki was so strong and wonderful."

I heard Gorgi whistle and knew that it was time for me to go back. I told Rokeena that I would meet her again as soon as I could arrange it, and that until then she had better say "I don't believe in demons" forty times every night before she went to sleep.

Raki, having to be with people like Rokeena! I was more sorry for him than I had ever been...*my* Raki, having to live with squaws who were so *stupid!* It was good to be Piyanah who was training to be a Brave, and knew that only fools and squaws believed in demons. I paused with my hand on the rough bark of a spruce, to thank the tree spirit for his protection.

Since Raki had been upheld by the Chief over letting Rokeena leave the tepee and be taken into the sunlight, and none of Nona's warnings of disaster had come true, the Old Women tried to avoid open conflict with him. Instead, they contented themselves with telling even more terrifying stories to the girls who were weak enough to listen, and we knew that if they had been in charge of the cooking-pots our tribe would have been made from skeletons.

Raki had found women's work easy, though if a single thread of a blanket he wove was crooked or the wrong colour, an Old Woman would pounce on the defect like a toad snapping at a fly; and they examined his moccasins in search of a misplaced bead that would make the pattern different from the second of the pair, with the eagerness of dogs rootling for fleas. The fact that Raki never burnt the food was a particular disappointment to them, and they began to believe that all men are born with the skill of women as well as their own, but are too proud to make use of it. It amused us that they never realized we had learned to prepare food, with many mistakes, in our little valley, and that Mother had taught us to embroider moccasins and set the threads straight on the loom.

They must eventually have decided that Raki had demons at his command who were stronger than their own, for they even pretended not to know that the girls who wanted to join our tribe sometimes left the tepees at dawn and did not return until sunset. Dorrok must have known that Gorgi and our other friends often joined the girls to help Raki teach them the things which would make them worthy of tribal brotherhood; but we were never sure whether he had consulted Na-ka-chek about it, or decided on his own responsibility that we should be allowed to carry out our plans without interference.

At first the boys were surprised that girls found it difficult to use a bow, but I explained to them that I had only been able to do it even when I first joined them because Raki and I had always done the same things. Gradually the girls became skilled with arrows, and about half of them showed real ability with a fish-spear. In some ways they had curiously strong bellies; one of them, called Cheka, who was only thirteen and very shy, gralloched a stag, and instead of being sick, as I expected, she let the guts run through her fingers as though she were admiring a new forehead-band. In a short time they all became good trackers, for this had always been a tradition with them...no doubt if I had had to look forward to being taken into the woods by a stranger I should have taken even more interest in learning the cunning necessary to a quarry!

Some of the boys did not like it when I said that they must learn women's tasks, but they agreed to try when I told them that in our tribe no kind of work would be considered inferior to any other. Gorgi found that he enjoyed making moccasins, and Tekeeni fringed quite a creditable tunic...though he admitted that he only did it to please me. I remembered Gorgi saying, ''May the Great Hunters be thanked that Piyanah cannot make a law by which men and women both have to bring forth children,'' and that led to a discussion as to what our laws would be.

''No man *need* take a squaw,'' I said. ''But if he does, he has got to accept her as an equal and let her share his life; and he must also share in the trouble of looking after any children they may have.''

"Can he have more than one squaw?" asked Tekeeni, and one of the girls said quickly, "Can a squaw have more than one man?"

"No," said Raki firmly, "they can't. Duck pair only once, and we have always been told that Great Duck is one of the wisest of the Lords of the Animals.''

"A stag has several hinds," objected Tekeeni.

"That's why stags fight each other," I said. "I think Raki is right. We ought to start with the same number of men and women, so that they can all have a chance of pairing if they feel like it.''

Then Kekki said, "When women are allowed to share the hunting, who is going to stay behind to look after the children...or will that be done by Naked Foreheads?''

"There will be no Naked Foreheads," I said. "At least, if any of them want to come with us, they are going to be given a fair chance like everyone else.''

"But *someone* has got to do the scavenging.''

"I know: that someone might be you, or Gorgi, or whoever can best be spared from something needing more skill.''

"But you said we could all choose what we most wanted to do," said one of the girls, "and no one enjoys cleaning cooking-pots or scraping hides.''

At this, Cheka said, "I like cleaning fish and things," and then she dived into embarrassed silence because everyone turned to look at her in amazement. She was the girl I had seen gralloch the stag, so I decided to arrange for her to have plenty of the same strange amusement...the sight of her fingering the steaming guts was still a distasteful memory.

"But who is going to do the scavenging?" repeated Kekki, who was always apt to ask the same question several times until he was quite satisfied with the answer.

"We have arranged that," said Raki, who until then had

left most of the talking to me. "Every moon we shall meet in council, to decide who has been the most, and the least, useful to the tribe during the previous moon. The ten who were most useful can do exactly as they like during the next moon, and the ten who have done the least for the rest of us can act as Naked Foreheads during the same period."

Gorgi then asked, "What happens if the first ten all want to sit by the river and do nothing?"

"It depends on what kind of 'nothing'. If they seemed just to be sitting, but at the same time were thinking, they might find an idea that was more valuable to the tribe than ten stags. If this proves to be so, they can go on thinking as long as they like. It is the amount of help they have given by which they will be judged...if the help is small, they can do scavenging, so that the tribe can be grateful to them because the encampment doesn't smell of rotting fish, or all the other smells that need burying."

"Who will do the choosing?" said Gorgi.

"Piyanah and I will always be in the council, as the Chief, and with us shall sit four others, two men and two women... selected because they have the most feathers."

"Oh, are we going to have feathers too?" said Rokeena, gazing at Raki with awe as she always did.

"Yes, but our feathers are going to be real. The white feathers will be the most honoured, for they can be won only for an idea, or a memory of the Before People, or something time does not spoil, which can be used to hold the bridge over the Canyon even in a thousand years. Yellow feathers can be for ideas too, but ideas which affect things we can touch: such as a better way of building canoes, or making pottery, or curing pelts; and they can be earned for discovering a new use for a plant, either as a food or for its value as a salve; or how to make a broken bone mend more quickly. Green feathers show that you have talked with a spirit and heard a message from the Great Hunters: it doesn't matter whether it's a tree spirit, or a water spirit, or just a friend who happens to be

113

dead. You also get a green feather for killing a demon, either by teaching someone not to believe in them, so that they shrivel up and vanish in disgust, or else by finding them when they are disguised as rattle-snakes and squashing their heads with stones...a white stone is the best for this, but a stick will do if you haven't got anything else.''

I looked at Rokeena to be sure she was listening...she was, and I reminded myself to ask her whether she had talked herself out of believing in demons yet. Then Raki went on:

''Brown feathers will still mean a proven skill in something which adds to the protection and well-being of the tribe, and Half-brothers will also wear brown feathers, for it is quite as important to make a cooking-pot as to fill it with meat. The women, or men, who do the cooking can earn a brown feather too, if their special skill has increased the pleasure and health of those they feed. We shall still have scarlet feathers, which can only be won by some special act of courage; but in our tribe they will have to be gained in doing something of real value, not just as a proof that the wearer has risked death for no reason. You could win our Scarlet by rescuing some-one, from a grizzly or from drowning in the rapids. If I had been the Chief I should have given a scarlet feather to Dorrok when he climbed down a precipice to rescue a fawn which had fallen down on to a ledge. It was starving to death, while its mother stood watching and wouldn't leave even when she heard Dorrok coming. He never told anyone, and seemed to think that he was a traitor to the tribe because he had risked becoming crippled, and useless as a Brave, for something that didn't matter. But it *did* matter to Dorrok, for I saw his face when the hind was licking her fawn and when he watched it trotting after her into the woods...and yet he thought he should be ashamed of weakness. And it matters to us, for I hope that Dorrok will come with us when we go to our own place of the corn-growing, to find the peace of the Feathers of Truth.''

114

Salt of Danger

If salt had been found in our territory there would have been no need for us to barter with another tribe. I think my father regretted even so small a dependence on strangers as was caused by the need to send, every year at midsummer, two Brown Feathers, and six Naked Foreheads who carried the salt-jars, to the Place of Barter, a month's journey to the South. Beaver pelts, moccasins embroidered with beads, and tunics of fringed doe-skin were used by us as exchange. In my grandfather's time we had sent bows and tomahawks, but Na-ka-chek said, "The wise man does not give weapons into the hands of a stranger, nor display a strength which may be taken for a challenge."

There was always a feast on the night the salt arrived, and even Naked Foreheads and children were allowed a handful of it, which they could eat like honeycomb instead of tasting it only from the common cooking-pot. It always surprised me that so much salt was given in exchange for things like moccasins, which could have no real value while there were hunters to kill deer and squaws to cure hides and do bead-work. There were stories of lakes of salt where it was plentiful as snow in winter; and a legend that in the Land of the Great Hunters salt was used to spread the paths of the encampments...but this even Raki and I found difficult to believe.

The day after the Feast of Salt in our sixteenth year Na-ka-chek sent for me, and I found Raki already with him in the Great Tepee.

"I have news for you both," he said, "which is not yet for the rest of the tribe. This year Dorrok has brought more than salt to savour our food; he has brought news of danger to increase our taste for courage. When I spoke to you with the dark smoke to remind you of your responsibilities, you thought I lied about the possibility of danger from the Black

115

Feathers, even though I showed you a forehead-thong from one of their warriors. For three years they have been slowly migrating westwards; and, knowing this, the Elders have counselled me that it would be wise for us to seek new hunting-grounds. This advice I should have accepted had I not pledged my oath to your mother that on the day that you two put on the Double Headdress I shall stand with you at the Pool of the Before People to tell her that I have fulfilled my word.''

''The Black Feathers will not respect our boundaries?'' asked Raki.

''During the memory of the grandfathers they have not sent a spokesman to the Gathering of the Tribes, which, as you know, takes place every seven years. It was because they lived so far to the East that many people had begun to think them only a legend. Dorrok heard at the Place of Barter that the Tribe of the Beaver, who are few in number and remarkable only for the quality of their pottery, have—disappeared.''

''How can a tribe disappear?'' I said. ''They may have migrated and not yet sent word of their new place of the corn-growing.''

''A tribe which migrates does not burn down its tepees, nor are human skeletons found under the brambles which have encroached on the planted fields: if they had died of a pestilence there would have been some who escaped to ask for help. The Beaver were massacred...by the Black Feathers, for any other tribe would have allowed the threatened Chief to send a spokesman to his neighbours, declaring the purpose of battle and asking that his women and children should be given shelter if his own men could no longer provide for them. It may be that this raid against the Beaver resulted in many of the enemy being killed and that they have learned to respect other men's corn; or it may be that this conquest will satisfy them for several years, and that if they cross the pass into the valley it will be to find it free

116

land from which we have already gone to the West.

"The threat of constant danger is too rich a meat save for those whose bellies are strong: so this news is to be kept from women, children, Naked Foreheads, and boys under fourteen, until such time as it is essential for them to know it. There will always be a Brown Feather watching the pass, and another four days down-river, though I think they will not come that way, for the falls make it impassable to canoes. Piyanah will continue to train with the boys over sixteen, for with them she will go into battle—unless she wishes to forget the promise of the Feathers."

"Of course Raki and I will fight together," I said. "We wanted to do that even when we were only eleven."

"Raki's part will not be so easy as yours, Piyanah. The best time to learn the colour of people's hearts is when they are afraid. When we are threatened, the squaws will forget the small preoccupations in which they conceal their thoughts; and it may be that if there is a leader amongst them, a leader whom they accept as one of themselves, they may discover qualities which will give them a greater recognition of their equality than they could ever learn in blind obedience. Raki will take them into the woods, not like a herd of goats in hiding, but as free women who must use their wisdom and strength to protect their children. I shall not even send Naked Foreheads with them. Those whom Raki has taught to use bow or sling will help him to provide their food; they will kindle their own fires, and this will do much to break the rod of superstition which the Old Women still wield. Raki has told me that there are already thirty girls near your own age who wish to join your tribe and that they have sworn to take husbands of their choosing and never to bear children to a man whose name they may not speak. The Black Feathers may come, and to many of us they will bring death; but to the rest they may help to bring freedom, from an enemy older even than the People of the Carrion Crow—the Lord of Separation."

I knew it had never occurred to Raki that he might have to stay with the squaws if the tribe were threatened, but we did not argue with Na-ka-chek, for we had both accepted that we must obey his laws if we were ever to be free to make laws of our own. Only one request did Raki make before we left the Great Tepee.

"From what I have already learned of women, I know that those who are strong in spirit can eat danger and keep a quiet belly better than a man. They are used to suspense, from having to watch the slow approach of pain which cannot be avoided...it is women, not men, who bear the children. Only those who wish to come with Piyanah and me do I wish to test with this news. If I am able to discuss my plans with them I shall be doing no more than give them the sense of shared responsibility which Piyanah will have from Dorrok and the Scarlet Feathers. Have I your permission?"

"It has been said that to tell a secret to a squaw, and to be surprised when the mocking-birds shout it in your ear, is as foolish as to leave a fire untended in a plain of dry grass and to be surprised when the wind rages with smoke."

"I am a woman and you trust the secret to me," I said indignantly. "Would you not have trusted it to my mother? How is Raki to teach the others to be free if you still repeat sayings without wisdom?"

To my surprise, instead of being angry he laughed, a harsh laugh like the creaking of a tree which has grown too old. "That was well spoken, my daughter, and I accept a just rebuke. You have played your part so well that Na-ka-chek had forgotten that you were not also his son."

Neither Raki nor I really believed in danger from the Black Feathers, for Father had used them to deceive us before.

"I expect Dorrok heard some story at the Place of Barter," I said, "and Father wants to believe it because it will make us all work harder. Do your women believe it?"

"Yes," said Raki, "they do. It makes everything much more interesting. I discussed it with Rokeena before telling the others, and she agreed that it was only right they should know and that they must swear not to discuss it except among themselves; so I told each of them separately and explained with whom they shared responsibility.'' He laughed. ''The others were furious!''

''But why, if they don't know anything about it?''

''Because they know there *is* a secret, and they keep on trying to find out what it is. Nona thinks it's something to do with demons, and I've heard it whispered that Dorrok brought back beads as well as salt and that I'm giving them to my friends to wear during the Choosing. They can't understand why our people want to learn how to carve and use bows and catch fish. They are very angry about it, for they say that if the hunters discover that women can collect food as well as prepare it, the squaw's life will be harder than ever. They jeer at us, and say that at least our foolishness will never be inherited, for no man will take us into the woods.''

''Do they *want* to be taken into the woods?''

''Yes: they think of little else. They don't know what is going to happen to them there, but they know that not to be chosen is considered an almost unendurable shame. Sometimes it is quite unendurable, for last year a girl killed herself because no man chose her...she ate death-berries.''

''Can't you tell them, Raki...what really happens, I mean?''

If it hadn't been Raki and me I should have thought he was embarrassed. ''Well, we don't know much about it, do we, Piyanah? I mean, you don't any more than I do...and you really *are* a girl.''

''Don't the girls talk about it...afterwards?''

''No,'' said Raki, ''they don't. Some of them seem sorry to be back with the squaws, and some of them are terribly glad. But they never say anything about what happens.''

''Aren't the girls told anything before the Choosing?''

''I'm sure they're not...they whisper and giggle and tease each other; some seem to think that the tree spirits make babies, but I'm sure that's nonsense. Do the other boys know all about it, Piyanah? I suppose they don't say anything about it to me because I wear squaw's clothes.''

''The boys boast how they will win the wrestling and earn the best squaw, but I think it's only important because it will show that they have become full members of the tribe. Perhaps they are told when they become Brown Feathers....I'm sure Gorgi and Tekeeni don't know anything, for they admitted it when they promised not to take a squaw until they joined our tribe.''

Raki sighed. ''It is very difficult for us, Piyanah, to have to teach men and women how to have children who can be free and happy, when we don't know how to have children ourselves.''

''I am glad we came back to the tribe,'' I said suddenly. ''I would like us to have children, and if we'd stayed in our little valley there would have been no one to tell us how to start.''

I was spearing fish in one of the hill streams, when the deep, ominous note of the Horn of Gathering rolled up from the valley. My heart leaped like a stranded trout, for the sound held the horror of a rattle-snake...the tribe was being summoned to hear that danger was closing in on them, to hear of the Black Feathers.

I caught up my six fish, threaded a reed through their gills, and ran down the steep hillside. When I reached the encampment the rest of the tribe had assembled, and Na-ka-chek was telling them that three hundred Black Feathers had been seen coming out of the East, from the country which had been called ''uninhabited.'' They were men in war paint, and with them came neither children nor squaws. When they heard this, the women huddled together and caught up their children as if to be ready for instant flight.

''It is not certain,'' said Na-ka-chek, in the same calm voice which might have been declaring something of minor importance, "that the Black Feathers will cross the pass into our hunting-grounds. If they go to the north-west I shall send runners to warn the neighbouring tribe that they may be the intended victims. If the Great Hunters consider us worthy, they will choose the Tribe of the Two Trees to cleanse the earth of the vermin of the Carrion Crow."

At this there was a murmur of assent from the Braves, and some of the squaws began to look less anxious as they realized there was a chance the danger would pass them by.

"Only the fool lets danger take him unawares," went on Na-ka-chek, "so our plans were made soon after the last salt reached the encampment. Those to whom I have given my authority will tell each of you what he is to do for the safety of all. Continue with your preparations, but do not let anticipation change the pattern of your lives until the Horn of the Gathering tells you that the enemy has crossed the pass."

The crowd dispersed, and I was able to speak to Raki alone before he went to give orders to the squaws.

"It has never before been so difficult to obey," he said, "and I have never been so close to understanding the courage, and the sorrow, of women. You can stay here, to fight; but I must hide with the women...hide, when I might be able to save you if we were together. Hide, because I am more useful keeping squaws from interfering in the battle than I should be if I fought beside you!"

"If we lose the battle, Raki, yours will be the greater danger. Even if you all manage to escape, how will you be able to look after a herd of women? The Old Women will be like a heavy stone round the neck of a swimmer, and the young squaws and the children will lame you as though you tried to wade through ant-hills. You will have to leave them, or starve with them...and I know you will never leave them."

"Don't you know I should welcome starvation if you had died? Do you think I want to keep you waiting in our little valley?"

"It will be difficult to hide the tracks of so many women, for only ours have been trained to walk in each other's footprints. The Black Feathers will not give you an easy death when they find you are not a squaw. They will torture you, Raki, and I shall not be able to help you from the other side of the water."

I heard Dorrok shouting for me, and knew we should not have another chance to talk alone. We both carried a weight of fear for each other, so much heavier than the fear for ourselves.

Dorrok let me take Gorgi and ten other boys to help Raki and our women to carry the things they would need to the chosen hiding-place. This was a large cave, its mouth hidden by a tangle of brambles, and near enough to the encampment for two journeys there and back to be made between sunrise and noon. There was no need to carry water up there, as a stream ran close beside it, but a lot of bread and pemmican was necessary, for it would be too dangerous to light a fire.

Na-ka-chek had warned Raki that the squaws must remain hidden until they heard the sound of the Horn. If it had not been sounded by the fourteenth day, they must try to make their way westwards to ask shelter from the neighbouring Chief...a journey that would take twenty days even if there was no sickness among them. He also warned us that though the enemy might be beaten off in the first attack they might withdraw only until they saw a favourable opportunity to fall on us again. Squaws who ventured back too soon were often carried off, and with Black Feathers even children would not be safe from massacre.

The approach to Raki's cave was up a steep slope of loose shale, without even a thorn bush to afford cover to anyone trying to attack uphill. The cave mouth was narrow, and partially filled by a boulder which would conceal three bowmen who lay flat behind it. Several of the girls were skilled with arrows, but I was doubtful whether they would find a human target so easy as the ones against which they

122

had practised. I was confident of their loyalty to Raki, but would they be able to keep free of the cloud of fear that wrapped the Old Women and the squaws who still clung to their superstitions?

Among the rest of us there was one question of supreme importance: would the Black Feathers use their traditional method of attack? On this depended the success or failure of our plans. Would they silently encircle our encampment, creeping forward through the darkness to pile dry grass against the tepees, then set them alight so that those who slept there would stumble out into the firelight, blinded by smoke, a prey easier than the animals stampeded by a prairie fire? Would they do this, or respect the honourable laws of battle? If they held to the laws of the Feathered Council they would give us a day's warning, so that our women and children could be sent to a place of safety: then the Chiefs would meet, to decide the number of Braves each might send into battle and to choose the landmarks from which, at dawn the next day, the line of warriors would approach each other, advancing under cover or charging across the last hundred paces according to their choice.

"The Black Feathers have been outlawed by the Council of Thirty Tribes for more than two hundred years," said Na-ka-chek. "We must remember that they are the children of the Carrion Crow, and have not even the honest cruelty of mountain lion. They will try to attack when we are asleep, setting fire to our tepees, massacring our women and children. We will let them think we are a fat and easy prey: they will find an encampment where everyone appears to sleep except the man by the watch-fire. This man will wear the blanket of an Elder, and the truth of a Scarlet Feather; he will know that the darkness is eager with death, yet he will sit, and smoke, and wait, until he gives the war cry by which we light *our* fires."

"Our fires," he repeated, "Beyond the circle of tepees shall be set tinder-wood and straw sprinkled with fish-oil.

Beside each of these a man shall wait with a smouldering torch, its light carefully hidden. It shall be the enemy, not ourselves, who is blinded by the light of a ring of fires, and we, ready in vantage-points on the cliff, shall let him slake his thirst for blood in the hot rain of arrows.''

Black feathers

''The Black Feathers! Wake up, Piyanah. The Black Feathers have crossed the pass!''

Still dazed with sleep, I found myself running with Gorgi down the steep path. Instead of a solitary figure by the watch-fire, the leaping flames showed my father wearing the feathered headdress, and round him gathered the Braves, to make before the Totem the dedication of arrows. On the fringe of the crowd I saw Raki, with the squaws who had not yet joined the others in the cave.

My father raised his right hand and the clamour of tongues was stilled. To the Totem he spoke, and the hearts of his people were open to listen:

''Messenger of the Great Hunters, in whose memory we live; at thy feet we set these our arrows, that they may fly in truth against thy enemies. Though we are but as a drop in a great river, we, the Men of the Two Trees, are of the morning against the darkness, and in the name of the people on the other side of the water we fight against the children of the Carrion Crow.

''If we die in thy name, may we deserve the right to enter the Happy Hunting-Grounds; and if we triumph in thy name, may the trees rejoice that we live among them, and the river rejoice that our canoes belong to their waters, and may the animals rejoice that in our country we have not betrayed them.

"May our courage and our endurance prove worthy of the Totem thou hast set amongst us. May our arrows have the vision of thy eagles, and the strength of our sinews be as the Great White Deer which only the chosen of thy sun has ever seen.

"Into thy care I commit my people, and I, Na-ka-chek, speak not only in the name of my Braves, for under your protection I place also the women, and the children, and the Naked Foreheads, declaring them to be my equals; so in the name of the Mother of my Sons, I ask that they, too, shall gain entry in honour to thy Country."

Then did the Wearers of the Scarlet, and the Brown Feathers, and all of us who would fight in the protection of our people, come forward to kneel before the Totem, holding in our outstretched hands the arrows, feathered in scarlet and yellow, which can be used only against humans who have been declared the enemy of the tribe.

Then did we kneel before Na-ka-chek, who made with his fingers upon our foreheads the tribal mark, the two interlaced blue triangles in the yellow circle, men and women under the sun, though except by Raki and me this meaning had been forgotten. And on the forehead of Raki and our thirty women he made this sign also.

Then I watched Raki take the path to the hills: and with him there were women who were young and proud; and women who were frightened; and women, with blankets drawn over their heads to protect them from demons, who shuffled along, dark as the shadows of sleeping bats. I watched them go into the woods beyond the firelight.

With Gorgi and Tekeeni, I climbed to our vantage-point on the cliff overlooking the encampment. We had been forbidden to talk, and thoughts began to race through my mind. "I must forget that I also am a squaw. Gorgi and Tekeeni are excited...to them the Black Feathers are a new quarry. They are right; Piyanah has sometimes wept in her heart at the death of a stag, but Black Feathers have not the nobility of animals, so she can watch her arrows drink their blood, and laugh and shout in exultation. Black Feathers are not real people, they are a legend, born of fear and shadows, who keep alive the curse of the Separation. Their squaws hate them and their children fear them: think of their squaws, Piyanah, whom your arrows will set free.

"I never thought I should have to fight without Raki beside me...we never really believed in the Black Feathers. Will Raki find the way to our little valley? Are the corncobs still there, waiting for us to pick them up? We were not afraid of crossing the water when we were eleven...we must not be afraid now. I can't be afraid, or I shouldn't have been able to eat of the 'feast of the preparation' without feeling sick. There is salt before battle, as much as you can eat... blood will taste salt too. My skin glistens with bear's grease...difficult for an enemy to grip in a wrestling hold, and if I am wounded, the grease will enter my blood so I shall gain the strength of a bear instead of weakening. I am glad that Pekoo remembered me, for the Lord of the Grizzlies will take me under his protection. An arrow will be hot as fire....Raki and I used to think it would feel like a hornet. I would rather feel an arrow than a tomahawk. If they take my scalp, I hope that I'm dead first. But I'm not going to be dead, because Raki and I are going to lead a new tribe, and this battle will be only a story we tell by the watch-fire when we are old."

I could feel Gorgi and Tekeeni tense beside me as we lay on the narrow ledge: the Scarlet Feather had put two fresh logs on the fire, the signal that the Black Feathers were sliding towards us through the woods with the stealth of vipers.

The circle of cliffs was taut with bows. A shadow moved down by the river, and I felt Gorgi notch his arrow to the string, though we were not to loose our bows until the enemy began to retreat towards the opening in the rocks on the east of the encampment. The man by the watch-fire seemed absorbed in his smoke.

The shadows moved closer. They were surrounding the

the Squaws' Tepees. The pool of darkness below the Great Tepee altered its shape...now there were men as well as rocks in the intensity of darkness. Now we should know if Na-ka-chek had been right when he said that the Black Feathers were obedient to their tradition and always surrounded the tepees before they attacked.

The man by the watch-fire threw on another log...the Black Feathers had surrounded the encampment. The Scarlet Feather knew that the three hundred pairs of eyes were watching him; he might well be the first victim, alone and defenceless; yet he had not moved, the smoke from his pipe was calm and unhurried, as though he were indeed an Elder, pausing in a story often told.

Suddenly he leapt to his feet and gave our war cry. The encampment was no longer in darkness, for the ring of fires we had prepared sprang into life...our fires, not the pyres of tepees for which the Black Feathers had waited.

In the sudden glare I saw the enemies: their bodies glistening with oil, their ribs outlined with charcoal so that they looked like skeletons from the Underworld. I saw the Scarlet Feather die, but before his body fell across the fire four of the enemy had died by his tomahawk. I saw Dorrok strip off a man's scalp like the pelt from a beaver: he held it above his head, then laughed and threw it into an empty cooking-pot before plunging after another enemy.

I learned that death can be grotesque, and a man run though his head lolls down his back. I heard that even a Scarlet Feather can scream when a arrow quivers from the socket of his eye. I heard Gorgi sobbing with excitement, and my hands were so slippery with sweat that I was afraid I might not be able to restrain my arrow from its leap.

The fires blazed higher. I could see my father in a press of fighting men. Quarters were too close for arrows, and I could hear the thud of tomahawks and clubs. I saw the skull of a Brown Feather split open and the white mess of brains slide down his shoulder before he fell. I could smell the hot, sweet stench of blood even through the smoke. Our fires were spreading and tongues of flame licked up one of the smaller tepees.

A wounded man was crawling up the slope towards me, trying to find the sanctuary of darkness. I was going to help him, but Gorgi pulled me back and I saw the black feather in his forehead-thong. He was coughing, a hard, dry cough like a sick animal; his body curved forward as though he were trying to retch. Fire suddenly ran up a pine tree and I saw the haft of a broken arrow sticking out below his shoulder blade: the light was so bright that I could even see the colour of the blood bubbling from his mouth. The coughing went on and on: I could hear it even above the noise of battle.

There were many of our dead before the few Black Feathers who still survived started to try to withdraw into the woods.

"Now!" shouted Gorgi. "Now! The first to pass that rock is mine."

I heard the sting of his bow, and a Black Feather threw up his hands and fell forward.

"Got him!" said Gorgi. "The second is yours, Piyanah....There! He is trying to hide in that shadow."

I held that man's life between my finger and thumb as though he were an ant. I could see the muscles of his back moving as he fumbled for an arrow. Killing a Black Feather is less than killing an ant. I felt the life go out of my bow, and saw the ant stagger and spin round...then try to crawl away. With my third arrow I killed him...the hunter does not let a wounded animal escape. It is beautiful to kill a Black Feather! At last I knew the meaning of a hunter, there was no pity such as had spoiled the killing of a deer. The blood of an enemy is hot and red and beautiful, and by it the brave grow strong!

"I am going to take his scalp," I said, and stood upright on the ledge.

"No, Piyanah, we are to stay here," said Tekeeni.

"I'm going to take his scalp, and get another for Raki."

I leapt down the steep slope, and Gorgi and Tekeeni followed me. The Black Feathers were trying to escape, otherwise I think we should never have been able to reach the place where I had seen my enemy fall. I caught him by the hair and pulled back his head, ready to slit his throat if his eyes moved. His jaw lolled open and his eyes were empty as white stones. It is more difficult to take a scalp than to skin a beaver....I cut too deep and tore away half his ear. The bone of the skull was white and clean with only a single streak of blood.

"They're gone," said Gorgi. "He must have been the last of them. He was a brave man, Piyanah, to have been the last to run."

"He's not a man," I said passionately. "He's less than an animal...do you think I would take a *man's* scalp?"

But I knew I lied. This coarse, strong hair was more than the scalp of a Black Feather, more than the sign that I could enter the ranks of the Young Braves. He was all the men who had jeered at me, all the men whom the squaws feared when they were taken into the woods after the Choosing. He was my father and my grandfather; he was the Elders without wisdom, and the Scarlet Feathers who had never known the loneliness of squaws. I must get another scalp for Raki....

"We must follow them. Look! Dorrok and the Brown Feathers are following them...none of them must escape!"

"But we must obey Dorrok's orders," said Gorgi. "He told us that we were to stay on the ledge and watch the eastern cleft."

"You needn't come with me...if you're afraid. You needn't come with me if you don't want to join my tribe... you can make your own tribe, where there are no squaws to lead you into danger!"

But they were obedient to Dorrok, and I was too proud to turn back when I realized they had not followed me. It was very dark, and the scalp tied to my belt was sodden and smelt of blood. The trees were black as crows and stood watching me. A clot of blood fell out of the scalp and I felt it crawl down my leg like a slug. I wanted to throw the scalp away, or bury it under a stone so heavy that I couldn't remember it even if I tried. But I knotted it more tightly to my belt, to remind myself that I was now a Young Brave. I should have to stay in the woods until daylight and then tell Gorgi that I had searched for a Black Feather to kill as I had promised.

I heard a sudden movement and swung round. The Black Feather must have lost his weapons for he caught me in a wrestling hold...it was one that Raki had taught me, so I was able to break free. He had a strong rancid smell: there was no moon and I could only see him as a dark shape against the darker trees. I dared not run for he would know I was a woman....

I drew my knife, but he must have heard me for in the next hold he twisted it from my hand and I heard it clatter against a stone. I tore his ear, that sudden twist of Gorgi's, and felt it strip from his head. He tried to bite through the big vein in my neck, but I twisted my head and his teeth sank into my shoulder until they grated against the bone. If only he would kill me before he realized I was a woman!

He tripped me, and I felt his knee pressing up under my ribs and then his hands thrusting towards my throat...breaking my grip on his wrists...and I knew I could not answer the death hold. Blood roared in my ears as though I had dived too deep...I was going to die and he would take my scalp. Would I still be mutilated on the other side of the water... would Raki recognize me in our little valley...would he grow old and I have to wait so many years for him?

Suddenly the terrible pain in my chest slackened, and I heard the Black Feather cry out. His head was being bent backwards across a knee behind his shoulders...thumbs, strong beautiful thumbs I loved, were driving into his eyes. His hands suddenly released their hold on my throat and I rolled clear. I heard his neck snap: as Raki's hands bent it backwards over Raki's knee.

130

And I was no longer Piyanah the Brave, I was a girl, crying because I had been frightened and now was so very happy. And Raki was saying that he was never going to let me fight any more battles. Then he picked me up, and carried me further into the woods.

new magic

No longer fear among the dark trees; but a peace I had not known since we were children. Here the only shadows were delicate as the small, singing leaves of the white birches, and instead of the slow glisten of blood there was the clean ripple of water over stones. Piyanah the Brave belonged to the land of shadows: I was Raki's squaw, and we were free in love.

I watched him soak in the stream the bandage I had used to bind my breasts, and it reminded me that my shoulder was throbbing where the teeth of the Black Feather had torn it to the bone. I wondered how we got here....Raki had carried me and then we had walked uphill along the bed of a stream. I was naked and my body was clean, so he must have washed off the blood.

The water cooled the heat in my shoulder, and Raki's hands were sure and gentle as he held open the edges of the wound to let the coolness drip into it.

"Did you take his scalp, Raki?" I said.

"Yes."

"Why?"

"Because I hated him...a scarlet hatred strong as fire. I had never felt that before, Piyanah; it's rich meat, for it made me grow up in a night. We're both grown up, Piyanah. I am a man and you are my woman...and this knowledge is stronger than any other law, for it is the great law of the Hunters."

"But will Father recognize it when we go back to the tribe?"

"We're not going back—yet. The Brave is allowed to take his squaw into the woods. Do you mind being my squaw, Piyanah?"

I laughed up at him. "Have I ever wanted anything except to be with you, my Raki? We have both killed an enemy and taken his scalp, so we are both Young Braves...a double right to be together, for Piyanah the Brave takes Raki for his squaw."

"That pretence belongs to the tribe, not to us. You are my woman, Piyanah, do you understand? *My* woman!"

He was so solemn that I wanted to tease him a little. "May I speak the name of the man who honours me with his attention, or should I keep silent and follow five paces behind you as a dutiful squaw must?"

"You need be obedient only if I think you are running into danger. If the Black Feathers come back, you will stay with the squaws. You would have been killed if I hadn't found you in time."

"But Braves have to risk being killed."

"I might let you fight beside me, because I promised that neither would keep the other waiting in our little valley...but I'm not going to leave you in danger again. You need never obey anyone but me, Piyanah, and I won't order you to do things unless I see that courage has deafened you to discretion."

Dear Raki! I had never heard him talk like this, and I found it enormously enjoyable. "What will you do if I am not obedient?"

"You will *have* to be," said Raki.

"You mean because you are stronger, that in a wrestling you would win? I have learned two new holds that I haven't shown you yet."

"It is not because I am stronger: it's because I am a man, *your* man."

Why did I love Raki more than ever before? The skin of his back was smooth as birch-bark and the muscles rippled like water. There was a frown between his eyebrows, and he was staring at a tree on the far side of the glade because he didn't want to look at me. A pulse beat in his temple as though he had been running, but he hadn't moved since he came up from the stream.

"I'm glad it was you and not Gorgi who found me," I said. "I'd much rather be here with you than with him."

"So should Gorgi be glad...if he values his scalp!"

"How rude of you, Raki," I said, trying to keep my voice serious. "Just because I've scalped a Black Feather it doesn't mean I'm going to start scalping my friends."

"You wouldn't have had the chance: I should have taken Gorgi's scalp if he dared to bring you up here!"

"But I have often been in the woods with Gorgi."

"Well, you're not going to do it again. Do you understand? That's an order, Piyanah."

"What a pity I'm so bad at being obedient!"

Raki was no longer staring at the birch tree: he was looking at me and the expression in his eyes was different from any I had seen before, hot, and fierce, and rather bewildered at the same time.

He caught hold of me. "You're going to learn to be obedient, now...and you'd better learn fast if you don't want your friends to be killed. You *are* my woman?"

My arms were round his neck, and under my hands the smooth skin of his back was vivid and exciting...."I have always been your woman."

My heart was thudding as though I had been racing uphill, but above it I could hear his heart.

"We needn't wait to share a star before we become one person," he said softly. Then my body and his weren't separate any more; the joy of them burst into warm, brilliant flame, and we were part of this new flame. In its light we could see each other closer and more clearly than ever before, and the joy was so sharp that we cried out, and let it lap over us in waves of warm light, warmer than the sun, softer than the depth of beaver pelts.

Then there was a peace, and a belonging that was the end of loneliness.

The dread of going back to the tribe kept on trying to creep into the glade, and in silence we fought it off. Neither of us wanted to kill anything, so Raki went to collect some fungus, the kind that can be eaten raw. When he came back he was whistling, and carried a bundle tied up in an old tunic.

"Where did you get that?" I asked.

"Gorgi brought it."

"Gorgi...but how did he find us?"

"He tracked us here, and when he saw you were wounded he went to tell Dorrok, who said that we needn't go back for three days and told Gorgi to bring us some food."

"That was nice of Gorgi," I said warmly.

"Yes, and clever of him to follow our tracks...especially as he can only see out of one eye."

"Was he hurt in the battle? He was all right when I left them."

"But not when I did! I hit him...hard. I tried to stay with the squaws, but I couldn't when I saw the fires and knew the Black Feathers had come. I only reached the encampment when they had fled....I couldn't find you and thought you had been killed. I was searching among the dead when Gorgi told me you had gone into the woods. He didn't believe you meant to try for another scalp; that's why they let you go alone. I told him—with my fist—that he was a fool. He followed as soon as he could, to help look for you."

"Which was nice of him, Raki, and nicer still to make things all right for us with Dorrok."

"Yes, I suppose it was," admitted Raki grudgingly, "though he deserves a lot more than a swollen eye for letting you go alone."

"Is his eye very bad?"

"Not nearly bad enough," he said unfeelingly; "in a few days it will hardly show at all."

"Perhaps he didn't follow me because he was afraid of losing his scalp...to you."

Instead of being angry Raki only chuckled, "Even Gorgi isn't that much of a fool!"

On the last evening before we must go back to the tribe, we were lying in the tall grass beside the stream. The trunks of the white birches were warm with sunset, and even the birds sounded drowsy, as though they had been practising our new magic.

"Do you think the Before People knew about it too, Raki?"

"I expect so: Mother said they knew all the secrets of happiness, so they must have known about this."

"It's terrible to think of generations and generations of people being content to live apart, just because they had forgotten something so beautifully simple."

"They can't have forgotten all about it, or there wouldn't still be a legend about two people becoming one star."

"But it would have been such a waste of time to wait until after we're dead."

"Do you think our people will understand when we tell them, or will it be difficult to explain?" said Raki.

"I hadn't thought about that. Perhaps it will be difficult...it sounds almost silly if you try to say it in words."

"Being a star sounds silly if you don't understand what it feels like."

"Yes, I suppose it does...sitting up in the sky, twinkling or getting yourself wrapped in clouds."

Two chipmunks were chasing each other along a branch. Suddenly I noticed that Raki was watching them intently. "Piyanah," he said slowly, "those chipmunks...and us... and the Before People. Do you think it could all be the *same* magic?"

I thought for a moment and then said emphatically, "I don't think so: anyway I'm sure it's nothing to do with the squaws going into the woods...for if it was, they wouldn't be glad to come back."

"You must be right," agreed Raki, "for if they had found our magic the men would never let them go back to the Squaws' Tepees."

"But *we've* got to go back...."

"Yes," he said, "we've got to go back. I thought last night of Rokeena and Gorgi and the others....The Before People have given us a secret we've got to share, for it's terribly important to have a secret from which a *real* tribe will be born."

"Shall we be able to use our magic again before we become Brown Feathers?"

"I don't think so. But we've got two heavens to remember now, this birch grove and our little valley. We can't live here and in our ordinary days at the same time....I couldn't bear to stay with the squaws if I let myself remember this magic, and I couldn't bear you being with Gorgi and Tekeeni unless you forgot it too, until we can be together all the time."

I tried to comfort him. "It will be only another year, now that we have become Young Braves so early."

"Do you remember how you felt when I said, '*Only* seven years'?"

"I know, Raki, but if I didn't say 'only' I might cry...and that would spoil our last night together...and it ought to be easier now that we've got so much more to remember, and so much more to look forward to."

Yet a year seemed longer than all the rivers of Earth, when, soon after dawn next morning, we came in sight of the encampment: Raki the squaw, and Piyanah the Young Brave, each with a scalp of a Black Feather knotted to his belt.

Death Canoe

I thought that the funerary rites would have taken place before our return, but, though the enemy had been buried by Naked Foreheads, in a disused clay-pit which would henceforward be taboo, the last of our dead had only just been brought back to the encampment, so his companions had waited for him until they could all go together to the land of the Great Hunters.

Seventy-three of our Braves had been killed; they lay in a semicircle between the Totem and the watch-fire, wrapped in their blankets as though resting before dawn. If the friend of a Brave killed in battle puts a hand on his cold forehead and speaks loudly, for it is difficult for the dead to hear, the words of the message will be carried by him beyond the sunset; and if a falling star is seen in the West it is known that the message has been faithfully delivered.

I wished I had thought to consult Raki as to whether we ought to ask one of them to tell Mother we had not forgotten the Before People. Was it easier for the dead to hear the dead than the living? Surely she could hear our voices when we spoke to her without the sound going through the ear of a corpse? But we could not be quite sure. She would be sorrowful if all the others who had gathered to welcome our Braves received news of the living, and she alone had no word from her daughter and her foster-son.

The encampment was hushed except for the sound of logs being split to make the funeral pyres down by the river. I went to lay my bow at the foot of the Totem, to thank him for sparing my life and to tell him that I had fulfilled the dedication of my arrows in the blood of an enemy. I decided to try to find a messenger before taking the scalp to the Tepee of the

Elders: if the dead saw it knotted to my belt they would recognize that I was now a Young Brave and so had the right to claim the privileges of a younger brother.

Only five of the dead had been scalped: they must have followed the fleeing Black Feathers into the woods, for I knew that the enemy would not have had the chance to snatch a trophy in the turmoil of a losing battle. These five bodies now wore new scalps, of bear pelt, to show that they were mighty hunters and had died in victory. The fur had been stitched to the flesh of the forehead. Little fires of aromatic twigs had been lit on each side of the row of Braves, but the smoke did not keep away all the flies: sometimes I had to brush them off before I could recognize the face they covered.

The Scarlet Feather whom I had watched smoking by the fire while we waited for him to give the signal for battle had taken his calm with him into death: the eyes were closed, and his strong hands still held the bow and the tomahawk which he would carry on his long journey. I did not like to disturb him, so I went in search of another messenger.

I saw a boy who had often speared fish with Gorgi and me: he must have died by a single blow from a tomahawk. His neck had been severed and was now carefully stitched to the shoulders with narrow strips of raw-hide, so that he should not stand before the Great Hunters as a cripple. I was afraid to put my hand on his forehead in case the head lolled to the side: I was ashamed of this dread and hoped he could not hear my thoughts.

The arrow had been taken from the eye-socket of Dorrok's friend whom I had seen die early in the battle, and a white stone, painted to look like an eye, put in its place. The lips were drawn back from the teeth and he looked as though he were snarling. I was sorry, for he had always been a kindly man, and his friends beyond the sunset might think he had grown ferocious, before he had time to make a spirit body to wear instead of this fading dream of flesh.

I did not realize that Barakeechi had been killed until I saw him lying between two Brown Feathers. His face was un-marked, but decay had made blue stains round his mouth, as though he had been eating elderberries. I drew back his blanket and saw an arrow wound above his left breast. I saw something move...there were maggots in the wound, maggots in Barakeechi who had always been more ready with laughter than any of us! He was kind and brave, and he had been going to join our tribe of the Feathers...his death was far more real to me than any of the others.

I put my hand on his forehead. ''Barakeechi, I know you can hear me because you have always been a friend to Raki and Piyanah. You are the first of the Feathers to go beyond the sunset. Will you tell my mother about the tribe, Bara-keechi? Tell her that Raki and I have always remembered the Before People, and that if they are lonely for Earth they can come back as the children of the Feathers, because our people are going to be happy together even as they used to be. Fare-well, Barakeechi, until we laugh on the other side of the water, when Raki and I have joined you.

''There shall be two enemy scalps in the Tepee of the Elders in your name. They killed you, Barakeechi, so I am glad that I helped them to die....You are smiling, because you have discovered that death is only the crossing of another mountain into a valley where there is no winter. I will re-member your smile when I am afraid....Tell my mother that we will remember.''

At noon the bodies were carried down to the funeral pyres, which had been lit since dawn so that when dry wood was heaped on the core of glowing logs it would flare up into a great intensity of heat. Each Brave was carried by two men, on a litter which had long poles so that the bearers could stand one on each side of the fire and lower it gently into the flames.

Na-ka-chek had given permission for Raki and me to per-form this last service for Barakeechi. For the first time in five years we were dressed alike, in the doe-skin tunics of Young Braves, and at the back of our forehead thongs were knots of hair from an enemy scalp, a symbol of authority nearly as important as a Feather.

Narrok had been sounding the death rhythms since dawn. Squaws lined the path to watch the progress of the dead: some of them should have been in grief for a son or the father of their child; yet though the hair was covered with the white ashes of mourning there was curiosity instead of sorrow in their eyes. Even our women, who stood a little apart from the others, showed no sign of emotion...why should they, when Barakeechi was the only one of the dead to whom they had spoken, the only one with whom they might have shared their future? They had often seen hunters bring home a kill; and to most of them a man was a more unfamiliar animal than a deer...and strangers are neither loved nor pitied.

The heat of the fire was so strong that it was difficult to lower Barakeechi gently. The stench of burning flesh made me want to retch. I found myself wondering how long it would be before I could eat roast meat without the same smell creeping into my nostrils.

Barakeechi was only the shape of a man, black and red with fire. Soon he would fall into ash, and only a few charred bones would show that a man and a tree had joined to light this torch of stars. In silence we stood to watch while the embers cooled.

Then came the Chief, in company with the Elders, to take from the place where each body had been consumed a handful of ashes. These were to be placed in the Death Canoe, which was carried on the shoulders of eight Scarlet Feathers. Na-ka-chek held the ashes up to the sky, speaking aloud the name of the man who had died that the tribe might live: telling of his courage and his woodcraft; telling of rapids he had conquered in a time of river's anger; telling of the animals he had killed and the bear's claws on his neck-thong. Then did he call on the Great Hunters to accept this man, his emissary, the Brave of Na-ka-chek, Chief of the Tribe of the Two Trees.

As he let the ashes fall into the Death Canoe the name of

the hero echoed and re-echoed, as we who had been his companions sent his herald to the hills.

At sunset the bearers waded into the river until the Death Canoe was borne from their shoulders by the current. Gently, and then faster it swept away towards the Great Rapid. In the West I saw a falling star; and knew that Barakeechi and my mother smiled together because we had remembered.

PART THREE

Brown feathers

Now that Raki and I were Young Braves, Na-ka-chek said that we could undertake the ordeals of the brown feather without waiting until we were seventeen. We hated being separated even more than we had done before the Birch Grove, so we accepted his offer eagerly...it might reduce the last year we must stay apart by several moons, and the Brown Feather had the right to claim his squaw!

The ordeals had to be undertaken alone, although the training for them was in company. I did not recognize how much I had relied on the presence of Gorgi or any of the others until I discovered how much more difficult it was to drive myself beyond what had seemed the limit of my endurance, or to make myself choose the more difficult of two ways up a cliff, without having someone to share his courage with me. And I knew it was not only their courage I wanted, but their admiration...the swift reward of pride felt by a friend, or the envy of someone who still refused to accept me as an equal.

The first ordeal sounded very easy...if someone else did it: to take a canoe up-stream as far as one could travel in three days. A Brown Feather watched your progress, but you never saw him. Dare you collapse exhausted, or was Dorrok watching, ashamed because you displayed this weakness? We had many other tests of endurance in canoes, but always a definite landmark had been assigned which must be reached in a given time. Knowing the distance you could say, ''Only one more bend of the river: only two hundred more strokes... only one hundred, before I can drop into the deep sleep that follows hard endurance.'' But now I should not know how much was expected of me: would I dare to sleep a quarter of

142

the time between sunrise and sunrise, or must it be a much briefer rest than this? If I went too far on the first day, should I be so tired on the third that I made little progress, and so betrayed that I had not learned how to use my strength to the best advantage?

Raki had completed this ordeal and returned to the encampment the night before I was to start, but Dorrok forbade me to see him, so I had no idea how far he had been.

I left at dawn and did not reach a rapid until the evening. The canoe was heavy to carry alone on the portage, but the bank shelved gently and gave firm footholds. This was further than I had ever before reached in one day, so I decided it would be safe to eat some of the bread and pemmican I had brought with me and then to rest until moonrise.

The river was low, for the autumn rains had not yet begun, so by keeping close to the bank where the current was sluggish I could drive the canoe steadily forward. Only the even beat of my paddle broke the stillness. To keep the strokes at an even pace, I listened to one of Narrok's drum rhythms inside my head; it would have been a waste of breath to sing aloud. There was a long stretch of river through open country and the moon laid a path for me to follow over the black water. Sometimes a fish rose with a splash, or a coyote barked in the distance; then again there would be only the faint sigh of my paddle leaving the water.

I slept in the canoe for a little while before dawn: I had tied it to the bank, intending to sleep on the ground, but the grass was sodden with dew and I could not find any other shelter from the chill wind. I wished I had brought a second tunic to sleep in, even though its extra weight might have delayed me, for I was too cold to sleep properly.

After sunrise I went on up-stream. The canoe seemed heavier at the next portage: perhaps because my feet kept on slipping in the loose gravel beside the rapid, or else my arms were getting tired. By noon I was so sleepy that I tied the canoe to a tree which overhung the water and dived until I felt more refreshed. I made myself chew some pemmican, though I was not hungry, and then lay on a sun-hot rock, longing to go to sleep but knowing that if I did so it would be sunset before I woke. If someone had been with me we could have slept in turn while the other watched, and this would have made the journey much easier.

Again I allowed myself to sleep until moonrise, but when I woke, the moon was high and I knew precious time had been wasted. Still half blind with sleep, I stumbled down the bank and dragged the canoe into the water. The paddle was heavy, as though it were made of cedar instead of birch. It was difficult to keep my strokes at an even rhythm, and several times I veered off the course and knew I had lost several paces of distance in needless effort.

A scream tore through the dark woods. "It is only a badger," I said aloud. But did a badger ever make a noise like that? A noise like a child in pain or terror? I wanted to reach the next bend which would hide me from the source of the noise. I quickened my stroke. The moon was obscured by clouds and only a fitful silver broke the darkness. I knew I ought to rest, but I kept on; to avoid going near the woods that suddenly held terror for me. I could not land on the far side of the river for a low cliff fell sheer into deep water where the current was swift.

The canoe jarred against something and nearly capsized. "Of course it is only a submerged log," I said loudly. "You are not a squaw who believes in water demons! You did *not* see a hand clutch at the prow, Piyanah. It was only a shadow....It was *not* a hand; if you think it was, you must be dreaming."

The sound of my voice scolding me only made the darkness wider and deeper...and it was not a friendly darkness.

"If you are too much of a coward to land, you will have to go on paddling, Piyanah, or else you will drift backwards on the current. Do you want Dorrok to be ashamed of you? Do you want to betray Raki and the Feathers, just because you are too lazy to paddle a little further?''

My shoulders ached as though they had been flogged. I began to chant a war song, to keep in rhythm, to keep awake. I saw a bar of yellow light reflected in the water: gradually the darkness dissolved to show the grey ghosts of trees, kind ghosts with whom singing birds were not afraid. Mist swirled up from the water like smoke. If it had only been smoke! Smoke of a fire by which I could sleep and be warm; smoke of a cooking-fire that would give me hot broth instead of a strip of pemmican I was too weary to chew.

The canoe was too heavy to drag up the steep bank, so I had to go on until I found a strongly rooted bush where I could make it fast. I could find nowhere dry to sleep; even under the trees the ground was sodden, but I saw a drift of dead leaves and crawled into it to get warm. ''I must only sleep a little while; tomorrow I can sleep...not now. Tomorrow at dawn I can sleep.''

It was noon before I woke: a noon which blazed with the heat of autumn whose flames had already begun to colour the woods. I dived into the water, but did not waste strength by swimming. The long sleep had refreshed me: I was greedy for bread and even pemmican was pleasant to chew.

At sunset I had to rest, but dared not sleep. I took a sharp thorn, and when I felt my eyelids getting too heavy for me to hold them open I drove it into my leg until I jerked into wakefulness. It is difficult to lie completely relaxed, so that your muscles can gather strength, when the ground is cold and hard; when rain is dripping off the trees, slow monotonous rain which makes it more difficult for your body to refuse the sleep for which it aches, sleep that it knows will be punished by the sharp pain of a thorn. I began to hate my body for tempting me to sleep, and to hate myself for being so unkind to it.

The rain stopped before moonrise. The canoe slid forward between dark ranks of trees that were no longer menacing. I pretended that they were people who had come to see whether I was worthy of the Feathers.

"They are sneering at you, Piyanah. Listen, they are saying that Piyanah is a squaw who pretends to be a Young Brave. Tell your arms, Piyanah; tell the muscles of your back and your thighs that if they plead with you to let them rest the watchers will hear and mock you. Do not betray me, my arms! Look, the moon has travelled a long way across the sky. Watch for the dawn which will soon come to tell you that we have won our rest. No, Piyanah, you must not look back; you will see the reflection of the sunrise in the water ahead. They should call it the Land beyond the Sunrise, that land where people go when their night has been long, and they are so very weary. Count the strokes, Piyanah, each hundred shall make a filament of your brown feather. On and on....The beat of the paddle is getting slow as the heart of a dying man. I can hear a rapid. Will the sunrise release me before I reach angry water? I shall never be able to carry the canoe even if there is a wide path without any rocks to climb. The moon is still very bright. No, Piyanah! It is the dawn; the dawn, Piyanah!"

I was close to the bank: I think if I had been in midstream I should have collapsed and let the current snatch from me some of the distance I had gained. I watched my hands making the canoe fast to a tree that grew close to the edge of the water. Slowly and deliberately my feet climbed the bank. I fell face downwards on the kind turf, and sleep wrapped me like a robe of beaver pelts.

I thought I was dreaming. There was a fire, and the smell of food cooking; and I was lying on a heap of dry grasses and covered with a blanket. I sat up and saw Dorrok putting another log on the fire; beyond him the river was red with the setting sun.

"Raki came as far as this, and so did I," he said. "None of the others came further than the place you reached at sunset yesterday. I thought you would reach the same place as Raki and I. That is why I waited here for you."

146

"So you are not ashamed of me? Oh, Dorrok, I am so glad!"

"No, Piyanah," he said gently; "I shall never be ashamed of my Chief."

I had already killed five stags which were beyond their fifth year, so Dorrok said I need only kill a grizzly to fulfill my ordeal of the hunter, and that with my tracking and woodcraft he was already satisfied.

Hunting a grizzly would probably follow much the same pattern as when I had found Pekoo, but now I should not have Gorgi and Tekeeni with me. If the grizzly attacked, I should have no hope of rescue; if I were wounded too badly to make my own way home, I should die, alone. The grizzlies were my friends; now I had to kill one of them to prove I was a hunter.

I think I should have failed in this ordeal if I had not seen the body of a child who had gone into a grizzly's cave. It was crushed to a bloody pulp, but the face was unmarked except by terror. The track of the bear which had killed her led into the mountains: and Dorrok granted me the right to avenge her death.

For sixteen days I followed these tracks; twice I saw him in the distance, a solitary male with no white marks, so I knew he was not Pekoo. He was wary, and every day moved to a new feeding-ground. Several times I tried to approach him, but though I kept in close cover he always moved on before I could get within bowshot.

Would he never choose a cave where I might hope to ambush him? The first snows had fallen. Very soon I should have to go back to Dorrok and admit failure. Unless Dorrok let me kill a spring bear I should have to wait until next autumn before I could hope for the brown feather, the brown feather and Raki.

To hunt a bear at night was against all the rules I had been taught, and I shall never be sure why I attempted it. I had

147

come to a place where there were many large boulders scattered on the open mountain-side. I knew the bear was hiding among them, but to follow him there would be to give him every advantage. It seemed madness, but I knew it was the only way to avoid another year of separation.

I walked slowly up-wind; arrow notched to the bowstring, tomahawk hanging ready from my belt. I asked Great Bear and Pekoo to forgive me for punishing this outlaw of their tribe. Perhaps they heard me and held him in sleep, for I saw him stretched out, half hidden by the denser shadow of a boulder.

A bar of moonlight fell across his shoulder, giving me a clear target to try the difficult shot to the heart....He tried to struggle up with the arrow buried under his foreleg....Then he lurched over on his side and blood trickled out of his mouth.

I waited with another arrow notched, but he did not move. I crouched, watching him until his eyes slowly opened. He did not blink, but was he watching me? Slowly I crept nearer: his eyes had begun to glaze, so I knew I should not be one of the hunters who die because they think a wounded grizzly is dead.

I hacked off the fore-paws, which would prove I had fulfilled the ordeal and earned the claws to wear on my neck-thong. Then, before I left him, I asked Great Bear to take him back into his tribe, for the feud between his people and ours was ended.

I put the bear's paws into the leather sack I had used for bread; on the third day I tied the thong more tightly round the neck of it, to try to keep the smell at bay. Every night I made a fire, and at dawn sent smoke signals to tell Raki I was on my way home. I knew how eagerly he would watch for the smoke, as I had watched when he was winning his bear's claws during the previous moon.

The mountains were already covered with snow, and even on the lower slopes it lay in the deeper gullies. Only two more ordeals remained—the winter journey, and the climbing of The Listener, the highest mountain of the range. I knew Dorrok would not let me attempt The Listener until the spring, but this did not matter because Raki and I could not be given our brown feathers until the ritual ceremony of the Sowing, which took place before the Moon of the Choosing.

To spend seven days alone in the great cold sounds very easy; seven small wooden tokens branded with the tribal mark sounds a trivial burden. But each token must be put in one of the seven places chosen for the ordeal, to prove that you have been there; and you must spend the seven days without the companionship of fire.

Cold can be more cruel than cougars: it can gnaw fingers from your hands and cripple your feet; it can rot away your ears and your nostrils; it can be venomous as a rattlesnake and scar like fire. It was bleak comfort that Raki and I were to start the ordeal on the same day, for the places allotted to us were so far apart that there would be no hope of either of us reaching the other in time if we sensed the stealthy approach of this quiet, white death.

We both chose the same kind of clothes: knee-high moccasins lined with beaver pelt; fur caps which covered the forehead and ears; and two tunics, the inner one furlined, the outer of oiled leather. We should carry our food, bread-sticks and pemmican, rolled in a blanket between our shoulders. Dorrok had advised us each to take a tomahawk, for cutting branches to make shelters, and a sling, which might be a means of getting warm, raw flesh which would help us to resist the cold.

We did not need to be reminded to take a second pair of snow-shoes, for we remembered the Young Brave who last winter had not returned from this ordeal. Gorgi and I were there when the melting snows gave up his body. He wore only one snow-shoe; we never found the other which had

149

betrayed him to the drift. Cold sometimes grows jealous of the living, but it is kind to the dead: the Young Brave looked as though he had only just gone to claim the right of entry to the Happy Hunting-Grounds.

The ordeal began at dawn. The first stage was easy, so I should be able to reach it in time to make a shelter before sunset. There was a clear, pale sun, and no wind. It might have been any ordinary day instead of the first of the seven days. Fresh snow scrunched underfoot, and the trees, wrapped in their white blankets, were solemn as Elders in council. I saw a snow-hare, and was glad that I was neither cold nor hungry enough to need a kill: it sat up on its haunches and then bounded away across the unbroken whiteness. Later I saw a stag. He stood to watch me; then walked quietly down a narrow track as though he knew I had not come as a hunter.

By noon there was real warmth in the sun. I took off both tunics so that my body could store the gentle heat against the night. I left the first token in a cleft of a high rock, then cut some pine boughs to make a shelter and spread more of them to lie on. There was a level space, from which it was easy to sweep the snow, protected on the windward side by the rock. If fire had not been forbidden, it would have been a friendly place; but I slept soundly, and woke hoping that Raki had been even more comfortable.

Until the fourth day the weather remained kind: then it began to snow. Under the trees I was protected, but in the open the rising wind drove into my face: the heavy flakes clung to my eyelashes and made it still more difficult to see the way. I think that if this stretch of country had not been very familiar I should never have found the next stage, for only those rocks whose sides were too steep to allow foothold to the snow were safe landmarks. The snow tried to drag me down, and swallowed my tracks before I had gone more than ten paces forward. Here there were no trees to give me branches for a shelter, so I cut snow into blocks and built them into a hollow circle; three tiers of these and then my blanket stretched over the top and weighted with stones. I knew that if the storm grew into a blizzard I might be buried, but if I stayed out on the exposed hillside I should never survive the knives of winter.

I dared not sleep, for I had to guard my hands and feet from the frost demons which crept up to attack them, keeping constantly alert to rub them with snow when they began to lose feeling. Pain is safety in intense cold, for numbness soon drifts into the greater numbness of death. When I felt the demons luring me to sleep, I stumbled outside, to swing my arms and stamp my feet until I felt the blood running free as water under ice.

I had to dig my way out in the grey dawn, and was so cold that I killed the first snow-hare I saw. Its blood was warmth, and salt, and life; the drops brilliant as a scarlet feather against the snow. I hated the cold that had driven me to colour its creeping whiteness with the bright blaze of death; hated it even more than I hated myself for betraying the hare who was also trying to withstand the challenge of the winter.

That night I huddled in a shallow cave and scraped a sleeping-place in the fine gravel of the floor. The snow had stopped, but there was still a high wind. Icicles hung from a branch which swept down over the narrow entrance and clattered against each other with the sharp sound of a skeleton hanging in a tree; a skeleton whose sinews still held the bones into a semblance of life. The idea of the tinkling bones grew stronger, until I could almost see the skeleton of the Black Feather whom Raki and I had found five moons after the battle. He must have climbed the tree to hide, and wedged his body into the crotch between two great branches, while the blood, which still stained the bark, slowly drained from his wounds. Even though he was a Black Feather I hoped that he had died before the buzzards came to clean his bones.

I felt myself sinking into the cold, and tried to send my spirit to our little valley to find out whether Raki was already waiting for me. If he had been trapped by the cold it would be so easy to join him; for the cold was kind unless you fought against it. To sleep would be so easy; to sleep would be to find myself in the warmth of our valley where it was always summer. I thought I could see the corn-cobs lying where we had left them. I called, "Raki! Raki!" But no one came down the path by the stream or from the friendly woods to answer me. If Raki had been there he would surely have come. "Raki must be alive!" I said aloud. And the icicles seemed to whisper, "Raki is alive."

I stood up, stamping my feet, swinging my arms until feeling returned to my hands and I could move my fingers. "Because of Raki I am stronger than the cold! He is my fire, my sun, my warmth; for love is stronger than cold, and separation, and darkness." I slept; and when I woke the snow outside was brilliant with sunshine and the sky a strong blue. I took off my sodden tunics and spread them on a rock to dry. The light and heat that were part of Raki soaked into me and gave me their strength. I knew that the Lord of Winter had challenged me, and because I had met his challenge I had been accepted as a friend.

I set off in a clean white world which blazed with light as though it reflected the watch-fires of a thousand tribes. I knew that Raki and I would both return to the encampment in safety; that every night I should find trees to give me shelter, that I should see the stars steadfast in the sky, while the grey clouds of death lurked beyond the mountains.

I knew this was true, and on the seventh day it was so. As I came down the western slope to the circle of tepees I saw Raki coming down the path from the east.

Never had a winter passed so slowly, but at last we heard the thunderous cracking of the ice as the river began to move with the urge of spring. I knew that soon The Listener would be ready to hear my challenge for the last ordeal. I had often been on the lower slopes of the mountain, climbing from steep slopes of scree into the high moraine; and the previous summer Gorgi and I had reached the foot of the last towering pinnacle, that looked like a finger of a Great Hunter pointing the way to his home. Raki had made the ascent in the autumn; I knew it must be very difficult for he was frightened for me. I promised to send a smoke signal when I began the climb and another as soon as I was safely down. Raki could not come with me, for the ordeals must always be undertaken alone; but he was going to wait near the foot of the precipice with Gorgi and Tekeeni, who had also passed this ordeal while I was hunting the grizzly. If they did not receive the second smoke signal they would know I must have fallen and come to find me.

The rock was honest, so that even a toe-hold would bear my full weight, but nowhere was there a ledge wide enough to rest on, so a precarious balance had to be maintained without a break. There was not even a thorn bush on the whole smooth expanse above me to give an illusion of safety. The whole of me was contracted to the urgent need of smoothly changing my weight from one hand to the other. I forgot every other texture except the wind-polished surface of rock as I desperately searched for a small projection or narrow crack strong enough for me to dare a shift of position. Once I nearly fell, and had to cling by one hand to a knife edge, which cut the palm so deeply that blood ran down my forearm and splashed my cheek before I could draw myself up to a safer hold.

An eagle dived out of the sky, so close that I could feel the wind of its wings. I hung motionless, knowing that if it attacked I should fall sheer to the rocks below. Twice I heard the sweeping of its wings, and waited for the deadly tear of its beak. Then it soared, until it became a dark fleck against the hard blue sky.

Because my left hand was slippery with blood it was increasingly difficult to keep a firm hold. I had been climbing in shadow, and for a long time had not dared to look down in case it made me giddy. Suddenly I realized that the sun was shining full on me. The knowledge that I must be nearing the top gave me courage to lean outwards so that I could see directly above me. There was a narrow ledge leading upwards and to the right. It was no wider than the palm of my hand, but after the sparse holds it seemed secure as the path beside a river. It led me out of the shadows, to the pinnacle rock which crowns The Listener.

Relief was so intense that I had to lie down, for my legs refused to carry me any further. My teeth chattered as though I was very cold, but I could feel sweat trickling down my body. It was not yet important that I was now one of the Brown Feathers, for they loved endurance and I only craved rest; rest on safe, flat ground where there could never be a danger of falling.

Then I thought of Raki, and of how there were no longer ordeals to keep us apart. Weariness was forgotten. I stood upright, my hands upstretched to the sky, and gave thanks to the Great Hunters who in love had brought me nearer to their country even than the crest of their Listener.

The Bridge

The day after Na-ka-chek gave Raki and me our brown feathers, he summoned us to the Great Tepee.

"You have fulfilled my commands." he said, "and earned the privileges of tribal brotherhood. I wish you to become the Chief of your own tribe next spring, on the Day of the Sowing, for that is the time of growth and re-birth. You will be eighteen, so you cannot say that I have burdened you with years before giving you authority. It is the Law of the Two Trees that the Brown Feather is free to make his own decisions...he has the right to take part in the Choosing which is at the next full moon. If you both wish it, I cannot any longer prevent you sharing the same tepee...."

My heart leaped like a young deer. Raki and I would be together again...the magic of the birch grove would come back to us. Was it really true that we no longer had to fear lonely tomorrows?

My father was still speaking. "It is no longer necessary for Raki to live with the squaws or Piyanah with the Braves: you are free to decide what you must do, but first I want you to listen to the advice of the man who is still your Chief. I shall not give you the double headdress until the spring, and that is ten moons distant. If Piyanah becomes Raki's squaw before then, the Young Braves may forget she is their equal. For six years you have given me much cause for pride, pride which has sometimes been almost impossible to conceal. I ask for ten more moons to complete my promise to your mother."

He must have seen my disappointment, for he said with a rare gentleness, "Compared to the past years, I ask so few restrictions of you both: only that you shall not share a tepee, only that you think more of the happiness of your future tribe than of your own immediate wishes. There are reasons why I ask you to do this...."

I saw that he was searching for the right words and was suddenly sorry for him. I had never seen Na-ka-chek hesitant before.

"What reasons, Father? Tell them, and we shall understand."

"When a man takes his squaw into the woods, or shares his tepee with her, children are born to them. I want you both to lead your tribe in equality, and during the first moons in unfamiliar country Piyanah must continue to think as a man. There will be many decisions which you must make together; and it is not easy for a woman to think clearly when she is heavy with child."

"I understand," said Raki. "Piyanah shall remain free,

155

so that together we shall lead our people to the country of their future.''

We left the tepee and took the path to the river.

''He meant our magic, didn't he, Raki?''

He nodded.

''Then it isn't only the Before People, and the animals, and us who know it...it is everyone's magic too?''

''Weather, and trees, and mountains belong to everyone, Piyanah, yet all people see them differently. A cloud can be a beautiful shape, or a song prouder than an oriole's, or a threat of rain...or *only* a cloud, ordinary and without any special meaning. Our magic is not the same to everyone: it can be laughter, and the end of the loneliness and the voice of the stars; or it can be cold as the cruelty of separation, drab and lonely...lonely as tears that are shed for something unheard which might have sung with the morning.''

''Why didn't we have a child after the birch grove?''

''I don't know, Piyanah. Perhaps because our children are not yet ready to enter the world through our bodies.''

''But you think our son might come now if we used our magic?''

''Yes...and it will not be easy to wait so long. I thought that when we had gained the brown feathers we should be free for magic. I have wanted you until I ached with longing, with pain more intense than hunger and keener than thirst. I know why stags fight in the autumn, for though I have often asked the Great Hunters to give me more understanding, I have sometimes wanted to kill Gorgi and Tekeeni, when I saw they were seeing you not as a Brave but as a woman, beautiful and magical.''

''Am I beautiful, Raki?''

''Is a white hind, or a birch tree, or a mountain lake, or a sunrise, beautiful, Piyanah? Think of them and know yourself to be of their company; then you will understand why everyone who looks at you should wear the feathers of the dawn.''

"It has been difficult for me too, Raki. I want to be your squaw so very much; to cook your food and even to think of new patterns for your moccasins....I should use very small beads, so many of them, even though they are such a nuisance to sew! I should like to do my hair in many little plaits to show that I was your dutiful squaw, though I won't put bear's grease on them, even to please you, because I don't like the smell!"

"Neither do I, my Piyanah. I like the smell of you, which is moss warm in the sun, and young leaves, and running water, and the white exhilaration of the first snows."

"It is not only to do useful things for you that I sometimes long to be a squaw. I am very fond of Rokeena, but when she looks at you like a sick gopher I suddenly want to smack her or pull her hair, to find out whether in spite of her placid smile she has the courage to fight for the man she wants!"

"Are you jealous of Rokeena?" He laughed. "How silly and how beautiful of you! Now I can stop feeling ashamed when I think the same things about Georgi...though mine would be much harder than a slap! It is a very strong magic, isn't it?"

"Yes," I said, "so strong that even if we buried it under a white stone that was larger than a mountain we should never be able to forget it."

"Wouldn't it be terrible if we did!"

And then we laughed at ourselves for being so solemn; the sun was warm and Raki and Piyanah had so nearly built their bridge over the canyon of the seven years.

Kekki, and twelve of the others who had been given their brown feathers at the same time as Raki and I, intended to go to the Choosing, though the women they would take into the woods already belonged to our tribe and would never go back to the Squaws' Tepees. Raki and I had been so sure that Na-ka-chek would give us the Double Headdress as soon as we had passed the ordeals that we had never considered the possibility of staying with the Two Trees until the next spring. Now I realized that if the other women used the magic they might be heavy with child, and so unable to go with us when we made the long journey to find the place where we belonged. Na-ka-chek had said, ''Piyanah must be free to think as a man when she leads the new tribe.'' It would be still more difficult for the other squaws to prove their equality if they were encumbered by babies, born and unborn, during the first moons of the Feathers.

Raki had gone hunting with the Chief and might not return for three days, the evening before the Choosing. The sear of disappointment had not yet cooled, so I knew the others would find it difficult to accept that they must wait nearly another year. It would be hard for the women to be told that they must stay under the shadow of the Old Women until we could set them free. Or need they wait? Na-ka-chek had said that Raki and I might not share a tepee yet, but he had allowed us to do everything else together. We could build a small encampment for the squaws who wished to come with us: there they would be free of the Old Women, free of the taunts and sly whispers of the squaws who still clung to the spider's web of false tradition and would not struggle to free themselves.

This idea seemed better the more I looked at it. The women would have a chance to grow used to freedom, used to being without the protection of habit: I knew that even Raki and I had found it difficult to feel secure away from the circle of tepees until we had found our little valley. They already knew the men with whom they would share the future, but they had always met them furtively, afraid of the wrath of the Old Women if they were discovered. It is more difficult for love to grow strong when it has to be kept hidden from the sunlight, for only the spawn of the Carrion Crow can thrive in darkness. Here they would be able to earn the right to magic, in friendship and equality. Magic would kindle their torches, but first they must find humour, and kindliness,

158

and shared experience to make brands for that kindling.

As Raki was away, I decided to find Dorrok; to discuss my plan with him. He was in his tepee, polishing a fish-spear with sand. He looked up as I entered, and from habit I gave him the greeting due to a Brown Feather. Then he laughed, and I realized that as we were now of equal rank there was no need of formality between us. I sat on a folded blanket at the end of his sleeping-mat.

"Dorrok," I said, "I want you to tell the others that they mustn't take part in the Choosing. I am not sure how much they know. Will you tell them?"

"About women, you mean?"

"About the magic that makes children...though I suppose to most people it isn't magical."

"Is it to you, Piyanah?"

"Yes....I thought it was a magic that Raki and I had discovered; until yesterday, when we realized that it belonged to everyone, and that it was also the way to make children."

"It was the day after the battle, wasn't it, Piyanah?"

"Yes. Then you knew about it all the time? That was why you sent Gorgi to tell us we need not come back for three days?"

"I followed you, Piyanah, when I heard that you had gone in search of a second scalp...but Raki was ahead of me. I saw him kill the Black Feather; I saw him carry you into the woods. And I knew you would find there the magic that so few of us ever find."

"Did you find it, Dorrok?"

"No, very dear, Piyanah. Seventeen years ago I fathered a son. It was my duty to the tribe: a duty like hunting or making a journey to fetch salt, and it was the only duty I have nearly failed to carry out. The girl was frightened of me; I tried to be kind to her, but I could not defeat her terrible docility. I think that if I had told her I was going to cut off her hands she would still have lain there, staring up at me with the same questioning obedience which tried to mask her fear.

I have often felt a traitor to the Great Hunters since I learned their laws from you...."

"You have never been a traitor, Dorrok," I said gently.

"I killed a doe in the breeding season because I was hungry: the fawn was alive when I slit her belly to gralloch her; it lived until the evening, and then I had to kill it too, so that it should not die for lack of the milk I had stolen. I have driven you and Raki nearly beyond endurance, because I was afraid that the love I felt for you might prove my weakness. I have been proud when I hardened my heart against love, and ashamed when I felt compassion. In so many ways I have betrayed the Great Hunters, but never so deeply as when I took that girl into the woods. I hated her because she would not cry for pity; I was afraid of her because that dumb suffering might make my body refuse to obey the needs of the tribe.

"Later I asked her how she learned such impassivity, and she answered, quite simply, as I might describe a fish-trap or the way to fletch an arrow, 'There is much less pain in the Choosing than I expected. I need not have driven so many thorns under my nails, nor worn a girdle of porcupine quills under my tunic, if I had known how easy it would be to keep impassive with a man.' It became a challenge to my pride to break down that impassivity. I tried to give her pleasure, and when that failed, to make her whimper with pain. But she remained obedient, and looked at me with the terrible patient hatred of the squaw."

"She had a son?"

"Yes," said Dorrok, "a son who never knew my name: a son she must have hated because he looked like me; a son she was glad to see leave the Squaws' Tepees for ever. I am glad that she died before he entered the Death Canoe: I should have seen her standing beside the path, smiling as his body was carried to the funeral pyre, smiling because part of me had died too young."

"Barakeechi was your son?"

"He *is* my son; and one day, when I have followed the

Feathers of the Morning, he will recognize the link between us.''

''He knows it already. He loves you, Dorrok, I know he does, as I do.''

He took my hand and held it for a moment between his own, then gently touched the callouses on the palm with his forefinger. ''You love me in spite of these? In spite of the scars on your feet where I never spared you on stony trails? In spite of the scar on your shoulder that came from the cliff I knew was too steep for you to climb?''

''Perhaps I love you because of the scars, Dorrok. You made me strong enough to fulfill our promise to my mother, and in loving me you have fulfilled your promise to your son.''

''It is a strong bridge that we have made over the Canyon...honour and endurance....''

''And love, Dorrok.''

''Yes, and love. Without love all bridges must crumble into dust.'' Then his voice changed, as though he was still afraid of the warmth of emotion. ''But you did not come here to talk about me: it was of the Choosing?''

''Yes, Dorrok. How much do the others know about making children?''

''Very little. I should have told them tonight, or tomorrow, what they must do in duty to the tribe.''

Then I told Dorrok of my plan, and of how Raki and I were not to use the magic until we had been given the Double Headdress.

''Na-ka-chek is a wise man, and you share his wisdom with your own,'' he said. ''I will tell those who are going to the South with us that they must all attend the Choosing, but only as a formality, in accordance with the laws of the Two Trees. They shall take the squaws into the woods, but only to save them from the Old Women. Tomorrow we will choose a place for the encampment, and build shelters for them to use until we have made new tepees. Gorgi and the others shall hear from me how they must win the right to use the magic, and that to betray it is to betray both the Before People and the Great Hunters. In love they shall be worthy of magic, worthy of becoming the ancestors of a tribe who shall be known as the Singing People, because of them the future generations shall be happy together.''

the thirty tribes

This was the year of the Gathering of the Tribes, to which all tribal brothers went with their Chiefs; and, if the distance was not too great, some of the boys, and women to attend the cooking-pots, accompanied them. Na-ka-chek agreed that the only women to go with us might be those who wished to join our future tribe, and now it was their turn to be envied by the squaws who had boasted of the Choosing. Dorrok told us that thirty tribes came to the meeting-place: Braves vied with each other in all kinds of skill and endurance; there would be combats and canoe-racing, and feasts which lasted until dawn coloured the sky.

Raki and I, as sons of a Chief, would attend Na-ka-chek at the Feathered Council, where all inter-tribal disputes were settled. This added to our excitement, for it would teach us much more than we had been able to learn from hearing our own Elders talking at the watch-fire...we might even get ideas for new laws of our own. For the first time we should meet people whose way of life was different from the Two Trees: we must find out as much as possible about their customs and their hunting-grounds, so that we could decide in which direction to seek our place of the corn-growing. Perhaps there were places where the winter was not so long, but a more kindly climate would be no advantage if the neighbouring tribes were hostile, or had Old Women still more ridden by superstition than Nona.

The journey took thirty-one days: it was slow and easy, for we did not start until after dawn and made camp before sunset; we even stopped at noon for a meal, when there was time to rest longer than most of us needed.

One of the Elders, a very old man who seldom moved from the watch-fire, must have found it difficult to keep pace with us, but though I once saw him take off his moccasins, and so knew his feet were covered with open sores, I never saw him limp. I suggested to Raki that we make a litter for him, for he was so thin that he would have been easy to carry even over the steeper tracks, but Raki said he would be bitterly insulted.

Game was plentiful, so the cooking-pots were full. Some of us went ahead towards evening, to collect wood for the fires and have the meat cut into chunks, and the birds ready spitted for roasting over the embers. Instead of the women walking forlornly behind the last file, as ordinary squaws would have done, they kept to the same long stride we had taught them. Young Braves helped them to carry their burdens; salt and corn-meal, and the things we were taking for barter.

When Na-ka-chek saw this, he smiled at me and said, ''That in itself is a triumph for you, Piyanah; for a Brave would have stood in hot ashes until his feet charred away, rather than be seen carrying a burden like a woman or a Naked Forehead.''

Fourteen years ago Narrok had come this way, not as a blind drummer, but as the Brown Feather seeking either the Scarlet or the Land beyond the Sunset. He still walked without hesitation if he rested two fingers on the shoulder of the one who went in front of him; usually I stayed with him, so that I could describe the cloud-shadows on the hills, or tell him of flowers I had not seen in our hunting-grounds. Narrok, who saw beyond the world of ordinary vision to the splendour of the West, and who yet was glad of the poor words by which I tried to share with him my sight; a flowering vine that had thrown a blanket of sky-colour over a great tree which had died in battle with the thunder-fires; a dance of insects through a shaft of sun between dark pines; a glowing pool of orchis in the dusk.

The last day of our journey was through thick woods, chiefly of fir and larch, where the pine-needles muffled the rhythm of our march until our two hundred were quiet as a solitary hunter. Raki and I had gone ahead with Dorrok; suddenly I saw the evening sun burning through the last ranks of trees, which ceased abruptly, as though they were meadow-grass cut by the sickle of the Lord of the Forest. The light was so brilliant after the sombre woods that for a moment I was dazzled; then I saw that the ground fell sharply to a plain, rimmed by hills so regular in outline that it looked like a food-bowl of the gods. Only once were these hills cleft; where a river gushed through a narrow gorge, to throw a coil of water like a sleeping snake across the plain.

Hundreds of fires sent up their smoke to the sky, grey smoke, as though the spirits of the trees had once grown there still guarded the earth which had given them life. I had been prepared to see many people, but had not realized how strange it would be to see hundreds and tens of hundreds; to see, not one cooking-fire, but more than I could count; to see, not one Great Tepee, but nineteen set in a circle round a watch-fire that was larger than a funeral pyre.

Na-ka-chek led us down to the plain. Raki and I walked directly behind him, and we were followed by the Elders and Scarlet Feathers, and then the others came in order of rank...so of course the women came last. Brown Feathers carried my father's tepee and the Tepee of the Elders; for these, being objects of veneration, increased the stature of those in whose care they had been placed. The tepees were not of double hides, for it was summer, but they had been freshly painted with scenes from the history of the Two Trees: there were pictures of men hunting, of deer and birds, and among these the symbols which only the Elders can understand. Now there was also the story of our victory over the Black Feathers, done in black and red on the right of the opening, so that all would know of our triumph without our appearing boastful. It is courteous for a man to give truthful answer to any question asked by a friend, but only a braggart tells, unasked, a story which increases the lustre of himself or his tribe.

As the Chief's sons, Raki and I could have shared the Great Tepee with Na-ka-chek, but he wished me to be treated as a Brown Feather, and thought it less probable that I should be recognized as a girl if we stayed with the rest of the tribe. This we were very willing to do, as it greatly increased our freedom.

The camping-ground allotted to us was to the west of the Great Tepees and near the river. Shelters thatched with pine branches had been prepared; this work, I found out later, being the responsibility of the Chief on whose land the Gathering took place. His tribe was much larger than ours and had many Naked Foreheads. Some of these were the sons of enemies captured in battle against the Horned Toad, a tribe which had been exiled from the Brotherhood of Tribes for betraying the Laws of Battle thirty years earlier.

A large stack of firewood had been cut for us, and cooking-stones left in a heap beside it; even a row of freshly filled water-jars had been set ready. After so much hospitality we were not surprised when two Naked Foreheads brought us five reeds, each of six fish, two haunches of smoked venison; and then, as though that were not enough, there was a basket of roasted eggs and a small jar of salt. Salt—and given casually, as though it were an ordinary gift like deer-meat or a blanket!

The camping-ground of each tribe was marked off by poles; decorated with carving, bunches of feathers, or bands of porcupine quills, glued to the wood, the joints covered with coloured leather. It was as though one of the Great Hunters had scooped up a gigantic territory in his hand and let the mountains and plains trickle through his fingers until only the people were left; people so different, yet who, because they were no longer divided by many days' journey, had become suddenly ordinary. No one expects a stranger to be like himself, but here there were so many strangers, and even their language was difficult to understand. Some had skins much darker than ours, and others were a sickly yellow, as though they had always lived in the dark. The women were stirring the cooking-pots and the Braves were appraising each other and pretending to find nothing extraordinary in the many things which must have been as strange to them as to us.

Instead of wearing the tribal mark only on the forehead, some had patches of colour on cheek-bones or chin, and others had been branded with the tribal pattern on the right shoulder or the base of the throat. How the women who had not come with us would have coveted the ornaments that I saw other squaws wearing! Necklaces of beads larger than a pigeon's eggs, made of stone in blue or red-earth-colour streaked with white. There were necklaces of shells, and of rare woods intricately carved; forehead-bands of beads or painted leather, or—and these were by far the most beautiful—of feathers which must have come from the breasts of rare and brilliant birds.

Many of the women had spread their blankets on the ground so that the patterns might be admired. Some of these had the blue of a jay and a dark, moss-green woven into them, so I knew there were dyes unknown to us. Our new tunics no longer seemed so splendid: there was finer doeskin, more elaborate embroidery, than any to be found in our tribe. We could not console ourselves by thinking that as we were a warrior tribe we had no time for decoration; for the Leaping Waters, warriors of great stature and renowned for courage, carried tomahawks whose handles were of the yellow metal that is found in the river from which they take their name and is worth even more than salt in barter. Their belts were studded with it and it hafted their spears; they

166

even wore armlets of the same rich yellow. They bore the scars of many battles, and their thin, proud mouths wore the secret smiles of victors, who are secure that tomorrow's conflict will provide yet another story to be retold at the watch-fires of their children's children.

When we saw a tribe who came from the far South, we knew it must be a land where food is very plentiful; for even the warriors were almost fat and laughed easily. Their women were sleek as dormice, with soft voices and small plump hands. They rolled a little when they walked, like pinioned ducks in a hurry. This was the only tribe in which we saw the men take any notice of the women. I saw a squaw bending over a cooking-pot, and a man slapped her on the buttock in a friendly way; she was obviously flattered at this mark of attention, for when he had gone she giggled and the eyes of her two companions were round with envy.

Every night the tribal story-tellers told the legends of their people, and all who gathered to listen were offered smoke or drink. Raki and I shared a cup of something dark and brown in the encampment of the Leaping Waters: it had a hot, bitter taste, and everything I looked at directly afterwards trembled as though in a heat haze. Later, Raki told me that he had felt the same. The stories we heard there were all of battle; the Leaping Waters even claimed to have driven the Black Feathers into the East, though this in the time of the ancestors. We were very doubtful if this were true, for they described them as being twice as tall as ordinary men, and having heads naked as eggs.

"That must be to explain why they haven't any of the Black Feathers' scalps," whispered Raki, and I nodded to show I agreed.

They had brought some other scalps with them, and these were passed round from hand to hand while the audience made noises of admiration or respect. The scalps had red hair, and were so old that the skin was hard as wood. They were supposed to have been taken from very dangerous enemies who came out of the sunset in long canoes more than five hundred years ago, and had the power of turning themselves into fish and escaping by river when pursued.

We listened to every story-teller in turn, hoping that one of them would have news of the Before People. We heard of courage and cunning, endurance and even laughter, but of the wisdom we sought we found nothing. There were the legends of the morning of the world, the same legends as our own, but with decorations that made them fit into the pattern of a different tribal lore; and the story of the first man and the first woman we heard again from a tribe of the south-west, who made pottery finer than I had ever seen...even Minshi would have had to admit that it was better than any he could make.

The last story-teller we heard belonged to the people from the South whom we had seen on our first evening. They were called the Smiling Valleys, and their stories were quite different from the rest. In one, the hero enjoyed sitting in the sun, having found a magical tree which dropped ripe fruit into his mouth whenever he opened it. In another, a woman was beguiled by a fire spirit, who in recognition of the pleasure she had afforded him, gave her a magic cooking-pot, which was always full of food so pleasing to the men that they were never discontented. Henceforward she had no need to work and could lie drowsing in the shade so long as she never brushed away the fly which settled on her forehead every seven days. The fly was sent by the fire spirit, to remind her that if she forgot to be grateful to him he would ask Great Fly to send a buzzing, biting cloud that would make it impossible for her to sleep even for an instant. It was a happy story, for the woman put a drop of honey on her forehead for the fly, so Great Fly was grateful for this courtesy to his people and told them not to trouble any of her tribe even in the hot weather.

Afterwards Raki and I talked to one of the Smiling Valleys; we were the only strangers at their watch-fire, perhaps because everyone else preferred to hear of killing, and scalps, and blood. Some of his words were different from ours, but not sufficiently so to make it difficult to understand the meaning. They were all very willing to talk about their own country, which lay seventy days' journey to the south; nor were they ashamed to admit that they, too, were awed at seeing so many strangers at one time and in one place; which made us feel even more friendly towards them.

I knew Raki shared my excitement as we listened. They could not tell us of the Before People, but they had news which was equally important to our future. They never saw snow except on the mountains which sheltered them from the north; their land was so fertile that they could grow three crops in the same year, and fish were so plentiful in their rivers that a hunter need not kill unless he felt inclined. They were proud of their leisure, proud of the smiling weather and their fertile earth; as we were proud that we could challenge the winter, and live through the long moons of cold on the food we had spent the summer storing as a bear stores fat for its winter sleep. There were no Scarlet Feathers among them, but instead of being ashamed they laughed and said, ''Why should a man risk death for no reason when life is pleasant?''

They were glad that their bodies were not lean and hard. ''Is not a fat hind preferable to a starveling?'' they asked. ''And does not a wood pigeon with a full crop make a more comfortable sound than a hungry jay?'' Instead of boasting of the deeds of their Braves, they told us with pride that the son of their Chief had made a new fish-trap, which was much less trouble to look after than any previously built and yet caught the same number of fish. Instead of scalps, they talked of shrubs and trees which had been brought to their valley to provide fruit and berries pleasurable to the tongue, and had been planted close to their encampment to be gathered without effort.

''How do you keep your people busy?'' asked Raki. ''If life is so easy for them, don't they quarrel among themselves?''

"If one of us is quarrelsome he is told to go away until he has defeated the demon which tried to make him bring discord to the watch-fire."

"What happens if he refuses to go?" I said.

"He does not refuse," said the Smiling Valley gently. "It is against our laws, and if he disobeys...then we have a feast to forget the sorrow we feel because one of us has been disobedient."

"Does he mind your feeling sorry?"

"No, he does not mind," said the Smiling Valley with the same gentleness. "Or if he minds, it does not worry us; for he is dead. It is the only sin which is punished by death among our people, the sin of deliberately making other people unhappy. It is our first law, for unhappiness makes people have pains in the belly and brings many kinds of sickness, and then they weep, and grow thin, and die."

"But you haven't told us how you keep busy," said Raki.

"We *think*; of the past, or of the future, or of today: whichever be more pleasant...if they are all of equal excellence we think of all three at the same time."

We did not ask the Smiling Valleys to come to our encampment, for we knew that our legends would be shocking to them. They were people who would be horrified to hear that we thought it better to run than to walk, to walk than to stand still, to stand than to lie down: who thought it gave merit to eat as little as possible, to climb a cliff where there are the fewest handholds, to run until you drop with exhaustion. These stories would not inspire them with admiration, but with sorrow and foreboding for a tribe so foolish that it must surely disappear from the Earth.

As we walked back to our camping-ground, Raki said, "They have time to think, Piyanah. We need not follow them in being fat or lazy, but we *need* time to think. Our winter is too long and cold...it is difficult to think when you are cold, except of how to keep warm and of whether your belly will ever feel comfortably full again...and so much of our summer is spent in preparing for the winter.''

''Yes, we all need time to think. Long thoughts, which are like the pinion feathers by whose strength a bird can fly.''

''Piyanah! We will take our people South, where they can learn that endurance is not all a man needs before he can be welcomed into the Land beyond the Sunset.''

''Yes, Raki,'' I said, ''we will go South.''

Feathered Council

Every evening another tribe arrived, until by the eighth day, which was the full moon, all the Thirty were assembled and the great feast took place which celebrated that the Moon of the Council had begun. Raki and I attended Na-ka-chek, sitting behind him by the watch-fire of the Great Tepees. All the Chiefs were splendid with feathers, their robes richly embroidered, some with beads, some with porcupine quills or feathers. Even among this magnificence, the Chief of the Leaping Waters outshone the rest, for his long green robe was covered with gold plaques, shaped like birds and fish, each so highly burnished that it glittered with life in the firelight.

Each Chief was attended by the son or blood-kin chosen to succeed him. The young men stared at Raki and me; perhaps they were surprised because there were two of us. Had I known it was the custom for each Chief to announce why he had chosen the name of his successor and the reason why he had been chosen, I should have been nervous before the feast. Perhaps so much rich food, and the kindly drink, made from honey and certain herbs which do not grow in our own hunting-grounds, gave me confidence; for it is difficult to be afraid when your body is content, unless it is directly threatened.

Each youth stared straight in front of him while his qualities were being extolled. I could not think of what they reminded me, until I remembered the squaws at the Choosing. At the end of each speech there was silence, the sign of agreement, though had he been considered unworthy to join the council, if the present Chief should die during the next seven years, he would be required to give further proof of his powers of leadership and his knowledge of the tribal laws.

My father was the last to speak. When I knew that Raki and I had to step forward, to be stared at by those proud, aloof faces which the fire beckoned from the shadows, my legs suddenly felt as though they had been running until they could not carry me any further.

"Steady, Piyanah!" Raki's voice was only a whisper, but my body heard it too and became obedient.

White and yellow, blue and green and scarlet; a wall of mighty feathers surrounded us. Eyes, implacable as hawks, cold, unwavering. Hands, placid as the smoke which rose from the long pipes. I, too, must be calm and impassive. I chose a star low on the horizon, and swore that my eyes should not turn away from it nor the lids flicker....

My father's voice was calm and unhurried: "I, Na-ka-chek, Chief of the Two Trees, have led my people to a place where the path forks, between the old way and the new. I am too full of years to go into the hills of the unknown future; but these two together will rule after me, and will take those of my people who wish to follow them, to find a new land under their own totem."

He paused, to give added significance to his next words: "Never before has a Chief chosen a man and a woman to rule in equality."

No one moved, but I felt the tension his words produced grow until I thought I could have touched it with my hands.

"I repeat: a new tribe shall be led by a man and a woman in equality, by Raki and Piyanah. They will act as one person, and speak with one voice in council. Those of my people who wish to keep to the old way will stay with me, and choose their own successor to take my place when I die. You have never seen a woman at your council, yet there is no law against it. It is said that a Brave must inherit: the training which Piyanah has undergone has been no less arduous than that of any other Brown Feather. She wears seven bear-claws, and has killed a running hind with a single arrow at two hundred paces. She has asked no clemency, and in battle she killed a Black Feather and took his scalp.

''All that she has done, so has Raki done also. They are the bow and the bowstring, the arrow and the quiver, the morning and the evening of their days. If anyone doubts her strength let him give her challenge; or else acknowledge the new tribe, which in the spring of next year will follow their dual Chief to the land of their future.''

The silence was deep as that which follows the roar of thunder. Then a youth, who belonged to the yellow-skinned tribe, said in a harsh voice:

''I, T'cha, will not sit in council with a squaw.''

''A man cannot refuse to sit in council with his equals,'' said Na-ka-chek.

''No squaw is a man's equal! You cannot turn weakness into strength by putting a brown feather in a forehead-thong. To have a woman in our council would be to dishonour the feathers. They have always been held in veneration, and now you turn them into an ornament for your squaw!''

''Her symbol is as true as your own,'' said my father. ''If you doubt its colour, why not prove its quality by giving her a challenge?''

The youth sneered, ''I do not fight with women...nor eat carrion.''

At this further insult some of the Chiefs turned to stare at the speaker in cold disapproval while the rest ignored him. I think they might have agreed with T'cha had he used words of suitable dignity; but the laws of courtesy were strict and not to be violated without rebuke.

173

Then spoke the Chief of the Leaping Waters: "It appears that this young man has been too occupied with learning the arts of the warrior to have had sufficient opportunity to learn the arts of the council, among which is a seemly choice of words. As he is determined not to sit in council with the Daughter of Na-ka-chek, would it not be agreeable to us all if contests were to be arranged between them; the winner to be accepted by us, the loser to be rejected from any place in our future councils?"

This speech won general approval, some of the old men even permitting themselves the indulgence of a smile. The Yellow Skin had to accept, though he did so with as little grace as he dared. He sneered at me, and for the first time I looked forward to the contest, for wiping the sneer from his face would be better than scalping a Black Feather.

When the oldest Chief rose to his feet as a sign that the council was concluded, I should have liked to stay to talk with some of the sons, but Raki told me, rather sharply, to come back to our camping-ground. I wondered what had annoyed him, until he said, as soon as we had gone far enough not to be overheard:

"Your father is a fool to let you take up that challenge. That man is more dangerous than a Black Feather; he will try to kill you."

"I am not going to be killed, Raki. I am going to lead a new tribe with you, to the South."

"You may be confident once too often, Piyanah! If I had let you meet any of the others, you might have given another challenge...that is why I hurried you away. You are feeling full of courage now, but by tomorrow you may feel differ-ent...and you will not have a chance to change your mind."

"I don't want to change it, Raki," I said indignantly. "I want to see those sneering eyes pop out of that yellow face because my thumbs are pressing into the corners of them. I want to see his canoe split open in the rapids, while mine rushes past and I turn to laugh at the expression on

174

his face as it is sucked down by the water.''

''The mead is talking out of your mouth, Piyanah. It makes you think that you like killing people, and you know you hate killing even a deer.''

''Killing a deer is much worse than killing that yellow horror...and I have always enjoyed killing snakes and spiders.''

''You are frightened of rattle-snakes.''

''Well, perhaps I am...but he is a snake that I am not afraid of...and I think it is unkind of you to try to make me think of being afraid.''

''Aren't you afraid?...it's never any use trying to hide your feelings from me.''

''Perhaps part of me is,'' I admitted reluctantly, ''but I shan't listen to that part unless it shouts so loud I can't help myself. I do wish you would stop being angry, Raki. If you don't I shall be miserable, and if I am miserable I shall forget I am a Brave, and then I shall never be able to remember the right holds in the wrestling. Will one of the contests be wrestling, do you think?''

''The Chiefs will decide that. If you had given the challenge, and it had been directly accepted, he would have had the choice; but now I suppose the council will choose them. I am not angry *with* you, Piyanah, but I am angry *for* you. Na-ka-chek had no right not to warn us of what was going to happen. When you had been Chief with me for seven years the council would have accepted you without question, and if they had tried to refuse you, then we could have kept away from the Gathering...it was the act of a fool to ask them to acknowledge you *now*.''

''Why do you suppose he did it?''

''Mead!'' said Raki. ''That is why I am so angry with him. Mead seems to breed conceit faster than dead meat breeds maggots. Na-ka-chek, a fool because he had drunk too much mead!''

''Could it really have made any difference?''

175

"If you don't believe me, I will soon show you what it can do."

Instead of continuing towards our camping-ground he turned east. Even without the full moon the night would have been brilliant, for many people were carrying torches which added to the light of the fires.

"There!" said Raki. "Mead can be strong as a tomahawk, though its effects don't last so long."

Three men were sprawled on the ground, breathing heavily through their open mouths. Raki jostled one of them with his foot, but he only grunted and went on sleeping.

"One of them is a Scarlet Feather," said Raki disgustedly, "and there is another of them."

This man was lying on his face. I thought he was dead until suddenly he rolled over and began to mutter incoherently.

"Not tens, but hundreds of them," said Raki. "When the sun comes back tomorrow she will think there has been a battle...but none of them will have earned a funeral pyre."

"I expect the yellow viper will drink so much that his arms will snap like dead twigs and his legs become weak as rotten fungus," I said hopefully, for Raki had managed to make me feel less enthusiastic for the contests.

"It will be his last feast in any case, for if you don't kill him, I shall."

"But you can't kill him, Raki, if he wins in a fair fight...though he is not going to win, of course."

He swung me round, and gripped my shoulders so tightly that I nearly cried out. "We were tricked into this, so it is not your fault. But this is the last time that I am going to let you come into danger. You are *my* woman, even though I am not allowed to claim you yet. I shall kill any man who hurts you; cripple any man who insults you; break the right arm of any man who annoys you! That is *my* first law, and with me it overrules all others. So if you don't enjoy

176

watching massacres, Piyanah, you had better not provoke insults...unless you want them to be avenged.''

The next morning, Raki said that until the Chiefs decided what form the contest between me and the Yellow Skin was to take I was not to enter for any of the other contests, in case I strained a muscle and so was at a disadvantage. When I protested that it was unfair to deprive me of this chance of proving that a squaw could be the equal of man in many things, he said:

''You will have every opportunity to prove that against T'cha. It is better that he should continue to think you an unworthy opponent, for over-confidence is nearly as dangerous a companion as fear. Let him continue to drink mead, and feast; let him boast of the humiliation he will give to the arrogant squaw...and then there will be more words to choke him!''

So I had to be content to watch Raki, and it was a rich contentment. In the wrestling bouts he was drawn first against one of the Leaping Waters, then against Braves from two of the northern tribes. Thereafter he was looked at with added respect by those who had been too stupid to recognize his quality before: a broken leg, a twisted shoulder, and a dislocated wrist are valuable as bear's claws when they belong to your opponent!

I should have liked to join in flighting arrows at the targets, especially when I saw that T'cha's skill was less than mine. I hoped that he noticed Raki got seven arrows, at two hundred paces, into the painted deer which was no larger than a man's hand, while he got only three. But they were in different groups, so it was unlikely that the Yellow Skin realized he had been outmatched by one of us.

Watching contests became very monotonous after the first two days. All the trained runners were so swift that the extra pace of the winner made little difference except to his friends. One wrestling bout is very like another, unless you have an urgent reason for minding who wins...watching Raki was a pride and an agony, and it was a relief when Dorrok, Gorgi, and Tekeeni all won their bouts. Gorgi suffered the only injury, a badly sprained thumb against one of the Leaping Waters, which prevented his taking any further part in the contest of arrows.

I was surprised to see that so many different types of slings were used: some tribes, instead of using any stone of a convenient size, had brought special ones with them, and other stones had a hole bored through them so that they could be carried on a thong. The contest of slings took place beyond the river, where there was a tract of marshy ground frequented by numerous wildfowl. Two men from each tribe took up position near the river bank, lots having been drawn to decide the order of their stands. Squaws, who had been sent out early in the morning to hide in the reeds until they were given a signal, walked slowly in line towards the hunters, driving the birds in front of them.

The highest score was fourteen, and neither of our men was in the first three. I was glad that Raki had not entered for this travesty of the art of the hunter. We had been taught that a man should kill his game instantly and without bringing it to fear, and the sight of this cloud of birds being driven blindly towards death disgusted us both. Often the kill was slovenly; a bird with a broken leg would escape to die slowly of starvation, another with a wing down would glide helplessly, and then try to run into the shelter of the reeds.

Every night the Feathered Council assembled, the Chiefs together with the Elders, to settle the inter-tribal disputes which two Chiefs had not been able to decide between themselves. The Two Trees had no petition to make, so there was not even the interest of trying to forecast what kind of decision we might expect.

The Elders were slow and deliberate of speech, their voices, devoid of any emotion, droned on, until several times Raki had to prod me to stop me falling asleep. Endless arguments and counter-arguments: as to the exact boundary between two hunting-grounds; whether a hunter had followed a deer on to the land of a neighbouring tribe without recognizing the landmarks, or had he deliberately failed to offer the customary haunch to the Chief on whose land he had made a kill? Was the deer wounded, and had the hunter followed it only to fulfill his obligations to a quarry? Was it more than five years old? How many deer had been killed in that season? Was the tribe in urgent need of meat?...So many words for so trivial a thing as a haunch of venison!

When I remarked on this to Na-ka-chek, he told me that before the law was passed which made it necessary for all disputes that could not otherwise be settled to be referred to the council, great battles had been fought for things no more important than this.

The following night they discussed a certain tribe in the south-west, who had recently been afflicted with a mysterious sickness which had caused more than half of their numbers to die. They had sent a spokesman to ask that their hunting-grounds should be reduced, and that in exchange they should be given grain and dried meat to save them from starving during the oncoming winter. This was granted, and then began seemingly endless discussions as to the exact limit of the new boundaries: which part should be taken by each of the three Chiefs who held the adjoining lands; whether they should give grain for three harvests, or would two years give the diminished tribe time to become secure through their own sowing?

The only time a squaw was mentioned was when one had been carried off by a Naked Forehead who belonged to another tribe. The Chief of the tribe to whom the squaw belonged had received the scalp of the Naked Forehead as a token that the incident was regretted, but he demanded further compensation. Eventually it was agreed that this claim was just, and it was settled at six doe-skins and forty arrows. No one bothered to state what had happened to the squaw!

Na-ka-chek told me that in the time of the grandfathers, before the Thirty Tribes had agreed to abide by these laws, only matters of far greater importance were brought to the council. Then, as now, a tribe who had suffered severely from an outlaw tribe might appeal for help, when the number of Braves considered necessary would be sent by the other Chiefs to bring vengeance. As the power of the Thirty Tribes became respected, the outlaws diminished, so now the most important work of the council was the allocating of scarlet feathers. These were given only at the Gathering; though a Chief, supported by his Elders, might declare any act of special courage that had been performed by one of his Braves, which, after careful consideration, could be awarded this highest honour.

On the fourteenth day the Chiefs were to declare the names of the Braves who wished to be allocated to an ordeal by which they could win the Scarlet. I had heard many stories of the terrible things that had been undertaken in search of this honour, and was very glad that neither Raki nor I needed such a feather to lead our tribe. I had seen the rock from which Narrok had dived into darkness: Raki and I had climbed to the top of it, and shuddered to think that anyone would essay that terrible plunge into so narrow a pool.

This year there were twelve who claimed the right of an ordeal. The first man was allotted the Ordeal of the Fire-Ants. The second, to climb the Cliff of Death. The third, to go down into a pit of rattle-snakes, his hands bound behind him, and to stay there from dawn to sunset...knowing that his only hope of escape was to remain motionless even if they crawled over his feet.

As each horror was spoken I became increasingly grateful to the Great Hunters that Raki and I would never have to undergo such an ordeal. Each man stood impassive as a totem while his sentence was spoken; then he raised his right hand to show that he accepted it. To refuse would have been to lose the rank of Brave, and to become a Naked Forehead or a

Half-brother, according to the clemency of his Chief: I knew there would be little clemency for one who brought so great a dishonour to the tribe.

What made these men risk a terrible death for no reason except the desire to wear a scarlet feather in their forehead-thong?   They were already Braves, honoured by their tribes: why did they want to gorge themselves with danger? Did they doubt their courage and feel driven to prove it to themselves?   Or was it love for their tribe and their traditions, so that their Chief might wear their Scarlet in his headdress and they be remembered by the generations?

Suddenly I heard my name spoken by the Chief of the Leaping Waters. My name and the name of T'cha. I felt Raki tense every muscle. I was almost relieved that at last I was going to know the nature of the contest, and was too excited to wonder why it should be decided on the same night as the ordeals. I stood up, as I saw T'cha had done, and walked forward into the fire-light.

''T'cha and Piyanah,'' said the Chief of the Leaping Waters, ''it has been decided by us that if you wish to attend our council in the future you can do so only if you wear a scarlet feather. If we give the Scarlet to Piyanah, then T'cha can no longer say that a squaw brings dishonour to our feathers. T'cha could not sit with us if he had been proved weaker than a squaw. So both must undergo the ordeal...or recognize that both have attended a Gathering of the Tribes for the last time. The ordeal is severe, but fourteen years ago it was attempted by one of my people.''

He paused and touched a scarlet feather in his headdress. ''His body died last year, but his courage lives here, with me. Where the river leaves the Place of the Gathering it flows underground, through caverns which are said to be haunted by demons of great malice. Little is known of these caverns, or of the tunnels by which they are joined, for very few have lived to describe them. I repeat, the Ordeal of the

181

Caverns of Darkness is severe…but not impossible. Do you wish to accept our decision?

I held up my right hand, and saw T'cha do the same. I had done so instinctively, not daring to hesitate lest they realize I was terribly afraid.

"You have two days in which to make ready," said the Leaping Water. "A canoe suitable for the ordeal shall be provided for each of you."

The oldest Chief rose to his feet to show that the council was at an end: and I tried to prepare myself to meet the horror in Raki's eyes.

the Caverns

I was glad that Raki had left at dawn to wait for me beyond the Caverns of Darkness; for if he had been there to watch me enter the canoe that might take me to the other side of the water, the sight of him would have drained away the last of that pride which would not let me refuse the ordeal. Even Na-ka-chek had tried to persuade me not to attempt it, telling me that the other Chiefs had proposed it only because they thought both T'cha and I would refuse and so lose our chance of joining the Feathered Council.

T'cha was surrounded by people of his own tribe; his voice was loud and arrogant, but I knew the sweat on his forehead was born of fear. I stood with Dorrok and Gorgi, while Tekeeni held the prow of my canoe. I saw his lips moving, and knew he was telling it to guard me. People from every tribe had collected to see us start; even the Chiefs were there. I knew very few would be with Raki, for most of them believed that we should never be seen again after we entered the tunnel that led into the cliff.

"I *know* there is a way through," said Dorrok again. "I

once spoke to a man who gained his Scarlet through this ordeal, though if I had known this was going to happen, I should have listened more carefully to what he said...it was seven years ago, but I think I have remembered all the essentials. You will go through underground caverns where the water spreads into lakes, so you have a chance to choose your way if you keep out of the main stream. There are places where the roof nearly touches the water; lie flat in the bottom of the canoe and guard your head with the paddle. Above all things do not let your torch go out, for without light you can only let yourself be swept along by the current. You *will* get through, Piyanah, because the others who failed believed in demons. Remember there are no demons...and you are not afraid of bats or echoes...echoes cannot hurt you even if they sound like an enemy. When you see bright water ahead and come into the open, keep close to the south bank where there is a clear run down the rapid. The rapid is easy; you and Raki have often gone down more difficult ones as a game. Remember the bright water is *beyond* the cave of the whirlpool...."

Until I heard the desperate conviction in his voice I had not realized he expected me to be killed. Did he think I ought to give him a last message to Raki? I could not think of one, for I had to conceal the fear that was growing stronger every moment, conceal it even from myself.

Lots were drawn to decide whether T'cha or I was to go first: it fell to him. He pulled off his tunic, and wearing only a breech-clout, got into his canoe. As it slid away from the bank, his tribe shouted encouragement...the shout being taken up by a few of the rest of the crowd which thronged on both sides of the river.

I watched his canoe gradually gathering speed; it looked as though it was sure to crash against the low entrance to the tunnel. He paddled across the current to the centre of the river and I saw he was making for a point where the entrance was a little higher than the rest. He ducked his head: a sigh went up from the crowd as the canoe swept out of sight.

"You see, it is easier than it looks," said Dorrok. "There is plenty of clearance, though from here it looks as though even a floating log would scrape against the roof. Hold the torch high as soon as you are in the tunnel...even if the light is dim, it will help you to know when to duck."

I walked down to where Tekeeni was holding the canoe. He looked up and said, "Everything is ready. I have put a knife, a rope, a spare torch and one that is smouldering and some strips of bandage in case you cut yourself on a sharp rock...loss of blood will weaken you, so tie it tightly if you have the chance."

"I hope you have put a double handful of courage in as well," I said, and managed a laugh which I think sounded convincing.

I turned to Dorrok. "Tell the tribe to prepare a feast to-night, to celebrate our victory over the Yellow Skins...and I shall be there to share it with you." But under my breath I added, "I shall be there, even though you cannot see me."

Would the spirit of Piyanah be welcome at the feast? Or would even the Braves be afraid of her, and shiver when she walked past them?

"The Great Hunters are with you," said Tekeeni in a low voice.

"Tell Raki..." I said, as I pulled off my tunic, and then, "No, I will tell him myself...this evening."

I felt the current draw the canoe away from Tekeeni. A great shout went up from the Tribe of Two Trees and it was joined by the voices of hundreds and tens of hundreds. Strength flowed into me with the sound...tens of hundreds of squaws had died of hunger, of childbearing, in sickness and in loneliness, died without acclamation. Their courage had never been acknowledged, but because Piyanah took a canoe into the darkness the Thirty Tribes would remember the bravery of squaws.

I paddled across the current as T'cha had done, and

reached mid-stream in time to choose the place where I would enter the face of the cliff. I made sure that the torch was smouldering, and that a second paddle was securely fastened to the side of the canoe, for if the one I held was wrested from me I should be helpless unless I had another to steer by.

The water was roaring, as though it were angry at being made to enter the narrow gateway ahead. I saw two small whirlpools and shot between them, knowing that had either caught me I should have been smashed against the rocks which guarded the entrance. The tunnel seemed to open like the mouth of a huge black fish; I ducked, holding the paddle over my head. My fingers were grazed by the rock above me, but lightly, so I knew they could only just have touched it.

The canoe suddenly swung round and nearly capsized. I had to risk hitting my head and kneel upright before I could bear with sufficient strength on the paddle to steady the canoe. When it was going smoothly forward I grasped the torch in my left hand and whirled it above my head. For a terrible moment I thought it had gone out; then I saw a few faint sparks, and a thin plume of flame streamed against the dark.

The roof was much higher than I expected, and walls of rock rose sheer out of the water...they seemed to be dry, for there was no gleam of moisture. The water was unbroken and it was easy to keep a level course. I began to feel more confident; then I saw the walls were drawing closer together as the canoe began to gather speed. I knew there must be a rapid ahead of me. The river was rushing towards the cleft like water gushing from the narrow neck of a jar. I could not hold the torch and go on paddling: if there were rocks among the rapid I should never see them in time...it would be impossible to steer at such a speed even in broad daylight...I must hold up the torch until the last moment to see as much as I can....I must tense every muscle to keep the canoe from turning over...in this black water no swimmer would have a chance.

The canoe lept forward. I flung down the torch and

strained against the paddle to keep the canoe pointing with the current...if the prow swung round, even very little, it must surely be swamped. The roar of water was louder than a thousand demons...it would be easy to believe in demons in this darkness, if there was time to think of anything except the press of danger.

The water buffeted the canoe until the breath was nearly driven out of my body. I gasped, and got a mouthful of spray that nearly choked me. I waited to feel the canoe twist beyond my control as it was clutched in a vortex. Just as the strain on my arms became unendurable the canoe began to slacken speed, and remembering what Dorrok had told me, I managed to drive it out of the main flow of the current. I expected at any moment to feel it jar against the rock wall. There was no jar, and in several strong strokes I came into still water, or water where the current was almost imperceptible.

I realized that I must have entered the first of the underground caverns where the river formed a lake. The torch still smouldered, and after I had blown on it the flame flared up. The lake was large, more than three times wider than the river in the open country, and widening as I drifted further on. Here the walls did not rise sheer, and at their feet was a narrow beach of sand sloping up to coarse gravel. I decided to stay there and rest before going on; now that the immediate danger was past my arms and legs felt suddenly weak and demanded time to recover from the strain of the roaring waters.

I used the rope which Tekeeni had given me to make the canoe fast to a spike of rock that jutted from the main face. After a few moments' rest I decided to climb along the shelf so as to find out the nature of the next obstacle I had to pass. It was an easy climb, though between the stretches of gravel there were outcrops of rock. The torch showed that in winter the water-level was much higher, for there were marks of erosion above my head.

For the first time I had a chance to think of demons; to

think how terribly alone I was in this echoing darkness; far underground with only a torch for a companion. A terrible sound wailed through the caverns.

"It is only a bat!" I said aloud, and heard myself answer, "No bat makes a sound like that."

The echoes answered, "No bat makes a sound like that...like that..."

"You are only an echo," I shouted.

"Only an echo...only an echo," the cavern agreed.

"I am not afraid!"

But the shout I had tried to make arrogant, answered, "Not afraid? Not afraid?"

Then there was silence among the sound of rushing water. I thought I heard Narrok's drum in the distance; and realized it was only my own heart.

Again came the terrible wailing cry. "It must be a bird," I thought desperately, "or the wind blowing through a fissure in the rock. It can't be a demon, because Mother and Bara-keechi would never let a demon attack me here, alone in the dark."

Again the wail echoed and re-echoed.

"Even if you are a demon," I shouted back, "I am not frightened of you. You sound unhappy and in pain. Are you in pain, you miserable demon?" The mocking echoes mimicked my voice, and I shouted even louder, "Are you in pain?"

This time the answer was louder...there was a word in it instead of only a wail...."Pain...pain."

Demons cannot speak in a human voice! Suddenly I realized what made that noise...it was a human voice distorted by echoes...T'cha the arrogant, calling to a squaw to help him!

Twice I had to wait for an answering sound before I could be sure of the direction. To my relief I saw that the river flowed into the further cavern through a much wider opening where the water was not very turbulent. It was too wide to

187

cross, so now that I knew T'cha must be on the far side of the lake I shouted to him that I had to go back to fetch my canoe but would soon be with him. There was no answer. I shouted again, but the echoes of my own voice dying into silence were the only response.

It was easier going back the way I had come for I knew the way over each jutting rock. As I had hoped, there was calm water again beyond the main current, but the lake extended so far beyond the narrow circle of torch-light that I never discovered its full extent. I secured the canoe as near to the entrance to the second cavern as I dared, so that I could search every part of the sloping shelf of gravel, which was wider here than it had been on the other side of the cavern.

I began to think that T'cha must have been swept away by the water since I last heard him. Once I had wanted to kill him, yet now I found myself hoping fervently that he was still alive....

He was lying half out of the water, and though unconscious he was still breathing. There was a thin trickle of blood down the side of his face, but this only came from a cut above the right eye. I felt his head and found there was no swelling on it nor any sign of a wound. I ran my hands down his arms and over his ribs. It was only when I took him by the shoulders to drag him further up the bank that I saw his legs. They had been crushed above the knees: splinters of bone were sticking through the flesh. I had seen men injured before, and Dorrok had taught me how to sew up long gashes in flesh with steady hands: but now I doubled over and vomited.

I had wanted T'cha to be alive; and now he was terrible because he was not dead. They might be able to cut off his legs. Perhaps Yellow Skins are kind to their Half-brothers... and he is the son of their Chief. If he were an animal I should kill him to set him free of his body; but he is a wounded man, and must be succoured.

He moaned; a terrible moan, of pain that is beyond the

188

limit of courage. I forced myself to examine his legs more closely. There was no chance of his being able to use either of them again; they were pulped above the knees. If I had not seen them myself I should never have believed that rock and water could have crushed with so savage a grip.

I could not leave him here to die alone....If I could take him back to his own people they would have nothing to offer him except pity; pity he would never be able to accept. He had sworn to make a mockery of an arrogant squaw who dared to demand a voice in the Feathered Council. If I rescued him, the mockery he would suffer even as a cripple would be more cruel than hornets....

"We are all the children of the Great Hunters," I said aloud. "Their laws belong to both men and animals. I must have the courage to show T'cha the same compassion that I would give to a wounded deer....I must send him to the other side of the water.

I must ask someone to look after him...."Barakeechi! Barakeechi! Because of our friendship, take this man and teach him the Laws of the West, for he is a Yellow Skin and may have no friends of his own in your country."

T'cha stirred. I thought he was going to open his eyes before I brought the pointed stone crashing down on his temple.

He sighed and his body twitched. Then he was free; free of the legs that could no longer torture him. The legs were only dead meat, and he could walk in freedom.

It was only then I realized that as I had asked the Great Hunters to take him in my name they would expect me to offer his body the proper funerary rituals. He was a brave who had died through an ordeal; he had earned the right of the cleansing fire and the protection of the Death Canoe. His body was still my responsibility even though it was dead, and my canoe must carry us both.

The ledge was wide enough for me to drag the canoe out of the water. He was heavy, but I managed to lift him into it and there was room for me to kneel across his body.

The canoe rode lower in the water, which added to the danger, but not sufficiently for me to be able to leave him. His head was in the stern; the eyes were shut but the jaw sagged open against the chest.

I could feel the pulped flesh of his legs against my knees. They were still warm, and slimy with clotting blood. I had gone beyond fear into a desperate endurance. I knew that it was already decided whether I was to escape from these terrible caverns or to die with the man I had killed. If I died, Mother would be surprised to see me enter the Land beyond the Sunset in the company of a Yellow Skin.

Steadily the canoe kept on through the second cavern. I saw ahead of me the opening into the third, and knew I had come to the Place of the Whirlpool. "It is round as a cooking-pot," Dorrok had said. "Keep close against the wall and try to reach the opening in the far side. Keep to the side or you will be drawn down into the black water."

I felt the prow swing to the left and had to fling down the torch so as to paddle with all my strength to keep close to the side. If there were any rocks sticking out from the face, I knew the canoe would be torn open. Twice I felt the canoe touch the wall and fended it off with my left hand. The whirlpool was trying to pull me into its vortex, as I swept round, trying to judge where the opening was that might lead me to safety…if only I knew where it was I could make a supreme effort to break out of the circle of death.

Suddenly I realized that at one place in the wall the darkness was not absolute…was there really a faint greyness? It might be the entrance to a tunnel…if I was wrong and managed to drive the canoe towards it I should smash it against the rock. Now…now…I thrust on the paddle and felt it bend under the strain. The canoe leapt forward… away from the whirlpool.

The tunnel twisted like a snake; the roof was getting lower, but the light was brighter. I had come through the darkness!

Ahead of me I saw a bar of brilliant light, close to the surface of the water. I had to fling myself flat on T'cha's body: the splintered thigh-bones crunched under my naked breasts. The roof was so low that as we shot into the open I felt a long strip of skin torn from my back.

Again I seemed to hear Dorrok's voice, ''Keep to the south side of the river when you come out of the darkness.''

I seized the paddle and stroked with desperate speed; close ahead was the white water of the rapid. As I came to the crest I saw beyond it people waiting on the bank. They must have seen me, for I heard them shouting above the noise of the rushing water.

Dorrok was right...there was a path between the cruel rocks...deep, green water such as I had often known; rocks that I could see in the clear light of day. Between two plumes of white water I shot forward into calm.

I saw Raki running down the bank towards me. He caught me in his arms...I forgot I was a Scarlet Feather; I was his squaw who had come home to him.

Raki, his arm round my shoulders, led me up the steep bank and past an outcrop of rock which hid us from the others who had waited there with him. I was shuddering, and my teeth chattered as though I were half frozen. He held me close, soothing me as though I were a child trying to wake from a dream of demons.

''I am so sorry, Raki. I wasn't frightened until I knew I was safe. It's my body, not me, that is frightened now...so don't be ashamed of me...please don't be ashamed. The others didn't see I was crying, did they?''

''They saw a Scarlet Feather who has gone to clean the blood from her wounds before she returns to receive their homage.''

''But I'm not wounded....''

''There is bright blood on your back, where a long strip of skin has been torn off. Your breasts and thighs are covered with dried blood...are you badly hurt?'' His voice was sharp with anxiety. "You couldn't talk if you were badly hurt, could you?"

I looked down, and realized that I must be a terrible sight to one who loved me. "It is not my blood, it's T'cha's. I had to lie on him when the roof of the last tunnel was so low. The blood-clots were like slugs, Raki." I heard myself laughing and couldn't stop. "Great purple slugs, that I had to crush with my breasts...."

"Quiet, Piyanah!"

I didn't want to laugh at T'cha, but the laughter shook me as though I were a tree in a gale too strong for it to withstand.

Raki picked me up, and I clung to him, trying to stifle against his shoulder the horrible sound I was making. I heard a splash as he stepped into a small pool; and then felt the sting of sharp water as he held me under a little waterfall. I gasped as the water poured over me, and then went limp.

"Lie still, Piyanah." He rested my head in the crook of his arm and scrubbed me with sand and then with handfuls of leaves until my body was clean.

Then I was lying on warm turf with him beside me: everything was safe and ordinary again. The caverns were no longer part of me; they were only a story to be told at the watch-fires of the future, for I could look at them through the eyes of a new Piyanah.

"Shall I tell them that I killed T'cha?" I said.

"Not until we have asked Na-ka-chek."

"Where is he?"

"Waiting to give you the Scarlet."

"Does he know I have won?"

Raki smiled. "He waded into the river to catch the prow of your canoe, but you seemed only to see me. Tekeeni and Gorgi and Dorrok were there too...."

"But they were on the other side of the caverns. How did they reach here so quickly?"

"Look at the sun. It has travelled a long way since you went into the darkness."

torch-light

Watch-fires were flowering in the dusk when I reached the encampment of the Yellow Skins. I went alone between the carved poles of the entrance, into the circle of silent people who waited round the bier of the youth whom they had hoped would lead their tribe after his father.

The men were naked, their bodies smeared with white ash in sign of mourning. They stared at me, their eyes heavy with hostility. They had known I was coming, for it is the custom for the victor of a challenge to say farewell to the vanquished. They hated me because I proved that the caverns were not an impossible ordeal: they hated me because they thought I had brought T'cha's body home to them only as a further humiliation: they hated me because they were no longer confident that it was safe to despise their squaws.

Pine torches were burning at the head and at the feet of the corpse, at the left hand and at the right hand, so that he should not go in darkness, whether he travelled to the north or the the south, to the east or to the west. The Chief, his face was stone, stood beside his son. Slowly he raised his right hand in greeting. He would fulfill the courtesies due to one who had gained the right to join the Feathered Council of the future, but I knew he would sooner have cut off that hand than raise it in greeting to a squaw.

If I spoke only the formal farewell that was expected of me, no one would ever know that I had killed T'cha...except Raki, and he would not tell even Na-ka-chek since I had decided that I must come to my own decision. The Yellow Skins might kill me; claiming that it was a just vengeance for the murder of a wounded man. But if I kept silence I should always know that the integrity of which I was proud had only been strong enough to show a small flame in the darkness of the caverns, and had flickered and died at the challenge of the sun.

I could hear my voice, but it sounded as though someone else was speaking, someone who stood close to me but was yet separate from Piyanah.

"Chief of the Yellow Skins, Father of T'cha, I speak to you in the equality of the children of the Great Hunters. Each tribe is protected by a different totem: yet all totempoles are but an echo of the trees which grow in the Land beyond the Sunset, and the spirit of all totems is an echo of the voice of the Lords of the Morning. In this recognition, all totems are carved from the same tree, and all men are brothers.

"Because T'cha and I are brothers, I gave to him that clemency which he would not have denied to me. He had called on me for succour and I gave him freedom. If I had kept him shackled to his body he would have known agony beyond the fortitude of warriors. If he had lived to be old, the pride of T'cha would have crumbled under the slow drip of pity, which is the only water he would have been given to slake his thirst.

"I asked the Great Hunters that I might judge with integrity. And when they answered, I asked that I might find within me the courage to set him free for the journey to their country. Water and rocks had crushed his legs and thighs: but it was a stone in my hands which crushed the bone above his temple."

A murmur spread through the watching crowd. "Death! Death to the woman who has killed T'cha! Death...."

Hatred was coiled like vipers in a circle round me.

"If T'cha could speak to you he would acknowledge my friendship!"

"Death! Death for the squaw who has killed T'cha!"

Their hatred was a dark flood lapping closer and closer towards me. I seized one of the funerary torches and held it high above my head.

"By this light in my hand I pledge my body and my spirit that I am not the enemy of T'cha, and that my people on

194

the other side of the water have heard my voice calling to them to welcome him in friendship."

"She has killed T'cha. Vengeance! Kill her! Kill her!"

Hatred was dark as wolves approaching a kill. The Chief leaned over the body of his son. "Speak, T'cha. Does she speak in truth? Or do you cry to us for vengeance?"

The sudden silence was sharp as ice. The Chief was staring down at the face of the dead boy. Did he expect the mouth to open and words to come forth that would bring me freedom or condemnation?

Slowly the Chief raised his head, but he was not looking at me nor at his tribe. It was as though he looked, with slowly increasing recognition, into the eyes of someone who stood beside me. He held out his hands, to set them on the shoulders of his son who to the rest of us remained invisible.

Then his hands fell to his sides. He lifted his head to watch T'cha go away from him, between the mourners, between the carved posts which marked their boundary, towards the river.

Very gently he took the torch from my hand, and held it above his head, as I had done.

"By this torch I pledge my word and the word of my people, that on this side of the water, and beyond the water also, the blood of T'cha is the blood of brotherhood between the Yellow Skins and the Two Trees. For my son, who was dead, has come home to me, brought home as was his body, by the courage of the Scarlet."

Then he took from his great headdress a scarlet feather and put it in my forehead-thong.

And I went the way T'cha had gone, and in silence the people watched me go...but Raki waited for me on this side of the river.

I had said, "We must go to tell Na-ka-chek that there is peace between us and the Yellow Skins," but when we reached his Great Tepee it was empty. Then I realized that the circle of the council was curiously quiet, and a solitary Elder sat smoking by the watch-fire. He looked up as we passed, and said:

"A Scarlet Feather should be as proud of his courtesy as of his courage." Then, as we did not answer, he added, "The Chief of the Two Trees gives a great feast in the place of his tribe. The Feathered Council wait to join with Na-ka-chek in honour of his daughter. The clothes you should both wear have been put ready in his tepee."

"I told Dorrok to prepare a feast," I said slowly, "but it was only to try to make him believe I was going to come back."

"The Chief can command his tribe without asking permission of his daughter." The words were cold, but the old man was smiling. "But I must not delay you with conversation, or those who wait for you will grow impatient."

I must have been seen leaving the Great Tepee, and some prearranged signal given: for as I turned towards our encampment the scattered torch-light began to flow into two streams, an avenue of fire to lead me home.

From every tribe they had come, to roar against the night the chants that welcome a warrior in victory. Now I knew why Raki had said he would run ahead to tell Na-ka-chek why I had kept him waiting. He would not share this triumph with me because the scarlet feather divided us. I wanted to tear it from my forehead-thong and break it in pieces: to show them that a squaw valued her love more than their insignia.

The sparks from the torches flared into the air like burning rain returning to the sky. Slowly I walked on, my right hand raised in greeting. The chants were like a strong wind driving me before it..."Piyanah the Warrior is triumphant...the bison call her brother...."

The chant of the Leaping Waters, "Piyanah is the brother of the strong river and the rapids are proud to give her challenge."

"The sun of her heart shall be warm even in winter, and

the trees of her years heavy with fruit," sang the Smiling Valleys.

Then ahead of me I heard the song of my own people. My heart felt as though it would break out of the stockade of my ribs.... "Piyanah has come home to us. Piyanah to whom the white birches are calling, 'Little Sister, take us for your canoe.' Piyanah, to whom the arrows are calling, 'Let us dream of victory in your quiver until we may leap from your bowstring.' "

This was much more than a surge of sound on which I was swept along like a twig in a swift current: it was the voices of people I knew and loved. Dorrok, who had led me in search of courage. Tekeeni, whose laughter had taken me out of despair. Gorgi who had shared with me his pride and kindliness. Narrok, who had let me see his far horizon and taught me to honour the vision of my own eyes. It was at their torches I had kindled my own; their light which I had carried with me through the caverns.

I had been unarmed, and they had given me the weapons that they now proclaimed as mine. The arrows of will; the bow of integrity; the moccasins of questioning and ambition; the forehead-thong of understanding; the shield of impassivity and hard endurance. They had shared with me their hearts, by which at last I could uphold a torch in shining company with them. I had thought that Raki and I were alone together, following the light of our single star. Now I knew that all stars are sparks from the torch of the Lord of the Morning. I knew that people do not belong to a tribe only because they need the protection of each other against famine and cold and enemies. They can give nothing until they have heard the singing. Neither have they courage, nor endurance, nor wisdom, nor the skill of a craft, until it has been shared with them. Each torch must be kindled from a living brand; and unless that torch seeks other brands to kindle soon does it gutter and grow cold.

For so long I had fought to prove that I was not a squaw

197

dependent on men, that I had forgotten that all men are dependent on mankind. I had been a drop of water, and now I was part of a great river: I had been a sapling stripped by the gales of winter, and now I was a forest: I had been a grain of corn alone in the grinding-bowl, and now I belonged to the rhythm of the growing field. I had been alone because I had been too blind, too proud, too deaf to know the company which sings beyond the cold lore of a tribe.

The knowledge of the company stayed with me through the night of feasting. The Chiefs were men of my father's generation, yet they were no longer remote because they were proud with feathers: they were men who had shared the judgments of the council and so could share more than mead and wild-duck basted with honey; they could share laughter and humanity.

The Scarlet Feathers and the Braves no longer stared at me in hostility, for I had been accepted as one of themselves. Our women joined in the feast as equals, and this had not happened even in the memory of the ancestors.

Raki nodded towards one of the Leaping Waters who was sharing a cup of mead with Rokeena, and whispered to me, ''If the stars see this they will think that the time of the Before People is returned.''

''Tomorrow they shall see that women can do more than share mead.''

And this was so, for Father agreed that our women could issue a challenge to twenty men from any other tribe with arrows and sling shot. Whether the women won, which they did three times out of fifteen, or whether they lost, they shared the sunset meal with their opponents...who a moon ago would have mocked anyone who said they acknowledged a squaw as worthy to join in a contest with them.

But this belonged to tomorrow, for Raki and I were still watching Rokeena and the Leaping Water.

''You are a man as well as a woman now, Piyanah,'' said Raki. ''You could lead a tribe alone....''

"No, Raki! I can do nothing without you. You know that, Raki, you must know it."

He took my hands in both of his. "Of course we shall be together always...I only said that you *could* rule a tribe alone. But if the Great Hunters remember their own youth they will never make it necessary."

Soon it was dawn, and the Chiefs were going back to the tepees of the council. The last of the torches were quenched, and those who drowsed with mead stirred in the grey light and slept on.

Raki and I went down to the river, where he spread a blanket on the short, dry grass. We fell asleep as the sun was coming up over the hills, for we had promised Na-ka-chek not to share a tepee.

Ordeals for the Scarlet

Although the Chiefs, and those who would succeed them in the Feathered Council, had gathered on the bank of the river to watch me enter the Caverns of Darkness, I had not realized that they did so only because it was their custom to watch the Ordeals of the Scarlet, until I went to Na-ka-chek's tepee the following morning. He warned me that it would not be easy to remain impassive if I had to see brave men die because the limit of their endurance had been passed.

"Remember, Piyanah, that to show sympathy would only make their task more difficult. I won my Scarlet by the ordeal of fire; twenty small tribal marks, branded into my body. The burns were not deep and healed before the next moon, but they chose each place so that it should bring the greatest intensity of pain...the soft skin of the arm-pit, inside the thighs, under the instep. It was not easy to breathe slowly and deeply, not to allow a single gasp of pain, to keep the muscles of my face smooth and untroubled.

"I was nearly defeated because I heard a woman whimper when she saw smoke curling up from my right nipple which the brand was charring. Until then I had been alone with pain, and could keep separate from it because it was an enemy I must fight. I was not Na-ka-chek, son of the Chief; I was Na-ka-chek the symbol of Man, who down the generations had fought with pain...and won. The compassion of that woman dragged me back to reality. I was no longer man against pain; I was a man suffering pain that was part of himself. Instead of being a solitary champion I knew there were people to whom I could appeal for help; there was no need for me to fight alone. Pain was an enemy whom I deliberately invited to pass through the stockade of my dwelling. I had summoned him to afflict me; how then could I call on the courage of the years to fight at my side? It was the last brand of the twenty, and my small mortality was just sufficient to endure it...had it been even the nineteenth, Na-ka-chek would have flinched, would have cried out, would have betrayed the Scarlet."

"If that woman had loved you," I said, "she would have given you strength, not weakness. She could have sent her courage and endurance to enter you, instead of whimpering with the pain she felt at the sight of your suffering. Raki and I learned this when we were undergoing the ordeals of the brown feather. He gave me his strength, not his fear; his belief that I would win, not his terror that I might fail. When I went through the caverns he was part of me: he made me believe that together we were stronger than the dark water. The love between us was clear as the star we shall set in the sky; his was the extra strength in my arms that held the canoe steady in the torrent, the thrust on the paddle which kept me out of the vortex, the bar of light which showed me the way out of the caverns; and it was his voice which called to me from the green water between the rocks of the last rapid. He took on himself the anguish we both felt when we knew danger might part us; he took my fear into his own belly, so that my body was steady and I could think clearly. It is very difficult to learn that quality of love, to be able to say, 'Give me your fear, and I will carry it'; instead of wailing because love has made you vulnerable to so many tears.''

''You share wisdom with your mother, Piyanah; and I am very proud that two such women have let me honour them.''

He saw that I was moved at this betrayal of emotion, yet instead of becoming immediately remote, as he had always done before when he found himself displaying warm humanity, he smiled and put his hand on my shoulder, saying:

''Na-ka-chek in his own way tried to give you his strength during the days when you needed it. When he parted you and Raki he lived again through the parting from your mother; when he called you back from your little valley he woke from his dream of happiness, which for three moons he had found in the birch woods of the summer weather. It has not been easy, my daughter, never to show you the kindliness and understanding that your mother had made part of your ordinary days: so many times I have longed to talk to you about her, so that in your words I might hear an echo of her voice. I wanted to cherish you because you are her daughter, and I have had to drive you to further endurance because you are my son.

''I made Raki live as a squaw not only because I knew it was vital to the building of the bridge over the canyon, but also because in him I made expiation. I betrayed your mother because I feared that if a woman shared my tepee the Braves would forget to honour the scarlet of my forehead-thong. Yet I made Raki become as a woman: I saw him pluck the arrows of mockery from his flesh, and clean the poison from the wounds with water from the spring of understanding. So many arrows he suffered, and his flesh is clean...and I, Na-ka-chek, the Chief honoured by his tribe, knew that I had fled from the threat of one such arrow, lest I die from the fester of the wound.''

''Dear Father!'' I smiled. ''Do you know I have never dared to call you that before, even in my heart? Since I entered your tepee only a little while ago, we have been sitting cross-legged on a coloured blanket, or so it would seem to anyone who watched, yet we have built a bridge over *our* canyon. There is no longer a gulf between us over which I can only see you proud with feathers against the night sky, as Raki and I saw you long ago, after we had made the first journey. We no longer have to shout commands, or promise obedience, or proclaim laws in loud clear voices: we can talk, Father, of the things that live in our hearts, softly, and without considering the words.''

''Yes, Piyanah,'' he said, very gently. ''We have crossed our canyon; and the first thing I must bring to you by that bridge is...Fear. The first thing I shall say to you as we stand side by side will betray a promise to Raki.''

I felt fear writhe inside me like a snake. ''What promise?'' I said, trying to keep my voice level.

''That I should not tell you he had demanded the right to an Ordeal of the Scarlet. He did so when he was sure that you were going to accept the caverns. He said, 'Piyanah and I will always be equals and wear feathers of the same colour.' It was not his pride that spoke, Piyanah, but because he knew there was a very small chance that you would live through the ordeal. If you came back from the caverns he would honor your Scarlet with his own: if you waited for him on the other side of the water the ordeal might let him join you without bringing dishonour to the tribe.''

The horrors of ordeals of which I had heard but not yet seen flashed through my mind. Raki smeared with honey while fire-ants covered him with a black pall. Raki's flesh charring while sweat ran down his expressionless face and his eyes spoke of pain which his proud lips would not acknowledge. Raki falling from the precipice, when his bleeding fingers slipped from the last narrow crack: his body turning over in the air before the cruel teeth of the waiting rocks crushed it to pulp.

''Which ordeal must he pass?'' And I was surprised that my voice sounded as though I was asking an ordinary question.

''The Eagle Rock.''

Narrok's ordeal! Then Raki might be blind too. Was he already thinking, when he looked at the sky, ''I must fill my eyes with that strong, clear blue and cherish the shape of the clouds, so that they will stay with me through the long night.'' Was he thinking, ''I must not stare at Piyanah, or she will guess that something is wrong. I shall always remember Piyanah's face, and the way she moves, and her skin, warm with the colour of deep autumn. But I shall never see her smiling down at our children, or her serenity when we are growing old.''

''The Eagle Rock is considered less dangerous than the caverns, Piyanah,'' said my father. ''You must believe, we *must* believe that the Great Hunters would not have brought us so far along the path only to lead us to a cliff that cannot be climbed. At sunset the tribe will rejoice that both my children are of the Scarlet.''

''Yes, Father, we must rejoice....''

I knew Raki would be wondering, ''How long can I keep Piyanah from knowing? Should I have told her yesterday, so that she had time to prepare herself for the ordeal of watching me...which will be so much worse than my having to dive? Will she understand why I did not tell her until the last moment, or will hurt bewilderment be the last thing I shall see in her eyes?''

Raki was with some of the other Chiefs' sons outside the tepees, waiting to join the procession to the Place of the Ordeals. I went to him, trying desperately to make my voice sound undisturbed.

''Tomorrow you will wear the Eagle's Scarlet.''

"Then...you know?"

"Yes, and I know you are going to win, Raki. You have never been afraid of heights, and I know the Great Hunters will make the pool deep, and safe...and easy."

"So you are not worried about me?"

"A little...but I have been afraid for you so many times, Raki, and nothing ever went wrong. This time I know we are going to be safe. The feathers of the future will be like wings on which you will glide down on the air...our wings, the past and the future keeping today in safety."

"I am sure I shall be safe, Piyanah," he said confidently. "I ought to have told you yesterday, but I was so abysmally frightened when you were in the caverns that I didn't want you to be disturbed by the same demon...the demon made out of imaginary horrors."

"I am glad you didn't tell me until today. It is so much more difficult to be certain of security when you are half asleep and very tired...."

There was no more time for us to talk, for we had to follow Father in the procession of Chiefs.

We stood on the edge of the pit of rattle-snakes. The man had been down in the pit since dawn, and now it was nearly noon. There were five snakes, sliding among the small stones at the bottom of the pit: one had begun to rattle angrily and was coiled to strike. Another was flowing over a bare foot whose toes were clenched to the sand with the effort of remaining motionless.

I knew the man was terrified, for his body was slimy with sweat and his coarse black hair clung to his skull as though he had been swimming. His feet were wide apart and the muscles of his legs and thighs were braced with the effort of standing still. A line of red on both wrists showed that he must have been clenching his hands to make the thongs, which bound them behind him, cut into his skin. I knew he had longed for this sharp, clean pain, to jerk him out of the swaying sickness brought by the crawling death in which he stood.

I am not sure how long it was before I knew that soon the tension which held him motionless was going to snap. The sun beat down into the pit and I could see the pupils of his eyes dilating and the flare of his nostrils as he tried to draw deep breaths to quieten his racing heart. The neck muscles stood out like thongs: then his head fell forward on his chest and he began to sway....

The first rattler got him behind the right knee and knocked him forward on his face. He fell on a second snake, and I saw it strike twice, full in the throat. He whimpered, like a frightened child, and tried to stagger upright, thrusting out with his pinioned hands.

A pole thudded down behind him and a Brave from the same tribe slid down into the pit and crushed two of the snakes with his tomahawk. Two other Braves flung fish-spears and killed the other snakes. When they carried the man up, the flesh round the punctured wounds was already beginning to turn black. They laid him on the ground and covered him with a blanket.

The Chiefs walked away. The man had failed in an ordeal; he would die; he was no longer of interest.

''Don't they even try to suck out the poison?'' I whispered to Raki.

''They would, if it would be of any use; but four rattlers got him, two in the throat. He will die soon...his tribe know it and so does he. They will be cutting wood for his funeral pyre before he is cold.''

Raki and I were part of a circle which might have been a council round a watch-fire, but instead of flames burning against the night a naked man stood motionless as a totem-pole, waiting for two Braves from different tribes to prepare him for his ordeal.

At a sign from his Chief—he belonged to the Thundering Herds—he lay on the ground, his feet wide apart, his arms outstretched on either side. His ankles and wrists were secured by thongs to wooden pegs driven into the ground.

On one side of him were placed two clay jars, and on the other a rush basket, plastered with mud and firmly covered.

One of the attendant Braves picked up the first jar and poured a stream of pale honey on the man's body; smoothing it evenly over the skin from the neck to a line midway between the navel and the dividing of the loins, from the shoulders to the elbows, and from the knees to the soles of the feet. Then from the second jar he scooped handfuls of what looked like heavy bear's grease, but it was nearly black and had a strong, pungent smell. With this he covered all the parts of the body that were not already glistening with honey, but left the face and head untouched.

When this was finished, the second Brave wrenched the cover from the basket and turned it over on its side. A dark stream that stirred like boiling pitch poured out; a stream which divided into spreading trickles...of ants. For a few moments they poured over the ground, questing in every direction: then they converged into three files and marched towards the feast which had been prepared for them.

The ants which tried to climb on the man's hand fell back and died when they touched the black grease, but the rest flowed steadily over their dead, to cover the body with terrible swiftness and purpose. A few strayed onto the face, which might still have been carven wood, even though I saw the lower lip begin to swell and a thin trickle of blood where an ant had torn a notch in the flesh.

Now he seemed to be wearing a tunic and leg coverings of black-red iridescence, that shimmered in the blazing sunlight as ants poured over each other in their lust for honey. I knew that if he moved they would attack as though a thousand war bows were loosed at the command of a Chief. Even if he managed to remain stock-still they might be hungry when they had finished the honey and decide to make a kill, to gorge on flesh; and ants can strip a carcass to clean bones with more terrible precision than buzzards.

Until then I had not seen the thread of honey leading away

from his right side to the half-empty jar. It was the narrow path which might lead them to march in search of fresh plunder; a narrow, shining path, which held the only hope of victory over this multitudinous enemy.

When I could no longer bear to look at the man's face, so terribly still above the quivering pall which covered his body, I tried to quell the queasiness of my belly by watching some of the Chiefs. There was a cold smile on the mouth of the Leaping Waters; to him this deliberate cruelty was a sensuous enjoyment, it held the warmth he had never found in women, the satisfaction deeper than a good smoke. The Chief of the Thundering Herds betrayed his inward anxiety only because his skin over his knuckles was pale with the strain of his clenched hands. He had taken care that his face was expressionless, that the muscles of shoulders and thighs were loosely flexed, but the hands betrayed his tension. Would he have understood a little of what I felt for Raki? Or was he thinking only of the honour of his tribe?''

Some of the older Chiefs, who must have seen this ordeal many times, did not have to pretend indifference: the ordeals were part of the tribal laws, a duty to be undertaken according to custom, but having no quality of horror or compassion. Only the Chief of the Smiling Valleys made no effort to conceal his repugnance; it was obvious that he attended the spectacle only because to refuse would have lost him the protection of the Thirty Tribes. He avoided looking at the ordeal; he let his pipe go out and then sent his son to fetch a brand from the nearest fire, and remained oblivious that this interruption was considered a breach of courtesy. He scratched his comfortable belly, slowly and reflectively, and then took off one moccasin and appeared to be entirely absorbed in taking a thorn from his foot. The pose of boredom was well done, but I knew he was feeling nearly as sick as I was. If we had not already decided that our tribe must go South, I should have known it then!

Suddenly a sigh went up from the watching circle. I

thought the ants had struck, and it was only with a strong muscular effort that I could turn my head to make myself see what had happened. The ants had found the new source of honey, and were surging towards it with such eagerness that in some places they were three or four deep on the ground. There were islands of skin showing among the black torrent; the islands widened, as though a river in flood was suddenly subsiding. There was still a thick black ring round his navel, where the rear-guards of the enemy host gorged themselves at the pool before seeking new hunting-grounds. Now less than a hundred remained; these seemed to hear an order from one of the leaders, for they scurried in the direction of the half-empty jar, plunging fearlessly off the precipice of knee or shoulder to stagger on through the forest of grass-blades.

The Chief of the Thundering Herds stood up, drew his hunting knife to slash through the thongs on the man's wrists and ankles, and lifted to his feet the man who had won new honour for his tribe. Then with his forefinger he traced the tribal mark on the forehead and breast of the Scarlet Feather. His son came forward and handed a lighted brand to the Chief, who set fire to the jar of honey on which the ants still feasted. The flames blazed up; it was the ants, not the man, which were no longer useful.

I expected to be able to speak with Raki before he went to prepare for his ordeal, but he must have decided it was easier for us both not to try to put our thoughts into words. A crowd had gathered on the slopes leading to the Eagle Rock, but I went with the Chiefs to join my tribe on the edge of the pool into which Raki must dive.

The deep water looked no larger than a long canoe and the crag towered into the sky above it. Could Raki see from up there that only a quarter of the pool was safe and that in the rest the treacherous rocks lurked just beneath the surface? Could he see them, or would the cloud shadows make him misjudge the colour of the water?

Dorrok, Gorgi, and Tekeeni were close to me, but I did

not notice Narrok until I heard a quiet voice say:

"He will not fail, Piyanah. He has not betrayed his eyes nor the light of his heart, as I had done. I was divided between the will to die and the will to live; that is why I was caught between the two sides of the water until you and Raki brought me fully to life again."

"He's ready!" It was a shout from someone in the crowd.

The height seemed to have made Raki look shorter and broader. Narrok gripped my arm: "In a moment he will be climbing out of the pool to stand beside you. Steady, Piyanah, give him your courage to keep him steady."

A groan went up from the crowd, as the body hurtled through the air, too close to the rock-face. Blank, unbelieving horror swept over me in a dark flood. I saw blood pouring like smoke through the water of the pool. Why does no one run forward to save Raki's body? I can't move. Why doesn't Dorrok go for me? Why are they letting a strange Chief touch Raki? Raki, whose face is only a pulp of red flesh....

I heard my father's voice, very far away yet solid as stone, "The Yellow Skin failed, Piyanah, but Raki will win!"

"The Yellow Skin?" I wanted to cry and laugh and scream with relief. The arm dangling from that crushed shoulder, from that dead body which T'cha's father carried in his arms, was not Raki's! It was yellow...it was not Raki's!

"Quiet, Piyanah!" Dorrok's voice, sharp and authoritative. I realized with shame that a convulsive sob had burst out of me.

"I'm sorry, Dorrok. I didn't know that two men were going to dive....I thought it was Raki. Why are they waiting, Dorrok?"

"For the blood to clear from the pool. It will not be long now."

A desperate call for help formed into words inside my head, "Great Eagle, please remember your rock and give the power of your wings to Raki. Great Fish, make him wise in water. Great Hunters, protect him, protect him..."

Raki stood far above me on the towering pinnacle; his hands stretched above his head as though he was thanking the Lords of the Sky. Slowly, so very slowly, he plunged down through the air; his body curved like a bow, his arms steady as gliding wings.

"He is going to do it! He is going to!" Dorrok was exultant.

I saw Raki flash by into the green water. I heard a shout of acclamation go up from the watching thousands. I saw him break surface, shaking the water from his eyes.

Then I felt his arm, wet and real and alive, round my shoulders. I was trying to thank the Great Hunters, trying not to fling my arms round him, trying to say calmly, "I knew you were going to be safe, Raki."

But most of all I was trying not to weep for joy; because our happiness was safe between our hands though I had thought it crushed to pulp at the foot of the Eagle Rock.

PART FOUR

Squaws' Choosing

The winter through which Raki and I waited as Scarlet
Feathers for the first spring moon, in which we should become the dual Chief of a new tribe, had the quality of that
pale quiet of early dawn which divides night from day. Since
childhood there had been barriers to separate us; now only
time kept us apart, time which flowed steadily as a river
without rapids, knowing neither spate nor summer drought.

Our women stayed in the small encampment we had built
for them away from the Squaws' Tepees, and the thirty who
had gone with us to the Gathering had now been joined by
five others who would make with us the journey to the South.
It was agreed that the men should also number thirty-five,
near our own age, so that each squaw should have a chance to
take a husband. There were, besides Dorrok, two older men
who wished to wear our tribal mark on their foreheads, Tenak
and Hajan, Scarlet Feathers with whom we had become
friends on our way home from the Gathering. Tenak chose to
come with us because he was always eager for adventure and
thought that in the South we might find a tribe even more
ferocious than the Black Feathers: Hajan because every year
he spent several moons away from the encampment to
explore country into which our people never penetrated. The
North and West were familiar to him, and he also knew of a
high pass over the mountains far to the South, to which he
would act as our guide.

We hoped that as many girls as possible would find
husbands before we made the journey, but neither Raki nor I
had expected that all thirty-five would be chosen by Braves
who were eager to fulfill the conditions of marriage under our

211

laws. Perhaps it was not only the squaws but also the call of far horizons that made them so eager to be accepted. No longer could young men wrestle with each other to see who should have the first choice of squaws; now they must play the same part as the males of the forest, using their feathers, their songs, their prowess to beguile the female; as though they were turkey cocks or stags instead of Redskins, who used to be so proud of being aloof.

Gorgi's choice surprised me. It was the girl called Cheka, whom four years ago I had seen gralloch a stag.

''You must not quarrel with her, Gorgi,'' I said, ''or she will take your hunting-knife to spill your bowels while you sleep. Is she still so greedy for the smell of warm blood?''

''No, Piyanah,'' said Gorgi gravely, ''I have made her forget her father, or at least the memory is fading—though it has been slow as taking a blood-stain out of white leather.''

''Her father? But surely she never knew his name?''

''It does not need a name to make a totem of hatred. He must have been very cruel when he took Cheka's mother into the woods, for it left the woman crazed with hatred. Cheka only joined us at first because she wanted to learn how to use a bow so as to revenge herself on men. It was not deer she gralloched, but the man who was her father; not fish whose bellies she slit open, but the belly of the nameless man who had driven her mother mad.''

''She hated Raki as she hated all men?''

''No, because she knew him as the 'not-man.' ''

''And were you a 'not-man' also, Gorgi? How did you make her long to put her arms round your neck instead of her hands to your throat?''

We were sitting on a fallen tree by a frozen stream, and, until I became interested, I had been drawing pictures in the snow with the end of my bow. Now I paused and looked at him.

''Tell me, Gorgi, *does* she think of you as a 'not-man' too?''

To avoid looking at me he pretended to be absorbed in taking a thorn out of his foot.

"Would you be shy, Gorgi, if you had tamed a mountain lion?"

"Yes, if it followed me only when I was running away! I expect it sounds very funny, Piyanah, so laugh if you want to; but I will tell you the truth even if it makes you want to laugh. I don't know why I chose Cheka. It was after I realized that no one except Raki ever meant anything to you—as a husband, I mean. I was jealous of Raki, and angry with you for preferring him to me; and being angry and jealous made me lonely. And Cheka was lonely too, for the other girls didn't like her, perhaps because they thought she was savage, or else because they recognized she was more beautiful than any of them. I did everything I could to make Cheka admire me; if I thought she was watching I would do the most dangerous thing—a dive the others said was impossible, or a rock climb that made me sweat with fright. I wore new tunics and put bear's grease on my hair. I made a canoe for her. But she remained indifferent. Then I fell out of a tree, of all the stupid, ridiculous things to do, and hit my head on a stone! It was noon when I fell and nearly sunset when I woke up; and I thought I must have died and gone to the Hunting-Grounds! My head was on Cheka's lap and she was kissing me and crying because she thought I was dead."

He sighed, "Women are difficult to understand, Piyanah, even when you love them. It was after she loved me that she told me about hating her father. Now she can't even see someone else clean a dead animal without feeling sick—much less do it herself."

I wasn't sure what to say about Cheka, so I said, "I'm glad Rokeena has chosen Tekeeni."

"Yes, I always thought she would after he stopped her being ashamed of the scar on her leg. They are like each other, Rokeena and Tekeeni, kind and loyal, and not very clever."

We sat in companionable silence for a while and then Gorgi said suddenly, "There is a question I have wanted to ask you for a long time; and if it's one you don't want to answer—well, could you forget I ever asked it?"

"Of course, Gorgi."

"Do you and Raki know exactly what men and women do when they go into the woods? I mean, have you done it yourselves, not just been told about it?"

"Yes, Gorgi, we have."

He gave a long sigh of relief. "After the Black Feathers?" I nodded and he went on, "Tekeeni and I thought you had, though we didn't know much about it then. At the Gathering some of the warriors from other tribes talked about women— usually it was after the feast when they were drunk. They boasted a lot, but they didn't say anything practical. Cheka says she wouldn't be frightened of me, but I keep on remembering the man who drove her mother mad. I'd kill myself if Cheka went even a little mad because of something I did. Is it dreadful for squaws, Piyanah?"

"It's lovely for squaws—if both people love each other. You have only to watch deer, or chipmunks, or even gophers, to see they both enjoy the magic. It only becomes squalid and dreadful when it gets snared in the cruel briars of taboos."

He looked so solemn that I tried to make him laugh.

"Lying down is very pleasant when you do it on moss or beaver pelts, but horrid if you do it on a thorn bush. Cheka's mother got thorns, but Cheka won't."

"Thank you, Piyanah, for telling me," he said fervently, "and could you tell Cheka too?"

"I think she'll have to wait to find out for herself. Raki and I discussed whether we should tell the others and he said no, because if we did they might refuse to wait until the spring moon. It's only fifty-three days now, so it won't hurt them to wait a little longer."

"But why should they wait?"

"Because," I said firmly, "women whose bellies are big

with child might be difficult on a journey. I want us to find our place of the corn-growing before we have babies.''

''But you and Raki didn't have a baby,'' objected Gorgi.

''That was very thoughtful of the Great Hunters; but now we know that babies are one of the things which happen when you use the magic we mustn't expect them to look after us again. Of course it may be quite a long time before they decide that the child Raki and I are going to have is ready to be born, but I don't think it's fair to shout to the child and say, 'We're ready for you,' unless we are. And I shall be too busy helping Raki, until we get the tribe settled, to be able to think enough about what kind of body our son would like, and how he would want to be born.''

Na-ka-chek

Na-ka-chek had gone to the pool of the falling water, there to tell my mother that at the fullness of the growing moon his oath to her would be fulfilled. I knew he believed that the dark water would suddenly become thin and luminous so that he could see through it into her country, as though he, from a narrow cave, looked on a scene of brilliant sunlight in the far distance. He would recognize her among the shining people, and call to her for a sign to show him she had remembered, and forgiven.

I had often tried to tell him that the Land beyond the Sunset is not remote, that those who dwell there can walk with us in close companionship, though their voice is silence and their laughter the dance of the leaves. But this he refused to believe, saying, ''I have made a vow, Piyanah, and only when it is fulfilled can I call to her again.''

I knew that my mother loved him, and so would not wait on vows. She would not think of him at the pool of the falling

215

water, but in solitude she must so often have tried to comfort him. So every night, as the moon flowed up the current of the sky, I went to the Great Tepee where he had lived alone with his thoughts of her. I talked to her aloud, though I knew that her people did not depend on sound for hearing.

"Mother, make him believe that you are close to him, as you are close to me; not only when I am in danger, or pain, or sorrow, but also in the ordinary days. He is staring down into the pool which took your body from him: a light gleams in the dark water; for a moment he thinks it is a faint reflection of the torch you are carrying through the echoing caverns which separate your country from this little earth. He is calling your name to guide you to him. Then there is silence, for he knows that the light is only the reflection of a star; a cloud drifts over the moon and the wind is sorrowful among the trees.

"Don't let him be alone any more, Mother. He is only austere because he dare not remember the joy he threw away: he is only aloof because he is so very lonely. I used to think he was cold and without understanding....I hated him, Mother, for I thought he was trying to take me away from Raki. I thought he was jealous of our happiness because he had lost his own. But he was not harsh because we were strangers, he was harsh because he thought we were part of him; and it is difficult, Mother, for a Scarlet Feather to be kind to himself.

"He has often said to me, 'The courage of your mother was so much greater than mine; and I betrayed her. Her wisdom was like a sun, and I tried to make her blind.' He thought you would only accept him if he gained even more endurance, that you could love him only if he gained the wisdom of a hundred Elders.''

I knew that she heard me, and yet each sunset showed me that he had not heard her: I waited for him in the forest clearing through which he would pass on his way home, and then when he did not come I went back to the tepee among the lengthening shadows.

On the fifth night I knew she was so close that she was almost tangible. Was it a shadow, or could I see her standing by the entrance? Then she was moving ahead of me past the silent tepees, and I followed her. Above the encampment she paused, by the rock beyond which she would not let us pass when we were children. I knew she wanted me to take off my clothes and leave them on the rock: for insignia which set people apart from each other did not belong to the path by which she was leading me.

The moss was cool and deep under my feet which were echoing the rhythm of her going. I was secure because she took me with her, as Raki and I had not been secure since we were children. Now I was running, swift and effortless, for I knew she tarried to keep pace with my mortality.

In the sound of the falling water there was singing, slow and measured. I went forward gently, no longer impatient, for the sound was free of time. In it there was the eagerness of fire yet no urgency, for this light need not tremble with the effort of giving heat unsparingly before the kindling-wood cut short its span. Here was growth without death, joy without sorrow, swiftness without tiring, for yesterday and tomorrow linked hands and knew themselves twin sisters.

Then I was standing near the foot of the fall, and could see Na-ka-chek through a mist of spray. He was sitting cross-legged, deep in thought. Or had he fallen asleep, for his head bent forward as though bowed by the weight of the feathered headdress. Another mist was rising beyond the fall: a bright mist like sunlight seen beyond a curtain of rain. In this mist there were people...two people, and they were young yet rich with years.

I knew that for them the moon shone always between the same two trees: and they were timeless. I could not see them, yet I knew their arms were warm about each other: I could not hear them, yet I knew they laughed, and whispered

217

the sweet truths of lovers united.

I knew that my voice, my sight, my hearing had become a bridge between them, though this in a manner I could not understand: and that my recognition would carry the reality even to the waking Na-ka-chek, whose body wore feathers by a pool while his spirit gloried in his freedom.

Slowly, as though still half-asleep, he stood upright. He lifted the feathers from his head and took off the heavy ceremonial robes. Naked and strong as a tree, he stood with his hands upstretched towards the sky.

"Great Hunters, I am no longer alone!" Warmth, and strength, and security were in his voice. Then he threw back his head and laughed; strong, resonant laughter of a man in whose heart gladness is an urgent spring which must gush forth.

He looked round, as though startled by the sound of his laughter; as was I who had never heard it before. He saw me, but without surprise, finding it natural for me to be there, as Raki would have done.

"It is not usual for a man to laugh because he rejoices that he was a fool...and I have been very foolish, my Piyanah... but what does it matter, now that I have come home? Narrok can see without eyes, but I had eyes and refused to open them. It is good not to be blind or proud or lonely. It was foolish to climb a mountain by a precipice when there was a smooth path to follow, but it is good to reach the peak. It was foolish to make a journey in winter, when the river would have been easy for canoes after the ice had melted; but even the fool may rejoice when he reaches the valley. Sit here beside me, my Piyanah, and hear why your father knows he was a fool and in that knowledge has found rejoicing.

"I caused myself, and all those under my authority, to suffer, to strive, to choose always the more difficult of two ways: and all this I did to try to become worthy of your mother. The scarlet feathers in my headdress, and your feathers and Raki's also, I strove for so that I might have something worthy to offer in exchange for her forgiveness. I was going to offer her my pride, my courage, my endurance, and the honour of my tribe; the courage, and enterprise, and freedom that you and Raki have won, and the future of your feathers, in exchange for a single word of recognition. I must give everything to her, and then perhaps, if it were enough, she might allow a bright gleam from her sun to pierce the darkness of the pool which hid her from me. So many fine and sonorous protestations I have made to her, here in the last five days...and none of them she heard!

"Then I began to think of you...you grow very like her, Piyanah, even in your body. I began to wonder what I should say to you if you were going away...as so soon you are going away, and I wanted to be sure you would remember me. Would you want to hear of the pride I feel in you, or the way I honour your courage, and your wisdom, and your endurance? Then I thought, 'How can I know what Piyanah would want unless I know my own heart? What would I want Piyanah to say to me before she went away?' It was easy then, for I knew above all things I should want to hear, 'I love you, Na-ka-chek.'

"You nearly said that once, on the morning after you won your Scarlet. Do you remember how you smiled and said, 'Dear Father'...and then said, 'I never called you that before...we have built a bridge over our canyon'? I wanted to say then, 'I love you, Piyanah,' but I thought a Chief and a Scarlet Feather could not open their hearts even to each other, without betraying them. Then I knew what your mother would want to hear, if my voice still held any meaning for her.

"I said, 'I love you'; over and over again, in an ordinary voice as though she were sitting beside me and could hear everything. The words seemed to find an echo in the pool, and I thought the water was throwing them back to me. But it was not an echo, Piyanah; it was her voice! I saw her; it was natural to take her in my arms, and for both of us to smile at the man sitting by the pool, the man who had tried to barter for love by the power of the feathers which had forgotten their singing.

"Once I thought that love was a word used only by a man and woman who in the summer weather had forgotten their duty to the tribe; now I have learned that it is stronger than war cries, and in it is the wisdom of the generations. It is the way of knowledge of the Elders, and the Scarlet of warriors; it is the feathers of the bird of the morning, and the canoe by which the living and the dead cross the great river. It is the full moon and the high sun, the living rain and the heat of the growing. Love!—the single voice by which the wearers of the Singing Feathers can know their kindred, and themselves."

Chief of the heron

During the winter our people had made for us the tepee of a Chief. It was of double hides, painted with scenes through which Raki and I had lived; two figures standing on a pass, watching a column of black smoke, the scalping of the Black Feathers, a canoe entering the Caverns of Darkness, Raki diving from the Eagle Rock; but much of it remained undecorated, for as yet our people had no tribal history to record. Instead of a centre-post it was supported by eight poles, of birch-wood, which is light to carry, carved with birds and animals between bands of the white and scarlet we had chosen for our tribal colours. On the day before we became Chief it would be taken up to the place where my mother's tepee had been set when Na-ka-chek came to this new place of the corn-growing. There we should begin the Moon of the Uniting, which henceforward would be the name given by our tribe to the first spring moon to commemorate that men

220

and women rejoiced together before setting forth on their journey to the South.

The preparations for this journey were almost complete. Each man had made a piece of tanned leather, his height by twice his height, to be hung over a cross-bar or a low branch to form a shelter in which he and his woman would sleep. Nearly everything we were to take with us must be new. The men had been making tomahawks, bows both for hunting and war, fish-spears, coils of raw-hide rope. The women were busy with leather sacks to carry pemmican or corn, water-skins, tunics, fur robes; in plaiting fishing lines, or collecting feathers to fletch arrows.

Ten of the squaws, led by Rokeena, were making marriage robes for Raki and me, and as they wished them to be kept secret until we wore them I had to whistle before entering the largest of the women's tepees so that they had time to hide them. I knew that they were of white doe-skin because I had seen a few shreds of this lying beside the blanket in which they were wrapped, and suspected they would be decorated with feathers, as Tekeeni had brought back a number of blue jays which he said were for Rokeena.

I made the ceremonial moccasins for Raki—though I often regretted the pride which would not let me give them to someone else to finish; setting beads, as I admitted to Gorgi, needs far more patience than stalking a mountain goat. He appreciated what I meant, for early in the winter we had gone into the mountains, and stayed there seven days before we killed the first of the eight rams that provided the fine, white fleeces which are used for a Chief's blankets.

All Chiefs, before they take their oath to the tribe, fast for two days and two nights; drinking only water at sunrise and sunset. They must not lie down or sleep, but sit cross-legged in a tepee set apart, so that if the Great Hunters speak to them, even in a whisper soft as a falling leaf, their voice will be clearly heard. For this fasting the tepees in which Raki and I had lived alone since we became Scarlet Feathers were taken up to opposite ends of the semicircle of cliffs. During this period of separation, which was a symbol of all that we had undergone to gain a yet closer unity, he wore the squaw's tunic that he had put on at our first parting, and I the breech-clout, breast-bandage, and roughly patched tunic which belonged to that same bitter loneliness.

I knew that below me in the encampment preparations for the marriage feast were being made, yet all was silence, for no one spoke above a whisper lest we who listened be disturbed. In thought I returned to that night when as children we had watched my mother and father looking towards each other, divided by so much more than the curve of the cliffs. Between Raki and me love sang like a bowstring, and the love of our tribe would be the arrow which should leap from that bow towards the sun.

A marriage between equals had not taken pace in any tribe during the memory of the ancestors, yet when I had asked Na-ka-chek what words Raki and I should use to pledge our oath of eternity, he had said, ''Your mother has told me it is her wish that I shall speak the words which will make you one at the dawn hour. Then, as the new Chief, you and Raki shall unite those men and women who wish to follow the path on which you are their forerunners.''

''What words shall we use to unite our people?''

''It is your hearts which must tell you that: but the words must be like living water fresh from the spring, for words and water grow stagnant if they are stored away. Your mother told me that the bright river which joins her country to our own must be ever flowing, that though the stream may echo the same wisdom, ripple after ripple, it must always be fresh and alive to keep its keen vitality.''

''Then, Father, is no wisdom of any value unless it is seen today?''

''Wisdom is always better than no wisdom; for is not stale water precious in a desert? But if we walk in company with the Before People we shall never know drought, for when we

222

are thirsty we can cup our hands at the ever-living spring.''

At moonrise on the second day I heard singing, many voices joined together, rising up from the circle of tepees. With difficulty I got to my feet, for my legs were cramped from sitting so long in one position. I unlaced the tepee-flap so that I could see out. Two lines of torch-bearers were winding up by the cliff paths, one towards me, the other towards Raki, coming to prepare us for the marriage.

The leading women carried logs of wood, soaked in resin to make them leap into flame at the first touch of a torch, and built a fire on the platform of bare rock outside the tepee. I had to keep silence until I spoke the oath with Raki, but it was good to give myself to their ministrations for I was tired after the ordeal. Four women, among them Rokeena, entered carrying jars of steaming water scented with balsam. On the ground they spread coloured blankets; then they washed my hair and my body and rubbed my aching muscles with pine-oil.

I lay naked by the fire, drowsy with the kindly heat until I was warm and dry: then I slept in the tepee until they brought the marriage robe. It was more beautiful than any I had seen—even at the Gathering—embroidered with white and scarlet beads, with the feathers of orioles and jays; stitched with the hair of the women who had made it. I was to wear my mother's necklaces, scarlet and blue and white, and a forehead-band of scarlet breast-feathers; even my hair was plaited with strands of white and scarlet wool.

Across the lake of shadows which lapped against the cliffs I could see the fire which the men had built for Raki. The moon was already low in the sky. Could Raki hear his heart thudding as I heard mine, thudding as though we had been climbing a high mountain and were nearing the peak? Suddenly, as though lit by a single torch, thirty other great fires sprang into life round the curve of the cliffs. This was the signal for which I had been waiting; for moons, for years, perhaps for generations.

As I walked down the path towards the Totem, the women followed, carrying their torches in single file behind me. I saw the moving plumes of Raki's torch-bearers: each procession so faithful an echo that they might have been reflected in still water.

The white stone, which had once been the boundary beyond which we must not pass, had been carried down and set before the Totem. On it were three bowls of red clay painted with white designs, and in front of these three wooden platters, all carrying emblematic objects to be used in the ceremony. I remember being surprised that I noticed even such small details as a single grain of corn which had spilled from the central bowl; for I had expected to be aware only of Raki.

Side by side we stood before the Chief: behind us the men and women to whom we in turn would hand on the unity which the words we were to hear would bring to us. In the torch-light Na-ka-chek's face had the same quality of time-lessness as had the Totem, both wood and flesh might have been carved by the same hand. The brown and white and scarlet feathers of his headdress seemed to have a winged life of their own. No one could have looked at him without awe, nor—and this I realized for the first time—without feeling a new strength, a new courage, and a new love, from some hidden source of life to which he belonged.

I had thought he would use words rich and sonorous, as though the Lord of the Trees spoke of the sky, but his voice was curiously gentle and intimate. He might have been alone with Raki and me instead of in the hearing of the whole tribe.

''Raki and Piyanah, the Great Hunters have allowed me to welcome you at my place of the corn-growing, so that we might learn of each other and remember that which was lost, and so search until it be found. The laws of my tribe divided you, but you have built a bridge over the canyon. That you are man and woman divided you, but by the bridge you have come to unity. You are the man and the 'not-man'; the

224

woman and the 'not-woman': being both you are one, and being one you are both. Now has the time come when you are to teach others that in duality there is unity, and that in unity there is duality.

"When you first came to me I thought you were young and helpless, children who had only to obey and to learn. Then I did not recognize that you already possessed the quality from which all others are born, the quality without which no others are pleasing to the Great Hunters. I saw the reflection of that quality in your courage, in your endurance, in your integrity, and it was reflected even in the skill you learned from others, woodcraft and the fletching of arrows. Then I began to ask myself, what was this quality which you possessed even as children? I knew it was the string without which bow and arrow are valueless. I knew it was the whet-stone without which the tomahawk becomes blunt. I knew it was the feather without which an arrow cannot fly to the quarry. I knew it was the river without which people perish of thirst. Still, though I could recognize its existence, I could not give it a name. It is a small word, and in my time considered unworthy for a man to use, even when young and foolish. Love is the name of the quality.

"Because you loved each other, you were able to love yourselves. Because you loved yourselves you knew yourselves, and in that knowing came an echo of the wisdom of the Before People, who long ago drove the Sorrow Bird from the land where they lived in peace. To this love shall you pledge your oath, and each day at dawn, and at noon and at sunset, you will say, 'I love us both, the male and the female: I love myself, the male and the female: and with eyes that are open to that love will I see others, the male and the female.' "

Then Na-ka-chek stepped forward to unite my forehead-band and Raki's forehead-thong: and he took my right hand and Raki's left hand and with the thong and the feathered band he bound them together, pulse to pulse: but first he took a knife from the white stone and made on each of our wrists a shallow cut so that our blood was mingled. Then he pronounced in a loud voice, so that all could hear:

"Raki and Piyanah are of one blood on Earth."

Then he cut off a strand of Raki's hair and a strand of mine, and these he put into one of the clay bowls, and taking a brand from the fire he set light to the hair so that it shrivelled into ashes. And from the second bowl he sprinkled water on to the ashes. From the third bowl he sprinkled salt into the water, saying:

"This oath shall endure after your bodies return to dust: for this water is the water of the river of life and this salt is the riches of wisdom which you have won through the years and which has become part of you."

Then he held out the bowl for us to drink, and when we had done so, he said, "Raki and Piyanah are of one spirit on the other side of the water."

Then four Elders, who had been standing to the north and to the south and to the east and to the west of the Totem, came forward: and each carried one of the carved ceremonial shields which were kept in the Tepee of the Elders and are old as the tribe. On the first and the second shields were the clothes of the separation we had worn during the fasting, and these my father took and held in his upraised hands towards the sky, saying:

"Of separation was born unity, and of earth shall be born fire."

Then he walked forward to cast them into the watch-fire. The third and fourth shields bore two feathered headdresses, alike as are the wings of a great bird. We went down on one knee before him, and he placed them on our heads, the sign of his authority and of our own, saying:

"In the name of these feathers, remember that you are pledged, now and for the generations, to look to the Bird of the Morning who alone can drive forth the Sorrow Bird."

And as he was speaking the sun flooded up over the hills

226

to fill the pool of the cliffs with light, and the torches were pale against the morning.

Then did he say, ''Because you have heard the song of the feathers your totem animal shall be winged.''

Then we all waited hushed and expectant, knowing that the first bird we saw would be our totem animal during the generations of the future.

No bird-call broke the silence. I saw two Elders glance at each other, and knew that if no bird appeared they would take it as an omen of disaster. Raki and I were the first to see the heron—two herons, flying very low over the encampment towards the river. The relief of the crowd was tangible as a wind.

''Raki and Piyanah, I, Na-ka-chek, declare in the name of my Totem, that now and until both of you have crossed the River, you are, and shall be, Chief of the Tribe of the Heron. What I have given to you, you shall give to your people. And to you they shall give that which they have given to me. Your honour shall be their honour, and your courage their courage, even as their feathers shall be in your headdress and their love in your heart.''

Raki and I knew that the unity to which we had attained was a degree for which all the others, save perhaps Gorgi and Cheka, were not ready. We had spoken in our names on both sides of the water, but they who came with us were building a bridge across the divisions of Earth, not yet the bridge between Earth and the stars. So it was in the name of their Redskin selves, not in the name of the generations, that we asked our tribe to pledge their oath.

First came Rokeena and Tekeeni, she upright and serene, so different from the crippled girl who had been scorned in the Squaws' Tepees; he a handbreadth taller than she, his mouth solemn—which hid the gap made by the ''friendship tooth'' which Raki still had on a neck-thong. The objects on the wooden platters had been placed there at our request, for we knew that they would help to symbolize the ritual we were

227

going to use. It was a ritual born of our hearts, yet well familiar, for our thoughts had polished the words many times during the past two years. On the first platter were two moccasins, a man's and a woman's, bearing in white and scarlet beads our new tribal mark of two interlaced triangles. With these were a thong and a forehead-band in the same colours, twisted together.

Then, speaking as one, Raki and I said:

"If we give you our moccasins, on what journey should they take you?"

Rokeena and Tekeeni answered, "Towards each other, towards our friends, towards the Sun."

And we asked them, "From whom should they take you away?"

They answered, "From the Sorrow Bird, from the Lord of the Carrion Crow, and from loneliness."

We gave them the moccasins and they put them on; then knelt and gave them back to us to be returned to the white stone.

Then we took the forehead-thongs and said, "What should they mean to you?"

"A sign that we should never forget that the name of each other is written on our foreheads; deeper than a brand, stronger than a tribal mark."

We asked them, "Why are these thongs twisted together?"

And they answered, "Because together they have the strength which cannot be broken, but divided they are no greater than their own substance."

Then from the second platter we took a cob of corn and a strip of pemmican and asked, "What is the riddle in these things that you can answer in yourselves?"

Rokeena said, "Corn is the wisdom of the future which should grow in the field that love has furrowed."

And Tekeeni said, "Pemmican is the memory of the past in which we are strong today and which can sustain us in a time of forgetting; as we were sustained until the Before People were clearly remembered.''

From the third platter I took firesticks and salt, and we said:

''What is the word of the fire, and the voice of the salt?''

Together, Rokeena and Tekeeni answered, ''The fire is the memory and the looking forward, that we shall take with us even to the places that are cold with today. The salt is the voice of the Great Hunters in which are remembered all the bright realities in the name of love, and in the eating of which we recognize that we may call both the pine-cone and the Lord of the Trees, both the rocks and the Great Hunters, our Ancestors.''

Then, as Na-ka-chek had done to us, we took her right wrist and his left and drew a knife over them until the blood flowed, and bound their wrists together to make them of one blood.

And this did we do also to Gorgi and Cheka; to all the seventy who were to come with us.

If a stranger had been looking down into the encampment from the top of the cliff he might have thought that the feasting he saw was familiar to any Redskin who had been to the Gathering of the Thirty Tribes. Young deer were roasting over glowing ashes and savoury steam rose from twenty cooking-pots; platters of salted fish were passed from hand to hand, and cakes fried in goats' butter and honey were piled on dishes of red and yellow pottery.

But let the stranger come down the steep path, and he would think himself bemused by tree spirits or drunk with mead. For he would have seen men and women eating together, talking together, singing together, in equality. And he would have seen two Chiefs, a man and a woman, sitting side by side on a white blanket woven from a fleece that she had brought back from the high mountains in winter. Yet even if the stranger had looked at the woman's moccasins he might not have known that it was a man who had embroidered them—a man in whose fingers dwelt the skill of both hunter and squaw, warrior and woman.

If the stranger had concealed himself in the shadow of the pine tree at the foot of the cliff to watch unseen he would have known that the feasting continued until sunset. He would have seen an old man, who by his headdress was a Chief also, go into the Great Tepee. And he would have seen the Elders go to the Tepee of the Elders, and the Old Women and the children, and many of the Braves, and the squaws, return to their own places as is the custom.

But he would have seen the man and the woman who wore the Feathered Headdress, and with them seventy and three, stay to put fresh logs on the tribal watch-fire that flared into a great blaze against the sunset. And as the shadows came down to guard the Earth against the Sun's returning, he would have seen these men and women go hand in hand to be alone together in the woods of their sunrise.

moon of the Uniting

I thought I had been dreaming of our childhood, when we used to sleep secure and naked in the robe of beaver pelts: but I was awake and it was not a dream.

Raki stirred and held me closer, murmuring, ''Don't let me wake up.''

''Wake, Raki, for this dream is not going to break with the morning.''

I think he could not believe it, until we stood together before the tepee to watch the sun of our tomorrows flowing down to fill the valley with light. His body was brave as fire against the red sky, while the great trees rose up from the mist as though the Hunters sent them to join with us in company.

''For a moon, Piyanah, we can forget yesterday and tomorrow. Where shall we go to share our being alone?''

''To the places where we still have a promise to fulfill; the places we expected to find again only on the other side of the water.''

''Where first, Piyanah? To the birch grove, or our little valley?''

''To the birch grove, for that had separation on both sides of it. It was like an island of a river in flood: every day we watched it getting smaller and smaller and knew that soon the current would sweep us away from each other.''

''Need we remember that sorrow?''

''Would you forget the joy, Raki? If you lose a few beads from your moccasins would you throw them away when they could so easily be mended? The moccasins of that memory will always take us back to youth and joy, and looking forward. It is for us to make them ready for our feet, and then, even when we are old and proud with feathers, we have only to wear them to speak in the voice of young love to those who have also turned aside from an arid path, to see a new star in a sky which had become too wide, too cold, for understanding.

''Now we can see that star as a kindled torch, but how shall we forget the time when it was cold as the drifts in which a lost hunter feels his humanity flicker?

''Because we have learned that the wisdom of the Great Hunters belongs to all ages, for the feathers of the bird of time can carry a man to all the days of his youth and of his age that he had known since before the first redwood. Do you remember, Raki, how, when we were children, we used to bury an uncomfortable thought and mark the place with a white stone to remind us never to dig it up again? Another white stone shall be the bead to complete these happy moccasins, so that we can wear them without fear of memory.''

''What shall we bury?''

''The grief of separation. Together we will dig a grave under the birch trees, and we, who are living, shall walk hand

231

in hand away from that grave, and laugh—as we must have so often laughed together when the bodies of our generations returned to the kindly earth.''

As we went down the path to the river an oriole was singing in a high spruce and we paused to listen.

''It must be Great Oriole,'' said Raki, ''for no ordinary bird could say so clearly, 'Raki and Piyanah are happy.' ''

''And that must be Great Chipmunk, hurrying off to tell all the people of the forests to rejoice with us who share their secrets.''

''Even the Lords of the Trees are with us, Piyanah.'' He took my hand and spread the fingers against the bark of a chestnut. ''The trees are warm with life; yesterday they were equally alive, and it was only ourselves who could not share in it, but today they are part of us.''

''And so is the grass...even the rocks are alive.''

He smiled, ''Do you think we could have died in our sleep and crossed to the other side of the water?''

''Perhaps being dead and being really alive are the same thing. Yesterday we were two people, but now together we are a child of the Great Hunters. Because we are that child our eyes can see the life in the trees, our ears can hear the laughter of the west wind, and our heart know that the words the rivers sing are, 'Love life: and live by love.' Yes, Raki, that is what has happened to us, we *do* love life...we never realized until now that life had to be loved before we could understand it. We have thought of it as something always there and never bothered to notice it; or else it was something to be endured, like an ordeal; or something which kept on changing its quality and was called by many names...birth, and childhood, and old age. It was always a background, never part of ourselves; a distant mountain that we seldom noticed because it was too far away to be climbed. I have never before seen life as something you can hold in your heart, warm and strong as sunlight: never realized it was something you could *love*, which, because you loved it, could never forsake you.''

''That is why everything is so different today, Piyanah. I always thought that if we could see beyond the little earth we knew, we should become grave and old with so much wisdom, but there is a simplicity about loving that I never understood until now. Both of us have thought and wondered about the laws we must make for our tribe, but now we can teach them to love life, and to do so they must love themselves and each other; then they will also have learned the great simplicity; to seek love, to act by love, to live love.''

''Then we shall have brought them home from separation. *They* will never have to be men pretending to be women, or women disguised as men. They will realize, as we have done, that each in himself is man and woman, and that from two of these are born the torch-bearers to whom the Great Hunters are no longer hidden by the mist of birth and death.''

It was sunset when we came to the place of the white birches, and the gentle green of evening was flooding up from the horizon to quench the yellow flames which still flared from the torch of the day. The air was very still and the young buds quiet, as though they listened for our returning. The moss grew close, here in the shade, and we moved silently as shadows.

It seemed that in a moment I should see Raki and Piyanah lying together by the stream. We had come to tell them that they might sleep secure from dreams of separation. A night bird called; its note sharp and clear as spring water.

''I thought I could see them there,'' said Raki, and I answered, ''Yes, so did I.''

He took me in his arms. ''They will come back to us Piyanah. Our life is a fire that will call them from the shadows. We have not been complete without them; they were waiting here, waiting until we came back.''

''While we were alone it was *that* Raki and Piyanah who kept our fire alive; they were much more real than the warrior

233

and the squaw, much more real even than the two people who yesterday took the oath of eternity.''

It seemed the sleepers stirred and got slowly to their feet; then came silently towards us, who waited for them. For a moment I could see the girl clearly, and pitied her for the fear in her eyes. I knew Raki could see the boy, who stood there trying to smile while the claws of separation, more cruel than a mountain lion, tore at his side.

''We have come back,'' I said, and heard Raki echo, ''We have come back.''

We held out our arms to the shadowy figures. Then Raki and I were together—alone among the birch trees.

As before, we stayed three days in the birch grove; but this time we left in peace on our way to the little valley. We had been travelling north-east through the forest since dawn, and were crossing a narrow game trail when Raki stopped and said:

''Piyanah, do you remember that tree—the one struck by lightning beside the big rock?'' Then he ran forward and pulled off a strip of lichen which uncovered an old blaze cut deeply into the bark. At the sight of it I could almost feel the sharp stone on which I had grazed my hand when I helped Raki dig up the bundles that he had hidden on the night we ran away together, so long ago.

''Seed maize and pemmican, do you remember, Piyanah?''

''Yes, Raki! And the tomahawk we brought to cut branches for our shelter, and the fish-hooks....Oh, Raki!—it's all coming back again, and now there is no fear to spoil it.''

''Do you remember how you hoped we should be able to cross on the ice? Now we can cross at the ford.''

''No, Raki—can't we go by the rapids as we did before? The cliff won't seem difficult to climb now.''

''Shall we laugh at ourselves for thinking we were such brave children?''

"We will laugh *with* ourselves, the real laughter we are finding together."

Soon we stood at the top of the cliff looking down at the galloping water. Because my hands were not cold with fear it was easy to swing down to the ledges. Then we were leaping from rock to rock across the river; soaked in noise and spray and sunlight; shouting to each other—though we knew the sound of our voices was snatched away like twigs by the thunder of the rapids. But it was good to echo the song of the water; we were part of its strength and urgency, for we shared the surge of freedom when the ice has melted.

We were not quite sure whether we found the same place under the bank where we had spent the first night of our adventure, but again we pulled down sandy earth with our hands to make a shelter against the north wind which came with evening. So as to echo our first journey we decided not to build a fire—but this time we had a beaver robe in which to sleep, a beaver robe in which to lie in Raki's arms and watch the stars.

"We have spent so long training our bodies to be obedient, Raki," I said sleepily, "yet now that we let them do exactly what they like best they are such indulgent masters!"

Raki chuckled, "I don't feel as though I had been submissive. I feel more exalted than if I had climbed a mountain which touched the sky."

"I feel better than that! I feel as though I had flown to the top of the mountain and so would never have to climb any more!"

By noon next day we reached the top of the pass. Here there were still patches of snow, and where it was melting in the spring sun we walked ankle-deep in slush, before we stood looking down the steep slopes into the "unknown country." In the distance we could see our Lake of the Wildfowl, glinting blue under the clear sky, but our valley was still hidden by a fold of the hills.

Raki smiled down at me, "No black smoke, Piyanah."

"I'm glad we saw it, Raki. Until now I was never sure whether, if we had the choice again, I would try to keep you away from the tribe. Our valley belongs to us more than it ever did before because we have made ourselves free to come back. It is not only that we are a Chief; it is because we tested our need of each other against everything else and found it stronger even than we knew. If the Great Hunters had answered my prayers, that I might be able to hide with you from the Black Smoke, there would always have been a barrier between us. You were never really happy when we had to hide; you would never have been happy if I had managed to keep you with me by saying that I would die if you went away—I always thought I should die if we were parted, Raki; did you know?"

"Yes; I thought so, too, and hoped that it would happen quickly to us both."

"It would have spoilt things for us if I had made you stay; or if you had sent me to the squaws while you became a warrior. It's better than being reborn, the thing that's happened to us in the last five days. It's the knowledge that if we met one of the Before People he would recognize us as belonging to their kind, for both of us know the two halves of ourselves and of each other. We have learnt everything we know as man *and* as woman; whatever we have of courage, or swiftness, or endurance, is male and female, instead of belonging only to either."

He smiled, "We both know how to strip the pelt from a gopher or the scalp from an enemy's head. And unless you had told me that you had made these moccasins I should never have believed that you were as good as I am at making patterns with beads!"

"I will race you to the rock where we used to watch the sunset, and then we will decide who has the swifter moccasins."

Across the slope we leapt like young deer; past rocky outcrops, through shallow snow-drifts, across narrow ledges which crumbled underfoot and sent showers of pebbles clattering down the hillside. He was gaining on me when I reached the stretch of mountain grass where the sentinel rock waited for us. I reached it in time to swing round, arms outstretched against the smooth stone, breathless, laughing—and more breathless still after Raki reached me.

I had so often thought of the valley as we had left it: the fish-trap above the second fall, the pine-boughs guarding the food we had stored for the winter, the firewood stacked beyond the shelter; the stripped corn-cobs, thrown down by the stone I had used as a grinding bowl when I had said, ''I want everything just as it is now on the other side of the water, Raki; everything just as it is now until I am used to being dead.''

Only the twin pine was the same, and at its feet a low mound covered with brambles must have been our wood stack, and shelter, and winter food store. The fish-trap had long since been swept away, and the dam we had built to make the pool where I filled the water-jar had fallen to the strength of melting snows.

''Look, Piyanah!'' Raki was pointing to the place where we had planted our first corn, where now there was a litter of dried stalks. ''It was a real place of the corn growing,'' he said softly; ''the cobs we hung to dry on our roof-pole must have scattered, and the ground we made was kind to them. Year after year they must have seeded themselves, for those stalks are not older than last autumn.''

''But the shelter is gone, and everything else,'' I said, feeling for a moment forlorn.

''The shelter was dead wood, cut from the tree; and why should the stream be tamed by the stones we set if we were not here to thank it for its courtesy? But corn is strong as a tribe: we brought it here and it has multiplied and flourished. Our tribe will be like that, Piyanah. It will start like a handful of corn, perhaps fifty or a hundred grains. And we shall take them to a new valley where the ground has never been furrowed, and when we leave them, because it is time for us to go to the other side of the water, they will no longer need us to look after them, for they are the seed of the generations who will be happier because we were born.''

''Raki, I think you have just found the question which all men and women have to answer before the Great Hunters let them enter the Land beyond the Sunset—'How many people are *happier* because you were born?' ''

the Bitter Mountains

At dawn we made our last offering, of grain and meat and arrows, to the Totem of the Two Trees. Henceforward we could no longer claim territory that was familiar, for the morning and the evening were the boundaries between which we travelled.

We were to make the first stage of the journey by river, before striking South to assay the pass over the mountains of which Hajan had told us. The tribe gathered to watch us go. The Old Women remote and vindictive, longing to mouth the maledictions they dared not utter in the presence of my father; the young men regretful that they could not come with us; the squaws scornful yet envious, the Half-brothers and the Naked Foreheads sorrowful because we who had befriended them were going away.

It was difficult to say farewell to Na-ka-chek and to display the impassivity that he expected from me. I knew he could have wept because he might never see us again, yet I knew he rejoiced because in our going we fulfilled his oath. I had begged Narrok to come with us for I knew he would be lonely for me, but he had said, ''Through your eyes, Piyanah, I have seen beauty which once I thought had forsaken me. When I was blind and in despair your father

238

brought me hope; now I stay to comfort him."

Raki and I knelt in the prow of the leading canoe, and at the bend of the river we let the paddles trail in the water, to look back for the last time to the place which for so long had been our home. Above the naked trees the look-out rock was carved against the sky; on it stood the Chief, watching us go away from him into the future. My vision of him was blurred by tears. I was afraid because I was leaving him, lonely because I was leaving him; yet how could I be lonely with Raki? And how could a dual Chief fear to go beyond familiar boundaries?

"Mother, don't let him be lonely! Mother, stay with him, very close so that he knows you are always there, even in the daytime."

I saw Raki pick up his paddle, and I bent to mine. Slowly the wooded hills swept down to hide us from Na-ka-chek. The silence of early morning was broken by more than birds, or water dripping from the paddles of seventeen canoes; we seemed to hear the heart of the woods beating. Then the rhythm changed, from a lament into a song of victory soaring in the sunlight, song of the Forgotten Ones laughing in the moonlight.

We lengthened our stroke to the rhythm of the drumming, and sorrow was lifted by the rhythm of the drumming; in the drumming there were high hills and looking forward; in the drumming there was laughter and new horizons; in the drumming there was friendship which a parting cannot sever.

"This is why Narrok was not there to say farewell to us," said Raki.

"This *is* his farewell," I said. "He is telling us that in spirit he joins in our adventure. He says that if ever we are in danger we shall hear his drum."

The rhythm beat like a pulse in my head, even when we were far up-river and my ears were deafened by the distance.

We kept to the river for eleven days; serene days when our cooking-fires were lit before sunset and no one woke until dawn. I do not know if the others found it hard to leave the canoes; to me they were the last physical link with the old life. The river was the same river in which we had swum and speared fish since we were children, but the country into which we were journeying had no link with us. We dragged the canoes up the bank, protected them with pine boughs, and tied three broken feathers to each prow to show that they were abandoned and could be used by anyone who had need of them.

The next eight days were through bleak country—bare hillsides with tracts of dense pine forest in whose shade the winter snow still lingered. Game was scarce, but several times we were able to kill a deer and so conserve the grain and pemmican we had brought with us.

On the nineteenth day we sighted the Bitter Mountains. They were much higher than those that guard the Valley of the Two Trees, and snow still lay thick even on the lower slopes. I wanted to suggest that we make a temporary encampment until the weather improved, but Raki and the others were so eager to press on that I did not voice my uneasiness. Hajan said that it would take us five days to cross the pass, so we waited until we had sufficient fresh meat to last us for that time. We smoked it over greenwood fires but did not cure it into pemmican.

Why should Redskins be afraid of cold? Did not each of us have two tunics, one lined with fur; and a blanket to sleep in, and moccasins of double leather? Why should I doubt the endurance of the women when they had not yet failed to maintain their equality?

The night before we were to start the climb, I walked beyond the friendly circle of firelight and could feel the snow crunching underfoot. Behind me I heard our people laughing and talking together; ahead of me were jagged peaks, black against the rising moon. I talked aloud, to try to fan my spark of courage into flame.

"Piyanah, don't see only the threatening peaks; look further, to the kindly valleys we shall find beyond them. Think of the fruit trees, Piyanah, the warm river and the lush meadows where your children will play. Take your people over the mountains, Piyanah, so that your son will know that even the winter is not unkind. Piyanah, don't let Raki know you are afraid, nor Dorrok, nor any of them. It was you who first wanted to go South; if they know you are afraid they will begin to doubt your judgment. If the mountains look difficult now they will seem even higher if we wait until the snows melt. You have made them wait until enough meat was smoked. There is no excuse to wait longer, Piyanah. Raki is ready to go. Would you make of yourself a burden instead of a companion?"

Next morning I saw a heron against the cold grey curve of the sky, a heron flying to the South. I took it for a sign that our totem was close. The faith that flickered grew strong. The mountains were only a barrier to cross—and had not Raki and I already crossed so many barriers to find each other?

The first three days of steady climbing, through the foothills that guarded the main range, were so easy that I was glad not to have betrayed my apprehension, even to Raki. The sky was a strong blue and the wind only enough to cool the sweat on our foreheads. Hajan said that the pass was between two peaks which we could see jutting up like the fangs of a wolf. It seemed guarded by a precipice, but he repeated that he knew the route by which this could be climbed.

On the third night we camped at the foot of the towering wall of rock. We were above the tree-line, but we had hoped to find the usual scrub or thorn bushes and so had brought no fuel with us. But there was nothing to give us fire. When the women realized that there would be no light to guard us in the dark they began to whisper together. Raki wanted to burn some of our arrows to quell their fears, but I told him that if he did, it would prove that we were tolerant of their super-stitions.

"All the tribes believe that it is an ill omen to pause in a migration without lighting a fire," said Raki. "The Chiefs believe it and the Elders; even the little fire that I could kindle from a quiver of arrows would comfort them—and it is so easy to make arrows, Piyanah."

Perhaps because I understood only too well what the squaws were feeling I said sharply, "If you encourage them in their superstitions I will go on alone, to show them that their Chief who is a woman is not so tolerant of their foolish-ness as their Chief who is a man."

I walked resolutely away into the darkness, praying that Raki would follow or call me back. The prayer was answered.

"As you feel so strongly about it I will do what you wish, Piyanah."

"Why listen to me when more than thirty other women are asking you to please them?"

"Aren't you being unreasonable?"

I knew this was true, but I replied, "Yes, if it is unreason-able to try to fulfill the purpose of our journey. You said that superstition was like a viper, to be killed whenever you get the chance. Now it seems that I am unreasonable because I don't feed it!"

"It is a good custom, the watch-fire of the traveller. The fire is the link between him and the sun—the place of the fire is his home even though the country is unfamiliar. Do you grudge them that small security, Piyanah?"

I wanted to cry out, "I want a fire more than any of them! No one else left people they love as I love Na-ka-chek and Narrok. I want to be back in the places I have always known, where even the grass is friendly. I don't believe Hajan knows the way over the pass. I think he is boasting. I think we are leading our people into a danger we are both too proud and too stupid to recognize."

I wanted to tell Raki all this, but instead, trying to make my voice sound amused and a little scornful, ''Give them their arrows, Raki; I had forgotten that children are afraid of the dark.''

He looked at me, hurt and bewildered, then turned to go back to the small patch of level ground where the others had spread their blankets. I sat with my back against a boulder and my chin on my knees, angry and miserable; watching the sparks from Raki's fire-stick and the pitiful little flames which crawled up the shafts of the arrows I had fletched for him.

The fourth day was slow and arduous. Thirty-seven times every load had to be hauled up to a new ledge by ropes; for the rock was friable and the handholds would not have borne a man's weight if he had been cumbered even by a tomahawk or a bag of maize. There were several places where we could rest, though with our legs dangling over a sheer drop. We dared not waste the daylight and so pressed on.

At sunset we came to a wide shelf, sufficient for us all to sit huddled together but not for anyone to lie down. We roped ourselves together so that if anyone slumped forward in his sleep he could be jerked back to safety. It was very cold and my jaw muscles ached from the effort to stop my teeth chattering; for the others might have thought they chattered with fear as well as cold—which might have been true though I would not admit it even to myself. We were all too tired to eat, though Raki gave each of us a stick of pemmican to chew.

Before dawn the wind began to rise, sharp as snow-water. I longed for the light so that we could see to go on. Anything would be better than this frozen waiting. Dawn showed a sky thick and grey as a dirty blanket. Snow began to fall, heavy sullen flakes, which froze as they touched the rock. Hajan again took the lead, but his earlier confidence had deserted him. The ledge on which we had spent the night ended in an overhang and we had to go back to try to find a new way up. We came to a perpendicular shaft which Raki decided would be possible. He went first and I followed him—feet and shoulders wedged across the cleft. It was painful progress, and all the time a question ran in my head, "Will the walls widen so that we can get no purchase, or narrow until we are wedged if we try to go any further?"

My moccasins were worn through before I reached the top, where Raki hauled me up to stand beside him on a wide platform; it was exquisite relief to lie down without fear of falling. It was easier for the others, for we let down a rope to them, but it was noon before the last load had been brought up.

Now the snow was falling faster and the wind bayed us as its quarry. When the clouds lifted for a few moments, we could see the pass above a steep scree, which looked easy compared to the last two stages. We even found a few stunted thorn bushes, which surprised me as the lower slopes had been barren, and there was a shallow cave which gave sufficient shelter for a fire. We all felt more cheerful after a hot meal, of pemmican stewed in snow-water and thickened with maize-meal. The weather was getting worse, so Raki decided we should spend the night there and start for the summit with the first light.

I must have fallen asleep while the others were still eating, for when Raki woke me I was still sitting half upright with my head on his shoulder. He had pulled a blanket round us. The others were rolled in theirs, huddled together for protection from the wind, which had veered to the northeast and was now blowing into the cave, the mouth of which was half covered by a snow-drift. I slept so heavily that Raki had been rubbing my hands and feet to warm them, without waking me. We baked bread in the ashes, and each had a piece to eat before the light was strong enough to move on.

Until about noon it was a slow, steady climb over loose shale. The wind came in gusts, sometimes so strong that we had to cling together to stop being driven down the perilous slopes. The women were uncomplaining as the men, though I saw that Rokeena's and Cheka's fingers were bleeding where the cold had cracked them open. All of us were scourged by the lash of the wind. Often the clouds lifted and we could see the twin peaks against the hostile sky. Then the clouds came down again and we could only plod on in the direction the brief glimpse had given us.

We only knew we had reached the top of the pass by the sudden increase in the fury of the wind, which roared between the crags as though enraged that anything dared to give it challenge. Hajan had been anxious for Raki and me to take the lead, but now he strode forward. I paused to let him go ahead; he deserved this triumph even though the going had been far more difficult than he had led us to expect. The snow-laden wind swirled round him like smoke. I suppose I should have been able to share his sense of triumph, but I was too tired and too cold.

Suddenly he stopped. I saw him shake his fist at the sky. As I came up behind him I heard him laughing. Hajan, the Scarlet Feather, the imperturbable, laughing as though laughter would break out from the cage of his ribs. Then I saw his face. It was the face of a man driven mad by his own betrayal—but he could still recognize me.

"I never came to the head of the pass! I lied when I told you that the southern slopes were easy! Look, Piyanah, you can see the land of your future; but to reach it you must borrow wings from your totem!"

He stood on the edge of a precipice; far below I could see the forests where we had thought to walk in peace.

"I promised to lead you to the South. I will keep my promise!"

With a terrible cry he ran forward and leapt. I saw his body falling...falling; his arms beating the air as though he were trying to fly.

Raki had stayed to see that everyone reached the summit in safety; I was the only one who had seen Hajan go to his death because he thought he had betrayed us. If the women knew what had happened they might panic, and to make our way down the cliff all of us would need everything we had of courage, and endurance.... ''I must lie, even to Raki, and say that Hajan had gone ahead. It will be true even if Raki does not understand my truth. I must tell him that I am going ahead with Hajan, and that he must somehow find shelter to light a fire; even if he uses all our arrows they must have the comfort of a little warmth.''

Raki, when I had spoken to him, was confident that our worst perils were over, otherwise he would never have let me go on without him even though he thought Hajan went with me. Hidden by a jutting rock I prayed as I had never prayed before, to the Great Hunters, to Norrok, to Na-ka-chek, to the Lord of the Herons, ''Please help me find a way down. Please help me to help them, for they have been so brave and have come so far.''

I shall never be sure whether it was the wind blowing through a cleft, or whether I heard Narrok's drumming with my living ears. The sound led me towards the face of the western pinnacle, and I saw that it would not be difficult to climb. I did not question why I should climb higher in an attempt to go down, but found myself scrambling from ledge to ledge on which, compared to the way we had come, was almost a series of natural steps. I reached a long horizontal crack, running east and protected from the worst of the gale.

Even above the battery of the wind the drumming was steady, the rhythm Narrok called ''new horizons'' and which I had so often heard come to life under his fingers. The crack ended in a ridge, curving down like a rib from a backbone. It was steep and snow-covered, but not impossible. From it I could see the precipice over which Hajan had plunged, falling sheer as water to the forest which he could have reached in safety.

The relief was more life-giving than a bowl of deer-stew. The journey back to Raki seemed easy. Three of the women were huddled together under their blankets in the shelter of an overhanging rock. They refused to get up when Raki gave the signal, and would not move even when their husbands ordered them. One of the men slapped his woman across the face, and suddenly she became the obedient, unquestioning squaw, who even a day earlier she would have despised. She scrambled to her feet, and followed him docilely. The other women did the same.

How soon Raki noticed that there was only one set of footprints ahead of us, I am not sure. He did not mention it, but I think he found it difficult to forgive me for having lied to him about Hajan. Soon we were on the lower slopes, and I was happy because I thought the ordeal was almost over and that Raki would soon be proud of me instead of angry.

We had seen two avalanches earlier in the day, but they had been too far away to concern us. Suddenly there was a crack, loud as the whip of the Great Hunters if they had been gathering all the herds of Earth. A great stretch of snow, marred only by the file of our prints, began to slide, faster and faster as the avalanche gathered speed.

"Run!" shouted Raki. "Cover your heads with blankets if it reaches you!"

Like bison in stampede, the avalanche thundered down. Clinging to Raki's arm I was deafened by the noise. It swept past us to crash among the trees below.

As the air cleared I saw men and women stagger to their feet. Swiftly I counted them, Raki and I and seventy and three—no two, for Hajan was dead. I counted them again. There were only seventy-one.

"Raki, someone is missing!"

Then I realized who it was. "Dorrok! The avalanche caught Dorrok!"

We were all digging with our hands, throwing aside stones and lumps of frozen snow, rolling away boulders, in desperate effort to reach Dorrok before he smothered. I tried to reassure myself, "People have lived for half a day under the snow. Don't die, Dorrok, we'll get you out very soon."

It was Gorgi who found him. He was still breathing, but

his life was running out like water from a broken jar.

"The pass I am crossing is very easy, my Piyanah. I never knew until now that it is so much easier to die than to live."

I thought that was the last time I should hear his voice; but he spoke again, smiling, "It is warmer, even than the South, on the other side of the water."

Black Spider

We buried Dorrok's body in an open glade of the forest whose shelter we reached at the sunset of his death. We slept that night by a blazing fire, but I could not get warm. The cold of the Bitter Mountains, the cold despair of Hajan, the cruel, relentless cold that had fallen on Dorrok and crushed to a bruised pulp those splendid sinews which he had tempered by fine endurance; this cold seemed to have become a part of me. I shivered and moved closer to the fire. Then it was the fire that seemed unkind, for my skin throbbed with heat and snow-water could not quench my thirst.

I slept fitfully, to dream that I was lost in a waste of snow; or parched, craving for water, crawling exhausted up a dry water-course, searching for even a small pool of moisture. By the morning I found it difficult to walk without stumbling and desperately tried to conceal my weakness from the others. They had seen Dorrok die, and last night I had had to tell them of Hajan's death. If they thought that I was going to fail them they might be afraid to go on.

Raki found a way to conceal my weakness from them. He wrapped my foot in strips of blanket and said it had been badly bruised by a loose boulder when I had been helping to clear the avalanche from Dorrok. He told only Gorgi that I was ill and dazed with fever, and they made a litter for me of one of the pieces of leather we used for shelter, slung from two tepee poles and carried on their shoulders.

I remember very little of the next few days, only the interminable sway of the litter and the soft thud of many feet in single file through the silent forest. Game must have been killed, for at night, and at noon also, Raki fed me with strong broth. They must have made camp early each evening, for I know I slept with Raki in the Chief's Tepee instead of the ordinary shelter we used on the march. It was set close to the fire and the light flickered on the pictures of Raki and me, and made them seem alive.

Sometimes I thought Hajan was with me, trying to make me jump over the precipice because he said I had shared in his betrayal by not telling the others that the mountains were too treacherous to dare. I tried to make him believe that we had found a way down and were safe on the southern side, but he always said, ''You will have to grow wings before you can reach that forest, Piyanah.'' And then he would run towards the edge of the precipice, and I was trying to hold him back. I would wake crying and shivering, and Raki would wrap another blanket round me and hold me in his arms, comforting me, saying that I was safe and only dreamed of danger.

On the sixth day I began to get stronger, but Raki said I must let myself be carried part of the day. I wondered why he did not decide to let us camp in one place for several days so that we all had a chance to rest. At first when I asked him this he pretended not to hear, but later he said:

''I dared not stay within sight of the Bitter Mountains, for every time our people looked back it would remind them of Hajan and Dorrok—and more important still, Piyanah, I dared not let them know you were ill.''

''But they must have guessed why I had to be carried?''

''No, they believed you had been injured by the avalanche. They are not afraid of an injury, but to them illness is a sign that the spirits are angry.''

''Raki, shall we never cure them of superstition?''

''We shall: but it may take years. They trusted Hajan to

guide them, and he failed. All the men had been trained by Dorrok: he was the standard by which they tested their strength. He had taught them to rely on their trained skill to overcome danger, and they saw him destroyed by a danger against which he was powerless. You and I, their Chief, are the only solid rock they have left. If they had realized that one of us was also afflicted by demons—for to them fever can come from no other source—they might have lost faith. If we had stayed in camp, even for one day, they would have known it was not lameness that prevented you from walking. Gorgi and I kept in the lead with you; and when at night you did not join the others round the watch-fire it aroused no curiosity, for it has always been the custom of the Chief to keep apart from the tribe.''

''Doesn't even Rokeena know I have been ill?''

''No, but she suspects, and so does Cheka. But they had the courage to keep their suspicions to themselves. I wish I could say as much for the other women!''

''They are being difficult?''

Raki's voice was suddenly bitter. ''Sometimes they have almost made me feel that we were fools to rescue them from the Old Women. If they had complained that the distances we made were too great I could have sympathized, for even Gorgi and Tekeeni were tired at the end of the day, as I was. If they had grumbled when the cooking-pots were half empty, or failed to collect their share of wood for the watch-fire, I could have sympathized; but their questions have been more irritating than a cloud of biting flies. The same questions over and over again. 'Where are the warm rivers?' Where is the valley which is never cold, even in winter? Why did you tell us we should find it beyond the mountains, when these woods are no better than our own?' And every morning they ask, 'Shall we find the valley today?' And when their husbands tell them to be patient or else to be quiet, they whisper together and sympathize with each other, and behave as though they lived in the Squaws'

Tepees of any of the Thirty Tribes!''

''How do the men behave, Raki?''

''If they grumble it is not in my hearing: habit is stronger than new laws and they have always been trained to obey their Chief. If I say that we start at dawn they are ready—at dawn. They follow me in silence, until I thrust an arrow in the ground to show them we have reached the site of a new watch-fire.''

''When we reach country that is kindly I think we ought to stay there for a while to let them regain their confidence.''

''To me we shall stay for something far more important. You need to rest in the sun, Piyanah, to sleep without measuring your dreams by the day's necessities. I think we shall soon come to such a place. I sent Tekeeni ahead as forerunner, and he has just come back to say that from the next hill he can see open grass-land stretching to the horizon. There is a lake, and he saw a herd of bison in the distance, so we shall not lack food; nor moccasins—and all of us need moccasins.''

I could walk all day by the time we reached the lake. It was fringed by reeds, and wildfowl were so numerous that we could have eaten three times a day with no more trouble than it takes to spread snares. There were no tall trees, but many bushes which afforded pleasant shade. They had grey-green leaves, and fluffy yellow flowers with a scent like warm honey.

Day by day the weather was warmer. We discarded our tunics and our skins soaked up new life from the sun. Raki and I built a shelter of dry reeds on the west of the lake while the others encamped on the far side. We felt the need to claim the Chief's privilege of being apart, and thought it might be well for the tribe to be independent of authority.

By the twelfth day I again had a body that was strong and obedient, instead of one which demanded irksome consideration; but I still found it curiously pleasant to be lazy, and so spent the afternoon basking by the edge of the lake. When I woke, a cool breeze was rippling the tall grass of the plain. I waded out through the shallows, intending to cross the lake in search of Raki. A swimmer was approaching, but the sun was directly behind him so until he drew closer I did not realize it was Raki. I went back to wait for him. His skin shone with water-drops as he came up the shelving bank. He flung himself down beside me, silent and frowning.

"You are troubled, my Raki?"

"Not troubled—impatient!"

"Who is the mother of your impatience?"

"Myself...and the women! For years, Piyanah, we have tried to train them to value freedom, and now they wail as though in taking away their abject dependence we had stolen their favourite necklaces! They seem to have forgotten that I used to live as a woman: now I am only a man, a man who must be obeyed even if his commands are foolish...and who has not even the sense to demand obedience! Squaw and husband are equal and I have told them they must share a tepee; but what do I find when I go to their encampment? The women all together, grumbling; and not one of them catching fish or hunting with the men!"

"The men are finding it difficult to share their work with the women, for their training has made them solitary."

"They didn't find it difficult to help me train the women after we had built an encampment away from the Old Squaws."

"Then it was an adventure to win a woman by more subtle means than wrestling at the Choosing...it was like finding a flint and turning it into an arrow-head, or teaching a coyote to act as a hunting-dog. At first they were content with a marriage of loins, but now they want something more. So do the women, but because they find this higher marriage more difficult they have begun to think regretfully of the old ways."

Raki sighed. "I wish all of them were like Rokeena and Tekeeni, or Gorgi and Cheka!"

"Three moons is a short time in which to kill the black

bear of custom. The women, even the most clear-sighted of them, saw men as mighty warriors who were rescuing them from the hatred of the Old Squaws. It is easy for a man to be kind to a woman who makes him feel a hero, much easier than accepting her as an equal.''

''And are men no longer heroes?''

''Why should they be? Every hardship, every achievement, has been shared by us all. Did the ice wind hold back its arrows from the women when we crossed the pass? Would the avalanche have turned aside if Dorrok had been a squaw?''

''Men and women have demanded equality, and we know that without equality they will never be able to sustain the bridge over the canyon...yet now they grumble because they lack the false totem-poles we cut down to make that bridge. Men are no longer heroes; and women are finding that hunting is not so pleasant when a careless arrow leaves the cooking-pot empty.''

''And men are finding women's work difficult,'' I said feelingly; ''I should never have understood how easy it seemed unless I had lived as a man. It is easier to tend a watch-fire than to keep an even heat under a cooking-pot... one forgets to add water and the stew burns, or ashes get into the dough to spoil the bread.''

Raki laughed, ''I know! Had you forgotten that I used to cook for the tribe?''

''Why was it so different when we were in our little valley?''

''Because it was natural for us to do everything together; you were better at some things and I at others, but not because we were male and female.''

''There has never been a canyon between us, so I suppose this is why we have never understood how it feels to look down from the bridge and feel giddy. If we had been leading a tribe in the old tradition, Raki, we should have consulted our Elders, whom we knew would agree with us, and no one would have questioned our decisions. The squaws would have known that if they complained that we travelled too far or too fast no notice would have been taken of them...they could have kept up with the rest, or stayed behind to die of hunger or grizzlies! The men would never have thought of questioning the word of the Chief...but now we give reasons for everything. Sometimes I wish we had never made it our first law that they must learn to think for themselves!''

''If they don't learn to think they will never be like the Before People. They will go on blindly following tradition, even if it cripples them. Do you remember the Brown Feather whose body was not found for two days after the battle? Dorrok had to break its arms and legs before it looked as though it was lying quietly waiting for its funeral pyre. That's what tradition can do to free people...break them to make them conform to a set pattern.''

''We have kept some of the old laws, Raki...like the hunter's law of never leaving a wounded animal to die.''

''That isn't a tradition, it's a real law of the Great Hunters. There are always some of the real laws in every tribe, but taboos have been added until very few people can distinguish between them. Even if one of the Great Hunters came down to talk to us, in a loud voice so that we could understand every word, and even if our children and our children's children remembered exactly what he said; if we hadn't also handed on to them the quality of thinking for themselves, taboos would creep into the laws and gnaw at them like termites secretly destroying the centre-post of a tepee.''

I saw he was discouraged and tried to comfort him. ''Anyone can lead a blind man...if he is really blind and not like Narrok. We must always have the courage to point to the furthest horizon we can see, so that those near us can learn to be far-sighted too, and follow the same path not because they tread in our footsteps, but because they are trying to reach the same landmark.''

"Perhaps we have never quite understood how difficult it must be to fight against taboos unless you can see them as barriers between you and a place you long for which is clearly in sight. You and I have always had each other to fight for; 'This will bring me back to Piyanah' was the light which carried me through the dark despair of living with the squaws; it was the rope which helped me to climb a precipice, the green water which led me down a rapid, the balance which held me in the dive from the Eagle Rock. We both saw the ordeals as obstacles which kept us from each other, never as an end in themselves. But if we had had no real horizon we should have believed that each stage of our training was terribly important in itself. That is why the Scarlet Feathers are solitary, more solitary than any of the others; they have climbed their highest mountain, and found the peak only a narrow platform where they are even more lonely."

"Na-ka-chek said that love was all the war cries of the true Scarlet...I suppose he meant that love was the first law of the Great Hunters."

"Love is the far horizon...the horizon we must teach our people to see for themselves."

"Yes, and it sounds so easy...love and have vision; love and be free of taboos. Why is it so hard for people to understand?"

"Because, Piyanah, they know also that to love is to accept responsibility; and people are more frightened of responsibility than of Black Feathers. We, the Redskins, honour courage, seek courage, almost we lust for courage, to conceal from ourselves our terror of responsibility. Men and women fear love more than they fear demons: they cannot hunt it with arrows, nor barter for it with salt, nor win it by an ordeal."

"We did not fear responsibility...we *wanted* to lead a tribe, we wanted to be free to use our own authority."

"Only because we had known love since we were born and have never feared it, even when it brought grinding

255

anxiety. Piyanah, at last I understand why the squaws cling to their superstitions and why men cherish tribal laws, however onerous. Obedience is a way of evading responsibility. The word of the Chief took the conscience of the tribe into his keeping. They need not question any decision he made: they were told that the man of endurance chooses the more difficult of two ways, so to them the steep way was *easier* because no choice had to be made. If they failed in an ordeal, again they were free of responsibility, for they said, 'My body has betrayed me.' They never said, 'I have betrayed my body.' Even if they lost a battle they said, 'The enemy was too strong,' or 'The demons were fighting against us.' It was the Gods' fault if the winter was too hard or storms spoiled the growing crops...so long as they could evade responsibility they never had to blame themselves!''

''Of course, Raki! And that's why the women cling so jealously to their customs and taboos. It is easy to say, 'Do not look at your reflection by the light of the full moon, or else a water demon will snatch your spirit,' or 'Do not let your shadow fall upon a woman who is heavy with child'... or any other of a thousand taboos. If taboos are broken and disaster follows, as it sometimes must, that makes it still easier for them to accept instead of to question.''

''We must tell them tonight, Piyanah, that every law which is blindly accepted instead of being tested against the feathers of truth is one more thread in the web of Black Spider, the wife of the Lord of the Carrion Crow. She is cunning, that spider; she offers freedom from responsibility...but whispers 'from responsibility,' so that the foolish hear only 'freedom.' She offers placidity; and whispers 'so that you will only see the hawk when it is plunging, too late to fight or run.' She offers the safe cave of habit; and whispers, 'safe until an avalanche closes the mouth and leaves you to starve, alone in the dark.' She offers expediency; and whispers '*my* expediency, in exchange for your integrity, of which I eat and grow fat.' She says, 'Be obedient, be secure, be content.' But unless Love has made your ears responsible for hearing *all* that she says, you will never hears her chuckling, 'Be obedient...to *me:* be secure...*in my web:* be content...*to wait until I am hungry.*' ''

''Yes, Raki. Tonight you must warn them of Black Spider, before you tell them that tomorrow we again go South.''

the Blue Smokes

For half a moon we travelled through gentle country. Flat grass-lands gave way to rolling hills; water and game were plentiful, and the suffering of the Bitter Mountains was forgotten in the easy marches. Raki and I were happy; for when we made camp the men and women shared in all that needed to be done, and the dusk was warm with laughter.

Raki smiled at me, ''Redskins who laugh, my Piyanah, and once we should have been surprised as though owls had spoken with the voices of Elders!''

Several times we saw traces of old camp-fires, but no human being until the fifteenth day. He was a hunter, and before he spoke we knew he could not be one of the Smiling Valleys, for his skin was too dark and his nostrils too broad. He told us we were entering the territory of the Blue Smokes and that the Smiling Valleys lived much further to the west. At this news we were disappointed, though the warmth of his greeting was enough to show us we had been wise to travel away from the hard North.

When we first sighted the encampment of the Blue Smokes we thought their tribe must number over a thousand, for the cluster of tepees, which were thatched with straw, was surrounded by between fifty and sixty wide strips of cultivation. It was only later that we learned they were less than three hundred and not sufficiently important to claim a place at the Feathered Council. To them, the cultivation of fields was more important than hunting, and they seldom killed for meat unless hides were needed for moccasins. Even their clothes were woven from plant fibres, though the method of preparation they did not tell us; it was a jealously guarded tribal secret, the cloth being their most valuable form of barter.

We were taken to the Chief, and found him to be a man past middle age. He expressed almost excessive pleasure at our arrival, and immediately gave orders for a feast to be prepared in our honour. We noticed that men and women shared the same encampment and the Chief displayed no surprise when Raki and I both wore a feathered headdress when we attended the feast. None of them had been to a Gathering of the Thirty Tribes, and they were eager for news of what had taken place there that year. It was late on the first night that the Chief admitted he had heard of us from the Chief of the Smiling Valleys. My ordeal had greatly increased in the telling! The caverns had been the home of particularly horrifying demons, which I, being possessed of curious magical powers, had been able to slay in hundreds. The Chief of the Demons had at last been driven to beg for clemency, which I had granted in return for an oath of allegiance from his people. I was now credited with being able to produce cloudbursts or droughts with equal ease, so that the crops of my friends flourished, while my enemies dwindled through famine.

I protested that Smiling Valley had been far too generous with his praise, but to my amusement, and Raki's also, this was taken for the natural modesty of a mighty warrior.

Each day brought further signs that the Chief dreaded our departure, for he was pathetically anxious that nothing should occur to offend us. Would we like tepees to be built close to his encampment, or would a site further up the western slope above the river be more to our liking? The diffidence with which he implied that a night of rain would be beneficial to his crops was almost ludicrous. I nodded, and then walked away as though deep in thought. He watched me anxiously, and then looked up at the sky to see if clouds were already hurrying to my summons.

It was with embarrassment that I woke in the night to hear rain drumming down, for I knew I should never be able to convince him that it was not due to me.

"I hope the Rain Spirits can laugh," I said to Raki, "and that they have heard my apologies for being credited with powers which belong only to them!"

It was difficult to make the Chief understand that we must have our own place of the corn-growing, and that this wish was not due to any lack of hospitality: at last he became reconciled, but clung to the hope that we should remain close neighbours. He praised the hunting-grounds adjoining his own to the east with words which might have described the Land beyond the Sunset. Nowhere else was game so easy to kill, or rivers so thronged with fish; nowhere were trees so noble, or the earth so lavish with crops. We realized why he wanted us on his eastern boundary...he was afraid that if we also adjoined the Smiling Valleys some of our beneficent powers might be deflected from him.

We needed time, both to explore the proffered hunting-grounds and to discover whether such neighbours would be healthy for our own people, so we told the Chief that it was our custom never to make an important decision save at the full moon. To this he acceded with haste, clearly upset that he had not understood so obvious a law without being told.

The superstitious awe in which the Blue Smokes held me began to spread even among our own people. Several of the women who had been troublesome in crossing the Bitter Mountains came to apologize for their past lack of faith in my leadership. I tried to make them see that I was the victim of a legend, but they did not really believe this. I tried being angry with them, and they became abject. I tried laughing at them, and they wept.

Only then did I realize how easy it had been for the Old Women to wield power: the passionate desire not to think, not to accept responsibility, was a plant with a hundred roots: you think you have torn it up and left the ground clean for personal integrity to flourish, and then shoots of the unclean weed appear and choke out everything else which tries to grow there.

The women of the Blue Smokes brought gifts to me, and when I thanked them, they said shyly, ''I have two daughters and I want a son,'' or ''My husband prefers another squaw,'' or ''My child is sick''...and then looked pleadingly at me to help them. I tried to explain that I was a very ordinary woman, who had no magic except that she belonged to a tribe who recognized that man and woman are the right eye and the left eye, the left hand and the right hand, the left foot and the right foot, of a third who is man *and* woman, and so greater than either. I told them that without this recognition both men and women are crippled, having the use of only one eye, one hand, one foot; and that by their own choice they could bring this recognition into their own tribe and share our magic. But they stared at me uncomprehendingly, and then went forlornly away, saying, ''Forgive me, that the gift I brought was not enough,'' or, and this was even more difficult to bear, ''Now I know that I am not worthy of your magic.''

Hoping to prove that I was ordinary, I went hunting with the men. But when my arrows brought down a deer they would not believe my skill came from long practice as did their own. They thought I had only to notch an arrow to my bowstring for a demon to carry it to the quarry's heart.

I realized more keenly than I had done before how lonely Na-ka-chek must have been. They were trying to thrust on me the loneliness of a Chief who deliberately kept apart from his tribe. Everything I did became hideously important: if I carried seven arrows in a quiver, the next day every hunter carried seven. If Raki and I went down to the river to swim at dawn, next morning the bank was thronged with people. They thought we had come to talk with water spirits, who, if they saw them in our company, would accept them as being under our protection. I could not break down their silent belief that I had powers I was not willing to use to help them. I began to be afraid that they would soon begin to fear me, and hatred is always born from fear.

Most of our tribe were happy with the Blue Smokes. After many hardships they enjoyed the easy way of life; they shared the awe in which I was held, and unless Raki had ordered them to do so, they need not have helped in the fields, or in hunting or setting fish-traps, for everything would have been willingly provided. Our squaws, who had been scorned and ill-treated by the Old Women of the Two Trees, were now envied and admired. They grew sleek and lazy with praise, and found it more pleasant hearing than they received in the company of their men, who laughed at them, or scolded them for feeding on credulity.

I began to lie sleepless at night, worried and indecisive about the future. Where should we go if we left here? The legend had come from the Smiling Valleys so we might expect the same treatment if we went to them. Both Raki and I longed to discover something wrong with the eastern hunting-grounds, but there was everything a young tribe could hope to find. We could not go further south, for the way was barred by a waterless desert, only five days' journey further on; a desert which in the memory of the Blue Smokes had never been crossed. Should we take the land so freely offered to us, and hope that in time we should be accepted as ordinary friends...or had awe already become too strong to destroy? Here there is everything they need, and because Piyanah went through an ordeal must she take them away from it? I felt very young and irresolute, and longed to be able to talk with Na-ka-chek as once the child Piyanah had longed for her mother.

Since Dorrok's death it was a council of six who made all

important decisions: Raki and I, Rokeena and Tekeeni, Gorgi and Cheka; for the others still found it easier to accept leadership than to share it. The moon when we must decide whether to go or stay was now at the full. We had avoided discussing this vital problem with the rest, so that our opinions should be unprejudiced. The six of us gathered in the shade of an ilex that grew on the crest of the slope overlooking the cultivation, and it was time to speak.

Cheka, the youngest and least experienced, spoke first. "It is difficult to be quite honest but I will try very hard. I want to stay here, because it is kind and easy. The country is safe, so Gorgi is willing to take me with him everywhere... and being with Gorgi is the only thing that really matters to me. But many of the other squaws no longer rely on their husbands as they did when things were more difficult." She pointed down the slope. "Look at that field...thirty of our women working there and not a man with them...and the rest will be chattering with the women of the Blue Smokes."

"She is right," said Gorgi, "I too would like to stay here, but the men of the Blue Smoke laugh at us for being dependent on squaws...though they think we do not hear their laughter."

"Their women laugh at us too," said Rokeena, "because they say we dare not let our men out of our sight. They say our men are children, who need our protection even when fully grown. They pity us, because our men are not strong enough to make us obedient! Because I stay with Tekeeni they tell me I am brave to bear so great an affliction as to have to follow a man who has the body of a warrior and the spirit of a child, who must cling to a woman's hand because he has not learned to walk alone." Then she turned to me and asked, "Have the Chief's women spoken to you like this, Piyanah?"

"Yes," I said reluctantly, "they ask, 'What has this equality you talk about given to your women?' And when I try to explain they nod their heads and say, 'The men of your tribe are clever, for they make you do their work as well as your own.' They believe equality is impossible...and so do the men.''

''Yes,'' said Raki, ''so do the men. I told the Chief that Piyanah wears the Scarlet in truth, and that she won it without using any weapons denied to ordinary mortals. He did not tell me in words that he thought I lied, but even though these people value courtesy he could not hide his disbelief. Though neither men nor women will acknowledge it, they are afraid of each other. The women fear the men because they need their protection against enemy Braves, against pumas, against having to think for themselves. Men fear women because they still resent the dependence on their mothers which they felt as children; they resent their physical need of women which drives them from the complete independence they covet above all things. They fear the unspoken power of women, which they think is due to their familiarity with certain demons...you will have noticed that in their legends the spirits, even the thunder spirits, are always female, and that only a woman can kindle a watch-fire.''

''They are afraid of each other,'' I said, ''and both are proud of inspiring fear.''

''Is that why they offered us hunting-grounds?'' said Tekeeni. ''If they fear themselves they must fear everyone else, and thirty-eight Braves within two days' journey would add to their protection...especially as the Chief must know his tribe are vulnerable after too much security. The Blue Smokes do not belong to the Thirty Tribes, but last year at their place of barter they heard of the massacre of the Beavers, and also that it was the Two Trees who defeated the Black Feathers. Our numbers are small, but those who might come to our assistance are many.''

''Of course that is why they are so willing to teach us their ways of cultivation, to offer seed, and help in preparing our future fields,'' said Gorgi. ''Honey to tame a bear...for a tame bear will still attack the stranger in the encampment.''

"It is easy to get grease from a tame bear," said Cheka. She pointed to a file of our women who were carrying baskets filled with weeds on their heads, "If we stay here they will sow the thistles of superstition in the ground we clean. Already our men and women are drifting away from each other...nothing important has happened, no bitter quarrels, yet the thistledown of separation is settling everywhere, and if we let it root we shall have to pull up a thousand thistles... while two thousand others grow."

"Then it is agreed we move on?" said Raki.

"It is agreed," said the others.

"To the east or to the west?"

"To the *south*," I said, and even Raki stared at me in astonishment, for had not the Blue Smokes told us that to the south was a desert which stretched to the end of the world?

"I have news for you from my father, Na-ka-chek. Last night he came to me while I slept, to say farwell before he went to join my mother beyond the sunset."

"He is dead?"

"I have never seen him so vividly alive, but his people have seen his body fall to ash and watched the Death Canoe borne away towards the rapids. He told me that beyond the desert we shall find our place of the corn-growing. There is a river, running east to west through open grass-land, and then a shallow valley guarded by wooded hills. He took me there, though I did not see the desert we must cross. He even drew a line across a meadow to show where we must cut the first furrow for our planting."

"Why didn't you tell me this when you woke?" said Raki.

"I had to be sure that all of you were willing to go on. I saw Na-ka-chek, but I cannot make you see him. He has shown me the country beyond the desert, but why should any of you believe what I have seen? The Blue Smokes have lived here for three generations, and they say that no one who has tried to cross the Great Thirst has ever returned. They are sure there is nothing beyond it, except greater thirst, and death. Why should you attempt such a journey because a woman called Piyanah had a dream?''

''Why?'' said Raki. ''I will tell you. The Tribe of the Heron was born of a dream, and we shall find our place of the corn-growing through another dream.''

Great Thirst

When the Blue Smokes heard that we intended to go South over the Great Thirst they were appalled at what they considered the deliberate suicide of an honoured tribe, until, after doing everything in their power to make us change our minds, they became, overnight, helpful and enthusiastic.

It did not take us long to discover why they had changed: the Chief had decided that I had at last been persuaded to use my magical powers. I would cause rain to fall so that the waterless desert became fertile; rivers would flow in forgotten water-courses, and as it would be a long time before other tribes came to know of such an extraordinary occurrence, the Blue Smokes would be able to extend their territory without hindrance.

Their women made water-skins for us, as we were each to carry two in addition to our customary load. They prepared a store of dried meat cured without salt; cheese made from goats' milk—their breed of goats was larger and more prolific than those we had tamed in the place of the Two Trees; and a store of breadsticks, bulky but easy to carry. They also gave us several skins of sour fruit juice, which was unpalatable, for it took on the taste of the hide, but they assured us it was excellent for quenching thirst.

All these gifts were made with diffidence. The Chief would say, ''I know well that the Chief of the Heron does not rely on the provisions needful to ordinary mortals. You thirst, and the clouds open; you wish for meat, and a sleek hind comes trotting towards you; it is over-warm, and a cool breeze blows from the north. And if the night is cold, you cause the thorn trees to burst into flame. However, most honoured Chief of the Heron, accept these gifts as a sop to my mortality. It pleases me to give you the best that I have, so be tolerant of me as would a river be if a squaw threw in a jar of water hoping to increase the roar of the rapids.''

I had despaired of ever curing him of superstition, so I accepted his offerings in gratitude and did not stress that I was well aware of the dangers of the Great Thirst.

During the preparations for this last stage of the journey, I became sure that the child who was going to be born to Raki and me was already strong in my body. By the signs in myself I knew that most of the other squaws were also with child, but decided it was as well that for a while they should continue to ascribe the thickening of their bodies to ease and plentiful food. They had been comfortable with the Blue Smokes, more so than ever before; but because they had won this security by crossing the Bitter Mountains they were prepared to undergo another ordeal to gain a greater plenty.

Na-ka-chek had told me that our place of the corn-growing was beyond the desert, and there my son was to be born; I could not betray my son, nor his father, nor his grandfather. Yet sometimes I found it almost as difficult in the hours of waking to keep the security of a dream as it would have been to prove its source to the others.

To Raki, my dream of Na-ka-chek was as vivid, perhaps even more so, than it was to me, and he was serenely confident that the Great Thirst was the last ordeal through which we had to pass. Gorgi and Cheka, Rokeena and Tekeeni, shared his confidence; the other men were obedient, but I knew they grumbled among themselves. We were taking them from hunting-grounds that were close and easy; we were depriving them of the admiration of the Blue Smokes, with whom they could feel mighty without doing anything to justify this vision of themselves they saw in other men's eyes. I told them the Blue Smokes despised them as weaklings who required the companionship of women, but they found it convenient to think I spoke in jest.

The Blue Smokes came with us to the last river north of the desert, five days journey from their main encampment. It was a small river, flowing between high banks and bordered by a belt of vivid green; but before we reached it we were already familiar with the flat lands that grew only thorn and sparse scrub, and where even a small breeze swept the loose soil into clouds of choking dust.

I thought they would help us to carry our extra load of water-skins for the first day's journey; the way was uphill over a stony ridge, which they told us, shut away the desert that would otherwise have spread like a forest fire to burn the sap from all that grew in safety beyond its protection. But they must have considered even the fringe of the desert too perilous, for they stayed on the northern bank; wearing their best tunics and waving blue and yellow pennants tied to poles. These pennants were significant of something very important in their tribal history, but when I questioned the Chief he seemed to have forgotten their meaning.

Some of the Blue Smokes had wept when they said farewell to us, but I was never sure whether it was because they thought we were deliberately going to meet death, or only because I was taking from them the magic, which, had we stayed, I might one day have used in their favour. They must have camped where we left them, for when at sunset we reached the crest of the barren hills we could see the smoke of their cooking-fires in the distance.

On the evening of the second day we reached a water-hole; it was brackish but drinkable, so we were able to fill the water-skins that were already empty. We caught some lizards, which the Blue Smokes had taught us were wholesome to eat, and though none of us liked the taste, we roasted them in hot ashes. During the next day we several times saw what in the distance seemed to be pools of water, but when we reached them they proved to be depressions filled with a white earth which resembled snow, for it had a hard, brittle crust. Crossing one of these a woman stumbled and fell. She had grazed her knee earlier in the day and I saw her flinch, and then stoop to brush the white flakes from the raw flesh as though they hurt her. I was reminded of the child Piyanah, thrusting her fingers into the tribal salt-jar, and finding that salt stings an open wound. I scooped up a handful of the white earth and tested it with my tongue.

Raki was ahead of me; I ran forward and caught hold of his arm, ''Raki, we are walking through riches for which the Two Trees would barter a year's work of moccasins and blankets. We are walking through *salt*, Raki—salt so precious that a man can be branded for stealing a handful from the tribal store.''

I was surprised he did not share my excitement. ''Yes, it is salt, Piyanah—and if we find water that may be salt too. Water is precious here; yet by our river it had no value. Unless the Great Hunters remember us, in three days we would barter more than blankets or moccasins for a jar of water.''

Subdued, I walked on in silence. Later I said, ''Raki, do you remember that we didn't believe it when someone told us there were places where salt had no value? And there was a legend that the paths of the Land beyond the Sunset are paved with salt; we didn't believe that either. Do you remember how wonderful it was to be given a little handful of salt to lick, once a year when the runners came back from the Place of Barter? It is strange how some things you long for don't seem to be worth anything when you get them.''

''It is like snow underfoot, Piyanah, almost the same sound and feel when you break through the crust; and it hurts your eyes like snow, when the sun is so very bright.''

''Don't talk about snow, Raki, it makes me thirsty. It is so hot already and it will be worse by midday. Everything is salt here—there is no wind, but the salt gets on my lips and stings the sun-blisters.''

''We can drink at noon. There are still four skins of sour juice, which are better than water.''

''And how many water-skins?''

''Fifty-three; sufficient for three days, longer if we are careful. There may be dew before dawn even here, and it will be cooler after sunset.''

Thirst was an unfamiliar enemy and our people feared it. They had been born within sound of water and until they joined the Heron every journey had followed the course of a river. At night we tried to give them the comfort of a watch-fire, but the leafless thorn bushes flared, crackled, died into white ash, seeming only to intensify the dark blanket of the night.

On the seventh day we found a second water-hole, but it was slightly brackish and too low to replenish all our water-skins. That night I heard a woman's voice shrill with urgency, and knew she was trying to persuade her husband to turn back. After another day of timeless endurance, Raki and I leading, while behind us straggled a file of figures plodding through the harsh sand, they were too weary for rebellion, so Raki need no longer stir them with tales of Scarlet Feathers.

Until I had drunk from the pool of the dry river-bed on the tenth day I dared not believe it was sweet. How it came there I cannot understand, but the water was real, waist-deep, and two canoe-lengths in breadth. It was encircled by stunted bushes, whose vigorous green—though I should have called them grey anywhere except in this pallid waste—had led us there. It was ecstasy to lie down to suck up deep, clear water; to plunge my face into water until my hair was soaked and it ran in kindly rivulets over my parched skin. When I suddenly doubled over and began to retch, and saw others do the same, I thought the water was poisoned, but Raki said it might only be because we had drunk too much after becoming accustomed to so little. He must have been right, for after we were careful only to drink slowly from cupped hands no one complained of any ill effects.

That night we lit a fire, and began to be happy because the Blue Smokes had been proved wrong in saying the desert was waterless. If there was one pool there were probably many; indeed this nearly dry river might be the northern boundary of the land we were seeking. The following morning, after filling all our water-skins and drinking deeply, we set off at dawn; singing, because even the least of us was confident of the future.

The flat arid ground shimmered with heat like scum in a gigantic cauldron, and at noon Raki let us each have a drink, which emptied three of the water-skins. Some of the skins had not been cured properly and the water was tainted. This reminded me of Na-ka-chek saying, when we had been talking about wisdom, ''Even stale water is precious in a desert.''

Three days later, several of the others said they could see a lake we would reach before sunset, and claimed there was no need to go short of water during the slow, hot march. Raki told them they could drink as much as they liked when we reached water, and this hope kept them going forward uncomplainingly. He and I were both sure that their lake was only another phantom, of which the desert demons had already sent several to dishearten us.

The ground was so soft that we sank ankle-deep at every step. If we wore moccasins the sand trickled into them and rubbed our feet raw; if we discarded them it was unpleasantly hot underfoot and the salt ate into every sore and blister. Towards evening we sighted a patch of scrub and hastened towards it, thinking there must be water. But the stunted bushes had been dead for years, if not for generations; and if they had once grown by water it had long since been engulfed by salt. Yet though they had held out a false promise we were grateful to them, for they gave us a fire to guard us in the great echoing waste of stillness, where even the stars had been lit by strangers whose names we had never known.

Seven water-skins divided among seventy-three is only four small mouthfuls. It is difficult not to gulp instead of letting it trickle slowly down the throat. It is difficult to chew pemmican or breadsticks when you are very thirsty, but we were hungry enough to eat even in spite of thirst.

When we saw the clouds massing on the dawn horizon we thought it was going to rain.

"We must spread out the tepee to catch the rain," said Raki. "If there is a storm worthy of those clouds each of us can drink well; and we may get enough to fill the water-skins."

The clouds were dark as bison against the pale sky. Suddenly one of the women cried out, "Look, we are coming to an encampment! I can see camp-fires; there is another and another!"

I too thought they were columns of smoke curling up from many scattered fires. I thought of water in cool jars; so much water that I could drink, sluice it over my body, and watch it running off me to soak into the dust, knowing there would be plenty more.

"It is dust, not smoke," said Raki, "dust caught up by the wind." And in a low voice, so that the others could not hear, he added, "The Blue Smokes say this is a sure sign that the desert demons are angry. I hope none of the others heard that foolish story, for in the desert it is easy to believe in demons."

The pillars of dust—and I had to say to myself, "Dust, only dust, caught up by the wind, Piyanah. You don't believe in demons, even in the desert!"—came steadily on, bearing down on us, blind and relentless as herds stampeded by a prairie fire. We heard the wind screaming defiance before the fury of it struck us.

"Lie down!" shouted Raki. "Cover your heads with blankets!"

Already my eyes and mouth and nostrils were filled with

dust. The scourge of the wind tried to tear the blankets from our bodies so that it could scour the skin from our bones. Clouds hid away the sun; we were lost in the blind hatred of a storm that was more cruel than any blizzard. Snow is always a clean enemy, content to lull her prey to sleep and to whisper, ''My death is kind. Sleep and forget to cling to life.'' But this hot wind gloried in its killing, with the hot, cruel hands of a strangler.

It made us cower, flat to the ground; for if we dared stand upright to give it challenge it would have snatched off our clothes to leave us naked and defenceless. Each breath was a laboured effort. We sucked in air through the blankets which we held over our faces. At last Raki had to sacrifice ten of our remaining water-skins to damp strips of blanket which we tied over our mouths and nostrils to keep out the worst of the dust. I knew what a wounded deer must feel with an arrow between her ribs. Each breath was a battle won: each pain a siege withstood against the demons of this unclean storm.

The wind dropped as suddenly as it had risen, and the dark, dust-laden air became slowly luminous. We scrambled to our feet, dazed and exhausted. The wind had grown tired of the dust and was letting it fall back into the desert. Now we could see the sun, heavy and round as a rising autumn moon.

''It is still daylight,'' I said slowly, ''the sun is not even low in the sky.''

I had thought it must be the morning of the next day: so much fear to be spanned by half a day's journey: so much courage needed to survive one desert storm.

We had to dig our loads out of the sand. The tepee was covered by a drift and we might never have found it if I had not noticed one of the poles, which had been snatched up by the wind and thrust upright like an arrow into the ground.

I tried to free my hair from dust by running my fingers through it, but it only trickled down into my eyes which were already sore and inflamed. There was coarse grit under my finger-nails, and it grated between my teeth. My tongue was so dry that it was difficult to talk without slurring the words, but when I tried to spit dust out of my mouth I could not even produce enough saliva.

Raki had to use five more skins of water before he could persuade everyone to pick up their loads and take their place in the file we led. Their shadow stretched forlornly behind them, as if they trailed their grave wrappings while seeking a place to leave their tormented bodies. I began to believe our track would be marked by shallow graves; beyond the last, two skulls, their scarlet feathers bleached to the colour of the bone.

Now the wind had dropped, the sun was mocking in a cloudless sky. I saw dark shapes ahead and thought they were bison. I broke into a run, notching an arrow to my bow-string. I thought of fresh, red meat, wet and juicy. Where there is blood and bison there must be water. Water running over stones, water in deep, clean pools, water cupped in my hands. Water—even a little muddy water! ''Great Hunters, who have so many lakes and rivers, please give us water. We don't need enough to float a canoe, only to drink. But please let us be able to drink knowing there is enough for us all.''

''Stop, Piyanah!'' Raki was running beside me. ''There is nothing there, Piyanah! Why are you notching your arrow?''

''Bison, Raki—fresh meat, and *water!*''

His fingers strong and insistent dug into my arm. ''You are dreaming, Piyanah. Those are rocks, not bison. Black rocks scattered over the desert. They will give us shade—we can rest there until nightfall for it will be cooler travelling under the stars.''

It was true we could rest in the shade, but the smooth, black rocks, polished by winds since time was young, stored the heat, so the shadows were little cooler than the direct rays of the sun. There were only five water-skins left when Raki gave the order to move on. The night was moonless, and between the great boulders there were small rocks, half-buried in the sand, which were difficult to avoid. I wanted to leave the tepee behind because the men were finding it so heavy to carry, but Raki said that if we abandoned it they would know there was very little hope of the tribe's survival.

I kept on remembering how the Blue Smokes had said, "The Great Thirst stretches to the end of the world." Some people believe there is fire at the end of the world, and others that there is a wall of water where all the rivers return into the sky. Fire or water? Fire or water? Blood throbbed in my ears as though my head were a cooking-pot bubbling over a fire. My body was fire: my feet and hands embers, my mouth ashes—hot ashes.

On the evening of the sixteenth day there were only two skins of water left, and for a long time we had dared do no more than moisten our tongues. Three of the women could not be roused when Raki said it was time to go on. Death had come for them while they slept. They lay huddled in the shadow of a boulder, tattered blankets drawn over their heads. Drought had stretched their skins so tightly over the bone that they looked very old.

I heard the sharp crack of their joints as their arms were folded to prepare them for burial. We dug shallow graves, and laid them curled on their right sides, facing the west. Their husbands put five grains of seed maize into their right hands, and beside each of them an empty water-skin. Even on the other side of the water they might fear thirst until they grew accustomed to the broad rivers of heaven.

In silence we trudged on, Rokeena and Tekeeni close behind us, the others following according to their remaining strength. I stumbled over a rock and fell sprawling in the hot sand. Sand thrust into my mouth trying to choke me. I thought I could hear water dripping into a pool among wet ferns. I held out my hands to catch the drops; slow and heavy they splashed against my dry palms. Slow and heavy and warm: warm as blood, salt as blood. It *is* blood, dripping from my nostrils....

I am floating on dark water, but when I try to scoop it up I find I can't move my arms. My body won't obey me any more: the tribe won't obey me because they know I have betrayed them. I am dying of thirst. Hajan had an easier death than thirst—but he didn't betray them, he only lost faith too soon.

I can hear Raki telling Tekeeni that they must go on alone to find water. If he goes we shall die without each other. I want to go with them, but they can't understand what I am trying to say. I can't speak clearly because my tongue is too big for my mouth.

Raki says I must stay to look after the others, for if we both go, the Heron will feel the Chief has abandoned them. Raki carries me to a great boulder and puts the last two water-skins beside me so that I can say when they may be used. He takes my feathered headdress from its wrappings and says I am to wear it to remind them that the Chief's authority must be obeyed.

I manage to smile at Raki before I have to watch him go away with Tekeeni: further and further away into the desert. Soon we are both going to die of thirst; soon we shall be safe on the other side of the water....

The feathered headdress seemed very heavy; too heavy for Piyanah to support. I felt my thoughts struggling to escape from my will, fighting against me as though I tried to pinion an eagle....I was trying to carry water in my hands, but it ran between my fingers and soaked away into the sand. I looked at my hands and they were dry; dry as ashes, dry as bones. The stars were so bright that I could see the huddled shapes of those who had followed us into the desert; the Tribe of the Heron who were dying because they had believed in me.

Raki and Tekeeni still believed in me. They had said that Na-ka-chek would never betray us, and so they will find water in time to bring it back to us. They have each taken six empty water-skins, a heavy load even for men who are not thirsty. I must forget Piyanah and think only of Raki; he will need everything I can give him, even my small strength, my flickering courage, may help him.

I am with Raki, sharing his thoughts, sharing his spirit; I *am* Raki....

"Piyanah must have water, so I shall find water. Piyanah will die if I don't find water soon. Na-ka-chek told her we should live in peace beyond the desert, but she is dying because she has lost faith in her vision. I will bring water, and then she will believe in herself again. The stars are very close. Tekeeni is with me; Rokeena is with Piyanah.

"I am glad Tekeeni and I tied a rope to our belts or we might have lost each other in the dark. If he falls I shall feel the rope jerk and know where to find him. Piyanah's face was covered with blood: I must bring water to wash away the blood. If I fall I might not have the strength to get up again: I must go on until I find water.

"The stars have fallen into the desert. Five stars, shining up from the sand. One of them may be Piyanah's star. She must be dead and has come back from the sky to find me. If I put her star into my mouth she will be alive again. I must be careful to take the star that is Piyanah or the spirit of a stranger will live in her body. Piyanah wouldn't like a stranger to live in her body. I wonder who the other stars belong to. I must tell Tekeeni in case one of them is Rokeena.

"I have tugged on the rope, but it is slack in my hand. Tekeeni has gone on without me. He must have known it was Rokeena's star and forgotten to wait for me. I can hear a sound that used to be familiar; splashing...splashing— water! Water! Tekeeni has come back. He is sluicing water over me—clean, cool water. Water for Piyanah! Piyanah, we have found water! Wait for me, Piyanah!"

I was again Piyanah, but refreshed by the water that I

knew Raki had reached. I went to Rokeena; she was so difficult to wake that I thought she was dead. At last she stirred and opened her eyes.

"Rokeena, they have found water! They will reach us before evening. They are safe, Rokeena, do you understand? Safe! I must go to tell the others."

"Leave them, Piyanah. Some of them may be asleep—and will the rest believe you?"

"They will believe me when they see I am strong because I know the water is coming. To *prove* I am sure I will divide the last water-skin among them!"

"It is empty," said Rokeena. "You gave it to them last night, soon after Raki and Tekeeni went away."

I went through the dawn to our people and to each I whispered, "The water is coming! Raki has found water!"

And they believed me. Some of the men wanted to go to meet Raki, but I said there had been wind during the night which might have covered his tracks, so they must wait here for water to come to them.

I climbed to the top of the high boulder beside which Rokeena was lying, and watched the dawn come green as water out of the east. The sun climbed slowly up the sky, and still the desert was empty. I was sure that Raki had found water, but would he reach us in time?

Rokeena was very still. I thought of waking her to reassure myself that she was alive, but realized it would be cruel when I had no water to give her. Had she already gone to the other side of the water by crossing a waterless desert? Or were deserts feared because people who died there could never find water to carry them to the Land of the Sunset?

Several times I thought I could see movement on the sandy waste, but it was always a rock shimmering in the heat. Now I could see two dark dots against the glaring whiteness. Demons had turned salt into water and boulders into bison, but surely these were men?

There was something moving...men. Raki and Tekeeni!

277

"But in this glare they may not be able to see you. Shout to them, Piyanah!"

My mouth was so dry that no sound came. "Blood is warm and salt, but blood is moisture."

I bit my arm, and then more deeply until a mouthful of blood softened my tongue, which had grown hard and swollen with thirst:

"Raki! Raki!"

I tried to shout louder than that pitiful croak.

"Raki!"

My voice must have carried a long way in that still air, for I heard their answering shout.

"We have found water...plenty of water...only half a day's journey to a river!"

They walked upright in triumph, as do men who have proved their vision. I saw our people stumbling towards them, towards Raki and Tekeeni who brought life out of the South.

Place of the Corn-Growing

We stayed three days beside the water that had given us life: only a series of shallow pools threaded by a stream, but to me stronger than a river of many rapids. During the second night I woke in the clear starlight, and saw three figures going into the desert. I shook Raki gently to wake him, for I thought they might be walking in their sleep, driven by a dream that they must still search for water.

"It is Kekki and the other two men whose wives died out there," said Raki. "They are going to put full water-skins beside the women, who may not yet have reached the Great River."

The others must have guessed why they had gone, for no

one mentioned their absence. The next night I heard them coming back. I do not know how deeply they mourned: they gave no sign of grief unless it was to become impassive as ordinary Redskins.

It was thinking about them that made me say to Raki:

"Why is it that we often hear our people quarrelling—and even sometimes quarrel ourselves? I never heard the men of the Two Trees raise their voices except in cold, disciplined anger, and though the women quarrelled among themselves they never did so in the hearing of the Chief or the Elders. And for anyone to weep even in privacy was bitter shame."

"The old rule taught us to conceal our feelings, for any emotion was a weakness to be overcome. But we have learnt that love is the source of life and that love cannot be shut away to be used by expediency. Love heightens feeling and changes the cold black and white of habit into many colours. There is no light without a shadow, and I think that every shade of feeling has its sombre opposite. The weak man may learn to be impassive, but the strong man can live by love because he is not afraid of hatred."

"Raki, I had never seen a man weep until Gorgi wept at Dorrok's death."

"He wept because he had learned to love, for we had taught him to feel."

"Will they be grateful, Raki, when they discover that in teaching them to accept emotion we have opened their hearts to hatred and quarrels as well as to love?"

"Do you love me less, Piyanah, because sometimes we disagree? Do you realize that when we were children we never quarrelled. You never slapped me, and I never pulled your hair?"

"Perhaps we never wanted to. Or was it because we had been taught that every action had an unnatural importance? They tried to teach us never to be natural, always to behave according to tradition."

"How many times, Piyanah, has a thorn worked deep

into your foot because tradition decreed that it would be weak to take it out before the leader of the file had given the signal to rest? Quarrels may be a way of pulling out a thorn before it works into the flesh, and impassivity the cause of a festering wound.''

I smiled. ''Then the Heron is moving in the right direction; for I have heard men quarrelling with their wives in a way which would have horrified the Elders.''

''Does it matter very much, when they have also learned to laugh with them?''

When we were ready to go on we kept down-stream, for although we had reached the southern boundary of the desert we were reluctant to leave the sound of running water. Gradually the scrub gave place to richer vegetation, and we could see hills in the distance. Then, twenty-two days after we had left the Blue Smokes, our stream led us to a wide river which ran through meadows thick with flowers. We might have stayed there if I had not so clearly remembered the place of the corn-growing which Na-ka-chek had shown to me.

The hills swelled into bold, well-wooded curves; of trees that were familiar and others whose names we did not know. We saw no sign of old watch-fires, and the birds and animals were so tame that we felt sure it could never have been a tribal hunting-ground.

It was against the rising moon that I saw the shape of a remembered hill. ''Raki! Raki, that is where we shall set our tepee!''

As I spoke two herons flew overhead, so I knew Na-ka-chek was well pleased. He had even made white and scarlet flowers grow in the meadow where he wished us to cut the first furrow for our corn-growing. There was level ground for more cultivation even than the wide fields of the Blue Smokes; and beyond it the woods rose to a grassy plateau, tree-shaded and sheltered by a great boulder creviced with ferns and gentle with moss. Here was our tepee set, and before it we kindled the first watch-fire of the Heron's place of the corn-growing.

I was glad that my child would be the first-born of the tribe, for I should need the authority of experience to calm the fears of other women. When Raki and I had decided that none of the Old Women should come with us, we had forgotten how much their birth rituals gave courage to the squaws; it had been easy for Piyanah the Scarlet Feather to dismiss this lore as superstition, but as the clean lines of my body began to blur I found myself sympathizing with fears I used to despise.

I kept on reminding myself that everybody had been born the same way, yet I felt that I was not only the first of the Heron who was going to find out what it was really like to bear a child, but the first of all women. I was afraid, more afraid, I thought, even than I had been in the ordeals. I *must* make the others realize that male children do *not* come out through a split in the belly. It *must* be nonsense that if a woman is not bandaged with the proper cotton and rituals, she will bleed to death.

Rokeena's child would be born soon after mine, yet I could not prevent myself sharing my fears with her.

"Rokeena, while you were in the Squaws' Tepees are you sure none of the women who had borne sons looked under their birth-bandages to see if there really was a wound?"

"If they did they never admitted it...how could they, when they believed that seeing the belly before the seventh day would let the baby be taken by a demon?"

"When do you think the belly opens?"

"They don't know. They are given a sleep-drink before the child is born so that they can't remember what happens... except that it is very painful."

"Raki says it is only superstition, and I'm sure he is right. Old Women don't know any real magic. Think of how they said you would always be lame. Did *they* cure you?"

"No, it was Raki who cured me."

"That proves he knows more than they do." I sighed. "It used to be so easy to be scornful of the things the squaws believed. I *know* a bear, and a hind, and a woman give birth in the same way, and of course it is not at all frightening... but sometimes one forgets it is quite natural and ordinary."

"If the skin splits it ought to leave a scar, and it doesn't, because I have often seen squaws naked who have had several children, and they didn't look any different to us."

I was ashamed of having to be reassured by Rokeena and said, in what I hoped was a brisk and confident voice, "We are fools...of course it doesn't split. I am a Chief, and yet because my belly is as swollen as a drowned rat's I behave as though I were blind as a maggot!"

If it had not been for Rokeena, who because of Raki thought I could never feel or act like a fool, those slow moons would have made me despair for the future of the Heron. Gradually I became further estranged from the other women, as they reverted to the superstitions of which we had hoped they were free. They blamed me for bringing them South, and so putting the barrier of the Great Thirst between them and the people of the old tradition. They were not bitter with Raki, for as he was a man they expected his decisions to be beyond their comprehension; decisions which were sure to be unreasonable but which must be accepted without question according to the custom. Yet now that my body showed that I shared the weakness of squaws they took little notice when I tried to reason with them. They whispered that I had a store of the sacred cotton and refused to share it, and some even dared to say that Raki had been taught the rituals by Nona and that I should be the only one who would live to see her son.

I was really angry with them when they began to ask the Great Hunters to send them daughters so as to protect them from the dangers of bringing forth sons, but it produced little effect. I knew I had failed with them when I saw they still refused to touch a knife, or an arrow, or a fish-spear; all of which are associated with the birth of sons.

Raki decreed that each woman was to bear her child alone with her husband, so that he would understand what it was like: the men were more afraid of this than if he had ordered them to collect the claws of ten bears in the season of cubs!

It was only when Raki kept telling me that it was as easy for a woman to bear a child as for a goat to have a kid that I realized he was just as worried as any of the others. I knew he would never lie to me if I asked him a direct question, and I determined that the barrier of pretence which had grown between us must be broken down...even if in so doing I added to my fears.

"Raki, do you really know anything about birth? Know because you have seen and not only just because you want to believe?"

"How many more times must I tell you that it is only reasonable that children of both sexes should be born in the same way?"

"I don't want to know what's reasonable, I want to know what's *true!*"

"Reason and truth are the same."

"Was it reasonable to take a tribe into a strange country without recognizing how ignorant we were? I didn't have a chance to find out the really important things...you lived in the Squaws' Tepees, I didn't! What did you think you were there for? It is very easy to laugh at superstitions, but it's no use being superior unless you know more than other people do."

Part of me could still stand aside watching Piyanah behave like the child who used to decoy Ninee into anger, but the rest of me was desperately serious, "Do you really know what happens...it's no use trying to pretend if you don't."

Raki was smiling, as he often smiled when I told him of a petty quarrel which belonged to somebody else, and he said soothingly, ''I thought that since you had watched the kid....''

I interrupted, ''If you tell me again that I have only to con-. sider how easily goats have kids, I shall forget that Scarlet Feathers are impassive or that a woman should honour the man who takes her for his squaw!''

Even then he did not realize I was angry, and instead of answering he pointed out through the open tepee-flap and said, ''Tekeeni is coming up from the river, and he has caught so many fish he can hardly carry them.''

He went on carving the haft of a fish-spear: calm and imperturbable, pretending he could change the mood of a woman by ignoring her. How dare he ignore me! Suddenly I remembered how I had often longed to throw something at the Elders as they sat by the watch-fire so aggressively undisturbed by the sound of quarrelling from the Squaws' Tepees. I was no longer Piyanah watching herself being foolish...we were one person: the angry woman and the angry child. Before we began talking I had been scouring a cooking-pot with sand....

I saw it glance off the side of his head. He put up his hand involuntarily, and then went on with his carving as though nothing had happened. Blood trickled from his hair above the right temple and dripped off the angle of his jaw. Suddenly I forgot everything except that Raki was hurt, and it was my fault.

''*Please* forgive me, Raki! Does it hurt very much? I didn't know it was so heavy and I didn't really mean to throw it at you. But I *knew* you were going to tell me about the kid again, and I couldn't bear it...please, Raki, don't hide things from me and I promise I won't be a coward any more.''

He took me in his arms, ''You are never a coward, my Piyanah. I am the coward, for I dared not admit even to myself that you might be in any danger. Nearly all the time I am sure that nothing terrible is going to happen; and then I start thinking about the Birth Tepee and the sound of women screaming before the cry of the child. And then I am terrified, Piyanah; that's why I keep on telling us both it's not dangerous, not even so dangerous as taking a canoe down a very small rapid.''

I wasn't frightened or alone any more: nothing could be horrible if Raki and I shared it, nothing could be really dangerous if we fought it together. I was strong and happy and free: I was his mother as well as the mother of his unborn child.

''I am so happy, Raki...and I don't think there is going to be a scar on your forehead, or only a very little one hidden under your hair.''

He laughed and held me closer. ''If our son excels at throwing we shall always know how he learned it!''

Throwing the cooking-pot at Raki taught me something I had not known before. It taught him something too, and after that he never hid his thoughts from me, for we both realized there are occasions when it is difficult to be both reasonable and a woman. I had not only lived as a man but thought as a man, and I had become intolerant. Although in a few days Raki's wound was healed, for the rest of our life if he thought I was being too adamant in my opinions, he used to put his hand to his temple as though to adjust the fore-head thong: and I would be more kindly in memory of an angry woman.

the first-born

Now that I could again tell Raki whenever I had even a twinge of fear, it was much easier to be sympathetic with the other women, for I recognized that the barrier had been reared by the resentment I felt when their fears increased my own. I was at last able to reassure them, and further increased their confidence by promising that if either my child or I died they should have some of the ritual bandages before their children were born. Gorgi and Tekeeni asked to be allowed to cross the Great Thirst to get these from the Blue Smokes. Knowing the quality of the Old Women we had seen there, I was sure they possessed all the trappings of superstition.

When this was known, even the most apprehensive women became confident; instead of regarding me as a tyrant they seemed to think I deserved another scarlet feather for risking my life in their defence. I laughed, and said it was Gorgi and Tekeeni who deserved the Scarlet, but they appeared to think that crossing the Thirst was nothing in comparison with having a baby.

I had expected them to protest when I told them that their babies were not to be wrapped like cocoons until the third moon, as had been the custom with the Two Trees. Instead they were eager that the new generation should have the same freedom as Mother had given to Raki and me. They made rush baskets lined with dry moss, wove blankets for coverings, and agreed that it would be much better for a baby to lie in such a cradle than to be carried everywhere on the mother's back.

Although our tepee was apart from the main encampment, I thought that as soon as the birth began, the women, and probably the men too, would gather round to hear without delay the news for which they were all so anxiously waiting. I remembered the screams which had been heard from the Birth Tepee...Piyanah the Scarlet Feather would never scream, but would Piyanah the woman have the same endurance?

I longed to go into the forest with Raki to have the baby in privacy, but we reluctantly agreed that if we did so the others might think we went there to work some secret rite by which I alone could be protected. It would be easy for them to start being superstitious again, for when I saw how tightly the skin was stretched over my round belly it was sometimes difficult to be sure it was not going to split open like a seed-pod.

For two days the valley had been ominous with the threat of thunder: the sky was yellow with heat and the sound of water oppressive as the drone of insects. Even my baby was drowsy, for he had not stirred since early morning. If I had been alone I should have stayed in the tepee during the heat of the day, instead of going with Raki to see how the new fish-trap was progressing. While he talked to Kekki, who had been driving stakes in the bed of a stream where it entered the main river, I walked further along the bank to a shallow pool where I could lie full length in the sun-warmed water. It refreshed me, and on the way home I lost some of the heaviness brought by the brooding heat.

Even after sunset it was too hot to sleep, so I lay with my head on Raki's shoulder. We talked of our little valley, and of how we had never really believed we should grow beyond the years of separation into this secure happiness.

"Sometimes," he said, "when I undo the flap of our tepee I still wonder what I am going to see. Will it be your mother coming to take us down to the river; or our Twin Pine; or the Naked Foreheads scouring the cooking-pots in which Raki the Squaw must prepare food for the Two Trees?"

"Dear Raki, our today is made of so many yesterdays...."

"And the Piyanah I love is made of so many people; the little girl, the Young Brave, the Chief."

"But I'm not the little girl any more; she died when we had to grow up."

"Yes, you are; and you are also the mother of my children. When you speak, or think, or act, you are *all* of you, for the child and the long-in-years are both part of the total you, like the thousands of strands which together make the pattern of a blanket. Our child is not yet born, but the arrows he will flight are already singing, and the colours of the feathers he will wear are instinct in his sunrise."

"Our son must often smile at the foolishness of his parents, for from his star he can command a much wider horizon than either of us. He can say, 'I am Miyak, the mighty hunter, the proud with feathers,' or, 'I am Miyak, who died when he was born.' He knows which it will be, but from us it is still hidden by the river-mist of time."

"Why do you always talk of our child as a son? It is our first law that men and women are equals; why should we value a son more than a daughter?"

"I am not yet ready for a daughter. A son will see with your eyes and a daughter with mine, and you have always learned to see things clearly before I did. If I had a daughter the others would still be afraid to bear sons...you are still afraid for me, aren't you Raki? Why should you be afraid? Why should either of us spoil the rejoicing by this prelude of fear?"

"Aren't you even a little afraid?"

"No, my Raki, I am strong and confident and *happy!* And you can't be happy and afraid at the same moment." As I said this I knew it was true, and splendid. "I am so very happy, Raki, and it's not just because I am hiding from fear. I have had several curious pains, they have a rhythm like a very slow drumming. I am sure that Miyak has decided to be born, yet the pains are beautiful and exciting, and *proud.*"

There was a sound of distant thunder. Raki went to look out across the valley, where fire was flickering in the sky above the hills. "The moon is rising," he said. "When the storm breaks, the air will be much cooler."

I knew he was only pretending he wasn't worried about my pains, so I lay still and waited for him to come back to me. Pain touched me again and then receded with the sound of thunder. I was restless, and longed for the clouds to let down their rain so that I could walk naked in the rush of clean water.

Without looking at me, Raki said, "Tell me when you have another pain...and you must tell me exactly how much it hurts, *please* don't hide it from me, Piyanah."

288

"It is much easier to have a pain in the belly than a pain in the heart...this is much easier than being parted from you even for a day. Come and lie down beside me so that we are very close and then the pain won't matter at all."

Later I found it so difficult to lie still that we went out into the friendly woods.

Thunder was still sounding but the rain clung to the sky. My body was sticky with sweat and I thought of going down to the river to try to get cool. Then I had a pain so strong and sudden that I had to hold on to a tree to stop myself crying out.

Raki led me back to the tepee. He wanted to fetch Rokeena, but I would not let him, and made him promise not to tell any of the others what was happening. He piled wood on the fire until light shone through the open flap. Usually in the hot weather there was only a thread of smoke rising from the watch-fire, but tonight, in spite of the intense heat, we both needed the security of flames against the darkness.

The thunder was louder than an avalanche, but I was grateful to the storm spirit because it drowned the whimper I could not hold back when the pain made me understand how it would feel to be crushed by a grizzly.

Raki crouched beside me, trying to shield me from the pain. I gasped and doubled up...it made me think of the women we had left in the Great Thirst, curled in their narrow graves. Thunder and Pain wore the same dark feathers and bore down on me with awful majesty.

I felt as though my body was being torn apart. "Raki, my belly *must* be splitting. I don't want to leave you, Raki. I'm not really frightened...but I don't want to leave you."

A last great crash of thunder; then a silence more profound than deep water.

The side of the tepee grew thin, like mist under the morning sun; I saw a man wearing the feathers of a Chief, and behind him a splendid company who shone with light, pale and clear as the moon. I ran towards them....

Then I heard Raki's voice above the rain that seemed to drum with a message from the Great Hunters.

"We were right, Piyanah! It *was* like the kid..."

His voice was more beloved even than the splendour of my vision..."Oh, Raki, I am so happy!"

I realized that I was back in my body, and it had again become important. "Raki, are you quite sure my belly didn't split?"

He took my hand. "Quite sure...but feel it for yourself."

"It feels very empty, and the skin is horribly loose. I told you Miyak was going to be a son...."

"He may be a daughter; I haven't had time to look yet.... Yes, he is a son! A very healthy, angry son by the sound of him!"

I felt too drowsy to look at him yet...I had seen Miyak of the feathers and he might be difficult to recognize in his little body. "Raki, you had better wrap him in something or he may feel cold."

"It is very warm tonight."

"Not as warm as it was inside me," I said, and then added urgently, "Put him down, Raki! Something else is happening to me....Have I had another baby? It didn't hurt nearly as much as the first one...."

"No," he said reassuringly, "it was only what I told you would happen...just the same as the goat."

I laughed and found it easy to laugh. "The next time I see a goat I'm going to apologize to it for not being properly sympathetic!"

Raki went out of the tepee and I heard the fire hiss as he threw something into it. Rain was falling steadily, but under the shelter of the overhanging rock the fire still burned. He came back, sluiced his hands in a bowl of water and then washed the blood off me. I was naked and comfortable; he put a breech-clout stuffed with moss between my legs, and covered me with a blanket for I had begun to shiver.

I suddenly wanted to see the baby: Raki put it in the crook of my arm and lay down beside me. The eyes of my son were dark as sloes with the blue bloom of the new born. I said to Raki, ''Now I know why a bear with cubs is more dangerous than the most savage of grizzlies!''

He laughed, the soft warm laugh of deep contentment, ''If the father bear felt as proud of his cub as I do no one would dare to come near his cave!''

Then, as we had promised, all the women came to see that the Chief's son was without blemish, and Miyak watched them with a wise stare as he received his first homage from the tribe.

ChilÒren oϝ the GReat hunteRs

Miyak, three years old and so like Raki that by looking at either I could see the man as a child or the child as a Chief, was teaching his sister to crawl. Already our children recognized a close friendship, and in them we were well content that the future of the Heron was secure. Raki and I were sitting in front of our tepee, looking across the cultivation to the river. It was evening: smoke was rising from the cooking-fires, and we could see men and women working together in the fields. I was sharing their contentment, already such a rich harvest of our sowing. Raki must have known that mine were long thoughts. He said gently:

''It is autumn, and we know that the winter will be kind. The woods will sleep lightly, for here snow is only a ghost that vanishes with the coming of the sun. If Na-ka-chek could be with us now he would be happy.''

''He is often here, Raki. Miyak saw him yesterday. He told me he had been talking with an old man who wore a Chief's headdress, like ours, but with feathers that shone, 'like moonlight on water.' ''

''Was Miyak frightened?''

''Why should a child be frightened of his grandfather?''

''I was foolish to expect it: I had forgotten that children who are born in love know that they who live beyond the sunset are their friends.''

''Raki, sometimes we think we have done very little since we came here. There have been no feats of endurance, no actions to make a legend at the Gathering of the Tribes yet we have achieved many small things; and though feathers may be small, together they can make the wings of the morning.''

''What are these new feathers?''

''They have become so familiar that they seem ordinary and unimportant: women working with their husbands, men and women laughing together, singing together—even weeping together.''

I paused to watch Gorgi walking down the hill with Cheka beside him, their son on his shoulder, their daughter clinging to her hand.

''Ordinary things, Raki—men and women going down to the river with their children. Yet you could search the Thirty Tribes and not equal that sight.''

Raki put his arm round my shoulders. ''Look, my Piyanah, at the reflection of another feather you have won for them. A man carrying a baby in his arms and a woman standing waist-deep in the river mending a fish-trap.''

''It is your feather, Raki, more than mine; or did we both win it at the same time? To us, such an ordinary law, but to strangers inconceivable; that men and women should recognize that in spirit they are already both male and female, as they will be when they enter the Land of the Great Hunters. Now in this recognition they can choose whatever work is closest to their hearts. They know it is nothing strange that a man should be happier—and so more useful to the community—looking after children, or cooking, or making tunics; or that a woman should be a mighty hunter, or skilled with words. Children live with their fathers and mothers and are happy...if I had to look forward to separation from Miyak when he is seven, the years would be only divisions of desolation.''

''We have given men and women to each other, and children to them both; but what have we taken away? The pride of endurance for the sake of endurance: and instead we have given them the strength to follow the ideas in which they believe. We have taken away the comfort of superstition; and given them the certainty that the Great Hunters are close and real. We have taken away the protection of impassivity; and given them kindliness in company. A rich exchange.''

''You forget that because there are no Naked Foreheads, warriors sometimes have to act as scavengers.''

Raki laughed, ''It is better to be a scavenger than a Scarlet Feather who is proud of being remote from his kindred. Now the Heron are more eager to win a white feather than once they were for the Scarlet, for they have learned that an idea may be more powerful than arrows against the Sorrow Bird.''

''It must have been a great battle,'' I said softly, ''between the Heron and the Sorrow Bird. And the Heron won, Raki. Perhaps only Narrok, who knows the language of the drums beyond the sunset, heard the cry of the Sorrow Bird in her dying. 'They have killed me, the People of the Heron, for they have learned to answer the Question of the Great Hunters—How many people are happier because you were born?' ''

JOAN GRANT

Joan Grant was born in England in 1907. Her father was a man of such intellectual brilliance in the fields of mathematics and engineering that he was appointed a fellow of Kings College while still in his twenties. Joan's formal education was limited to what she absorbed from a series of governesses, although she feels she learned far more from the after-dinner conversations between her father and his fellow scientists.

When Joan was twenty, she married Leslie Grant, with whom she had a daughter. This marriage ended soon after *Winged Pharaoh* was published in 1937—a book which became an instant best-seller. Until 1957 she was married to the philosopher and visionary Charles Beatty, who is the author of several books, including *The Garden of the Golden Flower*, a treatise on psychiatrist Carl Jung. In 1960, Joan married psychiatrist Denys Kelsey.

Throughout her life, Joan has been preoccupied with the subject of ethics. To her, the word ''ethics'' represents the fundamental and timeless code of attitudes and behavior toward one another on which the health of the individual and society depends. Each of her books and stories explores a facet of this code. As Denys Kelsey has written, ''The First Dynasty of Egypt once knew the code well, but lost it and foundered. Eleven dynasties were to pass before it was recovered, but those were more leisurely times when the most lethal weapon was an arrow, a javelin and a club. We feel that in the present troubled days of this planet, these books must be presented.''

THE FAR MEMORIES

Ariel Press is proud to announce that it has brought all seven of Joan Grant's "far memory" novels back into print in a uniform collection of books. They may be purchased either individually or as a set. The books, and their prices, are:

Winged Pharaoh. $9.95.
Life as Carola. $9.95.
Return to Elysium. $9.95.
Eyes of Horus. $11.95.
Lord of the Horizon. $9.95.
Scarlet Feather. $10.95.
So Moses Was Born. $9.95.

These books can be purchased either at your favorite bookstore or directly from Ariel Press (include an extra $1.50 for postage; $2.50 for Canada and overseas).

For those who prefer, the entire set of seven novels plus Joan Grant's autobiography, *Far Memory,* may be purchased as a subscription for $75 postpaid—a savings of $20. *No substitutions or deductions are allowed on subscriptions.*

All orders from the publisher must be accompanied by payment in full in U.S. funds—or charged to VISA, Master-Card, or American Express. Please do not send cash. Send orders to Ariel Press, P.O. Box 1347, Alpharetta, GA 30239.

For faster service, call toll free 1-800-336-7769 and charge the order to VISA, MasterCard, or American Express.

OTHER BOOKS PUBLISHED BY ARIEL PRESS:

Active Meditation: The Western Tradition
by Robert R. Leichtman, M.D. & Carl Japikse, $19.95

Forces of the Zodiac: Companions of the Soul
by Robert R. Leichtman, M.D. & Carl Japikse, $21.50

The Gift of Healing
by Ambrose & Olga Worrall, $7.95

The Secrets of Dr. Taverner
by Dion Fortune, $8.95

Practical Mysticism
by Evelyn Underhill, $7.95

The Light Within Us
by Carl Japikse, $9.95

Exploring the Tarot
by Carl Japikse, $9.95

The Betty Book
by Stewart Edward White, $9.95

Working With Angels
by Robert R. Leichtman, M.D. & Carl Japikse, $7.95.